The Last Shield

The Mercian Ninth Century
Book 6

MJ Porter

Map and cover design by Flintlock Covers

ISBN: 978-1-917374-09-5 Ingram paperback

ISBN:978-1-914332-35-7 Hardback

ISBN:978-1-914332-37-1 Kindle ebook

ISBN:978-1-914332-36-4 Paperback

 Created with Vellum

Contents

GWYNEDD
POWYS
DYFED
GWENT
CHESTER
GAINSBOROUGH
TORKSEY
BARDNEY
THETFORD
LICHFIELD
REPTON
TAMWORTH
PETERBOROUGH
EAST ANGLIA
ELY
WARWICK
NORTHAMPTON
GRANTABRIDGE
OFFA'S DYKE
MERCIA
WORCESTER
PASSENHAM
HEREFORD
KINGSHOLM
GLOUCESTER
LONDON
KENT
WESSEX
WINCHESTER
MAP OF EARLY ENGLAND
0
50 Miles

Prologue

AD875, Gloucester

The Welsh Lord Cadell has been as good as our agreement. The bridge spanning the River Severn at Gloucester has been repaired since our inauspicious meeting last summer. The bright, new timbers are easy to see in the dull winter light. But I can also determine that there's a make-shift barrier blocking the bridge, about halfway across, and from there, two figures guard the passageway. That's not how this was supposed to fucking work. I growl with my frustration at the damn Gwent Welsh. I should know better than to trust any of the bastards.

Knowing how much Haden despises bridges, I knee him forward firmly when we reach the beginning of the wooden planks that span the surging mass of water below. I'm not going to argue with him about this, not now, and not here.

Haden's first hoof on the bridge has him faltering as it echoes loudly in the quietness of the early morning. I lean down, prepared to offer him some words of conciliation in the hope of smoothing our passage.

'It's just a bloody bridge. You've done this before,' I advise him, already convinced that it won't work but determined to try, all the same. Haden surprises me by quickly placing his next hoof on the bridge, then the next, and the next as well.

I'm unsurprised when two sets of startled eyes peer at me from in front of the pile of casks and heavy pieces of timber lying across the bridge as they hear the sound.

At least they're alert, even if they don't hold weapons to hand, which they should. The fucking Gwent Welsh men will be watching and waiting for any sign of weakness.

'What's this?' I demand of both of them, hand extended towards the blockage in the middle of the bridge, as Haden walks sedately closer. I try not to notice that the bridge seems to sway over the echoing space below my feet. I wish I'd bloody dismounted now. I'm not enjoying the sensation. Typical that Haden has no problem with it now. I could have used him as an excuse to call the men to my side while I stood on firmer ground.

'My Lord King,' the first bobs and bows all at the same time. I detect Rudolf's stifled chuckle from behind me. I turn to glare at him where he perches on top of Dever, no fear on his face for all he's high above the surging river below. Rudolf meets my eyes without remorse. He's becoming as fucking cocky as the rest of my warriors.

I admire that. Not that I'm going to say as much.

It seems my face is becoming more recognisable. But then, I think, I have lived much of my life close to Gloucester. I've probably met these men many times before.

'The Gwent Welsh,' the guardsman gasps as though surfacing from beneath the water. His comrade is somewhat more assured, as he bows his head, although he doesn't remove his woollen hat, not that I blame him, and then meets my gaze.

'The Gwent Welsh, My Lord King. Up to their damn tricks again. It's just lucky that they haven't burnt the bridge. Again.' I twist my lips at the words. He's right to speak as he does. It is lucky. The Gwent Welsh have no sense. I swear they'd cut off their own hands and then try and wield a sword and be surprised when their enemy cut them down.

The men are dressed warmly, more thought for that than protection. I wish they wore byrnie and stood holding their shields. Better that that looking unprepared. They're a similar height, a similar shape, but it's all irrelevant beneath their thick cloaks.

'Would it not be easier to make your barrier at the end of the bridge?' Rudolf asks, his young voice high, confusion in the words, his humour, for once, thankfully, tempered.

'No, we've decided upon this boundary.' By that I take it he means the inhabitants of Gloucester. 'The Mercians from that side of the river,' and the guard points westwards, not into Gwent, but instead into the strip of Mercian land that lies there before the land belongs to the kingdom of Gwent. 'Are sheltering inside Gloucester. None of us wants the Gwent Welsh close enough to break through into the settlement itself.'

'Isn't it windy?' Icel demands to know, his words only just heard before being thrust away by the wind he speaks about. What Icel means is, 'isn't it windy on the bridge?' Another fair point to make. There's a stiff breeze ruffling my hair as I'm riding without my helm. If I had less hair, it would be too cold, and my ears would burn. Luckily, I have enough hair to provide some cover.

'And bloody freezing,' the first man complains, his hands deep inside the opposite armpit, as he hunkers into his cloak. He's hopping from side to side, trying to keep warm. They should have a brazier. But I reconsider. It would go out soon enough, and if it didn't, I don't want the Mercians to be responsible for setting fire to the newly rebuilt bridge should the brazier be toppled by the wind.

'Cynelm,' the man introduces himself, almost as an afterthought. I should have bloody asked but the situation perplexes me.

'There was a problem with wergild?' I return the conversation to the heart of the matter, trying to keep my mind on the task at hand.

'There's been no end of problems,' but Cynelm's words trail off as we all look into the shadowed gloom on the far side of the bridge. Something's coming. It can be heard, but more, it's felt in the trembling of the wooden planks beneath our feet. It could be a man walking, or perhaps twenty of them, a cart or even a few horses. I know the bridge shuddered at our passing. But I can't see, not yet, what comes this way. That side of the bridge clings to the darkness of a winter morning.

'Dismount,' I order my men. 'Take the horses back to Gloucester,' I command, aware some of the inhabitants of Gloucester have trailed the horses onto the bridge but unsure how many. I've kept my eyes forwards. A young voice sounds, one I don't know. I turn, shocked by the high voiced words.

'Aye, My Lord King. We'll do it.' A young girl, with her even younger brother, have followed us onto the bridge. They don't look as though they can control the ten horses, but the horses will go eagerly, I believe. None of them likes our windy vantage point. Neither do I, if I'm fucking honest with myself.

I hand Haden's rein to the girl with many misgivings, but I don't want Rudolf to leave my select band of warriors to accomplish the task.

'Do as you're told,' I caution Haden with a wag of my finger, and what I hope is a smile for the young girl. Haden shows me his teeth, a parody of laughter. I glance to the girl. She wears well-worn shoes, perhaps a size too small, and her cloak could be thicker. And that's not to mention the tangle of her long black hair which whips around in the growing gale. I can't be sure how skinny she is, but her lips are blue, her cheekbones easy to see. I'll handle that problem next.

Eagerly, she grips the reins, and Haden, shit that he is, bows his head and follows her sure steps as though she's a queen and he's hers to command. I huff through tight lips. I don't look to Rudolf. I know what expression will be on his sodding face.

'Right,' I state, once the horses and the children are well on their way back to Gloucester. 'Be ready for whatever the bastards have planned now.'

Edmund is already grimacing, for once, his face not the white of fear. Maybe, I should just let him take on the Gwent Welsh all the time. He's so keen to kill all the bastards, he doesn't have time to be fucking scared.

A handful of men eventually emerge from the gloom, grins on their faces as they sight the ramshackle arrangement at the heart of the bridge. Have they not seen it before? I should have asked more bloody questions of the two guardsmen.

The Gwent Welshmen come dressed for war; that much is immediately apparent. They dress little differently to the Mercians, but these men all carry a seax in one hand and a shield in the other. If they were banging the one against the other, I'd mistake them for Raiders.

The shields being carried aren't round like our own, but rather long and narrow, slightly concave as well. On the shields, rather than the animalistic representations of the Raiders, or the bright colours of Mercia and her eagle, they have white crosses daubed on a dark background. The crosses are easy to see, especially with the grey edges of dawn behind them.

They fight in the name of their God. That almost makes me fucking laugh aloud, as Rudolf would. I can imagine what Bishop Wærferth would have to say about that. I might keep one, show him, just to witness his reaction.

The words of my enemy ripple through the air, equally taunting and filled with humour. It seems they've not come to pay the outstanding wergild. I look at Edmund but quickly discard him as useless because of the angry lines around his eye and mouth. He's almost slathering to be upon the Gwent Welsh. If I even suggested a peace, Edmund would howl with the injustice.

I turn to Icel and Pybba, noting Goda, Sæbald and Leonath as well. Wulfred is chuntering away to himself while Lyfing winks at me, lips in a tight grin, hefting his seax and shield, ready for whatever needs doing now.

It's good to see we offer such a warm fucking welcome to our 'guests'.

It takes the bastards a long time to notice that the two guardsmen don't stand alone. Bloody fools. They really should have been paying a little more attention.

'What have we here,' the first one calls derisively. He's a squat man, heavily built around the chest, with wide legs and the confidence of a bull with a field of cows waiting before him. He speaks my tongue well, for a Gwent Welshman.

'I think we should be asking that,' Cynelm calls, trying to sound brave and bluff, even though I can see his knees shaking below the protection of the barricade, and worse, hear his seax tinging against his weapons belt. I shake my head at such folly. Men should know their fucking limits. Even I know mine.

'Stay out of the way,' I instruct Cynelm, moving to take his place, hoping my voice isn't quite as dismissive as I think it sounds in my ears.

'What are you doing here?' I demand to know, my voice rising, to crack like thunder over the howling wind.

'Who the fuck are you?' The second Gwent Welshman asks, this one tall and willowy. I'm surprised he can stand upright while the wind buffets us. It's growing in intensity as we trade words, not blows.

'We're asking the bloody questions here,' Icel shoulders his way beside me, his height almost matching mine. I would grin at him but now's not the time. I appreciate his support, all the same.

'No, we're asking the questions,' the first man counters, eyes flicking from Icel to me and then to those to our rear. I can feel someone breathing closely and assume Rudolf is behind me, shield to hand, should I need some protection from this motley collection of Gwent Welshmen.

'But you're not, are you?' Pybba counters, standing to my right. Edmund is there as well. I can feel his rage. If these fuckers aren't careful, Edmund will kill them all, and they won't even notice until they fall to the wooden planks of the bridge. If Hereman were here, they'd be dead already, I'm sure of it. He'd have used his spear, and everyone else's spear, to end their miserable lives.

He might even have just thrown pieces of the barricade. That man can throw anything to which he sets his mind.

'Who the fuck are you?' This is uttered as a howl of frustration. These Gwent Welshmen expected to see two Mercians on the bridge. Not twelve of them.

'We are the men of Mercia,' Goda states slowly, hands to either side, as though that explains everything. 'Now, who the fuck are you?'

'We're the Gwent Welshmen. Come to take what's ours.' Our enemy speaks with far more heat than Goda. He's as angry as Edmund.

'And what would that bloody be?' Icel counters.

'The money owed us by the thieving tanner?'

'Why does the tanner owe you money? And why does it take eight of you to resolve a minor problem with a transaction.'

'It takes this many of us because he didn't pay me properly, and these are my witnesses to that. Thieves must pay with their lives, if not with their silver.' The man who speaks stabs his chest and then points to the others as though that reinforces his argument. He doesn't explain how the debt came about in the first place.

I turn and eye Cynelm. He's shaking his head, eyes as furious as Edmund's at the accusation.

'Is there any truth to this?' I ask quietly through the corner of my mouth.

'None at all. The tanner paid what was due, and they killed the poor bastard anyway; strung him up, saying they had the right because he was a thief and in their kingdom, a thief pays with his life, although a murderer never does. Better to make a murderer pay for the death, and that can't happen if the man is dead.'

The complexity of laws in the kingdoms of the Welsh is often beyond me. But I believe a murderer should face the ultimate sanction, not so a thief. If the tanner paid what he owed, then that should have been the end of the matter. Perhaps this is something Bishop Wærferth can further investigate for me. Holy men have a love for law and order. It's probably because it involves writing and reading, not to mention slaughtering cows to skin them for their hide. Holy men are a strange breed if you think about it for too long.

'So, it's not the tanner you're after, then, if he's dead. I understand that you killed him and that the price of his wergild falls on you. That will outweigh any amount you believe is owed.'

'And who are you? The bloody king of Mercia come to resolve a business dispute?' The squat man cackles, but there's something about the stances of my warriors that makes the sound cut-off before it can really get going, the confidence to slide from his face.

'Are you the king?' he gasps, already trying to step backwards, only to crash into the man directly behind him.

'Do you have the wergild?' Goda enquires, the menace in his voice assuring me that he hopes they don't.

But now, the second man takes control.

'There'll be no wergild. The man cheated us, and he owes my friend here five silver coins.' He puffs his chest out as though that adds some sort of surety to the statement. 'Five silver coins with the face of Mercia's king on them.'

I consider that. These coins they want would have to show King Burgred's face. I sure as fuck haven't had any coins struck. Not yet. Again, this is something that Bishop Wærferth can resolve for me. Perhaps I do need to call a witan, as he suggests, after all.

Behind the front Gwent Welshman, there's a hurried discussion taking place between the others, and I think we won't have to fight the fuckers. Only the words become angrier and angrier, even the second Welshman gesticulating wildly, and for no reason that I can fathom, the daft sods begin to advance on us, drawing their weapons and holding their long shields before them. They're all well-armed, even if they don't have the protection of their byrnies that my men and I have.

'Fucking arseholes,' Wulfred complains. I'm inclined to agree with him. Of all the places to have a battle, on top of a bridge, in a swirling wind, isn't a good fucking idea. Not that I'll back down from the provocation. Bugger that.

It's not even in me to suggest we take the fight to the far side of the bridge.

'Watch the sides of the bridge,' I caution my men, pulling my seax from its sheath on my weapons belt, making an effort not to wince as the weight presses down on my unhealed cut from Gainsborough. I turn and peer behind me, noting that the inhabitants of Gloucester are no longer as sleepy as they were. Some of them stand on the bridge, while others behind try and join them, jostling those before them. Those at the front are pushed onwards, even though some have reconsidered the wisdom of such an action and try to backtrack.

It's too windy on the bridge, and there's about to be a bloody great big fight. I'm as angry with them as I am the bloody Gwent Welsh.

'Stay back,' I bellow, pointing with my seax to ensure they know what I mean, even if they can't hear my words. I don't want anyone else here thinking to play the hero. There's already twelve of us on the bridge. Trying to contain the two guardsmen is enough of a distraction for me.

At least our horses are out of sight.

I rub my boot over the wooden planks, noting that it's not as slippery underfoot as feared, considering how miserable the weather's been of late. Still, it's a long drop to the rumbling river beneath us, flashing darkly, the snowmelt raising the water level a good foot higher than usual. I don't much fancy taking such a drop, not in my byrnie and weighed down by my weapons belt and all the weapons that hang there. I'll drown even if I don't hit my head on one of the rocks that poke menacingly upwards.

'Do this quickly, and try not to kill the stupid bastards,' I advise my mouth to my warriors.

'They fucking deserve it,' Edmund snarls, but even he's calmer than I expect. Maybe he appreciates that this could badly end if we're not careful. I'd sooner not die because of some cheating Gwent Welsh cunt.

The two men we've been talking to are the first to start their advance. Unlike us, they don't stand shoulder to shoulder but rather come in a ramshackle arrangement, two in front of the others. I suspect those that hold back are as wary as we are. Maybe they're not all stupid arseholes after all.

'Get behind us,' I order the two guards. The collection of wooden barrels and haphazardly placed tree trunks don't offer any protection. They're merely there to obstruct.

'Which side?' I ask about the obstruction, the question directed to all my warriors—a mistake, I realise immediately.

'Inside.' 'Outside.' There's no consensus from them.

'Thank you,' I mutter. And then decide. 'On the outside. It'll get too messy if we stay where we are.' I return my seax to my weapons belt and hand my round shield to Goda, who stands behind me, beard rippling in the wind as though it's alive.

Quickly, I make my way over a slanted tree trunk, mindful that I'm forced even higher than Haden's back as I clamber over the barricade the people of Gloucester have forced upwards. The gusting wind is strong, and a large hand on my back assures me that I do wobble as precariously as I think I do. I turn and reclaim my shield, feeling naked without it, even if I don't believe the Gwent Welsh will attack me, not yet. They're still trying to goad on one another, those at the front shouting at the others further back.

'Fucking wonderful,' Icel rumbles as he stands beside me. Maybe we should have stayed where we were and allowed the Gwent Welsh the privilege of staring into the abyss far below us as they tried to get close enough to land a blow.

Rudolf scampers into place, the grin back on his face, his hair tumbled by the wind. I shake my head at the enthusiasm as he reclaims his shield from Edmund behind and stands, waiting.

Already, I can see that the footsteps of the two Gwent Welsh have slowed. Did they genuinely expect to come at us and have the barrier stay between us? I shake my head at their folly. I don't think any of them genuinely want a fight. Yet, not one of them hails me or makes an effort to pay the wergild. Sooner more deaths than they were forced to pay what they owed.

I might like the Gwent Welsh, in fact, all of the Welsh, but they are prepared to die for some fucking stupid reasons.

'This can be solved amicably if you pay the bloody wergild,' I try one more time because despite it all, I am king of Mercia and I shouldn't just have a fight for little or no reason. But then a spear flies through the air, menacing and grey. There's not enough sunlight for it to glint. I thrust my shield before me, bending low. I hope the two guards are bent double. I pray the people of Gloucester have listened to me and stayed behind us. If not, there'll be a scream of agony in a moment or two.

But no, the clatter of the haft hitting the wood reverberates loudly, and the Gwent Welsh are running now, the gap between us closing quickly.

'Stand firm,' I order my warriors, knowing they'll do whatever they want but won't risk their comrades.

And the Gwent Welsh attack collides with our shields. It's not so much a thundering attack, as something more like the patter of heavy summer rain on the roof of a dwelling.

'Fuck's sake,' Wulfred roars at the feebleness of it all.

A war axe impacts my shield, perhaps trying to hook it away from my body, but I merely force it away from where it's held firm. I notice in the growing light that it's a rusty weapon. Either that, or it's crusted with long-dried blood. I wouldn't be showing anyone a weapon in that state, and certainly not my sodding enemy.

I thrust my seax through the small gap between mine and Icel's shield, finding wood and having to work it aside to get between their shields which almost overlap. As their shields are concave, my seax is easily directed to the edges, and I stab hard, hoping to tear cloth, if not flesh, because my arm extends a long way. I should probably have gone to the other side. Equally, I should have used my hand that doesn't ache quite so much.

Beside me, Icel chunters under his breath, directing himself and his weapon. Edmund's movements are more violent. He feels no need for deception as he hacks away with his war axe. It's a wonder he still holds his shield. His face is set with fury. Again, I consider that he shows none of his usual hesitations. In future altercations, I'm going to hope that one of the Gwent Welshmen is there to incite such wrathfulness. And more, such resolve from my warrior.

Yet, the Gwent Welsh are fierce in their doggedness. I never expect an enemy to fall easily, but I'm surprised by how long the attack continues. I snatch my hand back when I can make no impact on my foe, and fearful that my hand might be trapped between the shield wall, opening the hated cut again, I decide to try something else.

Changing my seax for my war axe, I decide to hook the Gwent Welshman's shield, force it low, and, if I'm lucky, get a blow on his head. Not all of them wore helms, not when their shields went up, anyway. It's easy enough to catch the shield and drag it down. But the Gwent Welsh shield is cumbersome, and the man who holds it labours against my assault, for all he doesn't manage to remove my weapon.

Beside me, Icel attempts to get a low blow on his foe's legs, but the Gwent Welsh shields are longer than ours, obscuring more of the body.

I feel sweat starting to form on my back despite the chilliness of the day, even as my warriors and I shove and thrust at the enemy. I can't tell whether we're moving forwards, but certainly, we're not going back because the make-shift barrier doesn't press against my legs.

The Gwent Welsh call, one to another, but they're all trying to direct the others, and no one is listening to anyone else, even as they grow annoyed with their comrades for not heeding the instructions. It never works like that. All the same, I feel myself growing frustrated. This shouldn't be so bloody hard. They should be no match for us. Not that I like to think we're superior to others. I just know we are.

'For fuck's sake, do something,' Edmund blusters at me, and I turn to glare at him. His face, that which I can see beneath his helm, is red with effort, his hair streaming behind him. And then I realise what's happening. It's not that the Gwent Welsh are better at this than us. It's simply that the wind aids them. It gusts, coming from the far side of the bridge, making it hard to hold our shields up while giving the Gwent Welsh more strength.

'Bloody wind,' I huff, and Icel grunts in agreement even as he holds his shield in place, trying to find some way between the enemy guard.

'It's the fucking wind,' I mutter to Goda, and he, in turn mutters his agreement, before passing the revelation while Icel does the same. It's one thing to be overwhelmed by an enemy, but now the weather thinks to play its hand as well. Have I not battled enough of the fucking weather in recent weeks?

Not that I know how to combat the bloody thing. I just need to prevail against it, no matter what.

We still hold our places, but it won't be possible indefinitely. Something needs to change, Edmund is right in his demand.

'We should go low,' I think, wishing I could have an actual conversation with my warriors and make some reasonable decisions so that they all know what's about to happen. If we go low, I believe the Gwent Welsh will be unbalanced as they lean on their long shields, and we can stab into their legs. And the wind should be less mighty lower down.

'Down, on my word,' I lean close to Icel, straining against my shield, which threatens to bow backwards with the fierceness of the gale.

Icel makes no indication that he's heard.

Hastily, I tell Goda the same. His eyebrows raise at the instruction, but he nods and shares the news with Edmund. Still, I wait. There might only be ten of us altogether, but it'll take a while for the message to reach those at the edge of our shield wall. I think it Leonath to my right, and Sæbald to my left; two men I trust to do as I ask. And, more importantly, keep themselves safe.

But then I can wait no more because there's an ominous creak from someone's shield. It might be about to splinter. It might just have been that it was used as a weapon against our foe. I can't see, and I can't tell.

'Down,' I call, fearing my words will be whipped away by the wind. I drop down to my knees, wincing at the heavy impact, forcing my shield higher to cover my head and back, hoping my warriors follow suit.

Above me, an outraged shriek assures me that my foe has overbalanced as I hoped, that he threatens to fall on top of me. Quickly, I lash out, below the bottom of his long shield, where mud-encrusted boots speak of a man who's had a journey through mire and snow to get here. I bet his feet are bloody cold.

Blood wells, from the cut on his right ankle, and, because I'm an evil fucker, I stab downwards, all but skewering his foot to the wood beneath our feet. I spot Goda doing something similar, although his seax quests higher, perhaps seeking the top of his enemy's leg. At the same time, Icel merely continues his forward momentum for all he's crouched low so that his enemy buckles over him, forced upwards by Icel's body and downwards by the weight of his shield.

I rush to my feet, catching sight of an open maw and tears falling down a white face, as I stab into the shield-squashed man's back with my dagger. He shrieks, although all I see is his mouth opened in pain, the sound stolen away by the fierce wind.

They probably heard that in Warwick, let alone Gloucester.

My enemy glowers at me, a torrent of abuse falling from his lips as all around him, his comrades fall beneath our blades. Only then, I'm looking towards Leonath, my cry of terror fleeing from my mouth, as he precariously overbalances, standing too quickly and too close to the side of the bridge, to counter the blows of the Gwent Welshman he fights.

His horrified eyes turn my way, time seeming to slow, as I jump over bodies and flailing limbs, trying to fight my way to his side. The Gwent Welshman laughs at what's happening, even with Leonath's seax wedged into his chest, a torrent of blood blowing along the bridge as though an arrow leaks it in its wake.

But I don't give a fuck about that.

The Gwent Welshman will be dead soon, and his death will not be the direct cause of Leonath's.

'Leonath,' I roar, mindful that I can't follow him over the side of the bridge. Sound rushes in my ears, my heart thudding far too quickly. I know I'll be too late to catch him.

I catch sight of the shocked eyes of my warriors as they realise what's happening, colours blurring with my speed. I swear, at that moment, I move faster than the bloody wind.

What a stupid fucking place to hold a battle.

Chapter One

One week earlier

Blood fouls the air. Not mine, of course.

The sun has fully risen, the clouds, high and silent, a witness to the savagery of my attack. I'm just pleased it means I can see what I'm doing, at long bloody last.

Jarl Halfdan is down, dead, of course, his sword still in his belly, seeping his innards onto the cold ground, the blood just warm enough to melt the snow. But I'm not watching that. No. He brought his warriors with him, enticed them with promises of wealth and riches, of Mercia's wealth and riches.

They're not to have it.

But I don't mind if their flesh benefits the soil here. If the Raiders breathe their last on Mercian lands.

I just need to ensure at least one of them lives long enough to return north of the Humber, or better yet, to their homelands, far over the rough sea. Someone needs to tell the bastards that they'll only be met by a wall of iron and wood, and it'll be sharp and deadly.

There's nothing for them in Mercia. Nothing.

I've forgotten all about my wound, even though the blood has stained my glove, and I know it'll hurt when this is over. But for now, a little cut isn't going to stop me. Or my warriors.

Rudolf fights fiercely, his movements quick and precise. Hereman, as so often the case, brawls more erratically. He kills by chance, or so it seems. Anyone watching him would question his size but think him an easy enemy to subdue. They'd be wrong. Of course.

Seax buried deep into the chest of an enemy who huffs into my face, his breath failing him; I take a moment to suck in much-needed air, surveying the scene before me.

I infiltrated the enemy encampment. I had my warriors follow on behind me, and of course, the Mercians of Gainsborough are here as well. We're no match in numbers for the Raiders, but the Raiders are wedged between their encampment and the sullen river at their back. There's nowhere for them to go. A death thanks to iron, or one due to ice. I wouldn't welcome either choice.

And that's not the extent of my numbers either. Turhtredus has made a fortuitous arrival. His Mercians have rushed the fray.

'Get off,' I shrug my shoulder, dip the body low, and the Raider slips to the ground, not that his death acts as a deterrent. A wild-eyed man bolts towards me, his lips shockingly red in a starkly white face, the shreds of a beard doing nothing to cover his slashed and cut chin. This man has fought before, although how he's survived for long enough for his wounds to heal is beyond me.

He has a seax in one hand, a war axe in the other. His chest is covered with a thick byrnie, and yet it too has seen better days. His head is free from helm or hair. A slither of sunlight illuminates the snail trail of scars that cover him there.

I don't know who he is, but a reputation surely comes with him. It'll be my pleasure to be the one to finally end his life.

His eyes are red-rimmed, crazed even, perhaps driven mad by the promise of blood and death. A man needs to think more clearly than that to win every battle. Luck will only take you so far. I glimpse Hereman, his spear flying through the air, taking out an unsuspecting enemy, and I reconsider. Perhaps luck is a powerful tool to possess, after all.

My opponent skips into me, war axe swinging low to high, his intention evident. I don't take the invitation, preferring to step back, once, twice, to avoid the attack. I imagine his real purpose is to strike me with the seax, perhaps beneath my armpit or at the top of my leg. I decline such an ignoble death.

The ground remains slick, the snow and ice covering patchy so that it's impossible to be assured that moving a step forwards or backwards won't result in me slipping to my arse. Better a fall to the ice than a seax in my armpit.

The ice gives me an idea, and I flail my arms wide as though slipping. My opponent takes the bait, cackling with delight, licking his lips, scenting an easy kill. But I'm no more falling than the sun holds enough warmth to melt the snow and ice. As he drives towards me, I stab upwards with my seax, taking him beneath the armpit, even though the action sends a shockwave of pain thrumming through my hand. Not that it slows him.

The bastard still harries me, war axe wild, seax pointed, and this time I have to rear backwards. I don't slip, although I risk it, and still, his advance continues. One step, two, and then three and four, and only then does he come to an abrupt stop.

A flicker of surprise in his red-rimmed eyes, his mouth open in what I assume will be a roar of rage. But I've had enough. I spin into him, knocking into his jaw with my elbow, enjoying the sharp snap of teeth crashing together. At the same time, I retrieve my seax and move on. The sound of his body thudding to the hard ground reaches me as I raise my blade and begin to counter the next opponent who awaits his death.

This man is far more reasoned. If he's noted what happened to his comrade, it doesn't show. He's firm and well-planted, legs far apart as he prepares for the attack. His equipment is of excellent quality, his byrnie showing none of the raggedness of the dead man. Neither does he have any visible scars on his face or along the lengths of his hairy arms. Is he a better warrior? Or an untried one, or maybe just a rich man who plays at war in the hope of garnering more riches?

He carries a shield, the image of a wolf prominent, mouth wide open, saliva dripping from vicious-looking teeth. I hang back, take a moment to admire the bloody thing. I'm almost jealous of the skill of whoever painted the design.

The warrior nods at me when I meet his dark eyes, as though we can take this time to appreciate the image, even while screams ripple through the air, the unmistakable sounds of flesh being rent accompanying the cries. Fuck, we could be about to have a drink together, not try to kill one another.

He makes the first move, breaking the stillness between us, perhaps thinking to have lulled my senses. But I meet his questing seax with my war axe, thudding the hilt of my weapon into his shield. The blade won't pierce it, and even if it did, it would become wedged. I don't want to lose it. Not again.

My war axe batters aside his seax, a strike on his thumb severing it as the seax tumbles to the ground. It lands, blade in the ground, handle quivering, a fountain of maroon covering it. But my opponent hardly seems to notice his injury. Lightning quick, he bends to snatch it back into his hand, only it's almost impossible. He has no thumb to grip it, to yank it free from the frozen ground.

The attack deadens my hand. Briefly, we're both unable to resume the attack. His shield swings wide behind his back as he bends. I clench and unclench my hand, careful of the sharp blade. I could rush him, use my body, not my weapons, to tumble him. But he's thinking the same; I can tell in the way his lower legs tense as he hovers on his thighs.

I eye his shield, thinking he might use it to strike at my hand again, but he's finally realised the loss of his digit. Without seeming to consider the wisdom of the action, he casts his shield aside, reaching with his left hand for the seax, and just as he's about to grip it, I stab upwards with my blade, all feeling restored in my hand. The weapon pierces beneath his chin, up into his mouth, and I wince for the savagery of such a death.

Quickly, I hook my leg around his, upending him to the floor. Reaching for his seax, I stab him through the heart, the words of an apology almost on my lips. His eyes close, perhaps in thanks, as blood shudders around the blade. Gently, I reclaim my seax, wincing at the grate of bone on iron. But I don't rush onwards. My eyes are drawn to the shield. It *is* a fine piece of work. I should like to claim it, but of course, a wolf on the shield will mark me as an enemy, not an ally.

A roar of sound brings me back to the moment; the shield disregarded as my eyes settle on Edmund fighting beside Gardulf. The two battle against five of the enemy. Hereman is struggling to get close enough to help. We're not overwhelmed, not yet, but we're heavily outnumbered. While I've killed two men in a short time, there are still many more waiting for my blade.

I think to rush to Gardulf's aid, but Sæbald beats me to it. He strides into the mass of the enemy, hacking at backs with his war axe, while Goda protects his back from those who might think to attack him while he's otherwise occupied. I shake my head at the antics. There's no order here, none at all. The enemy did present us with a shield wall, but we never took the time to counter with our own. That might prove to be a mistake.

'My Lord,' Rudolf's shout reaches me above the crash of blades and the cries of the dying. Rudolf fights with Pybba as always; the two of them face a force of no more than four Raiders, I can't quite see them all, but that's not why Rudolf shrieks for my attention. No, there's something else going on, and I don't like it.

Turhtredus has led his warriors into the conflict. They're on foot, well-armed, but outstripped by the enemy. Our foe has turned aside from attacking my warriors and me, determining that it will be easier to get through Turhtredus and his men to their horses rather than risking their lives trying to get to the ship on the river behind them.

I'm not surprised, and still, it boils me. I need to help Turhtredus, and I must protect the horses. The area behind me might well lead into the kingdom of East Anglia, but first, they must travel through Mercia. I don't want them joining up with the Grantabridge jarls, and I don't fucking want them in Mercia either.

'Wulfred, Eadulf, Leonath, get your arses over here.'

With the aid of Beornstan and Ingwald, the three men have successfully beaten back the Raiders who faced them. They're not exactly having a rest, but neither have they chosen their next targets.

'My Lord?' Wulfred huffs. His face is both flushed and cold, the tinge of blue evident around his lips and in his eyes. It is bloody cold.

'We need to help Turhtredus. The bastards have their eyes on the horses.'

As he arrived so late, Turhtredus has abandoned his horses, and they're just visible, kicking at the snow and generally looking miserable in the next field over. It won't be easy to reach them, but neither is it impossible to do so.

'Protect the horses,' I order Eadulf and Leonath. They rush to follow my orders, calling to one another as they go, moving swiftly to avoid the wreck of the camp they must travel through. None of the tents remains upright. They sag like sodden clothes left out to dry in a rainstorm, and there are ropes and pieces of pole and wood everywhere. That's without considering the mass of dead or dying men and the smouldering campfires and discarded pots and cups that litter the space.

It looks like there's been a good party here, and someone needs to take control of tidying up. I spare a thought for my horses, Haden foremost, but we left the mounts in a more secure location than Turhtredus has managed, and they better still be there.

Fuck these bastards, always trying to steal my damn horses.

'We'll attack from the rear,' I caution my remaining men. I'd sooner stand face to face with my enemy, but they're so focused on Turhtredus and his warriors that it's an opportunity not to be missed.

Turhtredus labours up a slight incline, the ground treacherous beneath his feet and the rest of the Mercians. The Raiders have thought to make a stand on the slight rise. I'm not sure why they want the horses, not with the river at their backs. But then I remember. There was only one ship in the water. If more of the enemy has retreated that way already, there'll be no room for them.

Not unless they decide to swim, and that will be extremely cold.

With my three men, I move quickly to gain the rear of the assault. Rudolf watches me, one of his enemies mewing on the ground as though a small child. I'm pleased when he stabs down and ends the man's life with less suffering. Pybba's chest is heaving in cold air, expelling it quickly as he recovers from the two kills he's taken.

'Join me,' I call, and then reconsider, 'when you can.' Pybba nods, but Rudolf is once more engaged in beating back his enemy. It's a closely matched fight, but I'm confident Rudolf will prevail, and if he doesn't, Pybba will step in to assist him.

The ground is slick with blood and piss. I move lightly, allowing the battle joy to saturate me. I feel whole, here, on this battlefield. All my worries, and aches and pains from my neck wound, have disappeared. My skin burns brightly, my senses attuned to all around me. With a sharp snap of my elbow, I connect with one of the bastard's noses as he thinks to veer up from the ground. Turning the seax in my hand, I slice down through his neck, ensuring the wound is fatal.

He dies, but I focus on the Raiders trying to hammer their way through Turhtredus' defence. Why don't they go around it? I've no idea. Surely, it would be more straightforward. Or it would have been, but Eadulf and Leonath are in position now. They might not be able to cover all of the horses at one time, but they'll give it a bloody good go.

I eye the backs of the warriors and the expanse that leads to the river, and then I realise the problem.

The river twists here. I've not realised in the darkness when I journeyed along it during the night. It's much further to the river than it looks. And between the river, these warriors, and the ship they want, is a landscape of flooded fields, all icy, all impassable at speed. They could go around it, but the Gainsborough Mercians fight there.

These Raiders are trapped, and we're about to make their escape even more unlikely.

The noise of the battle makes it impossible to shout instructions to my warriors, but we share a look. We know what needs to be done. I streak off to the furthest part of the shield wall, my eyes noting those of our foes who already seem to struggle. The Raider shield wall is uniformly two men deep, one at the rear backing up the one at the front, but feet slip on the icy terrain. I bend and slice my seax into a few exposed calves as I carefully rush to my destination, the shrieks of pain adding to the general noise of the bloody battle.

Wulfred bends to do the same. I arch backwards, ensuring Beornstan and Ingwald are ready and confident that they are, I point my seax forwards. I hope the three men understand my intention. I use my seax to slice beneath a dirty, black byrnie, a flash of skin on display. Although there's so much hair, it's almost impossible to see the leathery skin as well.

The warrior rounds on me, blood dripping down his back, and before I can hammer home my advantage, he swipes at me with his spear. I'm forced to stumble backwards. The reach on the weapon is long. He can get hold of me from where he stands, but I can't get my seax or my war axe anywhere near him. The fucker.

Black eyes glance at me with disgust, the tip of a pink tongue showing between thick lips. He possesses a chin that looks large enough to be used as a shield, and a thin beard covers it, the hair, so light to be almost invisible when the sun lands on it.

'*Skiderik*,' he offers, and I nod. I'm used to the name.

'Fucker,' I retort as he menaces me with his spear, jabbing it one way and then another, mirroring my movements to get closer to him. A flicker of frustration begins to swell. I came to assist my warriors, not get caught up in a battle with a solitary figure.

But the spear is long and lethal-looking, the blackened ash of the shaft promising a weapon that's been well-used. The blade is far from smooth. Any cut from that will be painful, both on the way out and on the way in, tearing as well as slicing. I grimace. Nasty cock. A smooth edge brings a cleaner and quicker death. It will be done with the sharpest blade possible, and the smoothest edged if I must deal death.

I think to charge him, but my intentions are read, and his spear is there to stop me before I've even fully gained my speed. And then the shield wall shudders forwards.

'Bastards,' I exclaim, able to decipher the words of my Mercians as they fight for their lives. I'm doing fuck all to help, and that boils me.

I hope that Wulfred, Beornstan and Ingwald are having more success. I can hear some heated fighting, but I can't see it because the shield wall has become concave. I'm stuck on the far side, the rest of it billowing outwards to my left. All I can see is the river, and there's no one there. Not a single Raider has made it to the lone ship that languishes there. I can't think that'll last.

I can see nothing of the rest of the battle. I spare a thought for my warriors, even as the Raider taunts me. He must realise my dilemma. He grimaces at me, teeth blackened, no doubt with blood.

I turn aside and spit, reassess my options. Some might think it looks bleak. But I'm not going to give in. Doubt is as insidious as an enemy blade. I'll succeed. I just haven't determined how.

It's a stand-off. My foe menaces with his spear, and I have nothing long enough to get through his guard. Well, I do, but I don't want to lose my seax that day.

I could aim my war axe at his forehead or his chest, but he'd see the object long before it hit him. I'm sure he'd move out of the way. But and this cheers me, if I don't kill him, then I'll surely get one of the other fuckers in the shield wall.

Quickly, I determine where to aim and lift my war axe high and to the side. It's a heavy weapon, the handle flimsy compared to the weight at its head. All the same, the Raider, focused as he is on my seax, doesn't notice my intentions. I think it can't be so easy, and it's not. Something causes him to glance at my hand just as I release the axe with a heave of effort. He moves aside, chortling to himself at my easy miss. But I wasn't even aiming for him.

The man he was protecting buckles at the knee as my war axe thuds into the back of his byrnie. It bites deep. On the far side, I catch sight of my fellow Mercians, a tall man, head encased in an iron helm, seizing the opportunity to crash through the broken shield wall before it can be reformed.

I don't know the Mercian, but recognition flashes in his eyes, and before my enemy can think to react, a seax slashes across his exposed throat.

'Daft fucker,' I crow, rushing to assist the Mercians. The new warrior turns towards the extended shield wall, even as I direct my attention to the tail end of it. There are no more than twelve Raiders here, all fighting fiercely to kill my warriors. But they weren't expecting someone to come at them from the side.

It's the work of moments to stab into a tight chin with my seax, to take the seax from the limp hand, my war axe still in the back of the man I felled. I kill the fucker with his blade and kick him aside to get to the next Raider.

Startled eyes look my way, fury quickly replacing the surprise as furrowed brows and a thin face appreciate the danger in which they find themselves. I imagine the Raider thought himself reasonably safe in the middle of the shield wall. But he's now the end of it, not the centre. And he's not safe.

As I consider how to kill him, I can tell that the Mercian force under Turhtredus has sensed the change. They were winning anyway, but now it's only a matter of time before the Raiders realise that as well. It's a heady feeling.

I aim my seax at the man's throat, but appreciating that I'm the real danger, and not the man in front of him, shield against shield, he entirely turns, bringing the rounded wood between the two of us. He jabs it at me, an attempt to hit my chin or my nose. But I duck aside, mindful of the fresh blood pooling on the ground, of the heat that's turning the snow to water, of my injury that could do without the jolt from such an attack.

I catch sight of the Mercian, steadying himself as the weight he leant against abruptly disappears, but he moves on quickly enough, his focus on the next Raider.

'Fine, I'll bloody kill him then,' I huff beneath tight lips, considering the best way to end this altercation.

Once more, the Raider jabs the shield at me, but this time I stand my ground, surprising him when he impacts my body, and I grab the top edge of the shield with the fingers of my left hand. Quickly, I thrust it down towards the ground, satisfied when a howl of pain rings through the air.

'Daft bastard,' I offer, even as I step around the shield, to where the warrior is pinned in place, one foot beneath the round rim. He can't move, and quickly, I slash open his throat, only releasing my hold on his shield when I feel him weaken further.

Not that he falls. No. As sometimes happens, he stays standing, for all blood gushes from the savage cut, his chest a running torrent, the stench of hot blood and piss making me wrinkle my nose.

'To think, you nearly died a man,' I offer, a push with the back of my heel, sending him to the floor. I would sooner he'd fallen away from the shield wall, and not across it, but dead is dead. I can join the rest of the Mercian warriors now, but their work is nearly done. There might have been twelve of the enemy when the shield wall fractured, but now only three Raiders continue to fight, their blows increasingly frantic.

'I think you can manage this?' I huff under my breath, observing the man who left me to face the Raider has his hands on his knees and is busy heaving breath into his body. I note his build, his large hands, and where his belly hangs low beneath his too-tight byrnie. I can't help but think he needs to spend more time training and less time filling his belly with meat and ale.

I turn aside, dismissing my sour thoughts. There's more to occupy my mind than moaning about the fat fucker. The shield wall remains caved in, the Mercians closer and closer to success, and I'm forced to run, almost to the river's edge, before I can get behind the Raiders.

Only there do I catch sight of the rest of the battle. Rudolf and Pybba have joined Ingwald and Beornstan, and the four of them are cleaving through the Raiders. There huffs and grunts of effort reach me, but my eyes seek out Icel amongst the mass of warriors.

I can't sight him for too long, and I understand why I couldn't find him when I do. He fights back to back with Edmund, and that I never thought I'd fucking see.

Hereman and Gardulf are close by as well. They're heavily outnumbered and yet holding their own. The force from inside Gainsborough is also spread thinly, and I can't see Ealdorman Aldred, but that doesn't surprise me. No doubt he's quivering behind a locked door, waiting for the actual work to be done.

An unexpected surge from the Mercians and I'm forced perilously close to the edge of the river, my footsteps unsteady on the tufts of grass, long-dead weeds, and patches of ice.

I stab out with my seax, driving into one back and then another neck, pleased when the men stumble, and I have room to move once more. I meet the perplexed expression of Turhtredus over the heads of the enemy who still stand. I offer him a grin in place of an explanation. Only one of the men I thought dead suddenly stumbles to his knees, hands outstretched towards me. His neck runs with blood, and yet somehow, he lives.

I totter, with nowhere to go but through the fighting. I'm sure he'll thrust me into the water, his gloved hands coming closer, ever closer, but I step aside, holding my weapons tight to my body, and he doesn't have the control to stop himself. With a wince, I watch him stumble over the tufts of grass, slip on the ice, and then he's heading towards the river, and there's nothing I can do to arrest his momentum.

When he hits the icy water, the crash draws the looks of many, some fearful, others bemused, but it's the perfect opportunity to cleave my way through the shield wall.

With quick movements, I despatch the man who stands in my way, and then I hear the more familiar cries of the Mercians, their eager words urging me on. But again, this battle is all but done. I need to get to the rest of my warriors, where they're still outnumbered.

Looking down, the ground is slick with blood and other fluids, and I'm met with staring eyes and lifeless bodies. The majority, it pleases me to see, are Raiders. Not that the Mercians have come away unscathed. A man has stumbled to his knees, holding in his innards where they threaten to spill to the churned ground. I meet his eyes as I erupt before him. He nods, acceptance on his face.

'My thanks. You died a brave Mercian warrior,' I offer as I thrust my seax into his chest. His bloody fingers grip mine, driving the blade ever deeper, and then he shudders, the movement massive, as though he fights to live, only to still, his hand slipping away. I place my hand on his head, almost a benediction, only for a roar of outrage to ripple through the air.

I'm not sure what I expect to see, but it's not Leonath, on one of the horses, racing through the battlefield. I trace his movement, unsure what could have caused such a reaction. And then I see it.

A group of about thirty or forty Raiders have realised there's no escape. Their only chance of survival is to make it inside Gainsborough, and of course, fucking Ealdorman Aldred has left the gates wide open. The damn fool. The Raiders are spilling inside it.

Eadulf follows Leonath, hooves flying through the air as a chestnut mount almost knocks me to the floor. But they're right. There's no time to bloody waste.

Assessing the distance, I begin to run, legs pumping, arms powering me onwards. Leonath's cry has alerted Edmund and Icel as well. And they're running, Gardulf and Hereman as well. If only there were more men? If only Ealdorman Aldred had thought to hold some of his men back? If only I fucking had?

Chapter Two

Leonath's borrowed mount leaps over the ditch surrounding the settlement. The dirty white horse lands lightly and immediately kicks out with its front legs, first one and then the other. A Raider stumbles to the floor. Leonath's seax skewers another. Yet another falls beneath a spear, and I turn to glare at Hereman, where he runs in the same direction. With no thought for Leonath, the damn fool has sent the weapon high into the air. His aim might have been perfect, but equally, it might not have been.

'Perfect,' he shouts, even as he bends to pluck another spear from a body on the ground.

'Lucky,' I grumble, but now isn't the time to pick a fight with Hereman. I'm not sure there ever is a time.

From inside Gainsborough, I see a handful of men scurrying towards the gate, knowing even as I watch that they'll be too late.

'Fuck,' but I've seen something else as well. Perhaps Ealdorman Aldred isn't the craven I took him to be.

But more and more Mercians are making their way to the gateway from their place within Gainsborough. They've seen where the Raiders threaten to breach the settlement, and Ealdorman Aldred is amongst them.

He rides a black horse, darker than night and perhaps twice as tall as Leonath's mount. Even though I wish I didn't, I also note that he wears a polished helm, complete with dyed horsehair, a fair copy of my coronation helmet. It's no good for fighting in, that's for sure. As one, the Raiders who still live surge towards Ealdorman Aldred.

'Stupid bastard,' Edmund huffs the words at me as we run. Most of my warriors are now tearing towards the settlement. Behind us, I can hear the clash of weapons and the shrieks of the wounded, but I jump over a carpet of the dead, first one, and then another; the bodies occasionally rearing upwards under my weight, but they're all dead, and that's what matters most.

I think to defend the ealdorman, but I can't deny it, he is a stupid bastard.

'Hereman,' I roar as one of the Raiders attempts to mount Ealdorman Aldred's horse. Without the need for more words, the spear is once more flying. The Raider judders to a stop as the blade pierces his body. A splattering of blood covers Ealdorman Aldred's face, and his gaze turns my way. What did he want me to do? Let him fucking die?

By now, Eadulf has joined Leonath, and the two of them do all they can to forge a path to Ealdorman Aldred's side. Their blades send fountains of blood high into the air, the sound when it falls audible even above my harsh breathing. Finally, I stagger to a stop, watching the Raiders, determining the next move they'll make. There are enough Mercians inside Gainsborough to keep it secure, but Ealdorman Aldred seems unaware of that.

He bellows for his men to protect him, his spittle merging with the blood, his body telling of his fear. He might look the part, but this man is no warrior. Not when faced with so many against him and so few with which to defend.

Leonath disappears from view, and I fear he's been pulled to the ground by the enemy as Eadulf forces his horse ever closer.

'Fuck,' and Edmund hears me and understands the problem.

'Hereman, rescue the ealdorman,' I order him, but I'm not waiting for a response.

'Gardulf, Osbert, Wulfhere, with me.' I snap the instructions, hoping they hear them. Edmund calls for men to join him, and together, with Hereman at the centre, we begin a two-pronged attack. There'll be nowhere for the Raiders to go other than the end of my blade.

The ground is both frozen and slick beneath my feet, far from easy to traverse. When I crawled from inside Gainsborough in the dark, the ground was no hindrance, but now it is. The screams of fighting men deaden my other senses, and I act more on instinct than anything else. My seax flashes in the light from the sun, my war axe heavy in my hand, but useful. My arms ache, my legs as well, and I ignore the twinge at my neck. And don't even get me started on the dull throb my hand has become.

And then we're before the ditch, the view far from enticing, filled with murky water and other, hidden items, hinted at only in the disturbance of the water, the way the ice has formed half-heartedly. There's a downward-facing body floating in the sludge, and I grimace at the livid cut beneath the hairline. He must have once had a long mane of hair tied tightly there. But now, it floats beside him, more alive than him as it flows forwards and backwards with the disturbance of the water.

'Come the fuck on,' I encourage myself. Ealdorman Aldred is still in peril, even as Hereman rushes closer to him. Edmund has made it over the ditch, as have his comrades, a trail of bleeding men in their wake.

Wulfhere makes the jump first, landing with a jangle of equipment, his seax threatening to slip into the muck. But he grabs it, turning quickly.

'Fucking bastard,' he complains, and I don't know if he aims the words at himself or his seax. Probably both.

And still, I don't move. His head tilts to one side, a knowing look in his eye, hand extended over the breach in the mud.

'Fuck off,' and I tense to land beside him. I leap high into the air, hand on my seax, and fuck it, I'm compelled to grab for his offered hand as my right leg dips into the sludge.

He hefts me beside him, chest heaving, and I gasp around the agony of my burning hand.

'My thanks,' I offer, and he grins but says nothing else. That surprises me. My warriors are usually eager to crow over my miscalculations.

Gardulf lands next, his passage so light, he would leave no imprint in the snow if it hadn't turned to a filthy sludge. Then Osbert makes the same miscalculation I did, and I reach for his hand. For a moment, I think he'll tumble into the frigid water, but then our hands meet, and I pull him close, managing to use my undamaged hand this time.

'Harder than it looks,' he comments sourly, rather than thanking me, and I slap him on the shoulder.

'Too right,' I offer, turning to assess the situation again, pleased I'm not the only one who can't leap a damn ditch.

The Raiders still fight on the slaughter field, but their numbers are rapidly decreasing. The ship has yet to leave the quay, its mast visible even from such a distance. No doubt, those on board are waiting for others to arrive. They should leave. While they still can. They've managed to get the mast in place. Now all they need is the sail. The longer they linger, the more chance there is for my Mercians to kill every last one of them.

A shriek akin to that made by the wolf-eaten man close to London momentarily stills every seax, sword and war axe.

'Fuck me,' I exhale, the sound enough to send a judder down my spine.

'Hereman,' Wulfhere offers, although I would have guessed it, all the same.

I don't see what he's done, only the result of his action. One of the

Raiders is impaled on his spear, his mouth opening and closing in muted pain, for he's not the one making the noise. No, Ealdorman Aldred screams, and I grin. I can see why.

His horse is next to Hereman's victim. A handspan on either side, and it would be Ealdorman Aldred or his horse that was skewered. That's two of the bastards that Hereman has killed from a distance. Ealdorman Aldred's lucky to be alive. Or, perhaps he's not. Hereman is skilled with a spear. He always has been. Skilled with luck.

'Fucking cock,' I exclaim, eyes on the next problem. Hereman might have hit two of his targets, but others are eager to get their hands on Ealdorman Aldred. Why the man doesn't just spur his horse onwards, I have no idea. Perhaps there's something within Gainsborough he needs to protect. But no man should ever allow himself to be so vulnerable.

For now, Ealdorman Aldred remains in danger of being overwhelmed, but Edmund is close to him. Not that it'll be enough. The mass of Mercians and Raiders makes it challenging to see who triumphs, and that's no good. Not at all.

'Follow me.'

I cleave through the Raiders, eyes alert to the Mercians. I don't want to fell them in my haste.

Gardulf extends his legs, forging ahead of me, and for a moment, I fear Hereman or Edmund are in danger, but it's nothing of the sort. Gardulf has given himself over to speed.

'Shit,' and I surge after him. Between one blink and the next, he's subsumed by the Raiders.

'Shit and bollocks.' Osbert appreciates the danger. We aimed to save Ealdorman Aldred, but I can't allow Gardulf to take another wound. Edmund wouldn't forgive me, not this time.

Wulfhere keeps close to my back, the sound of a seax busy at work, assuring me that he's doing all he can to protect me.

'Damn bloody fool,' I expel, lifting my elbow high to knock aside a questing arm and then thrusting my helmed forehead at the next man to get between Gardulf and me. The warrior sags to the floor.

'Ware,' I warn Wulfhere. I don't want him to fall over the man. I would stab down, end his life, but I need to sight Gardulf more urgently.

Here, amidst the fierce fighting, it's impossible to know what's happening. Ealdorman Aldred might well have fallen, and I'd not know because I can't see the horse, or Hereman, or Edmund, or any of my men. I can see the Raiders before me and nothing else.

An elbow attempts to knock aside my seax, and I swing my war axe in the confined space, the shriek of agony assuring me my blow is true even before I glimpse its maroon shade.

I catch sight of a shock of colour and recognise it as Gardulf's tunic.

'There,' I bellow, aiming with my body, not my arm, for Gardulf. Two men block my path with their backs, held so tightly together, it's as though they're joined. Neither yields to my strike, and I only just manage to avoid taking my eye out with the stiff leather on the byrnie of the man on my right. Bastards.

I do catch sight of Gardulf. He's fighting as though possessed, seax and shield moving together, but he's surrounded, and these two men press around him, hoping to get closer.

I step back, reassess my options, but I want to be where the Raiders are. I have to get through them, round them, or over them, somehow in order to get to Gardulf. He might be holding his own for now, but he won't be able to forever. No one could. Not with so many hungering for his blood.

'Fuck,' I chunter to myself. Osbert is as stumped as I am, and then Wulfhere stumbles into my back.

'Shit,' we've worked ourselves into just as much of a mess as Gardulf.

'Not exactly gone to plan,' Wulfhere huffs into my face. I note the slither of blood on his bearded chin, the way he heaves air into his chest. He's fought hard to get us here, and for what?

'This way,' Osbert commands, shoulder cleaving a path through the Raider next to the two men, but it's just as impossible.

'Shield,' I order, and Wulfhere places it level with his knees, bracing his legs.

'Osbert, you first.' Startled eyes greet mine, but Osbert understands all the same.

'Fuck,' he exclaims, his unease evident in the way he speaks.

'Get to him,' I order, an almost lazy stab with my seax driving back one of the Raiders who's realised we're in a bit of a predicament.

'Aye, My Lord. Nothing like a fucking easy task.' But he runs the whole three steps and places his foot on the shield. Wulfhere uses all of his heft, and Osbert arches his back, turning in the air, and then he's over the immovable wall of the Raiders. His arrival is greeted with cries of dismay and a temporary lull.

'You next,' I order Wulfhere, but he's already shaking his head.

'Do it,' I flex my words with all the command I can, and still, he shakes his head, a wry grin on his lips.

'You go next. I'll fight through the bastards to get to you.'

'No,' but Wulfhere is immovable, and I need to assist Osbert and Gardulf.

'Damn you, you bastard,' I cry, foot on his shield, feeling the air beneath me. The movement is nowhere near as tight as Osbert's, and I more slide than land on the slippery ground. I leer into the faces of the two Raiders who blocked me. My seax takes its fill even before the one man appreciates that I'm no longer behind him.

His outrage dies on his lips, and I can see Wulfhere in the gap. Not that he can see me because he's fighting another Raider, back towards me.

'Shall we?' I ask the remaining Raider. His teeth clenched, eyes filled with hatred, he whips out his war axe, and I'm forced to veer away, bending my back once more, refusing to acknowledge the spasm of agony from my neck as I do so.

While his war axe sweeps wide, I stab upwards with my seax, catching a lucky strike on the underside of his extended arm. It's not enough to kill. It's not enough to stop his momentum, and yet, the leak of blood is immediate. It'll weaken him. Soon enough. I try not to grimace at the pain from my cut hand.

'Wulfhere,' now I need to get him to me while I can.

'Wulfhere, get the fuck here,' I cry, but he doesn't hear me. Instead, the opponent I face turns to my warrior, a sly grin on his face.

'Really, you're going to turn your back on me?' I crow, hoping to keep his focus, directed my way. Whether he understands my words or simply the mockery, he eyes me again, tongue poking between pale lips, more blue than pink.

'Yes, you want to watch me, not Wulfhere,' only I'm jostled from behind, losing my stance and stumbling low.

'Bollocks,' I expel, regaining my balance to see the Raider has gone for Wulfhere.

'Fine. If that's the way you bloody want it,' I shrug, back on my feet, shuffling forward so that there's some space between Osbert and me. Osbert fights with Gardulf, but both are wild with their manoeuvres, threatened on all sides. If I can just get Wulfhere to me, we'll overpower them all. If.

And then my eyes alight on something that makes it all that little bit easier. At my feet, a long spear lies on the ground, the shaft covered in blood and dirty water, but the blade is true and sharp. Hastily, I bend and retrieve the weapon. There's not the room to throw it at my enemy, but I just about manage to get it in position above my head so that I don't have to move from my hard-won place.

With a roar of outrage, I stab downwards with the spear, hoping for the Raiders back, but pleased all the same when the blade hits higher, through the hard muscles of his back, beneath the byrnie. His entire body quivers and the spear grows ever heavier in my hands. But he's stopped. His breath rattling as though chains fill his mouth.

'Wulfhere, get your fucking arse in here,' I bellow, and Wulfhere, abruptly free from this attack, nods.

'I'm coming. Make some bloody room,' he demands of me.

Only, the dying man isn't done yet. As Wulfhere steps to avoid him, the war axe swirls through the air, a final action from a desperate man.

Wulfhere doesn't see the war axe, his focus on staying upright over the growing pile of bodies at his feet.

'Fuck,' and I slash down with my seax, severing the arm just below the elbow. The war axe continues its trajectory but with the bleeding hand still attached.

'Down,' I roar. Wulfhere somehow hears my words and heeds them. The war axe thuds to the ground, landing on a cooling body with a wet thud, the clenched fingers slowly coming open, one after another, and I'm unable to look away.

Wulfhere stands, his eyes focused on the sight below him, as I run my seax through the dying man's neck to ensure no more of his antics.

'Ugh,' Wulfhere visibly shivers, and I grin at him.

'You don't see that every day,' I admit, tilting my chin to indicate the hand.

'I wouldn't fucking want to,' Wulfhere comments, 'but my thanks, all the same. I'll see that in my bloody sleep,' he continues, his words a whine of complaint.

I laugh at the outrage in his voice. All the things we've seen and done, and it's that which upsets him the most.

'Go and kill someone, banish that from your mind,' I order him.

'Aye, My Lord, I think I will.' With a final, backwards glance, Wulfhere joins Osbert in the mass of shoving men, even as I gaze from the bleeding hand to the dead man.

'You really should have had a bit more fucking control,' I comment acidly and then dismiss it from my thoughts. He's dead. That's what matters. How he met his death, and in how many parts, is irrelevant.

I can't see Gardulf in the confined space, but I can hear him, which means he still lives. Now, I just need to fight my way free from the Raiders.

With more room to swing a war axe, shield, or a seax, the fighting seems less frantic here. I'm not sure how many Gardulf has killed or

Osbert, but there's still enough foes to keep me busy. I spare a thought for Edmund, hoping he's not encountered such fierce resistance. Ealdorman Aldred has made a right fucking mess of this. But the time for recrimination hasn't yet arrived.

I dispatch a Raider who wears no helm with quick movements, a swelling blow on his left cheek revealing that he's lost it somewhere on the battlefield. Black eyes face me, a bloodied nose adding to the mess of his face. I stab into his chest where a rent in the byrnie has already done half the job. He stills and falls, lying across another dying man who howls with renewed pain at this fresh outrage.

'Shut the fuck up,' I offer, but there's no heat to the words. The man is all but dead. A nick on his exposed upper leg ensures it'll be quicker now.

His bloodstained figures grip a seax with a fine blade tight to his chest. I'd take it from him, but I have enough weapons already. I'll send Rudolf to retrieve it later.

There's a break in the press of bodies. Through it, I catch sight of Hereman and Edmund. They've surrounded Ealdorman Aldred, maintaining his place in the saddle, and are starting to fight their way out, not into the melee. Edmund must feel the weight of my stare because he turns and fixes me with an aggrieved look. His face is bleached of colour, or at least the small part I can see beneath his helm. I lift my chin, a challenge, not an admission that his son is beyond my reach. I hope the fucker can't read my thoughts.

And then the space closes in once more, Raiders rushing to die on my blade, and they do. First a slight man, his legs moving even after I've jabbed my seax through his chin, wincing at the sound as it emerges from his mouth, tongue still impaled on my weapon, so that I'm obliged to wrench it free from the mouth. The pinkness erupts through the jagged passage of my seax. It might make someone retch, but I flick it clear, a sharp twist of my wrist ensuring it leaves me clear to continue fighting.

The second is a larger man but as easy to kill. He squeals like a pig as I slash open his throat, having jabbed my helmed forehead against his nose, enjoying the crunch that accompanies the act.

My nose smarts and I turn aside, sneezing. I better not be getting a cold thanks to the crap weather I've endured of late.

Wulfhere cackles evilly, and I know it's at me. Damn fool.

'Concentrate on killing the bastards,' I huff. He cackles all the louder, even as he lifts his arm to bash aside a Raider's shield, slashing at his calf so that his leg is all but severed. The man thinks to run, but he can't, his right leg unable to move. Casually, Wulfhere stabs him through the chest, and the man's breath expels in one final cloud in the cold air, and then he's still.

With the man dead, I can see Gardulf once more, Osbert at his side. They continue to fight, but the Raiders coming against them have slowed to a mere trickle. They're no longer outnumbered. But, Gardulf is barely recognisable. There's no part of him free from blood or gore. His helm shimmers with it, larger pieces of flesh sliding down the slickness of the metal.

'Fuck me,' Wulfhere exclaims, his evil laughter no longer aimed at me. He stands and casually wipes his seax on his trews, careful to keep the edge away from his body. He'd look a bloody fool if he took a cut now.

'Use someone else's clothes,' I caution, voice dripping with annoyance.

'Aye, My Lord King,' but he does as I ask, bending to run his seax along the back of the man whose leg he ruptured.

'Well, are we going to stand here or help them?'

'I don't think they need us,' I advise, amazed at Gardulf's skill and speed. He doesn't fight like Edmund, and certainly not like Hereman, but there's something there all the same. I would name it skill, but I'm not sure it is. Moving as fast as he does, there's probably no need for skill. He merely decides on a target and goes about killing it, trying everything he can until his foe is dead.

It's fucking impressive.

'So we just fought our way to his side for fuck all reason.'

'If we hadn't fought our way to his side, he'd still be outnumbered.'

Wulfhere mutters something I pretend not to hear as I turn aside.

Behind me, the battle over Halfdan's camp is now a sporadic scene of fighting. There are four groups that I can see; one led by Turhtredus, another by what I take to be the other half of his force, another by the men from inside Gainsborough who joined the initial attack, and then there's Icel. He fights with seven of my warriors, all of them holding their own against the swell of Raiders. It ebbs and flows like the tide, and it's evident this has been happening for some time.

My warriors stand between the Raiders and the ship, still at the dock on the river. No sail lists on the mast. Perhaps those onboard mean to use the oars, or perhaps there is no one on board, not any more. Maybe some of my warriors have taken over the ship. The field is a glittering expanse of red and white, rubies and diamonds, but none of them has any value. It looks to me as though red snow has fallen, and yellow as well, if I'm honest, but mostly red.

'Well, they're all about fucking dead.' Rudolf has joined me, and he's elbow deep in blood, his chest heaving beneath his byrnie. 'The ealdorman is safe, for now,' there's menace in Rudolf's voice. I don't understand it, not at the moment.

'Good,' I state flatly. I'm thirsty now, cold as well, and more importantly, trying not to sneeze again.

'It smells funny,' Wulfhere comments, and I realise he's right. It's that which is making me sneeze.

'It tickles my fucking nose,' I complain, as Wulfhere lets out an almighty sneeze, head thrown back, snot flying through the air to land on my shoulder.

'Fuck, Wulfhere. Control yourself.'

'Can't,' is his gasped reply, as he sneezes once more.

'What the fuck?' looking around, trying to decide what it is that's made me sneeze so much. And then I catch sight of it, spilt over the body of one of the dead. I bend, pick up the small packet of powder, black spilling all around it.

'Pepper,' I offer, only just restraining myself from shoving it under Wulfhere's nose.

'Why would a Raider have that?' he demands to know.

'Maybe he fancied himself a cook or something. They can be funny about their spices.'

As Wulfhere sneezes once more, his nose running and eyes flickering closed and then open again, he tries to speak.

'Get it away from me,' he eventually gasps, and I nod. I can do that. I suppose.

'Gardulf, have you finished killing everyone yet?' I call, closing the packet and securing it beside my seax.

'What?' the word comes out elongated and confused.

I meet his eyes.

'Have you finished killing all of the bastards?' I speak more slowly as I indicate the mass he stands within with my hands. There are bodies up to his thighs.

'What?' once more, his eyes are unfocused. He's still far away, in his battle rage. Conversation is beyond him.

'Get a drink,' I call to him. 'Or wash your face with some clean snow. Bring yourself around,' he nods, and I move away, mindful of where I step. Blood, ice, weapons and body parts are all over the place. It would be too easy to fall on my arse, or worse, an upturned weapon.

Rudolf remains at my side. He breaths normally, without any effort, almost as though he's done little more than take a stroll. I wish I could recover as quickly as he can.

'Where's Pybba?' I think to ask. I can't see him when I glance around.

'Speaking with the ealdorman, or rather, demanding to know what this was all about.' Rudolf's voice is tight when he speaks, impossible to tell whether he's pissed off with the ealdorman or Pybba, although I can make a good guess.

Pybba. Never one to shy away from a confrontation with words.

'Well, I better see what it's all about as well.' My exertions from the previous night and throughout the day are starting to make my body sluggish. I could do with a night of good sleep, but there's no time for that. And after all, where would I sleep? The campsite is a mess, and Gainsborough is filled with dead bodies.

The shouting directs my steps. Edmund is standing back, no doubt deciding that Icel is welcome to this argument. And fuck. It's an unholy argument.

Pybba is furious and sheeted in battle dew. He hardly makes a conciliatory figure.

Ealdorman Aldred, looking as though he's done little but cut himself shaving, is puffed up and giving as good as Pybba but looks weak.

Around this altercation, the groans of the dead and dying make me wince.

'Can we not fucking finish the fight before we talk about it?' I mutter to Edmund, but he stills at my words. Again, there's something about which I'm ignorant. What has Ealdorman Aldred been up to? It can't be good if even Edmund disapproves. You've got to be pretty fucked up to upset Edmund with anything where my aunt, or his son and brother, aren't involved.

'Daft cunt,' Hereman huffs. He's stalking through the bodies, looking for anything he can use as a weapon, although his real hunt is for another spear. The problem with a spear is once it's thrown, you've got bugger all with which to fight. They're excellent weapons but too easily mislaid.

'Who?' I ask, but then I begin to hear Pybba's words.

'For this? You risked everything for this?' Pybba points downwards to something on the floor. I can't see what it is.

'Lives have been lost, injuries gained, just because you wouldn't ride out to help your king, your fucking king.'

Pybba's body flexes with rage. I'm in awe of his fury and his loyalty but equally astounded by the implication in his words. Why has Ealdorman Aldred delayed following my instructions? Why has he mounted a horse and made himself a target?

Light shimmers off something, casting Pybba's already reddened face, for he's discarded his helm, into a fiery glow, more like a sunset than a man. Behind him, the sunlight is weak and watery, but at least the clouds have cleared. We might get a day with no snow, and that would be a blessing. Although, well, it might foretell a cold night, when the ground will harden even beyond that of the bodies on the ground.

There'll have to be a fire to burn them all. Perhaps we can pile the dead in the ship, send the pyre along the Thames to the Humber. It would be good to have them gone, but equally, they might foul the water if they don't all burn. I don't want that, either.

'My lord king,' Ealdorman Aldred sees me first and immediately takes to one knee. Pybba, in a complete contradiction to his fuming words, stays upright, his words flowing without ceasing.

I pause, arch an eyebrow at him, waiting for realisation to percolate his senses. Only it doesn't.

'Shut the fuck up, Pybba,' Hereman bellows, perhaps the only one of us who could have said that without causing further outrage.

Pybba's jaw snaps audibly shut, and I incline my head towards him. He bobs his head briefly, but my eyes have caught what outraged him, and frankly, I'm surprised that Ealdorman Aldred still stands upright. We don't endanger our comrades for gold and silver, gems and priceless artefacts, but it seems that's precisely what Ealdorman Aldred has done.

The monasteries and churches might have their riches, and the monks and nuns might be prepared to die for their treasures and faith. But my warriors will die for one another, and, it must be admitted, for their horses. In the correct order, my warriors will die for Mercia, one another, and then their horses. Although sometimes, I think they'd rather die for their mounts than one another.

Ealdorman Aldred, it appears, doesn't hold to those same vows.

On the ground is a heavy-looking wooden chest, the lid thrown wide open, perhaps even cracked, and from it, spills a fortune in gems, and chains, coins and even some holy artefacts, no doubt stolen from a church. I find myself shaking my head.

I'm cold and wet and aching in places I shouldn't ache, my hand throbbing so much it's almost impossible to think clearly, and still, this disgusts me.

'Really, My Lord? Have you seen the wealth in discarded swords and seaxs, helms and byrnies? Why would you risk others when there's so much of it to go round?' I manage to edit out all the 'fucks' and 'bloodys' I want to add to the sentence, and Rudolf's smirk, from beside Pybba, assures me that he knows that, and therefore, so do all of my men.

'My Lord King,' Ealdorman Aldred stumbles, his eyes no longer showing the deference they should. 'These are the ealdordoms treasures. These are what fund it?'

'And so the lives of your men are expendable because they don't give you gold and silver.'

'They are my warriors. They fight to protect me and mine.'

'No, they fight to protect Mercia,' I intone, hoping my voice sounds as foreboding as it must. 'And when they fucking fight, they kill the bastards who come to Mercia, and in that way, grow rich. Have you not seen the wealth in swords, byrnies, helms and axes? These men, they wear their wealth. How else would they keep it safe? And you, you risk the lives of good men to protect what amounts to little more than the keepsakes of ten of these men. How many have we killed?' I direct this to Edmund or Rudolf. I imagine Rudolf will know.

'At least two hundred,' the pair reply at the same time. On any other day, such a feat would make me smile. Now it merely makes me menace Ealdorman Aldred all the more.

'Two hundred men. Their wealth is now ours. Jarl Halfdan's wealth is now ours, and yet Mercians have died, here, inside Gainsborough because your concern was with escaping and not with fighting. You left your gates open while the battle raged outside.' My words have slowed, my fury evident in the precise way I offer each new phrase. Damn this fucker. I didn't make him an ealdorman. Perhaps I could unmake him. I'm sure Bishop Wærferth would know how to do so.

'My Lord King?' Ealdorman Aldred gasps my title, not my name.

'How many Mercians are dead within Gainsborough?'

This time the reply is long in coming, and when it does come, Rudolf's voice is filled with the grief of ages.

'Seventeen.'

I say nothing else; allow the silence to fill around that word. Seventeen men and all for little more than trinkets and baubles.

Ealdorman Aldred stays defiant before me, before the eyes of my warriors, able to see behind us where the attack continues to rage, for all it's nearly done. I think he'll stay belligerent, refuse to acknowledge his error and fuck, I can't help wishing we'd expelled less energy to save the stupid turd.

Only then the ealdorman stands tall, his eyes flashing angrily, chest heaving, even as his horse nudges his shoulder, knocking him to the floor so that he lands, elbow-deep in the treasure chest that's fallen to the ground, no doubt tumbled there by one of the Raiders.

I turn aside, disgusted by the greed in his eyes, and the defiance on his face. Ealdorman Aldred has no genuine appreciation of what he's done here today. I thought him a better man than this. I was wrong.

'Come on. We need to ensure every Raider is dead, all of them.' Without pausing, even to kick aside the gold and jewels, to spill them over the disturbed ground, I turn aside. My battle isn't yet entirely won, and while there are Raiders to kill, I can kill them, rather than consider the folly of my sworn man, a man who pledged to fight for me and Mercia and who's allowed good Mercians to die rather than run the risk of losing his wealth.

It just shows how little he believed I would win this battle, and that sits uneasily with me.

I've never lost yet.

Why would I now?

Chapter Three

'My Lord King,' the voice calls to me from across the frozen expanse where yesterday men, and some women, were slaughtered because they followed a man who promised them what wasn't his to gift. They paid the ultimate price.

I squint into the harshness of the daylight. I've slept within Ealdorman Aldred's smoky half-hall, but not as well as I might like. I came here to organise removing the bodies from the slaughter field outside Gainsborough – not a pleasant task, but a necessary one. Already, I've heard the yips and squeals of wolves and foxes, the flap of heavy wings as battlefield feasts are interrupted, my thoughts returning to the wolf and her pups close to London. I hope they live, even as my lips curl at the hunger of these beasts. At their savagery. Yet, they didn't kill these people. My men and I did that. Perhaps I should reconsider who's the savage.

'I'm here,' I call, not considering the wisdom of that, and I hear Rudolf's aggrieved sigh.

'So much for keeping yourself safe,' he exclaims, Icel not far behind him, shaking his head, as all three of us watch the mounted warrior approach. He comes, not from the river, but the landward side, and it's not possible to see him. Not yet. He's all shadows and shapes. He might not even be a man at all.

But he knows me; that much is clear, as he picks me out amongst everyone else picking through the dead.

I imagine he's come from my aunt, demanding to know how I am, or perhaps from Bishop Burgheard, desperate to know that his diocese is secure once more.

'My lord king,' the man dismounts from a piebald mare with liquid ease, making me grimace even as I step forward to greet him. Icel has his hand on his seax, Rudolf pretending he doesn't, but his hand is behind his back. I fix them both with a firm glance, but neither quails—damn bastards.

Rudolf wears some bruises on his face but walks easily. Icel, I would expect to shuffle with the ease of a man of his age, twisted and bent, carrying the wounds from his clash with Jarl Halfdan, but of course, he moves more fluidly than Rudolf. Damn him. I know he's wounded, but Icel has kept the knowledge to himself, although I suspect Rudolf is aware of it. I need to watch those two. My youngest and my oldest warrior will make it difficult for me should they unite against me. Even if it's for my own good.

The man is dressed in a warm cloak, his face red and pink where it's exposed to the cold air of the early morning. I imagine he's ridden here from Lincoln. I can't see that he's spent the night beneath the stars.

'Bishop Wærferth sends his warmest wishes and hopes for success against Jarl Halfdan and the heathens.' The man, of average height, falters as he reaches the end of his sentence.

'Well,' and he laughs, although the sound is off, and he swallows heavily. 'It seems the bishop's prayers have been answered,' he admirably rallies as his eyes sweep the battlefield. Even I have to admit it's a grizzly sight. There are brittle bodies, frozen wounds, and the blood and piss have yet to entirely melt away. Should the thaw never come, this battle could be immortalised forever in the frozen shapes and sharp angles that speak of death. Painful death. I flinch as my eyes hook on a man, mouth agape, seax still showing through his bearded chin and into his toothless mouth. Those eyes. Fuck those eyes. They cry in agony although no water can form there, and probably never did.

'Yes, the battle is won,' I offer, feeling anything else is unnecessary and not trusting my voice to sound firm for a longer announcement.

'And, of course, you are victorious,' the man presses. And then shakes his head, as though the words don't need saying, which they don't. The outcome is obvious to anyone with the eyes to look.

'My name is Irfara. I'm one of Bishop Wærferth's lay brothers, able to conduct his business and leave the confines of Worcester.' I nod. I don't know much about monks or nuns. Some of them can leave their monasteries; others can't. I don't much care either way. If they stay locked up behind the doors and feeble walls surrounding some of the monasteries and nunneries, at least that gives them some protection from the Raiders.

The bishop seems to do whatever he pleases.

But Irfara says nothing else; his attention caught up by something happening behind us. No doubt the bodies, pale and gleaming after a hard frost the night before, stripped naked, are being moved, made ready for the pyre. It would take a man with a firmer stomach than I not to be worried by such a sight. Bled dry wounds expose too much. The greyness of the flesh, the blue tinge of lips and eyeballs, speak clearly of what awaits every one of us when our time on this earth has come to an end.

'And the bishop?'

'Ah yes, My Lord King,' and the man rubs one hand over his arm as though to ensure his limbs are still flooded with warmth. I can see that they are. His arms are pink, his hands enclosed in warm gloves.

'There are some problems. With the Gwent Welsh,' his smile is hesitant. No doubt he didn't want to be the one to bring me such news, and especially not now. I imagine I look less than kingly. I've not had the time to bathe, and why would I want to when the water would still be cold, if not entirely frozen. I've slept in my clothes. I've risen in my clothes, and now I prowl in those same clothes.

I've done my best with a rough cloth and water taken from the well. But the itch beneath my neck and along my arms is all I need to know that I'm covered in the rust of other men and my own salt.

My hand has been bandaged and tended to, my glove discarded while it's bound tightly, Rudolf sucking his lips when he saw the deep wound on the palm of my right hand. I ache to move it, to clench my fingers and assure myself that all is well, but Rudolf has forbidden it. While he watches me, I dare not take the risk that he'll send word to my aunt, occasioning her to ride here to tend to me, whether I will it or not.

I'm a bloody king, not some child to scold for picking his nose. I've endured far worse and I'm still hale and standing before my warriors. I can still fight. I can still kill. But bugger, it itches like mad.

'Problems. That makes little of them. Tell me, what are the fuckers doing?' Edmund has arrived. He still detests the Welsh, all of them, no matter from which kingdom they come. His words fall heavily into the cold air. I eye him, noting that he has managed to clean himself up, far better than I have. I would know who'd helped him, but I probably don't want to know too much. After such a battle, has his loyalty to my aunt wavered? I wouldn't be surprised.

Edmund's byrnie shows no signs of yesterday's battle. Not a speck of blood, or mud, covers his face, and I could be forgiven for thinking that he wasn't even there. I can't see a wound on him, and certainly no bruises. At least Icel and Rudolf look as though their clothes have been as involved in the defence as the rest of them.

'Well, the bridge at Gloucester.'

'What of the bridge?' I demand to know. They better not have attacked it again. I will personally ride into the lands of King Rhodri Mawr and set them ablaze if the stupid arses have played that trick again. Already, I'm considering how I'll punish Lord Cadell when I get my hands on him. As far as I knew, everything was progressing well. Now it seems not.

'It. Well, it was finished, but now the Gwent Welsh hold the people of Gloucester to ransom. They exact a fee from them when it's used.'

'Ah.' This shouldn't concern me. Not in any immediacy. I mean, I'll ensure the coins are returned to the people of Gloucester, but I think there's more.

'There have been some fights. A man was killed from Gloucester, and now the Gwent Welsh refuse to pay the wergild. I fear it might already have become a matter that can only be contained with violence. Or rather, Bishop Wærferth believes as such.'

Edmund opens his mouth to speak, but I'm quicker, eager to cut-off his string of complaints.

'Does the bishop believe there'll be war?'

This is the problem with the Gwent Welsh. One moment we're allies, the next, at one another's throats, and threatening to kill every man, woman and child within the confines of Gloucester, Hereford and no doubt, Worcester as well. Pestilent fuckers. Sometimes I admire them. They don't take defeat easily. And when it comes, they sure as fuck don't accept it. And there are nearly as many of them as there are Raiders.

'Alas, he does, yes.'

'Good,' Edmund manages to speak into the brief silence, hand on his weapons belt. It doesn't take a fucking genius to work out where his thoughts have gone. But my eyes travel to his seax, war axe and sword. Even they are spotless. Without Hiltiberht here to tend to me, I'm ragged and take as much care as I used to, before I was a king. I should probably have coerced someone else into cleaning my equipment.

'We'll return to Worcester,' I confirm, deciding that this is evidently something that needs my attention. 'In the morning. There's work to do here yet.'

'My Lord King,' the man bows once more, trying to back away from me, reaching blindly for his horse.

'We would be quicker with an extra hand,' I offer, knowing that the man won't touch the battlefield dead, no matter his calling to God.

'My Lord King, I, well, I,' and words leave him deflated, eyes wild as he realises he has no eloquent argument to make that will spare him from the burden.

'Go, eat and rest,' I take pity on him, even as Edmund grumbles beside me. 'There are enough for the task.'

Irfara trips over his feet in haste to be away from me. I chuckle, even as my thoughts turn to the damn Gwent Welsh.

'We had a fucking agreement,' I huff. I intended to return to Northampton and then London. I need to ensure Bishop Smithwulf knows where his loyalties lie. A diversion to Gloucester was not my intention. Not when the Grantabridge jarls are still around, and then, of course, there's King Alfred. What he's about, I've no idea? But I have my suspicions, and they're not good.

'You can't fucking trust them. It's always been the bloody same,' Edmund comments sardonically. He does like to be proved right. Bastard.

'I'll have words with Lord Cadell. I confess to being disappointed rather than furious. I thought he was one of the good ones.'

'None of them are good. Not one of them.' Hereman nods along with his brother, but Rudolf is less sure because he doesn't immediately agree. I'm with Rudolf.

I'd rather the Gwent Welsh were our allies, but, as enemies, they're at least predictable. Not that the Raiders aren't. There are just too fucking many of them.

Icel is also quiet. That surprises me. I turn to gaze at him but he ignores my scrutiny. Icel is free with his stories about defeating the men of the Welsh kingdoms in the past and yet today he offers nothing. That perplexes me but I'm not about to ask, not here, and not now.

My eyes scan the battlefield. Men bend to pluck the bodies from the ground, but the task is far from easy. The ground has frozen, the bodies stuck to it, and where flesh lies too close, the bodies stick, to each other, to the hard soil; the marbled redness of yesterday's spilt blood has become something less palatable.

And the fire has yet to start burning.

I sigh, rubbing my neck with my uninjured hand, thinking I never get the chance to enjoy anything for long. I could stand here all day and watch my enemy burn. I could probably manage a few days of it, if I'm honest with myself.

'My Lord,' Gardulf joins us, dragging something behind him. I fancy I know what it is. He's a vivid assortment of colours, every hue of a bruise from yellow to deepest black, and yet, like Rudolf, you could be forgiven for thinking he spent yesterday sitting on his arse drinking ale. I wish my steps were filled with as much ease and confidence as his.

Edmund turns to watch his son. I notice a flicker cover his face. Perhaps, after all this time, he can show some pride in his son's achievements. Gardulf is truly one of my warriors now.

'I thought you might appreciate this?' From behind his back, Gardulf produces the wolf-headed sword with which I killed Jarl Halfdan. A thrill floods my body. At least one of my bastard enemies is dead, along with all of the warriors he led into Mercia. I can hope that this carnage will be enough to dissuade others from following in Jarl Halfdan's steps. It's long past time that the fuckers were put to flight.

But there's something about Gardulf's stance that worries me, even as I reach for the sword with my bandaged hand. I test the weight, mindful that my hand aches, and Rudolf again huffs with annoyance at my actions.

It's a finely balanced weapon, even with frozen blood and ice marring a surface that should shimmer with the magics of the forge.

It'll clear away soon enough, and then the promised swirling design of the tempered blade will be easy to see. I slice it through the air, first one way and then another.

I'd like a weapon like this, but I do not need it. I have my sword, crowned with Mercia's twin-headed eagle. After all, a man can only fight with his two hands, should he be lucky enough to retain the use of them both. And a sword in both hands would be difficult to direct. I prefer a sword and a seax, or a seax and a war axe. Or a shield and a sword. For every possibility there is a time and a place.

'Tell me?' I demand of Gardulf when he continues to look uneasy. Behind him, I can see more of my men, standing, watching what's about to happen. I'm not the last to know but I'm hardly the first.

'Jarl Halfdan's body can't be found,' the words wrench from Gardulf's mouth with unease, and his eyes look downwards, gloved hands turning one inside the other.

'Fucking bollocks,' Edmund exclaims, already stamping away, his intention to see for himself evident. He marches towards Sæbald and Gyrth, Beornstan and Osbert. I consider then that they're all evil fuckers to give such a task to Gardulf.

At the same time, I absorb yet another blow. There's no reason for Gardulf to lie to me. But equally, I can't see how Jarl Halfdan could have survived. I saw his injuries. I witnessed him still in death. I smelt his last breath.

'He might have moved?' Rudolf suggests hopefully, but there's more hope than conviction in his voice.

I shake my head in denial. I don't follow Edmund. I can see where he argues with the four men, storming through the mass of bodies between the broken down and destroyed canvasses and all that remains of the building in which Jarl Halfdan sheltered.

'No, the bastard will have survived. All the bastards fucking survive,' I exclaim, a hand gripped tightly around the hilt of his wolf-headed sword, feeling the cut on my right hand, mindful that if I squeeze too tightly, fresh blood will well and then Rudolf will truly be angry with me.

It's all I have now. And it'll be enough. I just hope the fucker curls up and dies somewhere else. If he lives to fight another day, his desire for revenge is going to be even greater than mine.

And that does not promise me a long future as Mercia's king.

Chapter Four

'Ealdorman Aldred,' I'm mounted, although my eyes fix on the man. I don't want to leave him in Gainsborough, but he is the rightful ealdorman, for now. And anyway, I've commanded Turhtredus and his warriors to stay as well. He'll ensure that Ealdorman Aldred doesn't do anything else fucking reckless. I can rely on Turhtredus if not Ealdorman Aldred.

The ealdorman meets my eyes evenly. I'm impressed. I can't deny it.

'The Raiders are mostly dead and certainly fled,' behind me, the funeral pyres blaze, four of them containing a mass of broken and torn flesh and limbs. It's not a pretty sight, the smoke swirling in the cold air, the wood only just dry enough to take a flame. But I don't have the luxury of watching my enemy burn. I'll just have to be content that they're all dead. The smell will follow me as I pick my path back down Ermine Street. It's hardly a welcoming thought.

I still stink of the battlefield, and now I'll carry the smell of the pyres as well. I don't think I can look less like a victorious king.

The air is bitterly cold, the ground harder than the dead. I'll have to stop at Lincoln along the way to speak with Bishop Burgheard. I hope to set him to watch over Ealdorman Aldred as well as Turhtredus. If my followers aren't loyal, then Mercia will fall victim once more to the Raiders. That can't be allowed to happen. Not while I live and breathe. I'm not King Burgred to allow such slackness.

And Gainsborough would be a prime spot for them to choose again. It's close to the River Trent, and equally, within reach of the River Humber and the promise of freedom either north of the Humber, in Northumbria, or in their distant homelands, far over the brooding sea.

'Hold Gainsborough, and rebuild it, with firmer defences this time. Put those treasures you were prepared to die for to good use.' He flinches at the words, although I spoke without criticism. He's lucky to have the coins to pay labourers with, and he will use them.

'My Lord King,' he bows low, and for a moment, I admire his thick neck. How easy it would be to sever it here and now. I'd do myself some favours, ending a problem before it can truly become one. But no. I restrain myself. I'll not end a man's life when he's my ally. Or rather, when he's supposed to be my ally.

'Turhtredus will take command of the defences of the settlement until then. He acts with my authority,' and now I give my voice more force, ensuring it's loud enough that those who stand to watch the funeral pyres hear it as well. Only now does the ealdorman quell under my gaze. I'm too fiercely reminded of Ealdorman Wulfstan's disloyalty. I won't fucking have it.

'My Lord King,' he acknowledges my words, and I consider my conversation with Turhtredus the night before. I made it clear what he's to do, and he accepted it, although it's a task that could become impossible. I'll send Kyred to him if I can. Turhtredus needs others to stand beside him and against the ealdorman. The exhilaration of my victory has ebbed away quicker than the leaves, gone in a flurry during a winter storm, leaving the trees stark and naked.

'Come on,' I encourage Haden with a gentle nudge. I've checked his healing wound, Rudolf has as well. It has all but disappeared apart from a thin line. He steps out carefully, making his way to the ancient roadway, mindful of the hard earth and the wafting smoke. Luckily, because he's an arrogant sod, he lifts his head high, tail swishing, and makes me look like a king, even if I don't feel like one at this moment, let alone look like one.

My warriors call farewells to those they know as we depart. I keep my eyes forward, anticipating Jarl Halfdan rearing up before me or even lying dead, half over the road. Not that I'd mind that. And if he's still alive, then I'd welcome the opportunity to kill him again. I'd make sure of it this time by decapitating the bastard. I might even go so far as to skewer his skull on one of Hereman's spears and leave it planted in the ground as a warning to any who might think to emulate the Raider. One thing's a surety, we've not found his body, and we've all been looking for it. Icel has searched until it was too dark to see by, and then he took up a brand and continued.

That man's need for revenge could be dangerous if only I didn't share it. We both want him dead. All of us do.

Lincoln is not far from Gainsborough along Ermine Street, that of course, accounting for Bishop Burgheard's worry about events there. Not that I blame him. Lincoln is surrounded by water. It would be an easy target for the Raiders, if not for the old walls, so reminiscent of London's, differing only in that they're not a tangled pile of rubble. Those behind the walls might stand a chance of using them to keep the Raiders at bay. But the water means trouble. The Raiders could stay in their ships and still attack the walls.

While the sun begins to set in an array of cold pinks and purples, I ride into Lincoln, my warriors sullen behind me. It might not be snowing, but the wind brings its miseries, and I'm miserable. I'd sooner be standing beside the funeral pyres at Gainsborough. At least I'd be warm, even if I had to take shallow breaths.

'My Lord King,' a flurry of activity before me as I make my presence known. Haden is led away to a stable for the night, even as I'm ushered inside an ancient building, half stone, half wood, and all of it shadowed by the coming night.

'My Lord King,' Bishop Burgheard bows his head as he stands to greet me from beside the hearth, merrily blazing at the centre of the hall. I shiver at the warmth, and quickly remove my cloak and single glove, my other hand so heavily bandaged that no glove is required. I sniff and then wrinkle my nose. I stink of the charnel house, and I'm just pleased not to face the bishop in his holy church, which looms even more menacingly in the darkness.

'You were successful?' Bishop Burgheard asks me, the words flowing with ease. I think the sight of me tells him as much, but well, sometimes these things must be made clear. He tries not to notice my bandaged hand or the purpling bruises that cover my warriors. I try not to note that Icel is pale beneath his black cloak. Bloody fool.

'Yes, the Raiders are all dead or fled, but mostly dead. I'm surprised you can't see the smoke from here, the bodies made quite a pile.' A stunned look touches the bishop's face. Fuck. Once more, I forget that these people aren't used to the savagery of the slaughter field.

The bishop is far from a man of weak build, as I often assume holy men are. He didn't decide to become a priest because of his inability to defend himself in a battle. No, he must have chosen it because of his staunch faith, and that can be a weapon in itself. In the right setting. He's tall, angular, his head shaved, as it must be, but his eyes are fierce, and his hands are the size of a horse's hoof, a big horse's hoof. I wouldn't like to tangle with him.

From outside, I can hear the aggrieved neighs of the horses and know only too well who causes difficulties. Rudolf hurries from the room with an exaggerated sigh, throwing his only just discarded cloak back over his shoulders. It's not his job, but I didn't bring Hiltiberht north, so he must fulfil that role. Not that he minds. Pybba will inform him of what happens here.

'Jarl Halfdan.'

'Nearly dead,' I offer, a flicker of my eyelids belaying my fury that the bastard's not definitely dead. I would sooner hold that knowledge.

'And the ealdorman?'

'He lives, as do the majority of the Mercians.'

'Excellent, then I take it Bishop Wærferth's messenger found you.' Around me, there's a flurry of activity, servants bringing food and ale to my warriors, while others stand to give them places to sit and warm their arses. My stomach growls, and I wish I were being fed without the persistent questions.

'He did, yes. We travel to Gloucester.'

'The Gwent Welsh are a difficult breed,' the bishop offers as though it's a great secret he confers on me, even as he indicates I should sit, as a bowl of steaming pottage is laid before me. I sniff it, hoping for some hints of meat, but it's all onion and garlic. They better have more. My men are ravenous, and so am I.

'The Gwent Welsh have been Mercia's enemies for hundreds of years, as have those from Powys and Gwynedd,' I acknowledge, eagerly eating. I'd appreciate it if the bishop spoke and allowed me to eat rather than answering his questions.

'There is another messenger here. From Northampton,' the bishop offers. A slither of a groan escapes my mouth, even as the bishop beckons the man closer. I hurry to scoop as much food into my mouth as possible before being forced to listen to more unwelcome news.

I eye him, recognising him as Heahstan, one of the two men who saved me from a slippery death on Northampton's defences when I was weak from my neck wound. Due to that, I dredge a smile on my face, even as he grimaces. From behind me, Hereman laughs. I know it's directed at Heahstan's shock at my appearance.

'Hail Heahstan. Do you have news from my aunt?'

'I do, my lord... king,' and he adds the king when the silence hangs too heavy and Bishop Burgheard seems about to complain. I roll my eye at Heahstan, taking the sting from the need to use the title, even though I'm suddenly impatient to hear what he has to say.

'Tell me then?'

'She bid me inform you that the Grantabridge jarls haven't been sighted and that there's news from Bishop Smithwulf.'

'What is the news from Smithwulf?' It better not be about bloody King Alfred.

And now Heahstan looks uneasy. Bishop Burgheard moves his head as though to imply he can't hear, but of course, he can.

'Bishop Smithwulf says he acts as an intermediary with King Alfred of Wessex. Alfred still wishes to meet with you to discuss the Raiders.' My lips sour at the news, and I catch Pybba's eye. Of all my men, he's the one actively listening while they all eat and drink and generally make too much noise in a pathetic attempt of pretence that they're not ear-wigging.

'And my aunt's advice?'

'She didn't give any. Merely thought to inform you.' Heahstan puffs his chest out at the words as though to give him more courage.

I turn aside, gaze down at my food, using my spoon to hunt for a non-existent piece of meat or even fish. With all the water around Lincoln, a fish shouldn't be hard to come by, but there's bloody nothing.

I imagine my aunt thought I should be kept updated. Still, at least Heahstan doesn't bring news that the Grantabridge jarls have attacked Northampton. For that, I'm grateful.

'Ride with me tomorrow. I'll give you a reply for her. I'm bound for Gloucester.'

'Aye, My Lord ...King ,' and still the hesitation before 'king' trips from his tongue under the gaze of Bishop Burgheard. Heahstan bobs his chin and moves away, his shoulders firm now his task is complete.

'What's been happening with Bishop Smithwulf?' Bishop Burgheard asks as Heahstan joins the rest of my warriors, his head bent low to Pybba as they confer before he goes to Edmund. I smirk as Edmund sits upright, as though my aunt were in the room watching him. It pleases me to see that she has as much power over him, similar to me, even from such a vast distance. I imagine what she'd say to him if she knew of his dalliance with whoever it was in Grantabridge after the battle.

'He's struggling with his loyalties,' I announce. I hold Bishop

Burgheard's gaze with mine. 'He thinks that King Alfred of Wessex is his ally.'

'And he would be wrong to think such,' Bishop Burgheard hastens to respond.

'I blame the archbishop,' Bishop Burgheard continues. 'Sooner King Offa had managed to make Lichfield an archbishopric than have Bishop Smithwulf look to Canterbury in Kent for his spiritual leadership. Since Kent fell to the Wessex kings, it has been difficult to control. There was a time Mercia claimed Kent as well, and Canterbury amongst that. Sadly, not for these last thirty years.'

I'm sure Bishop Burgheard remembers those times, even if he didn't hold his current position during them.

'I do hear rumours that King Alfred is a pious man of learning.'

'Well, I'd sooner he could make a killing stroke than pray to our Lord God,' I mumble, wincing as my voice sounds too harsh, and I recall that I converse with the bishop and not Heahstan.

'All men must fight for their convictions,' Bishop Burgheard assures me, and I realise that I like the man, even as his words assure me that I'm correct in determining why he's a priest and not a warrior.

'And you, have you fought for your convictions?'

I think Bishop Burgheard will refuse to answer, but then he does.

'As I say, My Lord King. All men, and women, must fight for their beliefs. And I believe in Mercia. My Lord God absolves me of the stain of killing, as he does you.'

'I should like to hear your stories,' I continue.

'I'm sure that you would, but I'm a man of God now and not one to luxuriate in the blood and grime of the battlefield and in the feel of another's stilling heartbeat on the edge of my seax.' And he stands, bows, and goes to move away, as I hear the clang of a handheld bell and realise the monks have all been called away to prayer.

I watch Bishop Burgheard as he walks away. I should dearly like to know more about him. Perhaps I'll ask Icel if he knows anything about the bishop. They must be a similar age.

'Coelwulf,' Edmund clatters down on the chair just vacated by the bishop. His face is unreadable in the shadowed light from the fire and the candles held in their scones and on tables.

'Yes, my friend, what is it?'

'Your aunt?'

'Um, no, we don't talk about my aunt like this,' I hasten to stand, but his hand grips my wrist, effectively pinning me in place because he chooses the bandaged hand, not the hale one.

'What of her?' I complain, retaking my seat before Pybba walks over or any of the others become more interested.

'She sends a private message to me, but it was for your ears.'

'And what was that message?'

'She's sent some of her men to London to keep an eye on Bishop Smithwulf and the Raiders. And of course, by that, I mean King Alfred of Wessex.'

'Bloody bollocks.' I'm as angry as Edmund by the revelation.

'I didn't ask her to take such risks.'

'Well, she has, and I suppose we must be grateful that she doesn't go there herself.'

At that, Edmund's hand slowly releases from my wrist, and my eyebrows arc into my hairline.

'She wouldn't?' I denounce, shocked by his words.

'She bloody would,' Edmund is once more on his feet, hand on his weapons belt.

'Sit the fuck down,' I caution him in a loud hiss.

'That bloody woman,' but he does as I ask.

'Did Heahstan say as much?'

'No, but there was something about the way he looked at me that concerns me.'

'Then ask him.'

'No, I don't want to know,' Edmund confirms, sitting back in the high-backed chair, arms folded over his chest, the fingers on his right hand drumming on his upper left arm.

'She won't do anything stupid,' I confirm, even if I'm not sure. My aunt has always hated the Wessex royal family. She has nothing good to say about any of them. She doesn't blame them for what happened to my father or her father, but she would, given half a chance.

'Ealdorman Ælhun won't allow her to do anything she shouldn't.'

'And you think the ealdorman would be able to stop her?'

I grunt with annoyance.

'I must go to Gloucester, make war on the bastard Gwent Welsh, and I need you at my side.'

'I know that. I'm not rushing after that woman,' Edmund announces, but we both hear the uncertainty in his voice.

'Send Heahstan back to Northampton. I'll ensure he informs my aunt of what she is and isn't to do.'

And Edmund laughs, the sound harsh and abrasive.

'She will follow your orders?'

'I'll order her as the king, not as her nephew. That position is one she holds in some esteem.'

'Perhaps,' Edmund agrees half-heartedly.

'Certainly, it garners more respect from her than it does the rest of you lot.'

Edmund's lips part, showing me a wide grin.

'Aye, My Lord. Well, when you've seen a man shit down a mole's hill and be shocked when the little fucker complains, it's hard to respect a man, even if he is king.'

I can think of no response to that. I've seen my warriors, and they've seen me, in no end of ludicrous situations. No doubt, there'll be many more to come.

'I could recall her to Kingsholm,' I muse, eyeing Heahstan where he laughs with Icel, before deciding that the man once saved me from injuring myself. I would repay him poorly if I gave him such a task.

'We'll just have to rely on her sense of duty,' Edmund confirms, but neither of us is happy about it. We know her far too well.

Chapter Five

I call Heahstan to my side the following day. The temperature has risen overnight, and now the roadway is little more than a pile of sludgy snow; dirty and murky, the wind has returned, meaning it won't remain like that for long.

'My Lord,' his keen eyes face me evenly. I suspect he knows what I'm about to request from him. 'She is the king's aunt,' he offers, as though warding off my words already.

'I know what she is,' I concede. 'I also know what she thinks. Well, most of the time, I do.' Heahstan's gaze has slid towards Edmund, and I know what he means by that. Edmund and my aunt. It's never made sense, but so little truly does; why should I question it.

'Simply try and keep her safe,' I offer more softly. 'She would be a compelling target for the Raiders and the men of Wessex.' Heahstan grunts and I think he'll say something else, but he lapses to silence. I give him time. We don't need to rush this awkward conversation.

'I will do what I can and if it's impossible, I'll ensure she doesn't go alone but has the required resources.'

I reach over and clasp his upper arm with my bandaged hand.

Rudolf has made a point of checking it, changing the bandage and informing me I should do less with it. I grimaced at him. He glowered at me. Hereman merely chuckled. Damn them all.

'That's all we can ever do,' I confirm, pleased that Edmund has absented himself from our discussion. It would be even more fucking awkward if he were here.

'Travel safely,' I advise him, even though we have a way to go yet together until the Foss Way meets Watling Street. I'll be close to Repton. I could stop and ensure Ealdorman Ælhun hasn't seen any Raiders. I could also stop and speak with Bishop Deorlaf, but the feeling of urgency niggles beneath my skin. I won't do either of those things. I need to get to Gloucester.

'And you, My Lord. Ensure the bloody Gwent Welsh fuck off over the border. And, if you get the chance, ensure all is well at Kingsholm.'

I startle at the reminder of my home and the place where my warriors live out the rest of their days when too tired to swing an axe any more. I've not thought of it for months. That sits ill with me. I hope my warriors don't believe themselves abandoned.

I wouldn't be where I am now without them. A foolish man forgets those who've aided him in the past.

'I will. And you, keep the bastard Raiders at bay.'

His face splits with a grin.

'Always,' and he moves aside, making way for the bishop. He wrinkles his nose at the heavy smell of horse shit and sweat. It's never the most pleasant of aromas.

'My Lord King,' he bows low, showing me his shaved head, even as he holds his robes above his feet and the mess on the floor in his courtyard.

'Bishop Burgheard?'

'I came to wish you well and to thank you for your endeavours to date. I'll send half of my warriors to support the ealdorman at Gainsborough.'

'That's generous of you,' I acknowledge, my thoughts on the

rivers that converge at Lincoln. 'Is Lincoln not more open to attack than Gainsborough?'

A knowing twinkle enters the bishop's eye.

'We have means of protecting Lincoln. We have been doing it for many years. Why else do you think these ancient walls are kept in such good repair? Not everywhere can lay claim to such walls, and most of them don't take the time and effort needed to make sure they remain serviceable.'

'No, they don't,' I offer sourly, thinking of London. It's just too bloody big, London. And of course, it's grown outside those walls and dismissed them more often than regarded them—bloody fools.

'Travel with the good graces of your God,' he intones, and I think it over religious for my tastes, but the old bugger smirks as he says it. No doubt he knows what I think of that sentiment. But, hey, the Raiders intone to their endless number of gods. I may as well use the one I've got to hand.

And then we're outside, making our way back to the roadway, the cold wind making me wish I wore three cloaks and not just the one. Can a man never be warm? I sneeze loudly, and Haden startles beneath me.

'Sorry, lad,' I offer as we make our way between the River Witham to our right and Sincil Dyke to our left. I can't deny that it makes me uneasy. Raiders with their ships would too easily breach these watercourses, and yet, the ancient walls are impressive. The bishop is right to have confidence in them. A pity not everywhere within Mercia is so well protected.

I don't set a fast speed, as I did when I wanted to get to London or Gainsborough, and the roads were clear of snow. Instead, I allow myself to settle into a steady rhythm, not quite lulled to sleep but not far from it. Haden's breath steams in the frigid air, and I'm still not feeling as warm as I'd like. That said, at least my damn neck isn't itching. That gives me some blessed relief, and I'm grateful for it. I've managed to bathe, the bishop insisting on it, and although my hand throbs, it's almost a pleasant reminder of the many Raiders I've killed.

It also holds the promise that Jarl Halfdan is genuinely dead, even if not where I killed him.

Behind me, Rudolf and Pybba engage in a discussion about the many Welsh kingdoms. I smirk as Rudolf becomes increasingly confused. The history of the kingdoms that border Mercia is not for the faint of heart. If the Welsh aren't fighting amongst themselves, which is always better for Mercia, then they're trying to cause problems anywhere along the ancient dyke. Not that the dyke is a border, it was never intended as such, but it has become one, all the same.

The Welsh who think to live on Mercia's side of the dyke can never be assured of a warm welcome.

'So Rhodri Mawr claims the kingship of many of the Welsh kingdoms,' Pybba has returned to the start of the story because Rudolf has become so bloody confused. 'Once, King Coelwulf, the first of that name, claimed the overlordship of Powys and Gwynedd, but it didn't outlast his death. Now, Rhodri Mawr is the king of Gwynedd, Powys, and Ceredigion but would like to claim all of the kingdoms; to become the ruler of all of the Welsh tribes. He's an arrogant man, sure of himself.'

'And he has many sons who also rule with him?'

'Well, some say they do, and others say they don't. Rhodri has certainly given no authority to his brother, so I can't see why he would to his sons. And of course, in the Welsh kingdoms, all property must pass through the male line and not the female one. I disapprove of that. Women should hold what's theirs, just as much as a man should.' I smirk at Pybba's proud tone. As if he has land to worry about and a wife or a sister to leave his possessions to when he dies.

'But at least he hasn't killed his brother. Other kings have done so. Easier to rule without a brother to share the kingdom with, although, men who do that don't imagine the future when their flesh and blood once more becomes as ambitious in the shape of sons.'

For once, Rudolf is silent, but I wait. There'll be a question soon enough.

Haden moves through the slush covering the road. His steps are steady, his gait relaxed, but the gurgling noise of his passage is so loud it's impossible to hear if we're being followed or if there are people ahead of us. The drainage ditches aren't overflowing yet, but it won't be long, and the landscape has gone from one where there was little to see but white to one where the colours of winter are more evident, and it's much, much wetter. Water runs all around us, but, for once, it doesn't fall from the sky.

Overhead the sky is uneasy and sullen. I think anything is possible. The sun might even shine and warm me. That would be an interesting change.

'So, Rhodri is legitimately king of Gwynedd but rules Powys and Ceredigion by right of conquest.' Ah, Rudolf is back with more questions. I imagine the look on his face as he ponders the questions of the Welsh.

'Yes,' Pybba replies quickly, perhaps hoping that'll be the end of it, although he should know better. I do.

'So, his sons will need to fight to keep Powys and Ceredigion because there must be someone who claims the kingdoms by right of precedent?'

'Yes, or marry a daughter of their royal line, not that it'll do them much good, not if a woman has no right of inheritance.'

I'm stiff in the saddle, my body aches and complains with every movement. I never used to feel the effects of a battle. I wish I'd bloody enjoyed it more.

As Pybba is trying to explain to Rudolf, the Welsh kingdoms are a mass of heaving ambition and too many militant sons wanting what their father holds and is unprepared to share. I consider that? Would I share Mercia with another? To me, it would depend on their skill with a sword and seax and whether or not they were prepared to fight, risking all, as I do, against the Raiders and the Welsh. In time, I might have to battle against the warriors of Wessex as well, as so many of my predecessors did.

But, no, I decide, I wouldn't. Certainly, and no matter how much I miss my brother, I could never have ruled with him at my side. It would have resulted in too many arguments, and my answer to most of them would have been the point of my seax. My aunt wouldn't have approved of that.

Before night closes around us, we meet Watling Street stretching off into the gloom where darkness has fallen earlier, and there we leave Heahstan for him to turn towards Northampton. I note that Edmund has spent some time speaking with the other man. I'm glad I don't know the content of that discussion because what I can imagine is bad enough, and the reality will be worse.

I eye the sky, willing the moon to be bright enough to allow us to continue. I get my wish when the clouds part and a full moon offers sufficient light to highlight the dips and hollows of the ancient roadway. The forests close to Warwick call to me, promising enough blackness for a good night's sleep, but I ignore them. We're nearly back on familiar ground. From here, it won't be long until I could just leave Haden to direct the other horses, and we'd make it to Worcester without mishap.

But, as the evening presses on, the temperature plummets.

'We'll stop here,' I call, eyes picking out the well-known shapes of an ancient settlement that can still be seen in the tumbled walls and skeletons of stones that lie on the ground, a little above knee height in places. There's even the semblance of a low roof over some of the stones.

We've been here before. Under the advance of tufted grasses, a further trackway stretches to the north. I eye it thinking if the Raiders knew of it, they could use the distinct marks in the landscape to reach the heart of my kingship. But perhaps it's well covered now. Maybe the unsuspecting merely see it as part of the landscape.

Soon a fire is blazing beneath the low-hanging roof, the horses left to crop the soggy grass, and I tumble to the ground, every ache and pain from the battle, screaming at me, my hand throbbing in time with my beating heart.

'Fuck,' I huff, and Icel eyes me with a knowing look. I expect some wisdom from him, but instead, he stretches out his right leg and scowls before rubbing his upper thigh with rough hands.

'It only gets worse from now,' he comments sourly, his bluff voice missing its usual arrogance. At last, he reveals to me the nature of his wound.

Beyond the shelter, I can hear the murmur of my men as they go about the business of tending to their horses. The sound is comforting and routine, and yet my left hand never strays far from my seax, even though I'm not sure of my skill with it. I generally use my left hand for my shield or war axe, not the more precise seax.

Edmund arrives with a flurry of complaints.

'It's as though Sæbald has never sat a watch before. Damn fool. Facing away from the bloody road. As if the bastards would come any other way. Rudolf talks to that bloody horse like it's a person, not an animal, and Samson. Well, whoever left him out failed to secure his reins, and I've just had to release him. He could have broken a fucking leg.' Edmund spits as he paces in the confined space, head low so that he misses the roof that hovers so close to his head.

Icel fixes him with a stare, but some wisdom bids him remain silent as he pushes outside to check on his mount. Even I snap my jaw tightly closed. Not one of us is unaware of why Edmund is so cantankerous, and yet it doesn't make for harmony amongst my men.

I hear Icel calling to Sæbald, and then heavy feet marking a path away from the shelter.

'Sit the fuck down,' I command Edmund, noting how Hereman lingers in the doorway, unsure whether to risk coming inside or take his chances outside, despite the deep cold.

Gardulf avoids his father's eyes. When Edmund doesn't seem to hear me, I repeat my instructions.

'Sit the fuck down, Edmund. Stop pissing everyone else off.' Furious eyes bore into mine, and I shrug my shoulders at him, knowing it's most likely to elicit an explosion from him.

But he nods and sits, clamping his lips shut and gazing into the yellow heart of the fire.

I look at the ruddy cheeks of my warriors. The fire isn't as large as I might like it, and it smoulders more than burns, but every so often, flames lick along a dried branch, and shadows dance on the walls.

'People have been using this shelter for hundreds of years,' Icel rumbles, an attempt to restore the mood. 'Once, they say, there were many such shelters and even a bathhouse.'

'I wouldn't mind a fucking bath now,' Hereman grumbles, deciding it's safe enough to risk entering the same space as Edmund. 'Think of all that hot water easing away our hurts.'

My men are surprisingly hale after our encounter with Jarl Halfdan. Bruises are already starting to fade, and the deepest cuts to knit together. Even Eahric's nose is beginning to heal. He won't win a woman to his bed any time soon, but that's the least of our worries.

Rudolf doesn't seem to carry any wounds other than bruises, while Pybba has a deep cut on his remaining hand. It glows fiercely in the firelight, but it's healing well, and it's not stopped him from riding. Wærwulf has recovered from his stunning in the battle against Jarl Halfdan. Apart from a perfect egg shape on his forehead, he has nothing to show from the attack.

Bishop Burgheard provided us with food for the journey, and so we eat hard cheese and some rolled strips of meat. It would be good to have something warm in my belly, but that'll have to wait until we make it to Worcester and Bishop Wærferth. While the Welsh problem is his reason for calling me back to the western reaches of Mercia, I fear he might have other tasks he wants to accomplish as well. He might, damn the bastard, even force me to hold a witan.

That fills me with more fear than a battle ever might. I have no patience with the arguments of others, or even the demands the ealdormen and bishops might lay at my door for land or resources, for a reduction in financial burdens, or even to issue a coinage that shows my face.

No, I'd rather face the Welsh, wherever they might be.

Chapter Six

Worcester

'My Lord King,' Bishop Wærferth bows low as I stride into his hall at Worcester. I've risked inhaling deeply, but the stench of the river isn't rife today. Perhaps the cold has driven it away, or more likely, the rushing snow-melt waters, audible even from here, is busy clearing any of the muck that usually refuses to budge because the water levels are too low.

It's been a damp journey, cold and wet. About as pleasant as sleeping in the mud. Everything has been cloying, clinging, and my fingertips, both inside my glove and poking free from the bandage Rudolf insists I wear, are blue and about to become red and painful as heat begins to wrap around me.

Since my coronation, I've not seen the bishop, but he's not changed, not that I carried any expectation that he would. His hands are busy, even as he remains alert, his keen eyes taking in all he can with a swift glance. I consider that he sees a man who's done little more than fight, for many long months. Is this what Bishop Wærferth hoped for when he decided to make me Mercia's king. Certainly, there's nothing on his face to tell me his true feelings. It's a particular skill; being prepared for all eventualities.

It's been too short a space of time since I last saw Bishop Wærferth, since I last stood in this hall. Yet, it also feels as though a lifetime has gone by since I spoke with him. I was declared Mercia's king, adorned with a golden helmet and all the other items deemed fit to make me a king, but I feel no different. I'm still a warrior and a fighter. I continue to protect Mercia and to kill all who threaten her.

I stink of sweat, and I would have appreciated being able to bathe at Wall the night before, but I was in a rush, the need to rest the horses, a frustration and one I ill bore. Not that there are any buildings at Wall in which I could have taken a bath. But a man can dream.

'Bishop Wærferth,' I acknowledge him, hoping this won't be a protracted meeting. Most of my men have slunk away to find a bed for the night and some warm water. I envy them such freedom, appreciating Edmund, Icel, Pybba and Rudolf for remaining with me, even if I know Rudolf does it because he's a nosy sod. Not that the others aren't as well.

We've ridden all day, through roads and paths that have fluctuated between being snow-covered, or slick with snow-melt. Haden has been foul, refusing to follow my commands, and my hands both ache from gripping the reins tightly. I wish Haden knew I was a king and treated me with due deference.

'You look like you've been in a war,' the bishop tries to lessen the tension of our reunion as he remains standing. Irfara has come in with us, and I can feel his presence at my neck.

I appreciate the mark of respect, even as I settle on a welcome seat beside him. The heat from the hearth begins the tedious job of warming my body, my fingers starting to tingle as I pull my one glove aside. My left hand moves to toy with the bandage, but aware of Rudolf's interest, I move it aside, instead gripping the wooden armrest. Even the wood feels warmer than I do.

Edmund hovers behind me, Pybba to the side, whereas Rudolf thinks to serve me, but I shake my head at him, and instead, he faces the hearth, hands extended, his ears alert so that I know he listens to everything I say.

Immediately, I wrinkle my nose. Warm horse, damp horse, and the stink of a man who's fought for his life doesn't make for a pleasant scent. And certainly not in the confined space of the bishop's hall on a day when the hearth hasn't been allowed to dissipate to embers. It's warm in here. The river might not stink, but Rudolf does, and I imagine I do as well. I admire the bishop all over again. Not a flicker of disgust is evident on his serene face.

Irfara has moved aside, a flick of Bishop Wærferth's fingers ensuring a moment of privacy for the two of us.

Icel merely pulls up a chair, scrapping the legs over the wooden floor with a painful shriek, only to sit and cross hands over his flat stomach. His legs do the same, one over another, almost as though he's the king and not me. I notice that his boots are clean, almost shining in the light from the hearth and candles arranged on tables. How the fuck has he managed that in the short time between dismounting and coming before the bishop? Mine are merely brown, with some green patches. It seems I've mis-stepped in some horse shit. Bloody lovely. I miss Hiltiberht.

I suppress my mirth as Bishop Wærferth does his best to ignore Icel's presumption. It's not worth getting into an argument about right now. Not for the first time, I consider what Icel knows about the bishops who serve Mercia. Perhaps they were boys together. Maybe they once fought together against the warriors of Wessex, or the men of the Welsh kingdoms, or even against the Raiders. I don't know. Perhaps I should ask him.

'Yes, at Gainsborough,' I smirk. It's not as if Bishop Wærferth doesn't know my reputation well. 'Jarl Halfdan had brought Raiders across the River Humber, no doubt using one of the ferry crossings, because they didn't have enough ships for the job,' I mumble. At the same time, I accept the beaker of cold water offered me by one of the servants wearing a smart tunic, decorated with some holy images of doves and crosses. At least the bishop, or rather his servant, has remembered that I'm not likely to accept wine or ale, even as my warriors eagerly take warmed beakers of the stuff.

'And he's dead.' There's greater tension in those words. I eye the bishop, noting the way his thick eyebrows seems to jump as he speaks. It seems I'm not the only one to want Jarl Halfdan dead.

'He should be,' I counter, looking around the great hall, noting the shields high on the wall with their holy imagery, the brightly painted wood, the tapestries as well, in the light from the hearth and the candles. I hope Bishop Wærferth won't ask for more details. It still boils me that Jarl Halfdan might yet live. How, I've no idea, not with the wounds I inflicted. At least he doesn't have his sword any more. That brings me some pleasure.

The bishop's clerics are busy about their tasks beneath the brightest candles, if not as close to the hearth as I would expect. Some monks eat in near-silence, broken only by the sound of one of their brethren mumbling along in Latin, his eyes focused on a large book held on a lectern before him. I've no idea what he says. It sounds as though he runs a blade through a stone. I would recoil, but I don't want to upset my first ally by showing such disrespect for his faith, and for the faith that has made me king.

'And now King Rhodri Mawr demands your attention,' Bishop Wærferth continues as though we speak of little more than a horse in the stable.

'If it's not one of them, it's another,' I grin. I should prefer peace, but if we had peace, what the fuck would I do all day long? Speak to the bishop? Resolve land disputes? I don't think that would bring me any great pleasure.

And, I don't want to revert to what I was before my brother died. Admittedly, I could probably do without the title of king. But what's done is done. I can live with it. I pity the Raiders, who can't.

'Tell me of the problems?' I'm curious to see what he has to say. Irfara implied that war was brewing, but Bishop Wærferth seems too calm for it to resemble the battles I've fought since we last met.

'Something to do with the rebuilt bridge at Gloucester, and

wergild, and just a general mess, as it so often is with the Gwent Welsh,' Bishop Wærferth comments sourly. 'Although, well, I've heard rumours that they're troubled by the Raiders just as much as Mercia and Wessex.'

This is news to me. The Welsh kingdoms are not easy to penetrate, apart from along the coastlines, so I'd expect the kingdoms of Gwynedd and Dyfed to be most threatened. I note that Bishop Wærferth doesn't specifically name them. The phenomenon must be more widespread.

As much as I could do without the problem, I feel a moment of pity for them. The fucking Raiders get everywhere. They really are like fleas on a bloody dog, ants in the cracked honey pot.

'And King Rhodri Mawr?'

'He's not a man to cross.'

'And the Raiders have crossed him?'

Here Bishop Wærferth looks uneasy.

'I believe he and his brother are not getting on.'

'Fucking marvellous,' Edmund explodes from his place beside me. He's taken ale from the servant but has declined to sit. I'm not surprised by Edmund's reaction. He truly detests the Welsh and always has. There's a story there, one I've yet to hear, but I don't think I need to know it all.

'So, the king has been summoned back from beating back the Raiders in the north to attend some sort of family argument in the west?'

Bishop Wærferth eyes Edmund coolly. I consider whether he knows of my aunt's relationship with Edmund. Perhaps he just thinks he's an arrogant sod who doesn't know his place.

That's what I bloody think.

'Politics is only ever about families,' Bishop Wærferth states flatly, brokering no argument, making no sign that he's uncomfortable with Edmund's tone and the implication within it. 'The king knows that, as we all should.'

I don't glance at Edmund, expecting him to say something else, but surprisingly, he holds his tongue, preferring to swill his ale into his mouth. He sounds like a dog lapping at the stream.

'But Bishop Deorlaf hasn't been troubled by King Rhodri Mawr or Lord Cadell?' I press on. I need to know everything before I decide what to do next.

'No. I believe the hills, the River Wye, and the dyke make it too hard for any sort of attack. Especially at this time of the year. The Welsh, like the Mercians, aren't known for their river craft.'

I nod. I could hope the Raiders were as concerned by the weather as we are. I also wish the Raiders didn't have mastery over ships, rivers and seas because there are rivers crisscrossing Mercia and the Welsh kingdoms. Few are genuinely impassable, with the right level of determination. The Raiders possess that level of resolve.

'And you've had no problems within Worcester?'

'Not yet, no. Again, we have our ancient walls, and behind us, the river is not easy to cross without being seen. The bridge is well-maintained and guarded just as well.'

Rivers and walls. It seems as though more is needed to protect Mercian men and women. They need iron, and people prepared to die for their friends, family, and even their enemies. It takes a lot for anyone to put others before themselves. Unless, of course, they happen to like it. As much as I have men who enjoy the thrill of battle, I appreciate that not everyone revels in taking such a spin of the coin: life or death. Few would purposefully put themselves in harm's way.

'And, My Lord King,' and I meet his eyes, knowing I'm not going to appreciate the following words. 'A witan must be called. The ealdormen, the bishops, and the nobility all brought together to discuss what's been happening and what will happen in the future within Mercia. Not all of them rush from battle to battle, from one crisis to the next.' The words are lightly spoken. They bely what I've endured in recent months. I imagine that the ealdormen I'm not particularly close to see it similarly. After all, they don't get to smell the stink of battle, to hear the cries of the wounded and dying, or to witness men grown still and silent in death.

'Arrange it for Easter. A crown-wearing ceremony and a few days of hearing Masses and feasting will ensure Mercia remains united. Is there some saint's memory we can feast?'

A flicker of triumph in the bishop's eyes is quickly replaced by a calculating look that speaks to me of surprise at my easy capitulation, and some unease that I don't know the liturgical calendar as well as I probably should.

'Of course, My Lord King. I'll arrange it. And really, celebrating Easter will suffice. There is no need for other saints to be involved.'

'And ensure that Bishop Smithwulf of London attends. It's about time he remembered that Mercia is greater than London and that Mercia has strengths that Wessex lacks.'

'Very good, My Lord King.' And Bishop Wærferth nods along with me, a slow smile spreading on his lips. It seems I've pleased him. That doesn't delight me, and yet I can't deny that it brings me some satisfaction to have made one of my holy men content. With Bishop Burgheard in Lincoln my ally as well, it seems I'm winning as many friends as I'm killing Raiders.

If Bishop Wærferth and I can work together in such a vein, it will make it easier for me, even if I appreciate that there'll be a cost. There's always a bloody cost. And when the church is involved, that cost can be priceless. I've noticed that they can forget all to easily the Raiders I've killed to ensure their churches remain untouched, and when the threat dissipates, it's almost as though it never happened at all.

Chapter Seven

Kingsholm

We ride into Kingsholm as another wintry day comes to an end. The joy of being home seeps into my weary bones as soon as I'm allowed entry into the inner courtyard.

Perhaps I could stay here, rest my battered body. Haden could do with some time to heal. His wound is knit together but every so often, I feel his stride struggling. There's more than just the surface tear to heal.

But no.

'My Lord King,' I expect it to be Wulfred who hails me with a string of colourful words, but of course, bald Wulfred rides at my side, mounted on Cuthbert. Instead, it's a young lad who bows his head low, his shoulders narrow and slight, for all he's probably not much shorter than I am.

He opened the gates quickly when he recognised me. I wish I could say the same. I look to Rudolf in the hope he might know the lad's name. But he shrugs his growing shoulders, as perplexed as I am by the identity of the new gate warden. I suppose I have taken many men from Kingsholm in the last year, but surely Osmod or even Cuthwalh could manage guard duty.

'Fuck,' I mutter under my breath. Only for Pybba to come to my aid.

'Hemming, is that you?' There's wonder in Pybba's voice as he speaks from just behind me.

'Aye, it is. Well met, Pybba.' I'm still none the wiser, but Hemming doesn't notice my confusion as he walks to Pybba, reaching up to grip Pybba's forearm.

'He's Beornberht's son,' Edmund whispers to me, a meaningful look in his green eye as Jethson's movement forces Haden forwards. Fuck, how have I forgotten that? And fuck, I'm getting old if the sons of my warriors are almost warriors themselves. I don't object to Gardulf or Wulfhere riding at my side, but Hemming! The last time I saw him, he didn't even reach my chest.

I glance at Hemming, with his shock of long, dark hair, prominent nose, and broad chest. Now that I know, I can see Beornberht in the build of the son.

'I thought he was five,' I hiss to Edmund as our horses step forward and backwards, trying to avoid one another.

'He once was,' is the less than helpful reply from my surly friend. The further we've travelled from Northampton, the more difficult he's become. It doesn't help that we ride to fight the Welsh and he hates them all. Mind, he hates the Raiders as well.

We were all five once, I suppose. All the same, it shocks me. I've only been gone for half a year. In that time, he can't have aged a decade? Can he? Or maybe he wasn't five when I last saw him? I try to think, to remember my time inside Kingsholm, but it's impossible. I can remember the battles I've fought in, the cuts and bruises I've taken, but something as simple as when I last saw the lad is beyond me.

Kingsholm speaks of familiarity with its half stone, half wood buildings. I notice the roof of the great hall still sags and decide that I need to have it repaired before my aunt returns. Even now, the plume of smoke coming from the smoke hole is skewed. I really need to get it fixed. And then I catch sight of another who seems out of place here.

Werburg is no longer the dirty, thin and exhausted woman we found at Northampton, with chestnut eyes hinting at defiance. In fact, I think she might hold sway in my aunt's absence. She has that look about her, and not just because of the luxurious fabric that covers her thin frame, and rich fur collar that tops her cloak. There's something about the way she stands, how others defer to her. I find I don't object half as much as my aunt might when, or rather, should she decide to return to Kingsholm.

'My Lord King,' she curtsies to me, offering me a beaker of cold water, and I dismount from Haden, who's keen to be in his stables, and take the drink eagerly. One of the young lads takes Haden, and because he's home and knows what to expect, he goes without an argument. Damn surly beast. He wouldn't do that for me. But he's been better behaved during our journey here. He must recognise the tracks and roads we've travelled along.

'What brings you here?' Werburg asks, her hands now clasped tightly in warm gloves, one inside the other, not the clawed talons she had when I first met her. Around her is an aura of calm. She is once more a noblewoman. I could almost smile. I don't risk looking to see what Rudolf's response is. He might have felt intense sympathy for her. They might have formed a deep bond, but she'll never admire him the way he does her.

'Problems in Gloucester. Haven't you heard of them?'

She nods once, biting her lip and then leaning towards me as though to confer a great secret.

'I have, my lord king, but I worried that your arrival was something to do with Lady Cyneswith. Her health seemed more important than some of the Gwent Welsh.'

'No, my aunt is well. In Northampton, still.'

A slight gasp and I wish I'd not mentioned the place. But Werburg quickly recovers herself, and her poise returns with only a slight shudder for the unwelcome memory. It seems Werburg is content here, behind walls and with men to protect her honour. She could be a valuable piece for me to marry to one of my ealdormen, but I can't do that to her. Here, she has the best, if no longer active, warriors of Mercia to keep her safe. I'm pleased to provide such a sanctuary.

'All is well here. It's been bitterly cold, but the harvest was plentiful, and there's enough food until the better weather arrives.' I nod as she speaks. These are the sorts of concerns I should have, not who I'm going to have to fight next for the soul of Mercia.

'That pleases me, and now, if you'll excuse me.'

'Ah, yes, My Lord King, apologies.' And she moves aside, head bowed once more. I think I've upset her, only her voice rises in a sharp rebuke of one of the youngsters pulling on Samson's matted tail, upsetting the tired horse. I fear some injury if he's not careful. I'm surprised Icel isn't there to bat the annoyance from his piebald horse. But he's not.

'Leave the big horse alone before he kicks you.'

If I've upset her, Werburg's resumed her role of lady of Kingsholm quickly enough. The lad, no taller than Samson's head, has the good grace to look contrite, while Samson eyes her with respect. Another of the youths leads Samson away, and the youngster attends Werburg. She speaks to him softly enough that no one else can hear, and then he moves aside, Werburg shaking her head as she returns to whatever task our arrival has disturbed.

Hemming remains on guard at the entrance to the enclosure, the deep ditch filled with a hard crust of ice about halfway down. It looks firm enough, but I doubt it'd hold a man's weight. Here and there, stones and pieces of wood rest on the surface. It seems that the strength of the ice has been tested. In places, murky water laps at the edges of holes where the projectiles have cracked the ice.

The wooden walkway that tops the ditch looks grey above the shimmer of ice, and when Hemming walks away from his greeting, it's not just the creak of wood that fills the air.

My warriors quickly disperse, all of them keen to be doing something other than stand in the cold. I doubt there's even one of them who's not pleased to see them return to Kingsholm. Without my aunt here, I feel the odd-one out. I'm the king, and yet there's no one here to rush to greet me, not even my aunt's two dogs.

I sprint up the steps of the rampart and walk away from where Hemming has resumed his guard, the gates closed against any who might think to gain entry without permission. I sight the slightly removed River Severn, which is gilded with chunks of ice, although far from frozen and sluggish. I peer against the harsh brightness of the dying sun in the far distance, shading the horizon in a dull blaze of pink and violet only ever seen in winter, somehow thinking to see the Gwent Welsh there, weapons ready, just itching for a fight. Maybe they wanted me to come home. Perhaps they hope to make a name for themselves by tackling Mercia's latest warrior king.

There's nothing to see but the landscape, hints of browning-green beneath piles of sludgy snow, a few piles of white showing that the snow has been thick here as well as in the north. The weather has been no kinder across the river than here. I can make out the tops of the woodlands close to Gloucester itself but not the newly built bridge, and certainly, none of the Gwent Welshmen.

If they've got any sense, then the Gwent Welsh are at home, warming their feet and arses before a hearth; drinking their ale and sharing tales of their younger days when the world was better. It's always better with the help of hindsight.

I hear a giggle and turn to gaze inside the enclosure, noting the young woman who speaks to Rudolf, their heads so close together they touch. I'm surprised she can take the smell. I think to shout a warning to her, but then bright eyes look up at me, aware of my scrutiny. Oslac's daughter. She and Rudolf have been friends since she could toddle after him with a thin stick instead of the wooden sword which he carries. It pleases me to see that she seems recovered, at least physically, from the death of her father. Oslac was a good man. His loss haunts me, as does the loss of all of my men.

The cry of a babe also filters through the air, and I imagine it must be Athelstan's child, born after his death last summer. I'll find the child, ensure the mother has all she needs. Not that I believe she won't. It's not the way of the people who look to me as their lord. It has never been.

'It's good to be home,' Pybba joins me on the walkway. I don't mind his insertion into my thoughts.

'It is. But we won't be able to stay for long.'

'I know that, Coelwulf.'

I know he knows that as well. Perhaps I'm convincing myself, not him.

'I could,' he begins, but I shake my head, turn to meet his eyes.

'No, you can't. I won't risk it.'

'She's my daughter,' he argues.

'She made her choice when she married a Gwent Welshman. Not that I disapprove of her decision. He was a good choice for her.'

'It's less than a day's travel to where she lives.'

'It is, but it's not Mercia there. The Gwent Welshmen have no love for us, just as we have no love for them.'

'But.'

'No.' My tone is final. I only hope it stops Pybba from playing the bloody hero.

'We travel onto Gloucester tomorrow to determine what's truly been happening. I'll make a decision then.'

'I'm an old man, Coelwulf.'

'No, you're not. You're my warrior, and your loyalty is to Mercia. And anyway, Rudolf needs you.'

'Not any more,' Pybba tries to argue, a look on his face that I know only too well.

'We all need you, and Rudolf will always need you. I understand the pull of family, but this is war.'

'Bishop Wærferth correctly spoke when he said all war was about family.'

'He did, and he didn't. Wars with the Gwent Welsh, or those

from Powys or Gwynedd, are often family. The Raiders are just fuckers, all of them.'

Pybba's gaze rests on the faraway hill-scape. I don't know what he sees, but I doubt it's the river, grasslands, and sloping hills.

'I'll do as you say, My Lord King,' Pybba bows his head and moves aside. My eyes narrow at such easy capitulation. Abruptly, I understand how Bishop Wærferth felt when I gave in to his demand for a witan too quickly.

I doubt Pybba means his words, but for once, I hope he might follow my orders.

I hold my position, thinking of the years of war between the Welsh kingdoms and the Mercians, of how it never seems to stop, and yet, how there's always genuine respect between warriors. We might be prepared to kill one another, to make war, but when we war, it's not a slaughter, not like with the Raiders.

The fucking Raiders. Whatever uneasy peace exists between the Welsh and the Mercians, I can't see the same ever being said with the Raiders. And the men of Wessex.

Bloody bastards, all of them.

But, I confess, I quite like the Welsh. But you won't catch me telling Edmund that.

Chapter Eight

Gloucester

I ride to Gloucester as soon as it's light enough to see. I'm escorted by a handful of my men, Edmund and Pybba, amongst them. Hereman remains in Kingsholm, while Rudolf has to drag himself away from Werburg and Oslac's daughter – at some point, I'll remember her name. Not that it's anything more than friendship. I think Rudolf is more than aware of the problems of bedding a woman and the resultant children.

I hope he doesn't follow me in that regard. Perhaps a man should have a wife, or if not a wife, then an acknowledged heir to follow him. I've never considered it before. I thought it was about time my grandfather's line died out. It just goes to show that I know little and make piss poor decisions without even realising they're going to be wrong.

The horses' hooves sound loud on the frost-hazed road, and I'm not surprised when the head of a guardsman appears atop the old Roman walls.

'My Lord King?' his words end on a shriek of surprise, and I listen, even though I wish not to, as something heavy falls down wooden steps inside Gloucester.

I purposefully keep my eyes forward, wincing at the thuds and cries of pain, even while Rudolf chuckles behind me. I'd tell him to shut up, but if I do so, I'm going to have to look at him. And then I'm going to bloody laugh as well.

Unsurprisingly, it's not the head of the man we first saw who forces open one side of the wooden gate to allow us entry.

'My Lord King.' This man's hair is brown, bordering on red, and his cheeks are flushed, and his eyes crusted with sleep.

'My thanks,' and I knee Haden forwards. He willingly goes until I stop him.

'Have the gates been staying shut all day as well as all night?'

'Aye, My Lord King. The Gwent Welshmen have been causing problems. When don't they, aye? So, we thought it best to keep them shut as much as possible. The townspeople and those on the farms know to holler for entry.'

'Has it been that bad?'

'You need to speak to the reeve,' the man states, refusing to be drawn on the subject, even when it's his king who asks.

'Close the gate behind us then? And your comrade? Is he well?'

'He might be when he wakes up. Damn fool fell over his own feet.' There's no sympathy there, and I nod. Not everyone can have the grace of a swan, but it's to be hoped they can navigate steps without killing themselves. Not that I'm truly one to comment on that.

Rudolf continues to chuckle softly. Even the guard has a grin on his face. It won't be long, and we'll all be laughing.

Inside Gloucester, there are few people about their business. It's winter, and it's early morning. They'll all be lingering in their beds. Lucky sods.

The hooves of the horses echo more loudly inside Gloucester than outside. There could only be ten of us alive in the world, along with the two guards. It couldn't be more different than my last trip here when smoke coiled its way towards me, and it was difficult to determine what was happening. Now it's all laid bare before me as I make my way directly to the quayside and eye the bridge doubtfully.

. . .

The Welsh Lord Cadell has been as good as our agreement. The bridge spanning the River Severn at Gloucester has been repaired since our inauspicious meeting last summer. The bright, new timbers are easy to see in the dull winter light. But I can also determine that there's a make-shift barrier blocking the bridge, about halfway across, and from there, two figures guard the passageway. That's not how this was supposed to fucking work. I growl with my frustration at the damn Gwent Welsh. I should know better than to trust any of the bastards.

Knowing how much Haden despises bridges, I knee him forward firmly when we reach the beginning of the wooden planks that span the surging mass of water below. I'm not going to argue with him about this, not now, and not here.

Haden's first hoof on the bridge has him faltering as it echoes loudly in the quietness of the early morning. I lean down, prepared to offer him some words of conciliation in the hope of smoothing our passage.

'It's just a bloody bridge. You've done this before,' I advise him, already convinced that it won't work but determined to try, all the same. Haden surprises me by quickly placing his next hoof on the bridge, then the next, and the next as well.

I'm unsurprised when two sets of startled eyes peer at me from in front of the pile of casks and heavy pieces of timber lying across the bridge as they hear the sound.

At least they're alert, even if they don't hold weapons to hand, which they should. The fucking Gwent Welsh men will be watching and waiting for any sign of weakness.

'What's this?' I demand of both of them, hand extended towards the blockage in the middle of the bridge, as Haden walks sedately closer. I try not to notice that the bridge seems to sway over the echoing space below my feet. I wish I'd bloody dismounted now. I'm not enjoying the sensation. Typical that Haden has no problem with it now. I could have used him as an excuse to call the men to my side while I stood on firmer ground.

'My Lord King,' the first bobs and bows all at the same time. I detect Rudolf's stifled chuckle from behind me. I turn to glare at him where he perches on top of Dever, no fear on his face for all he's high above the surging river below. Rudolf meets my eyes without remorse. He's becoming as fucking cocky as the rest of my warriors.

I admire that. Not that I'm going to say as much.

It seems my face is becoming more recognisable. But then, I think, I have lived much of my life close to Gloucester. I've probably met these men many times before.

'The Gwent Welsh,' the guardsman gasps as though surfacing from beneath the water. His comrade is somewhat more assured, as he bows his head, although he doesn't remove his woollen hat, not that I blame him, and then meets my gaze.

'The Gwent Welsh, My Lord King. Up to their damn tricks again. It's just lucky that they haven't burnt the bridge. Again.' I twist my lips at the words. He's right to speak as he does. It is lucky. The Gwent Welsh have no sense. I swear they'd cut off their own hands and then try and wield a sword and be surprised when their enemy cut them down.

The men are dressed warmly, more thought for that than protection. I wish they wore byrnie and stood holding their shields. Better that that looking unprepared. They're a similar height, a similar shape, but it's all irrelevant beneath their thick cloaks.

'Would it not be easier to make your barrier at the end of the bridge?' Rudolf asks, his young voice high, confusion in the words, his humour, for once, thankfully, tempered.

'No, we've decided upon this boundary.' By that I take it he means the inhabitants of Gloucester. 'The Mercians from that side of the river,' and the guard points westwards, not into Gwent, but instead into the strip of Mercian land that lies there before the land belongs to the kingdom of Gwent. 'Are sheltering inside Gloucester.

None of us wants the Gwent Welsh close enough to break through into the settlement itself.'

'Isn't it windy?' Icel demands to know, his words only just heard before being thrust away by the wind he speaks about. What Icel means is, 'isn't it windy on the bridge?' Another fair point to make. There's a stiff breeze ruffling my hair as I'm riding without my helm. If I had less hair, it would be too cold, and my ears would burn. Luckily, I have enough hair to provide some cover.

'And bloody freezing,' the first man complains, his hands deep inside the opposite armpit, as he hunkers into his cloak. He's hopping from side to side, trying to keep warm. They should have a brazier. But I reconsider. It would go out soon enough, and if it didn't, I don't want the Mercians to be responsible for setting fire to the newly rebuilt bridge should the brazier be toppled by the wind.

'Cynelm,' the man introduces himself, almost as an afterthought. I should have bloody asked but the situation perplexes me.

'There was a problem with wergild?' I return the conversation to the heart of the matter, trying to keep my mind on the task at hand.

'There's been no end of problems,' but Cynelm's words trail off as we all look into the shadowed gloom on the far side of the bridge. Something's coming. It can be heard, but more, it's felt in the trembling of the wooden planks beneath our feet. It could be a man walking, or perhaps twenty of them, a cart or even a few horses. I know the bridge shuddered at our passing. But I can't see, not yet, what comes this way. That side of the bridge clings to the darkness of a winter morning.

'Dismount,' I order my men. 'Take the horses back to Gloucester,' I command, aware some of the inhabitants of Gloucester have trailed the horses onto the bridge but unsure how many. I've kept my eyes forwards. A young voice sounds, one I don't know. I turn, shocked by the high voiced words.

'Aye, My Lord King. We'll do it.' A young girl, with her even younger brother, have followed us onto the bridge. They don't look as though they can control the ten horses, but the horses will go eagerly,

I believe. None of them likes our windy vantage point. Neither do I, if I'm fucking honest with myself.

I hand Haden's rein to the girl with many misgivings, but I don't want Rudolf to leave my select band of warriors to accomplish the task.

'Do as you're told,' I caution Haden with a wag of my finger, and what I hope is a smile for the young girl. Haden shows me his teeth, a parody of laughter. I glance to the girl. She wears well-worn shoes, perhaps a size too small, and her cloak could be thicker. And that's not to mention the tangle of her long black hair which whips around in the growing gale. I can't be sure how skinny she is, but her lips are blue, her cheekbones easy to see. I'll handle that problem next.

Eagerly, she grips the reins, and Haden, shit that he is, bows his head and follows her sure steps as though she's a queen and he's hers to command. I huff through tight lips. I don't look to Rudolf. I know what expression will be on his sodding face.

'Right,' I state, once the horses and the children are well on their way back to Gloucester. 'Be ready for whatever the bastards have planned now.'

Edmund is already grimacing, for once, his face not the white of fear. Maybe, I should just let him take on the Gwent Welsh all the time. He's so keen to kill all the bastards, he doesn't have time to be fucking scared.

A handful of men eventually emerge from the gloom, grins on their faces as they sight the ramshackle arrangement at the heart of the bridge. Have they not seen it before? I should have asked more bloody questions of the two guardsmen.

The Gwent Welshmen come dressed for war; that much is immediately apparent. They dress little differently to the Mercians, but these men all carry a seax in one hand and a shield in the other. If they were banging the one against the other, I'd mistake them for Raiders.

The shields being carried aren't round like our own, but rather long and narrow, slightly concave as well. On the shields, rather than the animalistic representations of the Raiders, or the bright colours of Mercia and her eagle, they have white crosses daubed on a dark background. The crosses are easy to see, especially with the grey edges of dawn behind them.

They fight in the name of their God. That almost makes me fucking laugh aloud, as Rudolf would. I can imagine what Bishop Wærferth would have to say about that. I might keep one, show him, just to witness his reaction.

The words of my enemy ripple through the air, equally taunting and filled with humour. It seems they've not come to pay the outstanding wergild. I look at Edmund but quickly discard him as useless because of the angry lines around his eyes and mouth. He's almost slathering to be upon the Gwent Welsh. If I even suggested a peace, Edmund would howl with the injustice.

I turn to Icel and Pybba, noting Goda, Sæbald and Leonath as well. Wulfred is chuntering away to himself while Lyfing winks at me, lips in a tight grin, hefting his seax and shield, ready for whatever needs doing now.

It's good to see we offer such a warm fucking welcome to our 'guests'.

It takes the bastards a long time to notice that the two guardsmen don't stand alone. Bloody fools. They really should have been paying a little more attention.

'What have we here,' the first one calls derisively. He's a squat man, heavily built around the chest, with wide legs and the confidence of a bull with a field of cows waiting before him. He speaks my tongue well, for a Gwent Welshman.

'I think we should be asking that,' Cynelm calls, trying to sound brave and bluff, even though I can see his knees shaking below the protection of the barricade, and worse, hear his seax tinging against his weapons belt. I shake my head at such folly. Men should know their fucking limits. Even I know mine.

'Stay out of the way,' I instruct Cynelm, moving to take his place, hoping my voice isn't quite as dismissive as I think it sounds in my ears.

'What are you doing here?' I demand to know, my voice rising, to crack like thunder over the howling wind.

'Who the fuck are you?' The second Gwent Welshman asks, this one tall and willowy. I'm surprised he can stand upright while the wind buffets us. It's growing in intensity as we trade words, not blows.

'We're asking the bloody questions here,' Icel shoulders his way beside me, his height almost matching mine. I would grin at him but now's not the time. I appreciate his support, all the same.

'No, we're asking the questions,' the first man counters, eyes flicking from Icel to me and then to those to our rear. I can feel someone breathing closely and assume Rudolf is behind me, shield to hand, should I need some protection from this motley collection of Gwent Welshmen.

'But you're not, are you?' Pybba counters, standing to my right. Edmund is there as well. I can feel his rage. If these fuckers aren't careful, Edmund will kill them all, and they won't even notice until they fall to the wooden planks of the bridge. If Hereman were here, they'd be dead already, I'm sure of it. He'd have used his spear, and everyone else's spear, to end their miserable lives.

He might even have just thrown pieces of the barricade. That man can throw anything to which he sets his mind.

'Who the fuck are you?' This is uttered as a howl of frustration. These Gwent Welshmen expected to see two Mercians on the bridge. Not twelve of them.

'We are the men of Mercia,' Goda states slowly, hands to either side, as though that explains everything. 'Now, who the fuck are you?'

'We're the Gwent Welshmen. Come to take what's ours.' Our enemy speaks with far more heat than Goda. He's as angry as Edmund.

'And what would that bloody be?' Icel counters.

'The money owed us by the thieving tanner?'

'Why does the tanner owe you money? And why does it take eight of you to resolve a minor problem with a transaction.'

'It takes this many of us because he didn't pay me properly, and these are my witnesses to that. Thieves must pay with their lives, if not with their silver.' The man who speaks stabs his chest and then points to the others as though that reinforces his argument. He doesn't explain how the debt came about in the first place.

I turn and eye Cynelm. He's shaking his head, eyes as furious as Edmund's at the accusation.

'Is there any truth to this?' I ask quietly through the corner of my mouth.

'None at all. The tanner paid what was due, and they killed the poor bastard anyway; strung him up, saying they had the right because he was a thief and in their kingdom, a thief pays with his life, although a murderer never does. Better to make a murderer pay for the death, and that can't happen if the man is dead.'

The complexity of laws in the kingdoms of the Welsh is often beyond me. But I believe a murderer should face the ultimate sanction, not so a thief. If the tanner paid what he owed, then that should have been the end of the matter. Perhaps this is something Bishop Wærferth can further investigate for me. Holy men have a love for law and order. It's probably because it involves writing and reading, not to mention slaughtering cows to skin them for their hide. Holy men are a strange breed if you think about it for too long.

'So, it's not the tanner you're after, then, if he's dead. I understand that you killed him and that the price of his wergild falls on you. That will outweigh any amount you believe is owed.'

'And who are you? The bloody king of Mercia come to resolve a business dispute?' The squat man cackles, but there's something about the stances of my warriors that makes the sound cut-off before it can really get going, the confidence to slide from his face.

'Are you the king?' he gasps, already trying to step backwards, only to crash into the man directly behind him.

'Do you have the wergild?' Goda enquires, the menace in his voice assuring me that he hopes they don't.

But now, the second man takes control.

'There'll be no wergild. The man cheated us, and he owes my friend here five silver coins.' He puffs his chest out as though that adds some sort of surety to the statement. 'Five silver coins with the face of Mercia's king on them.'

I consider that. These coins they want would have to show King Burgred's face. I sure as fuck haven't had any coins struck. Not yet. Again, this is something that Bishop Wærferth can resolve for me. Perhaps I do need to call a witan, as he suggests, after all.

Behind the front Gwent Welshman, there's a hurried discussion taking place between the others, and I think we won't have to fight the fuckers. Only the words become angrier and angrier, even the second Welshman gesticulating wildly, and for no reason that I can fathom, the daft sods begin to advance on us, holding their long shields before them. They're all well-armed, even if they don't have the protection of their byrnies that my men and I have.

'Fucking arseholes,' Wulfred complains. I'm inclined to agree with him. Of all the places to have a battle, on top of a bridge, in a swirling wind, isn't a good fucking idea. Not that I'll back down from the provocation. Bugger that.

It's not even in me to suggest we take the fight to the far side of the bridge.

'Watch the sides of the bridge,' I caution my men, pulling my seax from its sheath on my weapons belt, making an effort not to wince as the weight presses down on my unhealed cut from Gainsborough. I turn and peer behind me, noting that the inhabitants of Gloucester are no longer as sleepy as they were. Some of them stand on the bridge, while others behind try and join them, jostling those before them. Those at the front are pushed onwards, even though some have reconsidered the wisdom of such an action and try to backtrack.

It's too windy on the bridge, and there's about to be a bloody great big fight. I'm as angry with them as I am the bloody Gwent Welsh.

'Stay back,' I bellow, pointing with my seax to ensure they know what I mean, even if they can't hear my words. I don't want anyone else here thinking to play the hero. There's already twelve of us on the bridge. Trying to contain the two guardsmen is enough of a distraction for me.

At least our horses are out of sight.

I rub my boot over the wooden planks, noting that it's not as slippery underfoot as feared, considering how miserable the weather's been of late. Still, it's a long drop to the rumbling river beneath us, flashing darkly, the snowmelt raising the water level a good foot higher than usual. I don't much fancy taking such a drop, not in my byrnie and weighed down by my weapons belt and all the weapons that hang there. I'll drown even if I don't hit my head on one of the rocks that poke menacingly upwards.

'Do this quickly, and try not to kill the stupid bastards,' I advise, my head turned to my warriors.

'They fucking deserve it,' Edmund snarls, but even he's calmer than I expect. Maybe he appreciates that this could badly end if we're not careful. I'd sooner not die because of some cheating Gwent Welsh cunt.

The two men we've been talking to are the first to start their advance. Unlike us, they don't stand shoulder to shoulder but rather come in a ramshackle arrangement, two in front of the others. I suspect those that hold back are as wary as we are. Maybe they're not all stupid arseholes after all.

'Get behind us,' I order the two guards. The collection of wooden barrels and haphazardly placed tree trunks don't offer any protection. They're merely there to obstruct.

'Which side?' I ask about the obstruction, the question directed to all my warriors—a mistake, I realise immediately.

'Inside.' 'Outside.' There's no consensus from them.

'Thank you,' I mutter. And then decide. 'On the outside. It'll get too messy if we stay where we are.' I return my seax to my weapons belt and hand my round shield to Goda, who stands behind me, beard rippling in the wind as though it's alive.

Quickly, I make my way over a slanted tree trunk, mindful that I'm forced even higher than Haden's back as I clamber over the barricade the people of Gloucester have forced upwards. The gusting wind is strong, and a large hand on my back assures me that I do wobble as precariously as I think I do. I turn and reclaim my shield, feeling naked without it, even if I don't believe the Gwent Welsh will attack me, not yet. They're still trying to goad on one another, those at the front shouting at the others further back.

'Fucking wonderful,' Icel rumbles as he stands beside me. Maybe we should have stayed where we were and allowed the Gwent Welsh the privilege of staring into the abyss far below us as they tried to get close enough to land a blow.

Rudolf scampers into place, the grin back on his face, his hair tumbled by the wind. I shake my head at the enthusiasm as he reclaims his shield from Edmund behind and stands, waiting.

Already, I can see that the footsteps of the two Gwent Welsh have slowed. Did they genuinely expect to come at us and have the barrier stay between us? I shake my head at their folly. I don't think any of them genuinely want a fight. Yet, not one of them hails me or makes an effort to pay the wergild. Sooner more deaths than they were forced to pay what they owed.

I might like the Gwent Welsh, in fact, all of the Welsh, but they are prepared to die for some fucking stupid reasons.

'This can be solved amicably if you pay the bloody wergild,' I try one more time because despite it all, I am king of Mercia and I shouldn't just have a fight for little or no reason. But then a spear flies through the air, menacing and grey. There's not enough sunlight for it to glint. I thrust my shield before me, bending low. I hope the two guards are bent double. I pray the people of Gloucester have listened to me and stayed behind us. If not, there'll be a scream of agony in a moment or two.

But no, the clatter of the haft hitting the wood reverberates loudly, and the Gwent Welsh are running now, the gap between us closing quickly.

'Stand firm,' I order my warriors, knowing they'll do whatever they want but won't risk their comrades.

And the Gwent Welsh attack collides with our shields. It's not so much a thundering attack, as something more like the patter of heavy summer rain on the roof of a dwelling.

'Fuck's sake,' Wulfred roars at the feebleness of it all.

A war axe impacts my shield, perhaps trying to hook it away from my body, but I merely force it away from where it's held firm. I notice in the growing light that it's a rusty weapon. Either that, or it's crusted with long-dried blood. I wouldn't be showing anyone a weapon in that state, and certainly not my sodding enemy.

I thrust my seax through the small gap between mine and Icel's shield, finding wood and having to work it aside to get between their shields which almost overlap. As their shields are concave, my seax is easily directed to the edges, and I stab hard, hoping to tear cloth, if not flesh, because my arm extends a long way. I should probably have gone to the other side. Equally, I should have used my hand that doesn't ache quite so much.

Beside me, Icel chunters under his breath, directing himself and his weapon. Edmund's movements are more violent. He feels no need for deception as he hacks away with his war axe. It's a wonder he still holds his shield. His face is set with fury. Again, I consider that he shows none of his usual hesitations. In future altercations, I'm going to hope that one of the Gwent Welshmen is there to incite such wrathfulness. And more, such resolve from my warrior.

Yet, the Gwent Welsh are fierce in their doggedness. I never expect an enemy to fall easily, but I'm surprised by how long the attack continues. I snatch my hand back when I can make no impact on my foe, and fearful that my hand might be trapped between the shield wall, opening the hated cut again, I decide to try something else.

Changing my seax for my war axe, I decide to hook the Gwent Welshman's shield, force it low, and, if I'm lucky, get a blow on his head. Not all of them wore helms, not when their shields went up, anyway. It's easy enough to catch the shield and drag it down. But the Gwent Welsh shield is cumbersome, and the man who holds it labours against my assault, for all he doesn't manage to remove my weapon.

Beside me, Icel attempts to get a low blow on his foe's legs, but the Gwent Welsh shields are longer than ours, obscuring more of the body.

I feel sweat starting to form on my back despite the chilliness of the day, even as my warriors and I shove and thrust at the enemy. I can't tell whether we're moving forwards, but certainly, we're not going back because the make-shift barrier doesn't press against my legs.

The Gwent Welsh call, one to another, but they're all trying to direct the others, and no one is listening to anyone else, even as they grow annoyed with their comrades for not heeding the instructions. It never works like that. All the same, I feel myself growing frustrated. This shouldn't be so bloody hard. They should be no match for us. Not that I like to think we're superior to others. I just know we are.

'For fuck's sake, do something,' Edmund blusters at me, and I turn to glare at him. His face, that which I can see beneath his helm, is red with effort, his hair streaming behind him. And then I realise what's happening. It's not that the Gwent Welsh are better at this than us. It's simply that the wind aids them. It gusts, coming from the far side of the bridge, making it hard to hold our shields up while giving the Gwent Welsh more strength.

'Bloody wind,' I huff, and Icel grunts in agreement even as he holds his shield in place, trying to find some way between the enemy guard.

'It's the fucking wind,' I mutter to Goda, and he, in turn mutters his agreement, before passing the revelation while Icel does the same. It's one thing to be overwhelmed by an enemy, but now the weather thinks to play its hand as well. Have I not battled enough of the fucking weather in recent weeks?

Not that I know how to combat the bloody thing. I just need to prevail against it, no matter what.

We still hold our places, but it won't be possible indefinitely. Something needs to change, Edmund is right in his demand.

'We should go low,' I think, wishing I could have an actual conversation with my warriors and make some reasonable decisions so that they all know what's about to happen. If we go low, I believe the Gwent Welsh will be unbalanced as they lean on their long shields, and we can stab into their legs. And the wind should be less mighty lower down.

'Down, on my word,' I lean close to Icel, straining against my shield, which threatens to bow backwards with the fierceness of the gale.

Icel makes no indication that he's heard.

Hastily, I tell Goda the same. His eyebrows raise at the instruction, but he nods and shares the news with Edmund. Still, I wait. There might only be ten of us altogether, but it'll take a while for the message to reach those at the edge of our shield wall. I think it Leonath to my right, and Sæbald to my left; two men I trust to do as I ask. And, more importantly, keep themselves safe.

But then I can wait no more because there's an ominous creak from someone's shield. It might be about to splinter. It might just have been that it was used as a weapon against our foe. I can't see, and I can't tell.

'Down,' I call, fearing my words will be whipped away by the wind. I drop down to my knees, wincing at the heavy impact, forcing my shield higher to cover my head and back, hoping my warriors follow suit.

Above me, an outraged shriek assures me that my foe has overbalanced as I hoped, that he threatens to fall on top of me. Quickly, I lash out, below the bottom of his long shield, where mud-encrusted boots speak of a man who's had a journey through mire and snow to get here. I bet his feet are bloody cold.

Blood wells, from the cut on his right ankle, and, because I'm an evil fucker, I stab downwards, all but skewering his foot to the wood beneath our feet. I spot Goda doing something similar, although his seax quests higher, perhaps seeking the top of his enemy's leg. At the same time, Icel merely continues his forward momentum for all he's crouched low so that his enemy buckles over him, forced upwards by Icel's body and downwards by the weight of his shield.

I rush to my feet, relenting and taking my seax with me, catching sight of an open maw and tears falling down a white face, as I stab into the shield-squashed man's back with my bloodied seax. He shrieks, although all I see is his mouth opened in pain, the sound stolen away by the fierce wind.

They probably heard that in Warwick, let alone Gloucester.

My enemy glowers at me, a torrent of abuse falling from his lips as all around him, his comrades fall beneath our blades. Only then, I'm looking towards Leonath, my cry of terror fleeing from my mouth, as he precariously overbalances, standing too quickly and too close to the side of the bridge, to counter the blows of the Gwent Welshman he fights.

His horrified eyes turn my way, time seeming to slow, as I jump over bodies and flailing limbs, trying to fight my way to his side. The Gwent Welshman laughs at what's happening, even with Leonath's seax wedged into his chest, a torrent of blood blowing along the bridge as though an arrow leaks it in its wake.

But I don't give a fuck about that.

The Gwent Welshman will be dead soon, and his death will not be the direct cause of Leonath's.

'Leonath,' I roar, mindful that I can't follow him over the side of the bridge. Sound rushes in my ears, my heart thudding far too quickly. I know I'll be too late to catch him.

I catch sight of the shocked eyes of my warriors as they realise what's happening, colours blurring with my speed. I swear, at that moment, I move faster than the bloody wind.

What a stupid fucking place to hold a battle.

But, I'm not the only one to realise the peril, and somehow Cynelm is there before me, reaching out and grabbing hold of Leonath's weapons belt, his legs wedged between one dead body and another. And Cynelm isn't alone. The other man has hold of Cynelm so that the three of them are poised, on a precipice, just one gust of wind from falling, Leonath's one foot on the bridge, but the other leg flailing wildly in the wind.

'Icel,' but he's already by my side, Edmund joining him.

I can't tear my eyes away from what's happening, but Lyfing has more sense about him, realising he can't get there in time but a length of rope lying atop the barricade can. The rope lands on the ground by the second man from Gloucester. He twirls his foot into it, managing to hook it around his boot, not once, but twice and then three times, and then five. Lyfing has Rudolf and Goda to assist him, the Gwent Welsh all dead or stunned into immobility.

The rope rears up before me, taut now, as the three pull it tight, and I add my hands to it, cursing the slickness of my enemies blood on them. But Icel does the same, Edmund following suit, and slowly, too slowly for any great relief, the three of them are pulled upright once more, over the side of the bridge, first the man whose name I don't know, and then Cynelm. Terrified eyes look my way, and then Leonath laughs, the sound grating and filled more with fear than joy.

'Fuck me, it's a bloody long way down,' and he collapses to the ground, being careful to put himself as far from the edge as he can, as though his legs can no longer hold him upright. I wince, the wet sound of the body he lands on adding a surreal feel to what's just happened. And then the body lets out a long, almost sonorous fart.

Silence fills the air, broken by Rudolf's chuckle. Like a dam breaking, we all laugh, the sound too high, too shocked, but it's what we need.

'Thank you, Lyfing,' and I march to his side and envelop him in my arms, unheeding of the blood that slicks his byrnie or the look of horror on his face at my actions. I hold him tight, my arms shaking.

Next, I stride to Cynelm.

'You saved my warrior. Thank you.' His broad face is too pale, and he starts to shake, even as I grip his forearm fiercely. 'And you, what's your name?'

'Elfwy, My Lord King.'

'You have my thanks as well. Such quick thinking was beyond the rest of us.'

Not that I'm overly surprised. The bodies of the Gwent Welsh show that we were busy with other tasks. All that it remains for me to do is grin down at the one man who remains alive.

'Finish him off, Leonath.' I offer, hoping that something as mundane as ending the life of one of our enemies will restore him to the here and now.

'My Lord King, wait.' The Gwent Welshman has his hand raised as though to ward off the blow.

'Why?' I demand, staying Leonath's tottering advance by thrusting my arm between him and the enemy.

'These fuckers might have had murder in mind, but I came with a message from King Rhodri.'

'King Rhodri?' I almost kill the bastard myself.

'Aye, My Lord King,' and the man attempts to stand upright while bowing. It doesn't go well, not with the wind still fierce at his back.

'What does he want, other than to cause trouble.'

And the man, his short hair cropped close to his ears, smiles in a sickly way.

'The Raiders, My Lord King. He needs your help with the Raiders.' And this, well, this is an entirely different proposition, and one that ensures the man lives. For now.

With less speed than I might like, we all return to Gloucester itself; the barrier partially dismantled to allow us through without having to climb over the top. After the near loss of Leonath, none of us wishes to take a chance on falling from the side of the bridge.

I ensure the Gwent Welshman comes as well. Haden has been taken to the stables by the young girl, the other horses as well. I seek out the reeve, hoping he can give me some answers as to why the children were on the bridge, alone.

The man bobs and snivels, his thick cloak ensuring he can't feel the fucking wind, and eventually, the story becomes clear. The boy and girl are the children of the dead man; the tanner.

'I'll take them to Kingsholm,' I announce, unease in my voice. More abandoned children for my home, but I'll not have them suffer because of their father's death. I'm upset no one within Gloucester has taken them in. Surely, someone must have realised their plight? The two children sit by the hearth now at Kingsholm, eating eagerly from bowls filled with oats and honey. Rudolf speaks with them, laughing along with them, and sympathising in equal measure for what's happened to them. At some point, they'll need to grieve for their father but that isn't today. Now, all they care about is being warm and fed. I catch stray words and know they speak about my bloody horse. Haden has won himself more adherents today.

I eye the young lad, no more than four summers old, and in him, I see a warrior of the future. It's hard to have his future laid out so clearly before me, Rudolf at his side representing what he'll become, but there are few alternatives. And the girl? Well, my aunt or Lady Werburg will see to her, I'm sure of it. Perhaps one of the childless widows will even take both under their wings. I hope so. They deserve to have someone who will love and care for them. They're too young to be doing it alone.

It's a struggle to turn aside from something so immediate, but I want to know what this Gwent Welshman has to say to me with his story of King Rhodri. I doubt there's any truth to it, now I've had time to think about it. But, well, I'm prepared to see what lies the man concocts to stay alive.

'What's your name?'

'Owain.' The man offers, wincing as his wounded arms are roughly cleaned by the none too gentle hands of the herbwoman. She's efficient and knows what to use to bind the twin wounds, one on the top of his left arm, the other lower down on the right. What she uses will keep them clear from the wound rot. She's already looked at his head wound and deemed it nothing more than a nasty cut that bled a great deal, as these things do. Still, it seems there's another who thinks as much of the Gwent Welsh as Edmund does. I admire her for such cruel efficiency.

'And you just happened to get caught up with those lot?' I ask. I'm sitting on a stool, elbows on my knees, watching him carefully. Edmund stands by the herbwoman, and I'll restrain the pair of them if it becomes necessary. Well, I will provided the man has something good to tell me that makes it worth my while allowing him to live.

'They told me they'd get me to Gloucester. I didn't realise the methods they intend to employ.'

'And what about the dead man?'

'That happened before I encountered them. I believed they intended to pay the wergild, and I hoped to take advantage of the goodwill such an act would create and gain access to someone who could get a message to you; the reeve, I hoped.'

'It's hardly a royal delegation,' Pybba sniffs. His face glows in the warmth of the hearth. I don't miss that the man who wanted to sneak to his daughter's home is now complaining about another stealing into Mercia. Pybba's argument would be that he's one of the king's men. Then again, if Owain is who he says he is, his claim would be the same. A stalemate then.

'Well, no. I'm not. Well.' And here I think we might be about to get to the truth.

'Lord Cadell sent me, not King Rhodri.'

At least this makes more sense to me. Lord Cadell and I at least know each other.

'And what does Lord Cadell expect me to do?'

'The Raiders are on the River Wye. They threaten Hereford.'

'But they threaten the Welsh of Powys first or Gwent?'

'Yes, they do.' That he doesn't differentiate between Powys and Gwent makes me think that King Rhodri has been busy expanding his dominions once more. That man will rule all of the Welsh kingdoms one day, and then he'll be as bloody lethal as Wessex.

'Cadell holds land close to the River Wye. He fears that if the Raiders gain a foothold, as they did in Mercia, then Rhodri will take the lands from him.'

'So there's no fear for his people then?' I arch an eyebrow.

'Of course he has, My Lord King. But he thought it better that I say Hereford was threatened. He thought it would make you more eager to help him.'

I shake my head, turning aside from the man, my thoughts running wild.

Bad enough, the Welsh on Mercia's western borders. I don't want the Raiders as well.

'It's not like the Raiders to try their luck in the Welsh kingdoms,' Pybba muses, and he's right, it's not.

'There's upheaval in Ireland.'

That's meant to mean something to me.

'Many of the Raiders come from Ireland, not just from the Northern kingdoms.' It's Rudolf who explains this to me. I try and sear him with my gaze, but as usual, it has no effect. I didn't even realise he was listening. I don't care from where they come. They just need to go back there.

'Our agreement wasn't one of mutual support,' I muse, and yet, Cadell is right. If the Raiders are on the River Wye, then Hereford could be threatened. Just like Worcester and Gloucester, and in fact, Northampton, Repton and Torksey, the rivers have been seen as a means of defence, but the Raiders make that irrelevant.

I stand, frustrated by yet another problem. I thought I came to drive back the Gwent Welsh, but it's the Raiders who are creating yet more problems. But before I move away, I have another question.

'Tell me, who leads these Raiders?'

'Two men, My Lord King, jarls Thorgills and Ottar.' I've not heard either name before.

'And they're from Dublin?' Despite Rudolf's words, I'm only too aware of the Raiders who've made Ireland their home. It's not as though I'm entirely bereft of knowledge. I did attend King Burgred's court as the ealdorman of my lands. Not that I ever enjoyed it. Not that I ever listened to the tedious transactions, only the news of war and Raiders, and Wessex, of course.

'Yes, My Lord King,' the man bobs. I find myself inclined to believe him, even if he is a Gwent Welshman. As I said, I have a grudging respect for the Welsh, and Cadell is high on the list. We made an agreement regarding the bridge at Gloucester, and he fought well against the Raiders at Repton and afterwards.

'Rest. I'll give you an answer soon.'

I turn and stride outside, immediately regretting the necessity. My enemy warms his arse before the hearth, and I'm forced back out into the blustery wind.

The rumble of cart wheels over wood reminds me of the dead Gwent Welsh. The people of Gloucester and this surprises me, have taken it upon themselves to transport them inside the settlement. I thought they might tip them over the bridge, but it seems they have some compassion, now the fighting is over. A pity they didn't show the same to the fatherless children.

Edmund is behind me, so close, he steps on my heel as I try to walk away.

'You can't go,' he huffs, rather than an apology. 'You're the king of Mercia. If you couldn't follow Jarl Halfdan to Northumbria, then you sure as shit can't go into the Welsh kingdoms.'

There's disgust in his voice, but I hadn't expected him to agree to Lord Cadell's request.

'I'll go,' Pybba announces. That, I did expect.

'You can't go,' Rudolf is already arguing, but then his words trail off, as though remembering that Pybba's daughter is married to one of the Gwent Welsh. His anguished face looks my way.

'It's not a matter of who goes, but rather if we should go,' I counter.

'You can't fucking go,' Edmund growls once more. I turn aside from him, looking to Icel. I can guess what his next argument will be. He might be able to argue without the bias of hatred or love.

'The Raiders are everyone's enemy,' Icel shrugs. He's right, and there's dawning realisation on the faces of all my warriors. Well, apart from Leonath, who has remained inside with Wulfred at his side. Wulfred isn't wounded, but he has been sniffing, his nose streaming in the wind. I should have left him at Kingsholm to be cared for by the herbwomen my aunt has instructed in the arts of healing.

I feel a flicker of annoyance. If Icel has realised this, why the fuck hasn't King Alfred of Wessex?

'Then we should help them, as Cadell asks.'

'You can't fucking go,' Edmund repeats, his words too loud, carrying even over the howling wind. I don't believe any of us will be going anywhere soon.

'We could split your force and reinforce it with men from Kingsholm.' Pybba offers the suggestion, his eagerness impossible to ignore. 'You can't send any of the ealdormen's men. They don't have the experience.' Again, he's right, as much as I don't like to admit it.

'What good would twenty men do against the Raiders?' I don't need the huff of annoyance from Rudolf to know I'm not winning myself any friends. After all, how many times have I fought with no more than my close warriors against superior numbers?

'The rest could travel on the other side of the River Wye,' I offer, hoping this might win me the support of more than Edmund.

'You're not bloody going,' Edmund roars this time, and I wince. He's right as well. Damn the fucker.

'Fine, fine, if I don't go, can I have your agreement for this?'

'I'm not going either,' Edmund puffs up his chest. 'The Gwent Welsh are all sheep-shaggers. If they spent more time learning how to fight with actual blades as opposed to lumps of stone, then they wouldn't have to beg their enemy to assist them.'

I snap down my immediate response. I'm not going to argue with him. I'll die before I get him to say anything nice about the Gwent Welsh.

'Yes,' Icel rumbles. He's cleaning his seax with a soft piece of cloth, but the blood doesn't want to come free, etched into the blade as though frost on the ground, only it won't simply melt into the blade as the frost would with the aid of some heat. It reminds me that I need to do the same.

'Yes,' Pybba agrees eagerly. 'But not Rudolf,' he states flatly.

I don't look at Rudolf. I can sense the betrayal there.

'You can't go without Rudolf,' I immediately counter. They fight too well together to separate them. The last time Pybba went into Gwent Welsh territory, he had two hands, and now he only has one. I won't allow him to forget that.

'Wulfred won't be able to go either,' I state, looking from Goda to Sæbald, interested to see what their thoughts are.

'I'll do as my king commands me,' Goda agrees, a smirk to take the sting from the words. Are my warriors about to fall over themselves, pretending they don't want to kill a few more Raiders?

'Fine, I'll make my decisions when we return to Kingsholm before we split our forces. What,' I ask, 'should we do about the bridge?' It's clear that Sæbald thinks the same as Goda.

'Leave it as it is,' Icel comments. 'The Gwent Welsh will think twice before attacking now, and anyway, the matter of the wergild has been resolved. The family of the dead Gwent Welshman will have to pay it.' That's what I like about Icel. He sees things clearly, more clearly than I do, where a blade isn't involved.

'And after all, that side of the river belongs to Mercia, not the Welsh bastards. If you want the barrier in place, then build it at the fucking far end of the river and not in the middle of a bloody bridge.'

My mouth drops open at his words, Edmund turning to scowl fiercely at him. It's not that I've forgotten Mercia extends over the bridge. It's just, well, perhaps I've overlooked that.

'I'll order that done,' I comment quickly, sounding more like the subordinate than Icel does. Sometimes there's just something about him that makes me believe he might be better at this than I am. Ruling that is.

With the wind shrieking ever louder, I return inside. This time Edmund doesn't step so close, and in fact, he's missing from my side. The daft bastard better not be rushing over the bridge on his own. As Icel said, the Gwent Welshmen are dead. There won't be others waiting to see how they fare. That's not how the Gwent Welsh go about their business.

'It's agreed,' I state, coming to a stop before Owain. He grimaces at my words. Not exactly the response I anticipated.

'I'll return to Lord Cadell, inform him of this.'

But I shake my head.

'There's time yet. The wind is foul. Wait, I will be. Nothing will happen for a day or two.' He slumps back in the chair at that announcement, and what rouses my curiosity is that he doesn't ask if I'll lead the expedition. Perhaps it doesn't matter. Maybe he just assumes I will.

I'm not entirely sure what that means.

Chapter Nine

I eye my warriors at Kingsholm. I can't say they look eager for our next foray against the Raiders, but then, it's becoming difficult to detect any change in their attitudes.

We've been fighting almost constantly for months now. We've lost friends in that time. I've paid my respects at the graves of my fallen warriors, gaining some solace in the fact that Eoppa and Hereberht have been reunited in death, their graves lying beside one another.

There are too many graves now, my fallen men, lost in battle. It's enough to dissuade someone from continuing in this vein. If only there were a fucking choice.

They know what's coming. I can't say that I still approve of the decision to split my force. Yet, Edmund is right. I can't go into the Welsh kingdoms. What if something happened to me there? I wouldn't be the first Mercian king to die on the blade of an enemy outside Mercia. Chaos and carnage have always followed each and every such occurrence.

I know my history. Or rather, my aunt does, and she's always ensured I know it as well.

'You all know who's going with who?' I ask, just to be sure. Edmund continues to scowl, probably because Hereman and Gardulf are members of the Gwent Welsh force, but also because he just doesn't like the Welsh. Why he keeps asking me, do we give a shit about the Welsh kingdoms and their fight against the Raiders? Sooner the Welsh had to battle them than the Mercians.

I've stopped answering him. The motivation is easy enough to decipher if he can just see beyond his hatred.

I'm forced to bolster my smaller force with some older and younger lads from Kingsholm. Hemming is overjoyed to be coerced into riding with me. The greybeards, well, white beards, really, Osmod. Cealwin, Eadfrith and Cuthwalh aren't quite as eager as I'd like them to be. It doesn't surprise me. It's bitterly cold even if the snow has stopped falling. Like them, I'd probably sooner warm my arse by the hearth. Not, of course that I say that.

A few of the much older men, those who can't see well or who need a stick to help them get around, valiantly attempt to join me, and I've been obliged to set them other tasks. While Lady Werburg watched me with a waspish glare, I had to soothe injured pride and ask them to guard Kingsholm for me, to help the youngsters train in my absence. I need more men. I can't deny that any longer. The last year has taken a heavy toll.

At least Lady Werburg and the other women were delighted by the arrival of the two small children. Here, I know they'll be safe and looked after. Already, they have new shoes and warm clothes to keep them warm, and more than one person to ensure they have hot food to eat and somewhere to keep away from the bleak weather.

As one group, we ride from Kingsholm to Gloucester, collecting Owain along the way. He's been given a horse to ride. I want my men to be able to move quickly. Walking just doesn't provide them with the ability to escape any altercation quick enough, and even though Owain stated he had a pony waiting for him on the far side of the bridge, I can't see the animal having the speed of a horse. The people of Gloucester watch us as we make our way across the bridge, the weather being kinder today.

I note that the barricade is now in place at the far end of the bridge, Cynelm and Elfwy watching with hooded eyes as we ride through the more formal gate arrangement that's been put in place. Again, I'm reminded that this isn't part of the Gwent Welsh kingdoms, that hardy Mercians make their home in this hilly and tree-filled landscape. They, I hope, will gain easy access into Gloucester. Certainly, some who sheltered within Gloucester have now returned to their homes to the west of the River Severn.

As one group, we ride further west. The sky promises rain, but it doesn't feel like rain will actually fall. It's one of those days when you need to be prepared for every eventuality. There's a strong wind, and I imagine it'll only gather strength. I would think back on the warm summer days spent riding, but all I did then was complain it was too hot, and my back was as flooded as the Severn threatens to become.

Beneath me, Haden bunches, ready to ride at the front of his herd, but Edmund is having none of it.

'I'll go first, with Gardulf and Hereman. You can stay in the middle of the group.' I bite down on my response. Edmund is still furious about the whole thing. Perhaps I should allow him some leeway.

The landscape here is as wild as when we travelled north. Quickly, we begin to move uphill through tightly packed trees. The trees keep the wind from my face. For a time, I could almost forget the purpose of my journey. It might almost be pleasant if not for the occasional wet splashes of melted snow that fall onto my head and down my back.

My men are alert but relaxed. As I said, this isn't yet Gwent. The Gwent Welsh shouldn't be close by, and if they are? Well, it'll give us all something against which to hone our craft.

That night, we shelter beneath the trees, the sound of rushing water assuring me that the River Wye is close. We share a cooked meal of pottage flavoured with onions and mushrooms, and I don't miss the wince on Icel's face at such plain food. I've seen it before. But he never speaks about it. I shrug it aside, eat my fill and roll in my cloak.

The night is dark and long, the rain coming at some point, thundering against the tree canopy far above my head. All the same, I wake with wet hair and shake it like a hound.

Rudolf eyes me with a smirk but says nothing further.

Owain is reunited with his pony, and I eye the animal carefully. It's much smaller than the chestnut horse he rides, and yet, it is clearly hardy and caring for it will be easy. It's survived for four days without Owain, and the beast looks none the worse for it.

'You can change your mount, if you prefer,' I offer, witnessing his indecision. Owain licks his lips, handing the reins of his borrowed horse to Hemming. I nod to accept the change. A spare horse will not be unwelcome.

Beside the banks of the River Wye, our force splits immediately, Icel and Pybba leading the majority of my warriors away towards where they can cross at a suitable location. The water is deep here, but there's an area of raised stones, not quite a proper crossing, but not far from being one either.

It pains me to watch them going their separate way, even if they laugh and joke, making light of my worry. And, in all honesty, I know they'll be fine without me. But it doesn't feel right.

I want to issue ultimatums, last moment instructions and orders, but Icel fixes me with a firm gaze, Pybba not far from doing the same. And I'm left with little option about where to vent my impotence.

'Rudolf, look after yourself,' I stutter, regretting the words as soon as I say them. 'And Dever.' I still haven't replaced the horse. Dever watches me as though he knows my thoughts. That horse misses nothing.

'I don't think you need to worry about me, My Lord King. But some of these other bastards, they could do with a caution.' His words are solemn. Once more, I feel as though I've lost the Rudolf who's been my squire for so many years. But then he grins, and the man he'll become one day melts away, as though snow beneath the sun's heat. Dever farts, the sound loud and long, and I grin as well. Neither of those two is concerned by what I've asked them to do.

'Okay, here we go,' and I turn Haden so that we can make our way further north. As we don't need to cross the River Wye, we don't need to find one of the few bridges further along the river's course. Hemming rides to my side, keen and eager, his face split in a broad grin, his hair tied back so that it doesn't get in the way of his eyes.

Edmund is behind me, speaking with Ælfgar, their voices low. I'm surprised that Jethson allows that. Usually, he and Haden vie to lead the horses. Perhaps, with so few of them, he doesn't feel the need to make a scene.

Haden is jaunty beneath me. I think he seems better for all the travelling we've done of late. His winter coat covers him, and although he looks to have gained weight, he hasn't. This year I won't need to run his gluttony from him or restrict the oats I allow him. It'll be the first time for a decade that I won't have to contend with a fractious horse when summer begins to make itself known.

Osmod joins me. He's a sour-faced man. He didn't used to be. A wound that festered in his leg has pained him for many years. Nothing my aunt does has ever fixed the ugly-looking scar. It perplexes her. It shouldn't hurt, the muscle knit back together, and yet it does. I used to like Osmod. It allows me to forget how cantankerous he can be.

'You need to find new lads for your force,' he begins, no hint of resentment in his voice. 'Hemming is a good lad, but he's only one.'

'I have Hiltiberht,' I counter quickly. Hiltiberht remains in Northampton, as does Penda. With the pair of them absent from my voice, there are few young lads, apart from Wulfhere and Hemming.

'And since I last saw you, Eoppa and Hereberht have died. That's only one to replace them.'

'There's Hemming as well.' Both of us look to the younger lad.

'He has much to learn,' Osmod comments, and I detect a trace of the bile I expected to hear. 'There simply haven't been the men to give him the full training he needs. He can fight us oldies, but pitch him against Rudolf, and he'd be lost.'

I can feel my eyebrows raise at the words. It's not even a criticism, not if I look at it the right way. What has come over Osmod?

He grins, a mouth full of missing and broken teeth greeting me.

'I'm not as grumpy as you might think,' he counters, seeming to enjoy himself. 'The bloody leg doesn't pain me as much as it used to, but I have the speed of a snail. I warn you I won't be much good to you.'

'But more use than Eadfrith or Cealwin?'

'Eadfrith spends most of the day sleeping, so yes. But Cealwin, well, he might have one more good fight in him.' Osmod smirks. His nose has been broken more than once, and now it seems to change direction halfway down his face. It gives him a skewed look. But I can't deny the intelligence in the eyes that watch me. Osmod was one of my father's warriors. He's seen a great deal in his time, and that's evident in the lines that wrinkle his face and the tufts of white hair that persist in clinging to the top of his head.

I glance behind me, sight Cuthwalh, where his chin bobs on his chest, as his grey mount, Aart, ambles along peacefully. We're not in a rush, not inside Mercia as we are. Equally, our path is more direct than for the rest of my warriors.

Cuthwalh is not as old as Osmod, perhaps by a good decade, but he's grown soft in his time at Kingsholm. I hope he need do little more than ride along behind me. I can't imagine he still possesses the speed and stamina that earned him such high regard under my brother.

'He'll be fine,' Osmod assures me. 'Quicker than he looks.'

And then Osmod moves to ride beside Hemming, calling to the lad and pointing out important landmarks by which he might find his way home if need be.

I ride in silence, hands on the reins, although I'm alert to any danger. The rivers. The bloody rivers. Without them, the Raiders would be stuck on the shoreline, unable to penetrate deep inside

Mercia. And it seems Mercia isn't alone in having such a problem. The Welsh kingdoms are about as uninviting as can be. There are little but sheep and steep hills to reward such efforts, but still, the Raiders come.

'I hope you know what you're doing,' Edmund has finally ridden close enough to speak with me. I knew it wouldn't take him long to continue his complaints.

'I never know what I'm doing. That's the route of my success,' I try and mollify, but unlike with most of my men, he doesn't appreciate my honesty.

'Northampton could be threatened, Gainsborough as well, and you're riding to the aid of a man you don't even like.'

'I never said I didn't like him,' I interject. 'Cadell isn't so bad.'

'I meant King Rhodri.'

'I've never met him. How can I say whether I like him or not?'

'And so you ride to war for a man you've never met. I just don't understand.'

'It's not Rhodri I'm helping. It's Mercia.'

'It's not right,' Edmund persists.

'No doubt Cadell's men said the same when they came to Repton, but they fought and lost their comrades. It's only correct to reciprocate.'

'What will you do if we lose two-thirds of your men?' This time my gaze is sharper. Damn bastard. But he's already shaking his head and raising his hand.

'That was uncalled for,' he comments quickly. 'It won't happen. I wouldn't be lucky enough to be left without Icel or Hereman.'

'But what are you going to do about London and King Alfred?'

'Bishop Wærferth is going to ensure Bishop Smithwulf knows the extent of his powers.'

'And when that doesn't work?' I don't mind such negativity this time.

'I'll order the walls rebuilt and repaired where they've tumbled down. That'll keep London safer, if not safe.'

'Will you nominate an ealdorman?' This isn't a demand to be given the position. It's an interesting idea.

'Ealdorman Ælhun already has command over a vast area.'

'But there's Æthelwold. He already controls Hertfordshire.'

'Yes, but his father died fighting for the Wessex kings. He might be susceptible to King Alfred.'

'I doubt it. He hates King Alfred. Didn't much like his father either, truth be told.'

'I didn't know that,' I counter. There are probably many things I don't know, but I would have expected my aunt to inform me of this development.

'He doesn't just tell anyone. There's some family loyalty there.'

'So, how do you know?'

'I know Æthelwold. I knew his father as well.' There's a story there, but I don't need to hear it, not if Edmund's aggrieved tone is any indication.

'I'll consider it,' I confirm. Perhaps it would be a good idea to make one ealdorman responsible for London. Then there'd be someone that Bishop Smithwulf would be accountable to who was much closer to him; and someone who would divide the loyalties of the inhabitants of London.

'But what of King Alfred?'

'Do we have to talk about him? Can't we just enjoy, well, this?' And I indicate my pleasant surroundings even if it's bloody cold. The track we follow is well-trodden, the sound of running water rippling through the air. The snow that's fallen so heavily has nearly all melted, no doubt accounting for the rushing river close by, which I can hear.

'When did you give a fart about your surroundings?'

'It's all a part of Mercia. I fight for Mercia.'

'So, you fight for the trees, and the clouds, and the roads.' His tone is so mocking, I want to smack him, hard, right in the nose.

'I fight for everything in Mercia, and Mercian. Are you telling me you don't?' His silence speaks to me.

'Fuck off, Edmund. I thought you understood what this was about.'

'I know that King Alfred is going to be a thorn if you don't deal with him quickly. He's not the sort to fuck off, unlike me.' And he knees Jethson forward, joining the rest of my warriors, while I linger at the back.

I'm furious with him, but equally, he's right. Wessex have slowly redrawn the extent of Mercia's influence for the last fifty or so years, pushing back against the advances of King Offa. She shows no signs of stopping, and the Raiders might just aid them further. I wish Pybba were with me. He has more of a head for politics than Edmund or me. I'm sure my aunt would also have ideas on what to do. I just want to cut Wessex loose, drive a wedge along the barrier created by the River Thames.

If only that were bloody possible.

Chapter Ten

I call a halt to our day's journeying as the sun threatens to sink quickly behind the hills to the west, causing shadows to stretch, making it difficult to differentiate between hollows and flatter land. I don't want to risk the horses.

We've happened upon a small structure at the base of the valley that just about accommodates us all. Hemming and Wulfhere rush around tending to the horses while I kindle a fire in a circle of stones, making use of tangles of sheep wool found outside, while Edmund presents me with stray pieces of wood. The heat is welcome after another bitter day in the saddle, even if the greasy smell isn't.

I would have thought my body would be used to the cold by now, but it seems not. And I'm not the only one suffering. Osmod and Cealwin dismounted as though it might be the last thing they ever do. They were so slow, I fear that if we're attacked, they'll succumb without even drawing their seaxs or shields. They might not even see the enemy before they're run through. They might be frozen in position. It's a bitter day to be out in the open.

But for now we're still within Mercia, the River Wye acting as a border, the Raiders, and the Gwent Welsh should be on that far river bank. I'm grateful for the presence of the river, as I eye my men without much faith in their abilities. They were all once men who could fight and kill, who fought in battles and importantly, who survived battles. But, the vestiges of their strength and stamina are only evident in the lined faces and battle scars they wear. It's not in sharp movements, or even supple poses.

I hope that we won't see the Raiders, even while I accept that hope is far from a sound battle tactic.

I think we might trade stories around the campfire, as my other warriors would so, those tasked with travelling on the far side of the River Wye. But no sooner has everyone eaten the warm, if tasteless pottage that I've prepared with some help from Hemming, than they all roll in their cloaks, content to sleep. The young, and the old, worn out by the day's exertions.

Only Wulfred and I remain awake.

'I'll take whichever watch you don't want,' I offer with a shrug to my shoulders, as I catch his eye over the smoking fire. It's finally starting to warm up inside the dilapidated structure that is more holes than walls.

Wulfred considers, one hand combing through his dark beard, his eyes dark in the gloom. Outside, I hear the nicker of the horses and the shuffling of their hooves over the wooden floor of the lean to they shelter beneath. They're almost under the protection of the steading, only the roof doesn't extend quite far enough for them to be covered entirely. They're at least out of the wind, which blows from the Gwent hills, the coldness of the faraway snow on the peaks making it feel colder than it should.

'Aye. I'll take the first bastard one. I'll wake you, and you can have the next one.' Wulfred used to spend his time at Kingsholm, just like Osmod, Cuthwalh, Cealwin and Eadfrith. I think that riding with me for the last few months has made him seem a younger man. I hold on to the possibility the same might happen with my older warriors, roused from Kingsholm to protect me on what should be a fairly simple expedition down the River Wye. Although, I realise, it's not going to happen overnight.

'Agreed.'

I'm not sure who I'll wake, but it'll probably be Edmund or Eahric. Hemming needs his sleep after the excitement of today. He snores now, the sound a gentle counterpart to the thundering noises that Osmod emits. I'm amazed he doesn't wake himself with such a sound. I've nudged him once or twice with my booted foot but all that happens is he stops snoring for a moment, and then starts up again. I imagine he sleeps alone at Kingsholm. No woman would put up with that. No man, beast or child either. Not that I think Osmod has children. Or, if he does, they've chosen a different path to their father.

Not that Wulfred ventures outside into the wind and I don't blame him. But he does take up a position where he can see beyond the blackness of the missing door, out into the gloom beyond. The trees whisper and shudder in equal measure as the wind knocks and shakes them. Come the morning, some enterprising youngsters will have twigs aplenty for starting fires throughout Mercia. Nights such as these make gathering kindling easy, provided you can sleep enough to have the desire to do so the following day.

I settle down to sleep rolled in my thick cloak, eyes on the leaping yellow flames in the hearth, my thoughts far away, wondering how my men are faring. As when we travelled along the River Trent to hunt the Raiders who escaped from Repton, I have a force on either side of the river. At some point, if we travel slowly enough, and they travel more quickly, we'll draw level with one another. I don't know if we'll be able to aid them when they encounter the enemy, but as I've been forbidden from travelling on the Welsh side of the River Wye, I have to content myself with believing that I won't be left feeling useless.

Wulfred's hand on my shoulder wakes me too soon, startling me so that my hand is already reaching for my seax, even as he bats it aside, his bald pate visible thanks to the glowing embers in the fire.

'What?' I ask, confused for a brief moment. Why do I sleep outside when it's the winter? Only, I'm not outside, it just feels as though I am.

'Shhh, you daft bastard. Your turn,' and he stifles a yawn with his hand, settling to sleep even before I've sat up, let alone stood to take his place.

My eyes burn with fatigue, my neck aching because of the strange position in which I've slept. My aches and pains from the battle at Gainsborough have mostly gone, although my right hand continues to heal slowly. It hurts now, the cold having seeped in through the open doorway. But, without Rudolf to fuss over it, it will feel as though it's healing more quickly. All I need to do is keep the bandage clean. That isn't always as easy as it sounds. Haden is a demand on me and he doesn't care about the state of my bandage.

I stand, only to wish I hadn't, and then make my way outside. The fire has burned low enough that I don't have to blink away the dancing flames to be able to see. I empty my stream away from the door and the horses, and when I return, I check the animals. Some of them sleep, heads bowed, vying for room, but Haden is awake and alert, his soft nicker calling to me somehow aware that I'm the only one awake.

'Aye lad, I know. It's bloody cold.' I run my hand along his nose and pause, forehead against his black and white nose, the white visible despite the darkness, enjoying the time alone with him. No one watches me. It's a relief not to be watched, for once.

I run my hands along his body, content that the skin of his wound is less puckered every day.

'Get some sleep,' I caution him, and turn to take my place inside, only I sense something moving in the shadows, and in the black spaces caused by clouds covering the bright half-moon. My body tenses, and I have to force myself to relax.

'Who's there?' I demand to know, reaching for my seax with my left hand, not my right because I can stab just as easily with my left hand, and not risk jarring my wood, or getting my bandage dirty.

When there's no reply to my call, I draw my blade. If this were one of my men, wakened because of the need to piss, they'd tell me. That means it must be a stranger, but not necessarily an enemy. After all, I still stand on Mercian land. I don't take any comfort from that.

'Come out, and I won't harm you,' I coax more softly, unsure if I mean it, but prepared to try. I creep towards where I think the sound came from, mindful that Haden has his head turned in the same direction. I trust his hearing more than mine.

But still, no one announces themselves, but the sound does continue. Intrigued by the strange noise, more a shuffle than anything else, perhaps even just heavy breathing, I creep forward, suspicions forming about who the enemy might be. Two small eyes peer at me in a shaft of moonlight as the heavy clouds part, and I chuckle with relief.

'A bloody sheep,' I announce loudly, pleased to put a name to the noise, and just in case any of the sleeping warriors have woken, concerned by the noise. I consider whether the animal is alone and why it's out here. But then I ponder the building, seeing it in an entirely new light as the moonlight shows me a feeder filled with hay, from which the sheep is eating, watching me with disinterested eyes. Ah. It all makes sense to me now.

'Apologies,' I comment, reaching out to try and run my hand over the sheep, but the animal startles at the action. Before I can stop it, it darts between my legs and runs inside the shelter where my warriors sleep.

'Fuck,' I mutter. I know sheep well enough to understand it's not going to be leaving, not now it's made itself at home, even if it has strange company.

'It seems we might have borrowed your barn,' I offer softly, wincing at the loud noises coming from inside. How none of the others has woken, I don't know. It doesn't exactly speak of men alert to every danger.

'What's happening?' Edmund sleepily asks as I re-enter the half-built steading that I now know is a sheep barn and find the sheep lying down and contently chewing in the far corner.

'Nothing, I went for a piss,' I reply, hoping he won't realise we have an addition to our number. Provided the animal doesn't wake anyone, it can stay for the night. It'll be daylight soon enough, and we'll leave.

Edmund says nothing further, so I assume he must sleep once more. I eye the sheep one more time and then turn my back on it, sitting in the doorway with my cloak tight around my shoulders. I shiver and place my hand in front of my face. The wound that Jarl Halfdan gave me was across the harder flesh close to my wrist, on the palm of my right hand. It was a deep cut, but it is healing. Yet, my hand feels tight as the skin knits together once more. I've taken to clenching and releasing my hand in the hope it won't remain as tight forever.

If my aunt were here, she'd rub ointment into it, but she isn't, and so I make do with some obnoxious pot that Lady Werburg gave me when Rudolf asked for it. I don't know if it's helping, but it smells bad enough that I think it must be. Nothing that tasted nice or didn't stink ever cured an ill.

Beyond the structure's walls, the wind continues to rush, to howl around corners and inside the shelter. More than once, I have to stand and add more wood to the fire or in the morning there'll be nothing warm to eat. The remaining pottage, nestling in the pot to the side of the fire, gives off a delicious smell, and it's that which keeps me awake as the broken night takes its toll on me. I could have done with sleeping all night.

As I stifle a yawn, a hand on my shoulder alerts me that someone is awake. Osmod grins at me in the grey light of dawn.

'Get some sleep,' he cautions me, half an eye on the other inhabitants.

'Is that a bloody sheep?' Amusement ripples through his voice. I'd expect disbelief, but perhaps this isn't the first time Osmod has woken to find a sheep sharing his bed.

'Yes, it seems we stole its bed for the night.'

'If that's the worse of our night time visitors, then I don't much mind.'

Gratefully, I return to my place beside the hearth and fall asleep again, the scent of sheep shit far from pleasant in my nostrils.

I doubt many realise the king of Mercia lives in such luxury.

Chapter Eleven

'Eh?' the less than articulate word wakes me, but seemingly no one else. I gaze at the open doorway in the light of early dawn, to be met with the startled eyes of a small lad, perhaps no more than six years old.

Osmod's snores fill the space, and I'd be pissed off, but more sheep have joined us while we sleep. They're nestled in close to my warriors, one even slumbering by the hearth, so close to it, I can smell the acrid stench of burning wool. My stomach rumbles at the thought of mutton in my pottage.

I lumber to my feet, biting back my complaints, and bow to the lad.

'My apologies. It seems we've stolen your sheep house.'

He nods, green eyes wide in a round face, mouth open, for all he carries a long staff, and it looks to me that he knows how to use it.

'Who are you?' he demands, as Osmod startles awake in the doorway, hand reaching for his seax, before realising he has a sheep lying on his other arm, and he's pinned in place.

'Warriors, for the king of Mercia,' Edmund states before I can. 'We ride to Hereford.'

There's no comprehension on the lad's face.

'Are the horses yours?' he asks instead, a soft look on his face.

'Yes, they are. Would you like to say hello to them?' Osmod asks, struggling upright, shaking his arm to get some feeling back into it now the sheep has moved. I was about to do the same. It's not as though I don't know how to win the hearts of small children.

The lad nods, brown hair covering his eyes as he does so.

'Are you alone?' I think to ask.

'Apart from Shep.' And a black and white nose appears between his legs, followed by a dog with a long coat and sharp eyes. It growls low, and this feels more menacing than the lad.

'Has he come for the sheep?'

'Yes, they've run away during the night. The wind blew a gap in the hedgerow and then knocked down the wicker fence that surrounded it.'

'Do you need some help rounding them up?' Hemming yawns as he speaks, leaping nimbly to his feet. I'm not the only one to snarl at such eagerness.

'No. Shep'll do it.' And before any of us can move further, the boy whistles sharply between his teeth and the dog darts inside, even as the sheep struggle upright, keen to avoid the dog's questing nose.

Osmod's sheep moves quickest of all, luckily, or he'd be flattened by the animals as they make a hasty departure.

I move outside, keen to be out of the way, looking for Haden and the rest of the mounts. But they're well, and the day is starting to clear, the wind, hopefully, having blown itself out. I shiver all the same. The ground is crisp beneath my feet and dotted with sheep shit. I didn't notice that last night. Neither did I see the frost. It must have come late while Osmod was on guard duty.

Edmund erupts next, followed by Eahric and Wulfred. Wulfred is pulling tangled pieces of fleece from his clothes. None of them looks impressed. I smirk, stretching my arms and stamping my feet to get some warmth into them.

'Fucking wonderful accommodation,' Edmund mutters to himself, just as two sheep rush by him, followed by more and more.

'How many of them are there?' Osmod asks.

'A herd,' I offer unhelpfully.

The lad appears then, and then more sheep, with Shep bringing up the rear.

'That's all of 'em,' the lad states confidently. 'I'll take them back to their barn. My father'll be pleased to see 'em all back. Pestilent buggers.' The words, coming from someone so young, make my lips turn upwards, but I don't laugh at him. That would wound his pride.

'Here, take this for the use of your sheep shelter. Tell your father that the king of Mercia was pleased to find the building in such reasonable repair.' Edmund hands the lad two silver pennies. Light glints off the surface of the coins, reflecting on the lad's amazed face, and he grips them tightly. He might only be six or seven, perhaps a little older, but he has a fine grasp of the wealth he carries.

'If you're going to Hereford,' he offers. 'You want to go that way,' and he points to the river side of thick woodland. 'This way is longer and doesn't follow the river.'

'Thank you,' Edmund continues. I think we should warn the lad about the Raiders, but Edmund does no such thing. I appreciate his confidence. There's a shriek from inside the shelter, and Ælfgar's outraged voice shouts as yet another sheep runs for freedom.

The lad glares at the sheep.

'It's always bloody you,' he complains to the beast, while Shep circles round to collect yet another of the lost animals. I can't detect any difference in the stocky looking animal. How the boy can differentiate between them is beyond me.

'The right hoof,' Hemming offers.

'What?' I turn perplexed eyes on him.

'The right front leg had a distinctive stripe on it. That's how the lad knows which one it is.'

'Oh,' I expel, but I'm none the wiser, and the sheep are quickly moving away, and up a gently curving valley side almost in front of us. I'm unsure how we didn't see it yesterday, but it was dark, and I doubt there were lights spilling from the covered windows and tightly-shut door. From halfway up, I can see a trail of smoke in the air. I take that to be the boy's home.

But my gaze fastens on the landscape to the west of me, turning slowly to eye the sweep of the broad river, the collection of trees and dead greenery that cling to the side of it. I can't see my warriors there, not yet. I feel a flicker of worry but dampen it down. It'll take them longer to find us. They have a much further distance to travel than we do because the river curves and bends, not at all like the River Trent.

'Where are the bastards?' Wulfred's words are hardly the reassurance I need after I've convinced myself that everything is fine.

'They'll be taking their damn time,' Edmund responds, his hands on Jethson as he makes him ready for the day. The horse manages to look as enraged as Edmund. That damn brute.

The pottage bowl is passed around, all of us taking our fill so that it's empty and ready to be swilled in the brook that flows close to the sheep barn.

Haden is eager to be gone, and I quickly realise why. Looking down, one of the sheep has made a bed between his front legs and still slumbers there. I gaze at it, considering what to do, only for it to jump upright and startle away in fright. Of course, it goes back down the track we followed yesterday, and not homewards.

'Bloody hell,' I make to follow it, but Hemming is already mounted.

'I'll go, My Lord King.' The words hardly are what I want to hear from one of my warriors, but at least I don't have to track the bloody animal. 'I have a way with sheep.'

I keep half an eye on his progress as I saddle Haden and then lead him back onto the crisp ground. Haden watches as well, almost as though he hopes the sheep will be found. Osmod chuckles at my side, Edmund scowling in annoyance, and then a black and white streak flees across the ground, and Shep is back.

With one or two sharp barks, the sheep has turned around and rushes to follow the others. Hemming looks crestfallen to have failed, but secretly, I'm relieved. If he's to be a warrior, he needs to excel in other areas. Collecting sheep is the work of the dog not one of my warriors.

'That dog's bloody amazing,' Eahric exclaims. 'Pity we couldn't employ the same tactic to herd the Raiders away from Mercia.'

I eye my warrior, noting how he watches the sheep, and the dog, disappear. His nose still needs to heal properly, but it is looking better. Maybe he fancies himself as something of a shepherd as well. I can just see it, Eahric and Hemming, in charge of the livestock at Kingsholm. At least, I think, they'd be safe then, with Werburg and the other women and children who shelter there.

'Hurry up,' Edmund presses my warriors, not at all interested in the sheep or the sheepdog, or in ensuring we leave nothing behind that we might need on a later occasion.

I think we need to do the opposite, linger, in the hope that the rest of my men will come into view in the far distance, but we've not yet made it close enough to the river's side. It feels like it twists and turns through the landscape, trees and hills doing their best to obscure any view.

A sense of urgency suddenly guides me as I consider the distance between my men and me. I mount up and look at the rest of the warriors. Hemming and Wulfhere are ready, Ælfgar as well, but Osmod and Cuthwalh are struggling to mount up. Osmod grunts as he tries, once, twice, before being successful on the third attempt, while Cuthwalh takes double that.

'Fuck. If the Raiders come, we're going to be buggered,' Edmund complains, for once doing it softly enough that only I hear.

One day, I want to tell him he'll be old and slow, but then I don't. There's a look on his face that makes me believe he regrets those words already.

'Ready,' Cuthwalh calls, a look of relief on his face. Now, we're all prepared, and I indicate that Edmund should lead. Perhaps he and Jethson could do with being at the front for a while.

He picks a careful path, weaving through the flooded areas and those that are slick underfoot, and slowly, the River Wye comes into view, as we take the path the young lad indicated. The River Wye isn't as wide as the River Trent, or at least, it isn't here, and I growl. We could have all gone together. It would hardly have been difficult to retreat over the river if we'd had a ship or even just a horse that was willing to swim.

But then I draw closer and gaze down into the water. It pools over the banks, the water creeping onto the lower lying ground.

I gaze into the distance, eyeing the snow-covered mountains.

'It looks bloody cold,' Edmund states, as though reading my thoughts. 'I wouldn't want to swim in that. It'd freeze a man.'

Peering back the way we've come, I can still make out the farm steading halfway up the hillside, but then the forest rears up before us, and we can see nothing behind, or to the side, only the opposite bank of the river. And my warriors are still not there.

'It's only been a day,' Wulfstan states, again, interpreting my thoughts correctly. 'They'll be by soon enough.'

But my attention has been caught by something else. In the far distance, I can see another billowing mass of smoke tumbling into the cold air.

'There,' I point, hoping Edmund can see enough to let me know if it's the Raiders or just a large fire, unfortunate but not as deadly as it could be.

'A fire,' he peers into the distance. 'We need to get closer if you want to see more.'

'Be wary,' I warn my men, hand on my seax. I direct Haden as near to the riverbank as I can. I don't want to risk him stumbling and upending me into the water, but I want to check for Raiders' ships. If they've made it this far inland, then they must have their boats with them. They'll have navigated along the river, and maybe they've even killed as they've travelled.

Edmund follows me, Jethson just in front of Haden, and for a while, we all ride in silence. I don't feel I'm being hunted, a strange sensation in itself, but there is something wrong here. Very wrong.

The far bank of the river stays devoid of all life, not even a bird at wing or a fish erupting from the water, and certainly no sign of my warriors.

'This could be a trap,' Ælfgar's words are ripped from him, as though he doesn't want to speak them, but he's not wrong. Just like Wulfred, Ælfgar used to spend his time at Kingsholm until I prevailed upon him to rejoin my warrior band. I realise for the first time that aside from Edmund, Hemming, Wulfhere and Eahric, all of my warriors are near old enough to be my father, let alone Hemming's. I swallow down my unease.

Perhaps this Owain has nothing to do with Lord Cadell? Maybe he was just one of the Gwent Welsh coerced by the Raiders to do their bidding? Or maybe King Alfred of Wessex wants me far from the heart of Mercia so that he can attack in my absence and take London as his own with the connivance of Bishop Smithwulf. There is a precedence for such a move on the part of a Wessex king.

Unease prickles along my back, and I can't stop myself from look-ing, time and time again, over my shoulder. Not that there's anything to see there, nothing but the silent swaying trees and the glowering, low hanging clouds that promise rain will shortly fall from their sodden depths. Even the smoke has disappeared.

'I don't fucking like this,' Wulfred mutters, jolting Cuthwalh from where he's nodding in sleep. Cuthwalh is exhausted and I feel both anger, and sympathy for him. I should have left him in King-sholm. If he's unaware of this sensation, then he's no good to me. Not any more.

What the fuck am I doing, I demand of myself, aware that this isn't going to go at all the way I believed it would.

And then there's no time to think about it.

Chapter Twelve

They surge from the river and the forest, vastly outnumbering us by at least four men for every one of mine.

'Fuck,' Edmund explodes, not even glancing at me, before encouraging Jethson to rush back towards me. Cuthwalh is wide awake now, flailing for his seax while his mount stumbles over the soggy terrain, startled and terrified in equal measure.

'To me,' I bellow, hoping my men are alert enough to heed my words, and if not the men, then the bloody horses.

How have I allowed this to happen? I should have set Edmund to ride in front and Ælfgar to the rear, but my focus has been on my other warriors. I thought them at risk, not me.

Leering faces greet mine. Only a handful of the enemy wear helms, and so I can see fierce eyes, bulging lips, and the grimace of sharp teeth. They look like wolves on the hunt. All they need is for slather to drip from their tongues.

Bastards, all of them.

They must have been watching our advance for some time because we're all but surrounded. More of the Raiders coming from behind us, as well as the side and the river. There's no way to go forward or to go back. Haden is steady beneath me, although I sense his vigilance. He'll do as I instruct him when I issue the command.

But and this is the fucking problem, I don't know what that's going to be.

Spears and seaxs, war axes too, are held ready in the waiting hands of the enemy. I glance across the river, wishing it were narrower here, the path to the far bank more inviting. But they've chosen well. The water gurgles and surges, two tree trunks caught in the mess of grasses to the side so that other rubbish piles up against them. There's no straightforward way of swimming across, and that's if we could even encourage the horses into the icy chill of the water that reaches its fingers towards me.

The enemy is dressed against the cold, legs wrapped in furs, while all of them wear a decent looking cloak as well, waterproof seal-skin making them appear as black wraiths.

'Fuckers.' I spit, still unsure, wishing I had Icel at my side, Pybba and Hereman as well, not to mention Rudolf and Gardulf. But they're far from here. I have a handful of old men, who last swung a weapon months, if not years ago, two young lads, one of whom has never fought before, and only a few of my warriors who've battled with me from Repton to Northampton, from London to Gains-borough.

I wouldn't be at all surprised to discover that the Grantabridge jarls sent these men. Perhaps it's all been a trick all along. And I've bloody walked right into it. What a fucking arse I am.

Edmund is beside me, Ælfgar to the other side, and we make a small, if tight unit, still on our horses.

I glance into the forest, half a hope that we might be able to escape that way, but the trees are tightly packed there, little but shadows visible from my viewpoint. It's dark and uninviting.

'King Coelwulf,' one of the helmed warriors grins at me, a tightly braided beard moving up and down when he speaks. It's blacker than the inside of the forest, darker than a moonless night.

'Who's asking,' Edmund responds, his words filled with menace. As so often in the past, even this small ruse confuses. The man glances unconsciously at one of the other helmed warriors.

I take it that this is Jarl Thorgills and Jarl Ottar, although which is which, I have no idea.

Both men are of average height, and from what I can see, they share similar tastes in clothes, as well as the same height. They could be brothers or cousins, but I doubt it. Brothers don't make the best allies.

'I am Jarl Thorgills,' the man confirms. He speaks with a hard edge to his words, as though the sounds aren't easy to make. His eyes still rake between Edmund, Ælfgar and me. I find it amusing that they can't tell a king from a warrior. The Raiders could learn from doing the same. They broadcast their status within the group, evidently not realising that it makes them a target.

'And I am Jarl Ottar,' the other states, tongue poking between his thick lips as though tasting the air. His words are mocking. He believes himself better than us; that much is clear. He stands in the centre of a line of men to my right. I take it to mean that while the jarls are united in this endeavour, the warriors they fight with have divided loyalties. Such knowledge is a weapon.

Perhaps, here, and right now, he might be correct.

'And who is King Coelwulf?' Jarl Ottar continues, scrutinising my men and me. I hold myself fluid, taking advantage of this conversation to devise a way of escape.

The Raiders aren't mounted, but they're slowly moving closer and closer. Not that I give a shit if the horses tackle them, leaving them mewing on the ground.

'I fucking am,' Wulfred states from behind me. His voice thunders with resolve, and I note the look of satisfaction on the faces of the jarls.

I want to ask them how they knew to find me here? Is it just a coincidence? Are there more of them close by?

'It's good to know who you are before we take your life. There's a price on your head.' And now I startle. It was the jarls at Repton who placed a price on my head. There's been no talk of such an incentive since the defeat at Repton. Have these men been here since last summer?

I open my mouth to speak and then snap it shut again. After all, Wulfred is king here.

'Tell me the price? And who offers to pay it?' he rumbles.

Jarl Ottar laughs.

'You must know that Jarl Halfdan wants you dead. Then he can rule Mercia without interference. I'm surprised you're not dead already. It's been many months, but then, I told my warriors that we should persist in our endeavours.'

'But, Jarl Halfdan is fucking dead,' Wulfred continues, and now there's some uncertainty on the faces of everyone there. It seems they don't know this.

'You lie,' Jarl Ottar laughs, but my face stays stony. And I imagine the rest of my warriors do the same. Jarl Thorgills looks to Jarl Ottar and then back to Wulfred.

'Now,' I mutter to Edmund, and he's ready.

Jethson surges forward, Edmund aiming him towards Jarl Thorgills. The jarl is taken by surprise, even as Haden skips ahead five steps and then rears, thrusting his hooves forward, once, twice, three times before he has to land once more. I swing my sword out wide, needing the extra reach to battle the line of four Raiders to this side of Jarl Thorgills. Thanks to Haden, two others, closer to him, are already down on the ground, and I hope they stay there.

The first man, caught by surprise, and even though he carries a shield and war axe, buckles as I swing my sword wide, catching him on the right ear and slicing downwards, across his neck, to his opposite shoulder.

His blood fills the air, shimmering for a moment, floating, before falling to the ground. The second man is only slightly more alert, managing to raise his shield to fend off my bloodied blade. The action threatens to topple me, but I grip Haden's side tightly with my thighs, while behind me, I can hear the rest of my warriors launching their attacks.

Here, in such a confined space, we all protect one another, provided we don't allow one of the Raiders to sneak behind us. Not that I think the Raiders will risk it because the horses are bucking and biting, doing what they can to help the rest of us. A horse has fucking big teeth.

With my balance restored, I aim my sword at the man once more, and because I'm higher than he is, thanks to Haden's strong back, I can reach inside his shield and stab him through the chest, not far from where his heart beats. His attack on me falters, his mouth falling open, and I kick him aside. He might not be dead yet, but down on the ground, while horses and warrior war above him, means it won't take long.

Edmund and Jethson fight next to me, whereas Ælfgar has the daunting task of attacking Jarl Ottar with his confidence. It's a pity Edmund and I rode as we did, but then, Ælfgar will have no difficulty in killing the other man. Poppy will assist him as well.

The third man I face is ready for my attack. His shield is before him, but I'm too close to be able to decipher the splash of colour on the wood. It might just be spilt blood from Ælfgar's battle with Jarl Ottar.

As soon as these two men are dead, I'll be able to assist him, or so I hope.

For now, Ælfgar and Poppy fight well together. She does her bit to snap and bite at any hand that comes too close while he directs her with heels and knees. Neither of them wants a wound. Ælfgar doesn't need another injury.

A sword flashes before my eyes, and I rear backwards, opening a space between Haden's neck and my body. The blade, a lucky strike from the man who's not tall enough to see where his weapon is, comes too close to Haden's neck. Quickly, I palm my seax and use it to hold the sword clear of the black and white neck. But now, there's a warrior to the other side of me. One of the others has pushed beyond the dead and dying men I've already encountered.

Now there are two swords aimed at Haden.

Without thought, I release my feet from the stirrups, leaning backwards and using my legs, unheeding of the coming pain, to kick the two weapons away.

The one leaps from the man's hand, high in the air so that I have to watch it to ensure it doesn't still impale my horse. The other sword doesn't move as well because my foe has a tighter grip on it. I grimace at the cuts that have opened on my lower leg.

'*Skiderik*,' my opponent screams, battle joy in his voice because he thinks to win, but I've been watching the other sword. At the last possible moment, I urge Haden to step sideways, and the sword, having turned end over end, nearly slices into the back of the man, pinning him in place.

I grimace at the laboured groan that tears from his mouth, body stiffening in agony, and death.

'Fuck,' I exclaim, even as I use my seax to slash open my other opponent's neck. He really was a very short man.

That leaves me with one man before I can get to Ælfgar. He glances at me, shifty blue eyes filled with fear, for all he has a helm and thick byrnie to protect him.

Only, my foe is jostled from behind, and another steps forward to take his place. This warrior is tall, well over my height, standing almost as high as Haden. He wears no helm, and I can see where his bald head and weathered face is crisscrossed with a snail trail of old wounds.

This man is a veteran, and veterans should never be underestimated. I know. I am one.

Poppy surges forward again, using her hooves to batter at the enemy, and the action forces me to check on Ælfgar. His hand wound hasn't long begun to heal. I can see where fresh blood coats it. I don't know if it's the same wound reopened or a fresh one, but I see the panic in his eyes, even as my enemy aims a large sword at my already bleeding legs.

Fuck, this is a mess.

I can't be in two places at once. But I have no choice.

Edmund attacks to my left while the rest of my warriors have their own opponents against which to fight.

At a time like this, I would welcome the aid of Hereman and his wild, but surprisingly accurate spear throws. But he's not here. Neither is Icel or Pybba, or Rudolf. Or any of the men who would make short work of killing these Raiders.

Grunts and cries of pain surround me, but it's Ælfgar who worries me. Poppy can't do all the fighting. Not that she's not trying.

Sensing my difficulties, Haden snaps his teeth at my newest foe, and the bastard responds by punching Haden in the face.

Fuck, that boils me.

As Haden rears, both by his wishes and mine, I reach out precariously, allowing Haden's hooves to give me the time I need, to reverse my hold on my seax, and stab down with the hilt on Ælfgar's enemy. It'll stun him, I hope, because Haden lands, and our foe hasn't so much as stepped back, even though Haden's hoof is on top of one of his feet, effectively trapping him.

The man simply leers and lashes out with his seax, aiming towards Haden's throat.

Fucker.

I turn Haden, releasing the man and kicking out at the same time. My foot hits the target of his chest, and he buckles, but not enough. Somehow, he keeps his feet, even as Ælfgar's opponent drops to the ground behind him. Ælfgar meets my eyes, thanks and relief in them, as he decides on his next opponent.

This is still a fucking mess, but at least I can concentrate on this man now. Is he one of the Raiders famous berserker warriors? I can't see it. He's calm, even as Haden and I both strike him. No, I think he just believes himself invincible, and men such as that are either lucky bastards or about to get a shock.

With Haden's throat away from the reach of the man's seax, I lean out, too far, and feel myself slipping from Haden's back. I grip tighter, my thighs seeking some purchase on the saddle, but there's nothing to be had, and Haden doesn't realise the difficulty.

I tumble to the ground, trying to do it as quickly as possible while avoiding the mess of dead bodies and my weapons. My enemy is quick to respond so that by the time I'm pushing myself up from the ground, his seax is perilously close to my throat.

I dip my elbows, thinking to go even lower, but instead, I surge upwards, elbow impacting the man's chin rather than his nose and my arm throbs uncomfortably. Somehow, I keep hold of my seax, and this time, I aim the punch, and it hits home.

But, once more, the tall man doesn't even seem to notice the attack. He can't be made from stone, surely, and yet that's all the reaction I get from him.

Haden spins, aware I'm no longer on his back, but the Raider stands between us. No matter what I do, I'm not going to be able to mount quickly enough to avoid a bloody wound.

'Come on, you bloody cock,' I exclaim, lacing my voice with disdain. The man's lip curls, all the reaction I've had so far, even as blood drips from his nose into the mass of a beard that hangs below his neck. Half of his cheek is missing the covering. Instead, angry welts attest to a man who's been burned in an incident.

I wish the blood from his nose came from a neck wound, but I still have to kill him, and down on the ground, it's an even bigger mess. Men lie dead or dying, and it's the dying that are the problem, especially those who're still alert to the danger around them.

A seax flashes darkly from the mass of the wounded enemy. It could be useful if only my opponent were to step on it, but he's just as aware of what's happening as I am. I kick the weapon aside, hoping to avoid the horses and my warriors as it flies through the air.

The dying man shrieks with agony, making me wince as I kick his hand. He tries to speak, but blood bubbles from his mouth in the wake of words. The other warrior takes advantage of my distraction to come at me with seax held tightly before him, legs apart, weight evenly distributed.

I'm really starting to dislike the sod.

I don't have my shield, but I have my seax and the other weapons that reside on my belt. But, what's the best weapon to use against a man such as this? It's not a weapon, at least not one with a sharpened blade.

I feint towards him, seax in the same position as his, using the time to think. How can I kill this man? I want to do it quickly, without too much fuss. It needs to be done unexpectedly because I can tell that he knows how to read a fighting man, determine his intentions even before they know what they're going to do.

Haden stamps his hoof, perhaps a demand that I hurry up or something else, but I can't look. Even such a glance would make me vulnerable.

I could veer left, or right, or attempt to rush away, but that would only mean another of my warriors would need to battle him. Apart from Edmund, I'm unsure who would be a match for him. No, I need to resolve this and quickly.

'Fuck,' and I grip my war axe in the other hand.

The man grins at me once more, showing me a line of surprisingly even teeth. Has the fucker never had his teeth knocked out? I think it's time to change that. And I lose my war axe, throwing it directly at where his head will be in a moment when he realises what I've done.

And fuck me, the sound of my war axe impacting those teeth sets a smirk on my lips. I've not won yet, but at least he won't be so proud of his damn teeth any more.

He grunts, his open mouth filling with blood to match that which floods from his nose. Then he spits. One of his teeth goes with the saliva, landing in a bloody mess on the floor, just to the side of my war axe, head down, handle swaying slightly, although it stays upright. It's too much of an open invitation to ignore, and again, this is what I hope.

As the man reaches for the war axe, his face bloodied, eyes flashing dangerously, I have all the gap I need. I want to get him beneath the armpit as his arm extends, but the luck doesn't all go my way. Instead, my seax embeds itself further down so that it dangles from his upper arm, blood flowing down it, but not enough to kill him.

Another groan of pain, and he's on me, my war axe in his hands forcing me to duck low, my eyes picking out a discarded seax sticking out from a lifeless hand. The iron calls to me, and I claim it. I lead with it as I stand. The war axe misses my head, but the warrior keeps his balance, hauling it back to his side, ready to start again.

The seax feels strange in my hand, the handle not fitting as close to my inner wrist as I'm used to, but it was quicker to take the weapon than fumble for one from my weapons belt. We face one another once more. He's bleeding from three places, and I note he doesn't remove my seax from his upper body. He knows enough to appreciate that such might cause more blood to flood from his body.

When the blow comes, I'm not expecting it. My helm protects me from the slicing motion of the axe, careering over the top of it without more damage than a loud ringing in my ears and the taste of iron on my lips. Fuck, I've bitten my tongue.

I suck on my blood, trying to see the warrior before me, but there's more than one of him. My axe sneers at me, promising me all sorts of pain.

'I think I'll have that back,' I announce, my voice thick with blood but not much. It consistently tastes like more than it is.

My words cause my enemy to grip the war axe tighter, and as he tenses, I shoot forwards, borrowed seax aiming for the line of skin above his byrnie. I anticipate him moving backwards, avoiding the blow, and I add extra force to it, determined to strike him, even if he does move. Only, he doesn't, and the seax buries itself deep into his flesh, close to his throat, but not quite close enough.

A wet sound of air escaping assures me the injury is fatal, but the man isn't dead yet.

My war axe comes at me again, the too-familiar wood wrong in the hand of another. And I'm too slow to react so that now he impacts the other side of my helm. I feel my helm slide, as though it'll fall from my head, but it doesn't, the chin strap keeping it on. But, again, the blow is heavy, and I see more of my enemy than just the one man.

I blink, try and clear my vision, but it's useless.

'Shit,' and the war axe rears up before me so that I have to step back. I only just get the seax before its sharp edge. Haden whinnies in alarm, but the sound gives me an idea as I realise my enemy is no longer between Haden and me. I stagger to his side, circumnavigating another thrust from the war axe. And then Haden's heft is behind me, and at least I know which way is which, even if he moves from side to side, avoiding other warriors.

'I've had enough of this,' I mutter. With the aid of Haden, I can end this. While my vision sways from side to side, I can narrow down where the man stands. The war axe once more comes for me, and even though I can taste vomit in my throat, my hand snatches out and grips the handle of my axe.

And it holds firm. My enemy tries to reclaim it, his hand firm on the haft, but he's still bleeding from the wound beneath his arm. All I need to do is hold on. Using it as a means of finding him, I walk along its length, stabbing his arm as I go, as many times as I can, and as quickly as possible.

His breath, already sounding wet and unsteady from the neck wound, comes ever faster, his eyes wide, almost bobbling from his head.

'Fucker,' and I hit him, full on the head with my forehead, and as he jerks backwards, I press the seax closer and closer to his throat until I sever his air completely. He drops without warning, his head hitting the floor with a bang louder than thunder.

'Fuck me,' I breathe deeply, pleased the bastard is dead. I suck in air for my heaving chest, Haden a comfort at my back.

'Come on,' I turn and mount up, the promise of space to do so because my enemy is dead.

On top of Haden, I gaze at the carnage around me. My warriors still stand, but Cuthwalh struggles, blood weeping copiously down his chest even though I can see no wound. His horse stands firm, snapping and biting at all those who come too close. I catch sight of the maroon shape of Hemming, weapons bright with the stuff. And Edmund, well Edmund battles four men, two to either side of Jethson, and still more of them come.

And there's no end to the number of Raiders who've yet to fight us.

Fuck. This isn't going to end well.

Chapter Thirteen

There's no chance of any help, not with my other warriors so far away. There's only us, and we need to retreat or find a place of safety. Or we're all going to die here, and my aunt will be fucking furious and might well say as much.

A war axe comes at me from my right side. I batter it aside with my double eagle-headed sword. My lower legs ache from where they're cut, but I can tell the wounds have stopped bleeding. I'm not going to bleed to death. Not yet. I've fought on with worse.

Again, my gaze is drawn to the darkness of the forest. It might be the only way we can attempt an escape, although it won't be easy. The man who leads us will have to find a decent pathway, while the man at the back will have to hold off the enemy. But, at least the tightly packed trees will make it impossible for more than two of our foe-men to come at us at once.

Equally, the river calls to me. But it's too bloody dangerous. Only a mad man would take the option of the water. I don't think I'm that desperate. Not yet.

I can't see Jarl Thorgills. With luck, Edmund has killed him. But

Jarl Ottar still lives. And he battles against Ælfgar. Ælfgar is giving his all, but he still bleeds.

I need to get to him. If both of the jarls are dead, the Raiders will lose heart. Why would they fight with no promise of reward? They might become desperate, but I'm counting on them just trying to escape with their lives.

I turn Haden towards Ælfgar. Jarl Ottar is on foot, Ælfgar not far from falling from Poppy's back, as he weaves his seax trying to get through Jarl Ottar's defensive shield. But Jarl Ottar holds the shield above his head, free to stab out with his seax. Only Poppy's awareness stops her from being slashed across her chest as she bucks and retreats, doing all she can to prevent Jarl Ottar from slicing open her flesh. I would say that she screams, but she's not terrified, far from it.

'Fuck this,' but it's impossible to manoeuvre Haden where I want him to be. There are too many people and too many bodies, and the ground is already churned and slick with the battle that's taking place. I don't want to leave Haden, but I do want to protect Ælfgar. I also hunger for Jarl Ottar's death. I'll bury him. I'll make sure he's bloody dead.

Knocking two men aside, a blow to a helm, and a slice to another's sword hand, which might, or might not, entirely slice his hand from his arm at the wrist, I slide down the left side of Haden. Slipping around his side, I knock aside another of the pestilent sods, and then I can see Jarl Ottar.

His dark eyes flash with malice, focus entirely on Ælfgar. Stupid sod.

He must believe his back protected, but it isn't. There's no one behind him because they've all rushed away to join the fray, and in the distance, the black maw of the forest beckons to me. This is our chance to escape because victory is beyond me.

As quietly as I can, I rush towards him, exchanging hands for my sword and pulling my seax loose. I come to a stop just behind him; hand raised to hold the seax tight against his throat. I can feel the coarseness of his beard against my hand. I grimace at the sensation.

He stills as realisation strikes. If he moves, his neck will slice open. If he doesn't, I'll do it for him. Jarl Ottar can't even risk lowering the shield because that movement will be just what I need for him to open his skin.

'Ælfgar,' I hiss at the other man. Poppy eyes me, something like pride in the glint of her brown eyes. 'Ælfgar,' I try again, and this time he hears me.

'My Lord?'

'I've got him. Lead the others away, into the forest. We're outnumbered. I have Jarl Ottar. He's not going anywhere.'

I could, I suppose, make Jarl Ottar my hostage for the good behaviour of the Raiders, for allowing us to live, but if I do that, I imagine they'll just come after me, eager to reclaim him. Especially if Jarl Thorgills is already dead, which I believe him to be.

'Tell the others, quietly.'

Poppy quickly trots to my side, Ælfgar's eyes boggling at the sight of his foe in such a compromised position.

'Lead us away from here. You'll have to choose the path, and I've no idea which is the right way to go. But anywhere is better than here.'

Ælfgar nods, and he's not alone now. Hemming, breathing heavily, and sporting a deep gash on his cheek, brings Perry next, and all while Jarl Ottar is helpless beneath my seax.

I feel my arm begin to shake, the exertions affecting me, and Jarl Ottar must feel the quiver of the blade because he holds ever more still, his neck rigid between my blade and my head.

I suppose I could just knock his head and send him tumbling to the ground, but no, I need him alive, for now.

Osmod follows Hemming, a tired smile on his face. His helm is askew, his mount flashing darkly with blood as he follows on behind, although I don't believe he's injured.

The Raiders have yet to realise what's happening, and Ælfgar is almost out of sight, below the dark expanse of the woodland fir trees.

I feel Jarl Ottar move slightly, and suspecting he's trying to issue a warning to his warring men, I breathe into his ear.

'Don't even fucking think about it,' and I press the blade ever closer, knowing he fears to swallow. This time, I allow my hand to shake even though my exhaustion has faded away now I have a plan that might be successful.

The Raiders, blind in their rage and with no one to offer orders, instinctively move to the next of my warriors, no thought for where the others have gone.

'Cealwin,' I hiss, and he looks at me, from where he's been trying to hold off one of the Raiders, using his shield and war axe to hold off the wild thrusts of his opponent. Aart turns quickly, seeing the opportunity to escape, and he takes his rider without any more urging. Thank fuck for the horse.

Now, the fighting centres around Eahric, Wulfred, Wulfstan and Wulfhere, with Edmund in the midst of it all. From where I stand, I can't see if Edmund faces the same men as before or if he's already vanquished them.

'Haden, you next,' and I urge him to hurry away. For a moment, I think he'll stay in place, jostled slightly by the backs of the remaining horses, but then he picks up one hoof, then the next, and he's walking into the woodlands, without even a backwards glance. I mean, it's what I wanted him to do, but all the same. That horse has no loyalty.

Eadfrith notices what's happening, and he follows Haden, eyes squinted in concern, but I shake my head. Now isn't the time to argue.

But I have the problem of my other men. Wulfhere is pressing against one of the Raiders, and I watch as he forces him, with the use of his mount, closer and closer to the river's edge until there's nowhere else to go. The man tumbles backwards with a shriek, and the loud splash assures me he's in the water.

Wulfhere swivels, looking for the next man, and realises what I'm doing.

'Wulfred,' he urges. Now all of my men are alert to what's happening, although not the Raiders, not yet. Jarl Ottar remains under my control. Perhaps I should just kill him. But that won't give me what I need.

Eahric and Wulfhere peel away from the fighting and encourage their mounts away quickly. Wulfred is next, leaving just Edmund and Wulfstan.

This is the perilous moment. My two warriors could be overwhelmed here, lost to me forever, but I'm relying on their skill, Edmund's years of training, Wulfstan's sheer determination that makes up for his lack of skill.

Judging the best moment to order them away is difficult. There's no let-up in the attack. I have no idea how many Raiders attempt to tackle just my two men, but it's too many. Shields, blades, war axes, and some swords all aim for them and their horses.

I could order Jarl Ottar to call his men off, but again, that would only draw more attention to what's happening. No doubt, they'd all surge into the woodlands, and I need to give Ælfgar more time yet to find a path through the tightly packed trees.

'Get on with it,' Jarl Ottar seethes, his arm trembling, where he holds the shield.

'Fuck off,' I breathe into his ear.

But then there's suddenly the opening that I need.

'Edmund, Wulfstan, now.' I roar the command, hoping it penetrates the fug of battle. Both of them jolt, and Wulfstan responds the quickest of the two. Berg thunders into the woodlands, one of the Raiders falling to the ground as he aims a strike with his war axe at a man that's no longer there.

Just as he's opening his mouth to shout a warning, Jethson gallops over his back, the man bucking with the weight on him, head and legs thrown upwards even as his cheeks purple. And then I'm the only one remaining. A ragged cheer fills the air, thinking they've won, only for someone to notice Jarl Ottar, and there's no choice, not any more.

'Enjoy your hell,' I whisper as my blade slicks over his throat, blood following in its wake and drenching my bandaged hand.

I kick him downwards before turning my back and sprinting after Edmund. This is the moment where it might all fall to shit. If the Raiders follow me, I'll be alone, facing all of them. Alone.

I run from daylight to darkness, the trunks of the trees and the trailing branches of the fir trees, funnelling me into the only available path, the brown of dead ferns as far as the eye can see. I keep my eyes focused on the way ahead. I can't risk falling over tree stumps. Then I'll be dead. But I'm alert to the sound of pursuit, and although it takes longer than I think it will, I can still hear it all the same.

A man follows me, perhaps three or four. It's impossible to tell without looking.

My seax is steady in my hand, blood running from its surface onto the ground. Ahead, I can glimpse Jethson's chestnut arse making his way through a shadowed patch before disappearing. I hold the place in my mind, not wanting to become any more distanced from the rest of my men.

I hold out hope that the Raiders will grow tired of the chase, but that's not the case. If anything, there are more and more of them on the path. I imagine they run, one behind the other, to do otherwise would require more skill than I possess to ensure they don't run into a branch, a tree, or trip over stray shoots in the richness of the loam.

The fresh smell encourages me onwards. Remembering my fall in the woods near Northampton and the time it took me to recover my feet and stop vomiting, I err on the side of caution. Slower, provided the Raiders don't gain an advantage on me.

My breath hitches, my chest uncomfortably tight, and the pain of the wounds on my legs, and my hand, make the experience uncomfortable, but I can't stop. Not until I've found my warriors or escaped the Raiders, whatever comes first.

I wish then that I'd kept Haden close to me. He'd have made short work of the forest floor, and I'd have an advantage over the Raiders on foot.

I glance down, sight a root on the ground, and leap over it, landing with a clatter of weapons and a jolt of pain up my legs. But I quickly regain my speed, once more catching sight of Jethson's arse far in the distance. I consider taking a different path, leading the Raiders away from my warriors, but I don't. Without Haden, I'll stand no chance. And while I want my men to live, I also need to do the same.

The sound alerts me. I strain to determine from where it's coming. I squat low, moving to the left, and a seax shudders to the ground where my foot would have been had I not moved. Footsteps thud closer, and a movement to my right, has me moving to the left to avoid the reaching hand.

They're getting too close. I spur onwards. Moving from side to side with each long stride, trying not to make it too predictable. Another weapon thumps to the ground. My chest is heaving. My breath too harsh. I can't go on like this, not indefinitely.

Something flies through the air in front of me, just over my head, and a huff of air, and a tumbling sound, almost makes me turn. But I don't, because another missile appears, and there's another toppling sound, this one wetter and harder. Broken bones, not that it probably matters. I assume the man is dead.

A hand from out of the darkness ahead encourages me onwards, from who, I don't know. And then the area up ahead becomes even darker, and even though I'm still running, there's no light with which to see.

'You can stop now,' Hemming whispers the words, finger to his lips, in the dull light.

'What?' From somewhere, I can hear the thunder of running steps, and my hand goes to my weapons belt, but there's no need. Not here.

The smell of horses is rife in the air, but it's the eyes of my warriors that I seek. Edmund is close to the entrance to this cave they've found. The mouth of the cave is entirely covered in branches. How they found it, I can't determine. One moment I was running through the forest, as fast as my legs would take me, and now I'm sucking in the rich smell of the ground, the stink of horse shit, and fear.

I walk to Edmund, my mouth open to ask the question, but his eyes remain focused elsewhere, and Ælfgar stands with him.

Of course, Ælfgar found this cave. It's him I need to speak to, but not yet.

The sound of running footsteps fade away, the silence of the wood, or rather, the noises of the forest, slowly filling in the noise of the battle.

'How?' But I get no response, but instead, more fingers on lips, and even Haden walks into my back, nudging me with his head as though to force silence from me.

I nod, concentrate on slowing my thudding heart and harsh breathing. As I do, all the hurts of the battle make themselves known, and I run my hands along my lower legs, questing for blood. But, if there is any, it's dried.

I hunt for my warriors. Some have their heads bowed where they've slumped to the floor. Others are still mounted, the horses as winded as I am. Hemming nods to me, his face dark with blood. Cealwin moves to dismount, the actions slow and laboured. I go to his side quickly, offer him my strength so that he all but falls into my arms. I stagger to hold him, and as one, we sink to the ground. It reaches up to cushion me more quickly than I think possible.

When I open my eyes once more, Edmund is above me.

'What a fucking mess,' he complains, his words soft. I gaze towards the entrance of the cave. Ælfgar remains on guard, Wulfstan beside him.

'At least we're all alive,' I mutter, taking his hand and allowing him to haul me to my feet. It hurts. It really does.

'For now. What were you fucking thinking?'

I have no response to that. I didn't believe we were in danger. I should have known better.

'Cadell said the Raiders were on the other side of the River Wye.'

'Then he bloody lied, or these are different Raiders.' Edmund is pacing in the space. It's surprisingly large, and there's enough room for the horses to move around and for the men to sit or lie down as they decide. Cealwin holds out his hand, and I help him stand, noting the glazed look in his eyes.

'You need to drink,' I advise him, reaching for his water bottle on Aart's saddle. I remove the stopper and hand it to him. He swigs it thirstily as I lick dried lips, tasting the salt of my exertions and the rust of the men I've killed.

'How did you find this place?' But Edmund shrugs. 'Ælfgar did, not me. It's a damn good job he did.'

'What if they come back?'

'Then they bloody come back,' Edmund counters. I can see he's in no mood to help me.

I look around the space. I feel both safe and trapped. I can't help but think that we should leave now, while we can. But what if we find the Raiders again. What indeed?

'We'll stay here,' I announce, meeting the eyes of every one of my warriors, Ælfgar and Wulfstan, taking it in turns to look my way.

'We'll hunt the fuckers down, one at a time if need be.' Edmund's face lights with a glimmer of respect. 'Two of us at a time, no more. The rest here, guarding the horses and one another. When they're all dead, we'll leave and resume our journey. Now, who's badly injured?'

I should have asked that first, but it felt more important to be decisive, to determine a means of leaving here with our lives. At the moment, we're trapped, and it's not the same trapped as inside Northampton, where we had the upper hand.

Hemming speaks first. 'I'm bleeding, and Cealwin has a deep cut on his upper arm.' I glance at both of them, quickly determining how they fare.

'Anyone else?'

Wulfhere looks at me with weary eyes, face unnaturally white.

'On my stomach,' and he points and winces but doesn't disturb his byrnie. Fuck. That could be serious, and dread pools down my aching legs.

'Anyone else?' We all have bruises and cuts. It's the deeper ones that are prone to wound rot. Not that I mention my legs, not yet.

No one speaks.

'Get some rest and help those you can,' I urge, kneeling beside Wulfhere where he's slumped against the wall of the cave.

'Show me,' I demand, Edmund close beside me. Tears have formed on Wulfhere's face, leaking down his cheeks and onto his byrnie, reminding me of just how young he is.

I know he's terrified. I find a smirk, level my voice so that it's not filled with the fear I feel.

'We need to get it cleaned. It'll hurt like a bastard, but once it's clean, you'll feel better.'

I think Edmund might help me out, offer some words of encouragement, but his presence is a menace behind me. I know the words that will trip from his tongue if this wound is mortal.

'Here, I'll help you.' Pulling my glove from my hand, trying not to wince at the blood-soaked bandage on my right hand, I help him remove his byrnie, grimacing and moaning all at the same time. Immediately, I can see a lot of blood. His pale tunic is sodden with the stuff. Yet, I also feel a spark of hope. It's not a deep cut. Just a long one, running almost from his belly button to his back. Poor bastard, that's got to hurt.

Fearful eyes greet mine as Wulfhere's byrnie releases him, and my initial joy fades because there's more than one wound on his belly. The other is deeper than the first one.

'Let me look.' Edmund has already moved away, and I imagine I know his thoughts. We need a fire to clean the wound, but if we have a fire, it'll lead the Raiders right to our side. Bastards.

But, well, there are other ways, as Eowa showed me in the woodlands close to Warwick.

'Is it bad?'

'The one is long and shallow. It'll heal well enough. The other, well, it's smaller but deeper. It needs stitching, as happened to Haden.' Of course, Rudolf did that, and he's not here.

'I can do that,' Cuthwalh states from his nearby place. 'I know how to tend to deep wounds. Give it a good clean.' He advises, and I nod, finding another smile for Wulfhere. Confidence is almost as much as a balm as bandages and spiced drinks. For a moment, I wish Tatberht were here to help his grandson, but while it might aid Wulfhere, I wouldn't enjoy the accusations in his stare.

'There you go. I'll clean you up, pack the cut with some moss and honey, and Cuthwalh will stitch you up.' I take comfort in that I can't see more than skin and blood through the deeper cut. Certainly, I can't see the coil of intestines that can so often be lost through wounds such as these.

Edmund returns to my side, a beaker filled with water and other items in his remaining hand, a pot of honey and a collection of moss as well.

'Thank you.' I'm surprised by his helpfulness, but I shouldn't be. That's unfair. He might be a grumpy bastard much of the time, but my aunt has taught him a great deal about healing. At least I have some idea of how they pass their time together.

'I'll do it,' he mutters, laying out his items in a close circle on the floor. 'I'd tell you to lie down, but that'll hurt, so I'll just ask you to move forwards or backwards,' Edmund's words are soft and reassuring. My mouth drops open in shock.

I grip Wulfhere's shoulder, hold his pained gaze with my eyes.

'You'll be well,' I reassure him. 'Let Edmund and Cuthwalh help you, and then keep your movements as little as possible.' He nods, swallowing heavily. I pity the lad all over again. He's become a warrior too soon, and now he has the wounds to show for it.

Rage burns deep inside me, but I keep the smile on my face until I'm back at the entrance to the cave. I peer outside, noting how the branches of the tree run into the cave, hiding it from the view of any who don't know it's there. Once more, I'm in awe of Ælfgar.

'How did you find it?'

Ælfgar's face lights with a wry smirk.

'Poppy found it, not me. Something startled her, and she just galloped, and I couldn't stop her, and then we were in here. I raced back to direct Hemming.'

'Then I'll thank Poppy and not you,' Ælfgar smirks and then chuckles softly. 'I'll stand a watch if you want to rest,' but he shakes his head.

'No, I'm fine, for now. We could do with water for the horses, though,' and Ælfgar's right to remind me of their requirements.

'I can hear water,' he offers. But of course, the water is outside the cave.

'I'll check the rear of the cave first. There might be a spring.' I'm not scared to leave the cave, but if we can avoid it, that would be better.

Walking back through my men and horses, I see that Wulfhere has his eyes all but closed as Edmund and Cuthwalh tend to his wounds. Haden greets me with a soft nicker, and I run my hand along his black and white body, checking on his old injury, but the flesh has knitted together now. The flesh is a little puckered and red, but there's no indication of the wound rot. I flinch, feeling the cuts once more on my legs. I need water to wash them.

The horses remain saddled, and I turn, thinking to call Hemming to the task, but he sleeps, mouth wide open, a soft snore coming from him. I shake my head. Gone are the days when I can sleep like that. I envy him.

I do see Wulfred talking to the horses while Cuthbert has his saddle removed. The horses crop at the stray shoots that snake across the floor of the cave. With so much green foliage, I'm sure there must be water somewhere in the cave. Either that or the place must flood when it rains. Not a happy thought with the amount of snow still lying on the higher ground.

I'm amazed by the size of the cave as I work my way backwards. Quickly, any light from the entrance leaks away, and I'm struggling in the dark. But, the sound of flowing water reaches my ears. I press on, hands out to the side so that I can use the cave wall to direct my steps. I don't much fancy getting lost here. And then I can smell the water as well as hear it, and I bend down, gritting my teeth at the ache in my legs, and run my hands through chill water, startling as it works into my bandaged right hand.

I scoop it into my mouth, and it tastes fresh. The horses will be happy to slake their thirst. I also notice something else, the hint of growing light. I'd follow the light, but the only way to get to it is through the water. That'll have to wait, but it offers the opportunity to escape a different way to what we first used. I don't miss that it might mean there's another means of coming into the cave.

Walking back to the horses, I lead Haden and Cuthbert to the water. Haden doesn't appreciate the darkness, but Cuthbert's nose quivers as he smells the water. He pushes onwards, and Haden has no choice but to follow. They drink for a long time, and I allow it while considering the haze of light in the far distance.

I decide then that I'll mount Haden and make my way towards it, but not until all the horses have been watered. I keep a close eye on my warriors as I take the horses away and return them. Wulfhere has been stitched up and rests against the wall, his chest exposed, for the time being, a cloak around his shoulders to keep him warm. Cuthwalh nods at me, eyes sunken with exhaustion while Edmund has forced Ælfgar away from the entrance to the cave.

This is such a fuck up, and yet, I can't help but think that we've had a lucky escape, even if we're trapped, for now. We could never have overwhelmed so many. But, with Jarl Ottar and Thorgills dead, the Raiders have no one to lead them. Will they nominate another or simply run freely over the landscape, attacking any unfortunate enough to encounter them?

I can't hide here while Mercia suffers. Damn bloody Lord Cadell and his worries about Hereford. He should have come to me months ago, informed the bishops of the problem. They could have sent their warriors much more quickly, and then the Raiders would have been long dead.

Eventually, every horse has been led to the water, and now some of them sleep on the ground, while others stand upright to eat whatever grasses they can find. Most of my warriors sleep, and I know it's time to look at my leg wounds.

I've already refilled the beaker of water that Edmund first had, and now I slump to the ground, behind Haden, and peel back my trews. Fuck, it hurts, the crust of blood sticking my clothes to my skin. But, once pulled back, I can see that there's not as much blood as I feared, although black bruises are already starting to form along the edges of the wound.

I hiss through my teeth, cleaning away the scraps of clothing stuck in the wounds, one just below my knee, the other more towards the ankle on my left foot. It hurts, but nothing compared to other cuts I've taken. Critically, I examine my lower legs. These aren't the first wounds I've taken on them, and I note the fine white line that denotes where Hereman accidentally cut me beside the River Trent.

'Why are you hiding away?' Edmund crouches down beside me, his eyes seeing my wounds and dismissing them just as quickly as not of concern.

'They'll heal,' he mutters, running his hand through his hair, single eye fierce.

'What are we going to do?' he demands to know.

'What I said, but I think there might be another means of escaping. There's a light at the back of the cave.' Immediately Edmund stands, as though to investigate straight away.

'You'll get wet feet,' I mutter, wrapping a strip of linen around the cut on my right leg.

He pauses, looks at me as though contemplating whether to continue or not.

'It'll wait then.'

'It will, yes. I'll stand a watch if you want some sleep.' His stomach growls in response, and I arch an eyebrow.

'I'll eat and sleep. Don't do anything fucking stupid while I'm asleep,' Edmund orders me. I grin and cock my head to one side.

'You won't know because you'll be asleep,' I taunt, and he reaches over and grips my shoulder, arresting me with his gaze.

'Don't do anything fucking stupid,' his words are measured, weighted, and fuck me, I find myself nodding.

Bastard.

Chapter Fourteen

I n no time, my exhaustion makes itself known, and I have to move around to stay awake, even while I keep my gaze fixed on the muted world beyond the cave.

The light plays tricks on my eyes as the day advances, some areas shadowed, others grey, and all of them hold the promise that I'm being watched. It's unsettling. I'm pleased when Haden joins me, the soft sound of his hooves over the ground, waking no one, although I'm alert to his intentions.

Together, with my arm looped around his black and white neck, we stand and watch as the sounds of snoring and farting fill the air, accompanied by the odd moan and groan. Responsibility weighs me down. I worry about the rest of my warriors. I must hope that if they encounter Raiders as we have, they have the numbers to overwhelm them. I should never have split my force.

Eventually, as I'm nodding to sleep on my feet, Eahric appears, yawning and stretching, face still sheeted in blood, or rather, his lower face. It's as though only half of him has been in a battle. The other half, where his helm covered his head, is unscathed, well, if I can ignore his still healing nose.

'Get some sleep,' Eahric encourages me, turning to rub his hand along Haden's nose. Haden turns away smartly as though Eahric was speaking to him.

'I've seen nothing and heard even less,' I advise him. Fatigue drags at me, but as I make my way to a space to lie down, I check my warriors. Most of them sleep, but of course, Edmund is missing, and I know where he'll be. I'd go after him, but I'm just too damn tired.

When I wake, Haden's colossal head is resting on my chest, the scent of sweet grasses ripe in my nostrils, as well as other, more earthly scents.

'What?' and I try to move him aside, but he stays there. I'm forced to shuffle sideways, which reminds me of all my aches and pains, especially along my legs, which sting, for all the cuts were shallow.

'Thanks,' I huff, suppressing a yawn, looking around me. Eahric is no longer on guard duty, Cealwin having taken his place. Of Edmund, there's no sign.

'Where's the bastard,' I ask Haden, leading him into the cave for more water, now that he's decided to move. The darkness is complete. Night must have fallen in the woodlands and will probably last for a long time here. It adds to the feeling of protection and isolation. Inside our hiding place, we're almost apart from the world. Perhaps we should stay here, emerge in years to come when some other poor bastard has sent the Raiders back to their kingdoms in the far north.

A pretty fantasy but not one I can allow to gain any traction in my tired mind. It's my role to save Mercia. It probably always has been, or some such. Certainly, I can't see that my brother would have had the capacity, even as skilled a warrior as he was.

I see a shape ahead of me, more by the fact it's darker than the rest of the space than anything else.

'Where the fuck have you been?' I ask, but it's not a voice that responds but rather a nicker of outrage.

'Jethson?' I know it's him as soon as I rest my hand on his neck. His fur is rougher than Haden's, even though the horses are about the same size. Of course, the fact that Haden shies away from Jethson helps with the identification.

'Where's Edmund?' I don't expect an answer, and I don't get one.

I gaze around me, seeking the lighter part of the cave I saw before, but it's not there. In fact, it's challenging to determine which way leads into the darkness and which out.

'Shit.' Has Edmund really done this? Has he fucked off and left me with so many injured men and only a handful of my warriors to forge an escape? I can't believe it, and yet there's no other conclusion.

'Bastard,' and I lead Haden and Jethson on to where the tinkle of falling water assures me there's another source of fresh water. I'm furious. I didn't tell Edmund of my suspicions so that he could leave me here. Had he gone to find help, I might not object, but how can he have? The rest of my warriors are on the other side of the River Wye. That he's left Jethson boils me further.

And I know why he's done it as well. He's left us all so that he can go to my aunt. I hope she flays him with her tongue because I'll be doing the same.

The fucker.

'Where's Edmund?' It's Ælfgar who asks, eyeing Jethson with consternation.

'Didn't he go into the woodlands?' I direct this to Eahric and Cealwin, but I'm unsurprised when they both shake their heads, looking as confused as Ælfgar.

I sigh, threading Jethson's rein across his saddle and tying it tightly before starting to remove it. The other horses wear no saddles. Was Edmund hoping to take Jethson with him? I wish I could direct my ire at Eahric and Cealwin, but they were to watch for someone trying to get into the cave, not trying to escape.

'I believe he's found an escape route in the cave,' I'm forced to admit.

'What, he's left us?' There's a hint of panic in Hemming's voice as more and more of my men wake at the unease running through the cave.

'I'm sure he's gone for help,' I try, but my heart's really not in it. 'He wouldn't leave Jethson.' I attempt again, but Wulfred is watching me, fury on his face, his bald pate as red as his cheeks.

'That fucking cunt,' he explodes, and I don't argue with him. There's no point. I feel the same way he does. Edmund has left us. I would never have expected it from him, but it seems I don't know him half as well as I think I do.

'Well, we should see if we can get out that way,' Osmod states defiantly.

'Yes, we should, but if the horses could make it, then Jethson wouldn't be here.'

Osmod grunts, agreeing with my conclusion. But he's right. We should find the exit. Perhaps, after all, Edmund hasn't left us. I've jumped to conclusions about him before and been proved wrong. Maybe the same will happen this time.

'We'll look when there's more light. For now, I can't find it because the cave is as dark as night.'

'He'll come back, won't he?' Hemming demands querulously, and I nod, just the once words beyond me.

I lift Jethson's saddle and place it on the ground, close to the others. We won't be needing the horses for a while.

'Has everyone slept and eaten something? I want to send two men out to seek the Raiders. Well, I want one man to come with me. There's murder in my heart. It's the only way I'll recover my good humour now that Edmund's deserted us.

'Yes, aye, a bit,' the responses assure me that while I've been sleeping, the others have been looking after one another, not that it's much lighter here than inside the far reaches of the cave. It must be the middle of the night, and I'm sure the moon will be little more than a slither tonight. We can't always rely on it being bright and free from clouds.

'Then I'm going to find the bloody enemy.' My words are tight with fury.

'I'll come with you,' I'm not surprised that Ælfgar offers, but I'm looking at Wulfstan. He shrugs his shoulders.

'Aye, I'm ready,' he agrees. He protected the wolf cubs close to London. Now I'm going to rely on him to protect the rest of my warriors and me.

'I've heard nothing while I've been on watch duty,' Cealwin offers as I prepare myself to slip back amongst the trees. It will be difficult to see out there, but hopefully, there'll be some little light from the moon or the stars. Maybe the fuckers won't have been quite as keen to spend the night without the aid of a fire. The smell of smoke will make it easier to find them.

I check my weapons belt, noting the seax that doesn't belong to me. I should like to go back for my lost weapon if I can. But first, there are Raiders to hunt down before they find us, and one blade cuts as deep as another. If you know what you're doing.

Wulfstan checks his weapons belt as well, and seemingly content, looks at me.

'Shields?'

This is a difficult one. A shield will be heavy to carry, but it's better to have one than not have one if it comes to a pitched battle. But I think speed is more important.

'No,' I announce. 'We need to find the Raiders before we kill them.' Wulfstan nods, his eyes keen. 'A good idea. And then we can determine how the fuckers will die.'

I grunt and turn to my warriors once more.

'Stay safe. We'll be back as soon as possible.'

I don't wait for them to reply. They're my men. They know what's expected of them. I do hold Haden with a lingering gaze. He, of them all, might be the most difficult to contain. For now, he seems content enough.

'Watch my horse,' I urge Ælfgar in an undertone.

'Wulfhere and Hemming are good with him,' he mutters. It seems my men know my horse as well as I do.

Carefully, I peer out of the concealed entrance of the cave, noting that there's just enough light by which to see. I press my body against the nearest tree trunk, mindful of the branches that hang below my eyesight, the rippled texture of the wood. I inhale the scent of the trees, sharp and biting, and yet a comfort all the same. Wulfstan follows me, his movements so quiet I startle as I realise, he's beside me.

I look behind, but already, I can't see the entrance to the cave. It's just dark and then darker, with no hint that there's any rocky formation, only more and more trees. I can't hear my men, or the horses, or the stream that flows through the back of the cave.

'Fuck, we'll never find our way back.'

'Mark the tree trunk,' Wulfstan suggests.

'We don't want others to guess what it is?'

'I'll make it look like one of the animals did it, but I'll make it bigger.' And he proceeds to sheer away some of the brown bark, in just such a way that it does appear natural and not placed there by a man with a seax. It's more a scratch than a cut.

'It'll have to do,' I huff, not at all sure that it will. I've led Wulfstan out here, and we could go back now and be assured of finding my warriors again. But, if we hide away at some point, we will run out of food. No, I need to do what I suggested, no matter Edmund's betrayal.

'Which way?' I have no idea which direction we came in or which way the Raiders might have gone. Beneath the canopy of branches, little rain or snow has fallen, and the ground is dry. It's worked in our favour until now. I can't see any horses hooves in the leaf litter, but equally, there are no footprints either.

'That way,' Wulfstan points to the right. I nod. It's as good as any other suggestion.

'Stay close,' I instruct him, wishing that I had fifty men at my back and not just one. 'I think we should mark a few other places as well,' I huff once we've taken no more than twenty steps. Turning, it's impossible to see which way we've come.

'I'll cut more marks as we go,' Wulfstan confirms, a flicker of unease making its way over his face, even in the half-light. My stomach feels leaden. Perhaps Edmund had it right. It would just be easier to escape with our lives and release the horses into the woodland in the hope they'll stay together and could be found later.

There's a creeping sense of dread I've not felt for a long time. This is fucking stupid and equally imperative. There's no choice here.

I forge a path through the hanging boughs of the evergreen trees, noting how tall they are and how lush with branches and pine needles. This must be a good place for them to flourish, with the river close by and water pooling from the higher land behind us. A good place for trees, if not for two Mercians being hunted by an unknown number of Raiders.

Where the fuck has Edmund gone?

Has he gone to my aunt, or has he gone to find help? I wish I knew. For now, my fury keeps me pressing on through the trees. Fingers of fear shudder down my spine when unexpected branches or spider's webs touch my face or hands. Wulfstan is the same, more than once, I turn, weapon raised, just to watch him shrug aside a spiders web that's hanging between the trees, only just visible when I know where to look.

'This is fucking hopeless,' I mutter, just as I catch a whiff of smoke.

Eyes wide, I raise my finger to my lips and seek out Wulfstan's white eyes in the gloom. He nods. He smells it as well.

Ever more silently, I work my way towards the smell, the soft tones of men growing more audible. A crackle of flame, no doubt caused by a handful of pines thrown onto the fire, and I can see my enemy.

There are no more than eleven of them, hunkered down around a roaring fire, the smell of which permeates the woodlands. They're not trying to hide; that much is clear.

It's only then that I regret not having Wærwulf with me. He'd be able to tell me about what the Raiders are talking. Their voices fill the woodlands, drowning out all sound. There could be fifty of my enemy behind me, and I'd not know.

They have no horses, and no one seems to be on watch duty, but I might be wrong. It's impossible to see far in the gloom, with the flame casting some areas into shadows that seem to leak all the way back to the river in the far distance.

Carefully, I work my way close to a tree trunk where the branches only begin far above my head, and Wulfstan follows me. I'm not going to send him off on his own. Then we'd both end up lost. No, we need to stay together if we're going to succeed.

'We wait,' I mouth at him, and he nods, eyes never leaving the scene before us. The Raiders are no more than seven horse lengths in front of us, but they're oblivious to being watched.

I don't like to kill men when they sleep and can't protect themselves, but I'll make an exception on this occasion. I need them dead. I pity them for all of a heartbeat until my fury returns. They had a choice; I mustn't forget that. There was no need for them to come to Mercia.

Eventually, some of them roll to the side and find sleep, all but one of them. The guard sits with his back to the fire, staring out to the opposite side of where Wulfstan and I stand ready. The flames begin to die away, and he doesn't replenish the wood or throw more dried pine needles on the smouldering remains. I watch his head, urging him to fall into sleep, but after a long time, I realise he's more alert than that. He plans on staying awake until he's relieved of duty.

This is a problem.

With the fire a ruin of its former self, and without the cover of conversation, the woodland has become preternaturally quiet. I'm worried that if I breathe too loudly, he'll hear me. The ground might be spongey underfoot, but a man with weapons is likely to be heard, even when he moves silently.

I want to infiltrate the campsite, but there's only Wulfstan and me, against eleven Raiders. Yes, some of them might sleep, but how quickly will they be fully alert? Do they even all sleep, or is this a ploy to draw me out from my hiding place? Maybe they know I'm here.

I argue with myself for a long time, wishing the man would sleep, and just as I've decided to attack anyway, the opportunity too good to miss, the man's head nods forward, his neck visible where his hair's cut very short, as his chin rests on his chest.

'Thank fuck for that,' I mouth to Wulfstan, and he snorts quietly. I'll leave it a moment more, but no longer than that. I can't risk one of the others waking.

'We go together, protect one another's backs, kill them all while they sleep. If they wake, we'll fight together.' He nods, his mouth a tight line of concentration.

I like Wulfstan. He's always been a fierce warrior, and now I need him to be the most vicious he's ever been.

'We can do this,' I reinforce before starting to move forward. I glance from where I need to stand to where the man sleeps, checking he stays asleep, pleased when he does.

And then the warmth of the fire reaches me, and I'm close enough to stab down through the chest of a man who sleeps with both arms flung above his head, legs wide apart. He doesn't even open his eyes. Behind me, Wulfstan bends to kill the next man. We crab our way through the campsite, slicing throats or stabbing through chests, and then I'm facing the watchman.

I look at him, startled that he seems to watch me, even though he makes no move. Forehead furrowed, I reach my hand out, but there's no air coming between his lips. Poor bastard. He's died, just like that. I note then that he was a grey beard. The Raiders chose their guard poorly. I wish I'd known he was dead.

There are only four sleeping men to kill, and I think we're going to manage it successfully. Only then the man before me opens his eyes wide, alarm in his dark eyes, weapon to hand immediately.

'*Angreb*,' he hollers, but it's too late for the man that Wulfstan kills. That leaves us with three against the two of us, and while my enemy is alert and, on his feet, the other two aren't. One is so tangled in his cloak that he dies on Wulfstan's blade trying to free his weapon.

This is a fairer fight now.

The warrior glances around furiously when no one leaps to assist him, his face turning angrier and angrier.

'Olafr,' he cries, his eyes on a younger man I've already killed. I arch an eyebrow, no hint of apology as I rush him. Only now could I do with a shield, as a seax flashes before my eyes, the blade sharp and deadly in the hand of the warrior. He's not an exceptionally tall man, but his upper arms hold silver rings, three on the one side, four on the other. He might just be a jarl. Certainly, these men were his to command.

'Egil,' the other man desperately cries, and the clash of weapons fills the air. Wulfstan has a battle on his hands, but I'm sure he'll prevail. Now I just need to do the same.

'*Skiderik*,' the man huffs, but there's resolve on his face. He means to kill me or die here. I know which option I prefer.

I counter his seax with mine, coming in closer to the warrior, thinking to use my fists to wind him, but he darts back, bending as he does so. His movement is so quick, I don't appreciate that he's flung a handful of dried pines into the fire until the flames leap high, blinding me to whatever he means to do next.

'Bastard,' I reply, trying to blink the bright light from my eyes, expecting an attack at any moment. Only it doesn't come.

'He's gone,' Wulfstan informs me, as I try and attack with my seax, despite not being able to see.

'He's run away,' Wulfstan continues as though an everyday occurrence.

'Is everyone else dead?'

'Aye, My Lord. All of them. A few put up a fight, but not many.'

I turn. Most of the Raiders haven't moved from where they slept. The watchman still nods in death, and three of the remaining men have slumped to the floor, having tried to protect themselves.

'Where the fuck's he gone?' I complain, frustrated that such a trick has worked on me. I would have preferred it if all of the Raiders were dead.

'I doubt he knows,' Wulfstan comments laconically, bending to inspect something on the ground. I look around me. It wasn't my finest work, and I don't like killing men when they sleep, as I've said. But I must do so for Mercia to survive.

'What's that?'

'A ruby, I think,' and he shows it to me.

'It just looks like a stone to me.'

'It needs the light,' he argues, as a loud crack rings through the air. How someone's managed to find the only twig to stand on, I'll never know. The ground has been remarkably clear of them until now.

'Over there,' and Wulfstan points one way, while I think it's another.

We're completely exposed. Slowly, I bend and send a handful of dried pines onto the fire. As before, the flames leap into the sky, hopefully blinding whatever or whoever tracks us.

'Quickly,' and I rush back into the trees, pleased when the darkness swallows me, even as I hold my seax ready, just in case, I'm running at whoever made the noise.

My chest heaves with the speed. I only turn aside when the light from the fire has noticeably dimmed. I turn then, looking back the way I've come, while Wulfstan rushes to join me. The woodland might be protecting my warriors, but suddenly, it feels too tight, as though the trees press in on me. Only then do I see what's caused the noise. There's a wolf, or rather, four of them, nosing amongst the dead.

'Fuck, they can smell blood from a good distance,' Wulfstan exclaims as I worry at my lip. It was just a pack of wolves, but in running as we have, I have no idea of the way we came. Everything looks the same, especially in the dark.

'Shit,' and Wulfstan glances at me, eyebrows furrowed.

'What?'

'I don't know how we got here. I don't know which way to go.'

Wulfstan pivots, looking all around, and for a moment, I think he's going to have an answer for me.

But when he meets my eyes, I see the acceptance in them.

We're lost.

Fuck.

Chapter Fifteen

'We'll stay together and try and find our way back,' I state, deciding that confidence will make it happen.

'We stayed together to get fucking lost,' Wulfstan attempts to joke. I grin, but it's more of a grimace.

'We did, yes. But provided we stay together now, at least we won't lose one another.' I've been peering down at the ground, trying to decide if there's a way of retracting our steps that doesn't involve getting anywhere near the wolves. The sound of ripping cloth and chewing is enough to keep me away from the fire.

'So, did we come through there or through there?' I point, trying to decide which is the best way to go. If there was some light or even the sound of the river, I feel I could re-orientate myself, but there's only the noise of the feast the wolves are enjoying. I hope they eat well and leave nothing behind but bones. I don't want to come back to such a gruesome site.

'I thought it was that way,' and Wulfstan points directly across the campsite. If only there were a bloody tree or some sort of land-mark we could look to, but there isn't.

'We have three choices then. Which one should we take?'

Wulfstan shakes his head, running his hand through his dark beard.

'We may as well just try one and see what happens.'

'So, which one?'

'This one,' and he turns and walks away. I appreciate him making the decision, even if I think it is the wrong one. One of three things could happen; we could find the river, the cave or the Raiders. I would sooner one of the first two.

I bend and wipe my bloodied blade through a handful of the rich loam before following on behind Wulfstan. There's no clear path. None at all. The trees are sometimes widely spaced, but more often than not, narrowly spaced, so we have to slide between the low hanging branches. In places where the branches start higher than my head, it's easier going, but only until we encounter the next lower hanging branch. For all I know, we could be walking in circles.

'This is fucking useless,' Wulfstan explodes, long after I've started thinking the same.

He's right. I've seen nothing I recognise, and it must still be night time because there's no lessening to the gloom.

'Perhaps we should just stop and wait for it to get lighter?' I state, not that I'm going to follow my words. My neck's aching from constantly flicking forwards and backwards, side to side. I don't think we're being hunted, but there are so many small creatures in the woodlands that I might just be mistaking their scrutiny for some of the Raiders. At least we don't stumble back upon the campsite and the wolves. Neither do we find other Raiders. Not here.

'We should stop,' I state again, but then Wulfstan turns and grins at me, his speed increasing.

'What is it?' I demand to know, but he's too quick, and I risk losing him as well. Hastily, I follow in his tracks, avoiding the tree roots and upturned ground where burrowing animals have made their home. And then I hear it, first as a soft rustle, before it becomes the rumble of falling water.

We've found the river.

Thank fuck for that.

Now the grey light of dawn begins to permeate inside the tree-line, and Wulfstan instinctively slows, giving me time to catch him.

'We need to be careful,' I caution. Wulfstan's pointed look tells me all I need to know about wasting my time with those words.

'I'll look,' and Wulfstan is gone before I can call him back. I follow on behind him with more caution. There's little point in me lingering. If all of my warriors were here, then yes, caution would be required, but if Wulfstan gets set upon by the Raiders, I'm not going to leave him to face them alone.

The first thing I notice is the expanse of the river. It's wide here, far broader than I've seen so far. I take that to mean we're further along than we need to be. We must have headed north when we needed to go south. That's not a problem, provided we're not too far away from the initial battle site.

Wulfstan has hunkered low, squatting down so that he's all but merged with the remnants of brown ferns and struggling green plants trying to survive the winter. I can see him, but I think that's only because I know where he is.

I stay just behind him, trying to scout along the riverbank, seeking out the sign of any ships. But there's nothing to be seen because it's still too dark to be able to pick out details that are smaller than the river or the trees.

'It's fine,' Wulfstan whispers to me. I join him then, helping him to his feet.

'I thought we'd never find the river,' he rejoices.

'Me neither. Now we just need to make our way back to where we encountered the Raiders.'

'Let's hope it's not too far. My feet are aching.' I'd call him weak for such an admission, but my feet are throbbing as well. It makes a strange counterpart, pounding feet and aching cuts on my legs.

I'm reminded of our trek through the snow, such is my pain. We're too used to our horses to get us over long distances.

Staying just inside the tree line, we strike out once more after emptying our stream into the river. I'm thirsty, but the water is too far down the bank, and I risk sliding into the water. I decide to wait until we come across a smaller stream merging into the larger river. With the snowmelt and the rain of recent days, I can't think it'll be long.

We walk in silence, alert to the changing daylight around us and to the potential for the Raiders to have stayed on the riverbank as the most accessible means of navigating. As we've proved to ourselves, it's not easy when you don't know the landscape intimately.

By the time the sun has fully risen, we've still not found the site of the battle, and my belly's beginning to rumble and my lips are dry, my mouth parched. Yet, it's still impossible to get close enough to the river without taking a considerable risk.

'Well, this is shit,' I exclaim eventually. Our silence has gone from being comfortable to sullen. I'm not blaming Wulfstan for our predicament, that's entirely my fault, but I fucking wish I could.

'Shhh,' his warning comes just in time. Not that I was talking, but neither was I stepping carefully, my thighs have grown heavy with having to lift my feet so high to clamber over the weeds and ferns and strange lumps in the ground.

I follow where Wulfstan points, out to the side of the river, and there are more of the Raiders. They walk together, fully armed, murder on their faces, as they call one to another. I recognise none of the men from yesterday, but then, I killed every man who tried to kill me. These must have been the Raiders who never got close enough to take a stab at us.

I count them. There are five that I can see. None of them looks happy, from where I stand. Their stances are tight, and blades glint in the daylight, but they're not coming any closer to the treeline. They're content to stay by the riverbank, but they're not searching the riverbank. No, their gazes are fixed inside the woods. They're hunting for us.

How many of the bastards still live? I thought I'd killed more than this.

'Stay still,' I caution Wulfstan. They're not moving slowly, for all their intention to find us. The Raiders move with too much speed for it to be a fight they genuinely welcome. Not for the first time, I consider why they don't just leave? Their jarls are dead. Why don't they just take the ship and go? There might not be enough of them to row, but I know their boats have a sail as well.

It might take them a while, but they'd make it home, eventually. Unless the Raiders don't know where home is. That, I realise, would be a huge problem, just like mine in these woods. I don't know where to go. I might have the means to get there but no one to direct me.

When I think the Raiders have moved off far enough, I tap Wulfstan on the shoulder, and we emerge from our temporary hiding place behind a wide tree trunk and continue on our way.

We must be close to the battle site. It surely can't be much further? I just can't see that we walked that far during the night, especially when we could hardly see.

When we find a stream, I urge Wulfstan to bend and drink before taking my fill as well. There's a handy piece of stone to stand on so that we can dip our hands into the water and then lift them to our faces. My thirst surprises me. After all, it's far from warm.

We press on, and I'd have walked beyond the site of the attack if not for my eyes catching sight of something glimmering in the growing sunlight.

'Wulfstan, here,' hand on my seax, I stalk to the river bank. Gazing all around me, or as far as I can see, I step out confidently, sure the place is home to no one but the dead. The dead are still here, lying where they fell. No one has thought to steal their weapons or riches. It seems the Raiders are running scared. I smirk as I dip low to collect my lost seax. The sound of the weapon ripping free from the dead man makes me judder, the sound harsh even when the man is long dead and solid in his everlasting sleep. The weight of my seax is a comfort. It does a warrior no good to lose a much-loved weapon.

Wulfstan watches, eyes alert, relief on his face when I return to his side.

'We went this way,' and now I can see signs of our headlong passage. There are bits of broken branches and splatters of blood, but also hoof prints. Alert that we might be watched, we weave a path away from where the horses took us, and eventually, I moan with relief. I can see one of our marks in the tree bark.

Hemming is on guard duty when I finally step through and into the cave. I've been aware of his gaze on me for some time, and so there's no blade held at my throat. There's a look of delight on his young face.

'We got fucking lost,' Wulfstan offers as an explanation even though no one asks us.

'We killed some more of the bastards and got lost in the dark.' I gaze around the cave, hoping to find Edmund returned to us, but he's not there. I should have known not to think he might reappear.

'It was a quiet night here,' Ælfgar informs me as I riffle through my saddlebags, looking for some cheese to ease my hungry belly.

'Good. There aren't any Raiders at the site of the attack.' I'm considering returning that way. Better to be out in the open than hidden away here. But one look at Wulfhere, and I appreciate he can't be moved, not until he's healed some more. His face is drawn, sweat-soaked, and Eahric tries to mouth something to me from his side.

We need to stay here. There are too few of my warriors to risk leaving a handful behind, especially when one of them would be so severely wounded, he still might not live. Impatience claws at me, but Wulfhere isn't Haden, and even Haden needed some ease to help him when he was first wounded.

'I need to sleep,' I announce, rather than making any other decisions. Even this is met with a wave of happiness from some of my warriors. I never thought they'd be so pleased to have me away from them or sleeping.

Quickly, I finish my cheese and strips of rolled meat, wishing I had more to eat but grateful all the same.

I roll on the floor, close to the entrance so I'm still between my wounded and any attackers who might attempt to infiltrate us, and then I'm asleep as soon as my eyes close.

It's dark once more when I wake, the noise of men and horses snoring and moving in their sleep assuring me that all is well. Eadfrith is on guard duty. He stands or rather moves from side to side, just a few steps before he retraces the same distance. He's trying to keep himself awake.

I stand, even though my feet are throbbing, and go to his side.

'I'll take the watch,' I offer, and he agrees far too quickly, but I don't object. I'd sooner be the one to guard them than the older man. I doubt he'll ever leave Kingsholm again. I don't blame him. This was supposed to be an easy task, not one where Raiders attacked us. I almost apologise, but I don't. If he didn't realise it might happen, I'd be surprised. After all, he's ridden as one of my warriors for long enough.

I move outside the cave to empty my stream into the mulch of the spongy ground, having peered into the gloom. There's no one out there. Nothing moves, not even the wolves of last night. I'd be surprised if they don't still feast. They'll have been joined by the birds and other small creatures as well.

Moving back inside, I detect a change in the darkness and hold steady. No one could have come through me, not unless they've used Edmund's escape route. But it's just one of the horses, not a Raider.

My thoughts turn to my plans for my men. I said we'd hunt down the Raiders, and Wulfstan and I have killed more of them and seen no others. Is that it, or are they hiding somewhere else? Does it even matter while Wulfhere can't be moved? I consider Edmund. I should investigate where he's gone. I was too angry before, but what if he's stuck somewhere? Maybe he went to explore and became trapped, but I doubt it.

The night drags, and when the rest of my warriors stir, I'm no closer to a decision. We'll have to wait, at least another day, perhaps two, and then we'll have to take Wulfhere away, no matter whether he's well enough to move.

Chapter Sixteen

B efore we leave, Eahric and Wulfred scout the area. They're able to make their way back to the riverbank and without seeing anyone. I can't hope for anything better. I've checked the passageway I believe Edmund took at the back of the cave, and there's no sign of him. I even risked calling his name into the gloom, raising my voice far too loud so that it echoed back to me. He's not there. He never was.

With the aid of Ælfgar, I manage to get Wulfhere in his saddle. His wound has begun to knit together remarkably well, his fever passing as quickly as it descended. He grins, reassurance that he'll heal making him giddy, even as he grunts in pain as we force him into his saddle.

There's no need to tie him in place. He can sit remarkably well with the padding around his waist, made from the spare tunics I carry in my saddlebag. I know a moment of remorse for the delicate embroidery, but my aunt would approve of my using them to better purpose. And it's the cleanest thing any of us have.

I stink. I can't deny it. As soon as it's safe to do so, I plan on dunking myself in the nearest pond—anything to drive the smell of stale blood and sweat from my body. I'll risk the ice-cold water.

'It's not that far,' Eahric reassures everyone. 'It might feel as though we rode from Gloucester to London to get here, but we didn't.' I don't know if I'm pleased by the reminder of how little progress we made before being set upon by the Raiders.

I've arranged the men in the following order. I'll lead, with Wulfstan at my side. Behind us, Jethson will be riderless, Wulfhere to one side, and Hemming to the other. Osmod and Cuthwalh are next, with Eadfrith and Cealwin behind, and at the rear, Ælfgar, Wulfred and Eahric will have the most challenging role of us all.

'If the Raiders attack, form a tight circle if we can't use the horses to escape.'

I decide to continue to head for Hereford. It must be closer than returning to Gloucester, but if we need to, we'll reverse our direction and go back home to Gloucester and Kingsholm. Then, I'll summon Bishop Wærferth's men and ride to Hereford to hunt down the remainder of my warriors.

I'm not going to leave them to fend for themselves. If I make it to Hereford, I'll avail myself of Bishop Deorlaf's men as well. They're used to fighting on the border with the men of the Welsh kingdoms of Powys and Gwynedd. I'll welcome their local knowledge.

'Stay alert,' I caution before setting out. It's daylight beyond the enclosing trees. It's light enough to see, and that means the Raiders, if there are any, will be able to see us just as well as we can spot them.

I ride with my shield in place over my right leg, seax poised in my weapons belt, and I've checked to ensure my war axe and double-headed eagle sword are accessible as well. Of course, Haden's in a foul mood, so I have an angry horse to assist me if needed. Bloody wonderful.

'Calm down,' I urge him, as he dances first left and then right, head moving from side to side, keen to be released from his captivity. The lack of good grazing has made him as irritable as me. With little but cheese to eat, my belly feels hollow.

Berg is far more amiable as Wulfstan follows on just behind. There's still not enough room between the tree trunks and branches for us to ride side by side.

It doesn't help that I've decided a gentle speed is the best. I don't want to rush or be overly cautious. Haden doesn't like that. He wants to gallop, no matter the objects that block the path.

The two of us fight our way to the riverbank, the gurgle of the water directing more than any visible trail through the undergrowth. But then, almost within sight of the river, Haden stops, refusing to go any further. Berg all but collides with him, and still, he won't move on.

'What is it?' Wulfstan hisses.

'I don't fucking know. Come on, Haden, not now.' But then I hear it. A low growl, nothing else, and the snap of sharp jaws.

'Fuck, the wolves are here now.'

'It's not like them to be out in the daytime,' Wulfstan counters, as though I don't know the unmistakable sound of a wolf eating, or that they normally come out at night.

'Well, they are. We'll have to go round.'

But which way? With the wolves on the river bank, I have to commit now to Hereford or Gloucester as my destination, and I don't know. I'd sooner reach Hereford, and the remainder of my warriors.

'Bugger,' and I dismount, leaving my horse with Wulfstan to stalk through the treeline as though the decision is to go to Hereford. But, I'm still well hidden when I hear voices from further along, and they're not speaking my tongue.

'Fuck,' I pause, trying to catch sight of the men, assess their numbers. But they move about on the riverbank, and the tree trunks and the men merge, the bright sunlight making it impossible to get a true reckoning of how many we face.

I gaze at the men, undecided as to what to do. Another altercation with these Raiders could be problematic. But the thought of abandoning my warriors on the other side of River Wye worries at me. I said I'd meet them. What will happen to them if I never arrive?

But I have wounded men. I can't risk it.

Resolved, if unhappy with the decision, I return to Haden and Wulfstan.

'Gloucester,' I announce.

'Aye, it's for the best,' but Wulfstan sounds far from happy about it. It sits uneasily with me to do the sensible thing. That's not what my men expect from me.

Mounting Haden once more, I veer away from the wolves at their banquet, and the Raiders who are to the north of the wolves. We need to arrive on the riverbank far enough away that they won't scent the horses, or at least far enough away that the wolves will think it too much effort to hunt us down if they do smell them. They have a feast. They should enjoy it.

The sound of chomping, whining, and general yipping follows me for longer than I like. I itch to burst free from the drooping branches and lack of clear sight. Hereman would be useless here. There's not enough room to aim his spear, let alone have it fly free to its destination.

Only when Haden stops his prancing do I deem it safe enough to emerge onto the river track.

I pause one final time, listening and looking, but there's nothing other than the far distant yip of the wolves and the thunder of running water. The wolves are keeping the Raiders away from us. I should be grateful for that.

Wulfstan emerges first, shielding his eyes from the sudden brightness and then peering all around him. He takes Berg to the riverbank itself, leaning over to study the water, as I beckon for the rest of my warriors to join us.

'It's risen a lot,' Wulfstan comments. In the far distance, the snow-capped peaks of the hills are visible. All that snow is yet to melt. I feel a flicker of worry for those who live so close to the water's edge. I hope they're safe. The River Wye might yet breach its banks. It's not far from doing so now.

'It's fast-flowing,' Wulfstan adds, moving away to the front of the group while I linger at the back. We're still vulnerable, even now, and until Wulfred, Eahric, and Ælfgar have come out from beneath the trees, I'll watch our rear.

When we're all once more in place, I return to Wulfstan's side and set a steady pace over the damp grasses. It's taken longer than I'd like to win free from the trees, and the amount of daylight remaining to us is debatable. Still, I hope we can at least return to the sheep shelter we borrowed on our journey here.

As the distance between us and the place where we encountered the Raiders begins to grow, I allow myself to think we've avoided them. Leaving Wulfstan to lead, I move amongst my warriors, ensuring all are well, even Wulfhere, who rides with a scowl on his face but shakes away my question about stopping. Only then Wulfred calls to me.

'Coelwulf, have a look at that fucking cloud?'

I groan. It's black and menacing. In fact, the entire skyline is shadowed. I'd just thought the sun was close to setting, but no, it's swamped by black clouds promising not just rain but a deluge. With the river already so close to flooding, I need to be careful. When the rain begins to fall, the soggy ground will quickly become too wet, the trickle of the smaller streams leading into the larger River Wye will expand into every dip and hollow that the land offers the water.

'Shit,' I return to Wulfstan, increase Haden's speed to a steady canter that allows me time to check the foreground for burrows that might trip him, but all too soon, a steady trickle of rain starts up. It smells cold, and it is fucking cold, falling almost like snow.

'Are we near the fucking sheep hut?' I ask myself, visibility already poor enough that it's difficult to see anything but grey lines.

'Yes,' Wulfstan huffs. 'I recognise this place. We should be there quickly from here.' It's far from ideal, but if we stay out in this, we'll only get lost and risk getting stuck on land that's quickly flooding.

'Lead the way,' I call to Wulfstan above the growing thud of the rain. The drops are so huge, they hurt as they hit me, and Haden is already sodden, shaking his head as he attempts to avoid them. I wish

I'd scouted the weather as well as for Raiders. I've given up my refuge only to ride into a storm that might still trap us for days to come.

Wulfstan veers to the left, and I follow on behind, a glimpse behind me, assuring me that I can't see my warriors at the rear. But, they're good men, seasoned. They might not be the warriors they once were, but they know how to ride in a fucking storm. It's not as if it's an isolated occurrence, not here on the border with the Welsh kingdoms of Gwent and Powys.

Yet, for all Wulfstan's reassurance that we're close, by the time we find the shelter, I'm soaked and cold and wishing for my cave once more.

'Well done,' I praise Wulfstan, pleased to see that there don't seem to be any sheep to argue with us for room in the crumbling building.

'Aye, it was still bastard further than I thought it would be.'

He stays mounted, watching for the rest of my warriors, while I check the interior of the shelter. Happy that it's empty and no Raiders hide there, I move to Wulfhere's side and help him down. He lands heavily, and with a groan of pain, the weight of him doubled because of the rain that's leaked into his trews, clinging to his cloak.

'Good lad,' I offer words of encouragement as the remainder of my warriors arrive. While I take Wulfhere inside and settle him in the driest corner, the rest of my warriors force a long branch that Wulfred has dragged closer over the leaking gaps in the room that the horses will occupy. I go to help them as soon as Osmod is there to aid Wulfhere.

'Where did you get it?' I call to Wulfred as soon as it's in position, and the horses look a little happier at where we're leading them.

'Just over there,' Wulfred explains, pointing back toward the river bank. 'It looks as though it's been cut just for the task, but they didn't complete it before the rain began.'

'Well, Haden's pleased not to be wet,' I smirk. I'm so wet, just unsaddling Haden is agony, my tunic and byrnie stuck to my skin so that I just don't have the usual movements freely available. I'm not alone in struggling with such a simple task. I force myself to do the same for Jethson and Wulfhere's mount before I allow myself to slump to the floor inside the other half of the shelter.

My warriors have removed as many of their clothes as they can. But without the heat from a fire, they're cold. I consider the wisdom of alerting the Raiders to where we are, but Hemming is blue, Wulfhere so white, it's as though he lights the room. I bend and gather some dried hay together, bits of fleece as well, using the same stones as the other night to hold the fire in place. There's even some pieces of wood left to burn as well.

At least, if the bastards come, we'll be warm enough to fight them.

Chapter Seventeen

The world has turned watery and grey when I emerge with the weak light of a new day.

Everything is drenched. Everything.

Even the tiny brook which the sheep must use to drink from is three times larger than when I last saw it.

'Fucking weather,' Wulfred gripes even as he farts, his face as clouded as the sky the night before. I'm with him. We've had nothing but crap weather. If I were a religious man, I might think my Lord God wanted me to fail. But fuck him. I'm not going to.

'Are we moving on today?' Osmod calls from inside the shelter. I growl at the question.

'We fucking should,' Wulfred continues, no enthusiasm in the words. 'But whether it's possible is another matter entirely.' My eye has been caught by what I hope is a trickle of smoke coming from the steading halfway up the opposite hill. If we could make it there, I'm sure there must be a track that would lead us away from the river. But getting there is the problem. Water surrounds us. The small brook is the least of my concerns.

The river has burst its banks, water stretching with glowering menace almost to the sheep shelter. We can't go forward, neither can we cross the small brook, and where there must have been a stream, there's now a torrent of water surging towards the river. We're trapped. Just what I didn't want to happen. Fuck.

'I'm going to scout up there,' I call to Wulfred, pointing where I mean to go, listening to the squelch of water every time I take a single step. Now, I can see why the sheep aren't here. The farmer wouldn't have taken the risk with so much rain, especially not when he knows the fields must be prone to flooding. A pity I took less care with my men.

Behind the sheep shelter, there's a low hill stretching into the clouds that hang low, promising little warmth for the day. Not that I think it's going to rain again. But the water that already lies on the ground has nowhere to go other than into the river and then out again, spreading once more over the fields. And so it will repeat until there's some heat to dry it all, or the river succeeds in taking it away to the distant sea.

The air is ripe with the scent of rich earth, shit, and dampness. I wrinkle my nose, watching where I step carefully. I don't want damp feet when I've managed to dry myself during the night, thanks to the small fire that warmed the sheep shelter nicely. I scamper up a handful of large grey and white rocks, hoping for a vista that shows me a possible way of escaping.

The river stretches out as a dirty stain across the landscape, patches of white snow still visible, but they're few and far between. Water has claimed almost every field that borders the river, spreading further and further inland. In one of them, as I hold my hand above my eyes, there's a family of ducks making use of the water, and deer drink from the shallow pools, wariness constantly making them look up to ensure they're not being watched.

Towards Hereford, I can see the beginnings of the forest where we encountered the Raiders and sheltered in the secure cave. The treetops glint in the weak light, covered in water that the slight breeze can't dispel. It's grim and gloomy, and then my heart sinks because as

I turn towards where the open sea lies some distance away, along the track we took to get here, a sudden burst of sunlight through the clouds highlights the one thing I didn't want to see.

'Fuck,' I mutter, an eye fixed on the object that makes its way slowly upstream, oars to either side as they battle the raging current.

'Bastards. Why are they coming upriver when it's in flood?' but I don't need to answer that. It's obvious. We're still being hunted, or rather, I am.

I turn aside. There's time yet. I just need to find a way to escape this place. And I need to do it quickly.

Only Wulfhere is mounted. The rest of us scrabble up the steep hillside, Haden away in front, while I help Stilton keep his footing. Wulfhere wants to walk, but he can't move fast enough. I don't like risking Stilton, but I'm all out of options. I don't have the numbers to counter the Raiders in their ship.

As evident as our passage might be on the stone-laden hillside, as we snake our way up the steep hillside, I'd sooner that than hide away again, especially when our only shelter is a crumbling sheep barn.

My breath is harsh in my chest. I know my face is red from my exertion, but if old Cealwin can force himself up the slope, then so can I.

Without us on their backs, most of the horses are doing well, choosing the best paths for themselves. Wulfstan stays behind Wulfhere and Stilton, his eyes alert because too much sweat drips into my eyes to make it easy to see. I refuse to remove my byrnie or my weapons belt, and it only adds to my difficulties. As quick as I want to escape the watery expanse, I'm not about to take stupid risks.

'It's still a good distance away,' Wulfstan comments, not for the first time. He's been keeping a running commentary on the advance of the single ship. I can tell it's a Raider craft because it wallows low in the water, making it easy to advance along the river, oars extended to either side. More than once, it's been forced to stop, no doubt tangled in tree roots or other objects washed away by the ferocious storm water. I hope there are more and more of them. I hope it rains once more, sending a torrent into the river, making it so rough that it's impassable.

'Fucking good,' I exclaim, urging Stilton upwards. I can't see how much further we need to go, not from my position, but I do know that this stony part of the hill doesn't last all the way up its side. At some point, the ridge flattens out, and grasses take the place of the rocks. I just wish it would come fucking sooner.

'Nearly there,' Hemming calls from somewhere up above me.

'About bloody time,' I huff, as perplexed as Stilton as to how we're going to make our way up a particularly steep part of the hillside.

'Go right,' Wulfstan points, better able to see from his distance away. 'There's a sheep track you can follow.' A sheep track makes it sound well-trodden, but really, it's just a slight definition in the rocks and stray pieces of grass where the sheep have travelled the previous year. But still, it does offer a less direct path and Stilton and I slowly emerge to see the rest of my men.

They're all sitting on the hillside, water bottles in hand, drinking and recovering their breaths. The horses have taken to the lusher grasses with a frenzy, keen to fill their bellies. I wish I could live on grass, but then, I won't appreciate the smells the horses emit when they fart.

'Well done, Stilton,' I pat the horse's long nose, and Wulfhere reaches down to do the same. His face is pale. I'm not surprised. There were parts of our journey up this hill that were terrifying for me, and I wasn't hanging onto the back of a horse.

'Do you want to get down?' I ask him.

'No, I'll stay here, but I'll let Stilton crop the grass.'

I turn then, gazing down at the river.

'Bloody bollocks,' I exclaim. The damage looked terrible enough from my vantage point behind the sheep shelter; from here, I can see much, much further along the fields that nudge up against the river and most are covered in brown and grey water. I spare a thought for my missing warriors on the far side of the River Wye. I hope they're somewhere safe.

'That was some storm,' Osmod confirms as I shake my head in wonder at the power of a little bit of rain.

'Poor bastards,' and Ælfgar indicates an area of raised land, upon which no more than five or six black and white cows stand. They can't escape, not from there.

'Can cows swim?' I ask, perplexed.

'If it's that or drowning, I imagine they can,' Eahric offers, although it's not really the answer. I confess I'm not much of a cow person. I should probably know such things, but I don't.

But my eye is drawn to the river, seeking out the Raider ship. Only I can't see it.

'Where've they fucking gone now?' I look north and south, but the brown craft seems to have disappeared. 'Have they fucking sunk?' I can't keep the hope from my voice.

'No,' Wulfstan quickly dispels my optimism. 'They came ashore where we stopped last night, look,' and he moves closer to the edge of the hillside, pointing down. I don't want to look, but I do. From here, the ship is small and looks far from menacing, but figures are moving in and out of the sheep shelter, and one points up the hillside, even as I duck down, keen not to be seen.

'Will they come this way?' I pray they won't, but I know better than that.

I turn back to my warriors, eyeing them with concern. I thought we were merely travelling to Hereford. I didn't appreciate the danger we'd all be in on such a journey. And now my warriors look tired and hungry. I don't know where we are, not from here, and we're prey. I've fucked up this time. Again.

'We'll move on when we've recovered. We should be able to ride for some time from here.' The top of the hill is flat, some collections of stone making me think that it might once have had one of the old forts on its summit. But nothing is remaining for us to use, even the ditch, which I half see, filled with grass and probably, tumbled rocks at the bottom, perhaps even the odd sheep carcase. No, we can't stay here.

In the distance, I glimpse a rainbow, colours bright in the dull day. It leads my eye inland, to where Worcester might lie, or Gloucester, although there'll be another river to forge as well. For all Mercia has so few coastal lands, there's a fucking lot of waterways to flood at will. And there are many hills as well, to crest. I sigh, running my hand through my grubby beard.

'Come on,' I urge my warriors, keen to be away. I prefer to be the one doing the hunting, not the one being hunted.

It's much easier going when we return to the horses. The hill slopes gently down before meeting another lower hill so that by the time the gloomy light of the day is fading away to complete darkness, I feel as though we've made good progress. Behind, I've caught no sight of the Raiders, and Wulfstan's doleful tones haven't filled me with alarm. I don't think we're yet free from them, but at least we stand some chance.

We rest that night amidst a dilapidated stone building, long since fallen to ruin, and in far worse condition than the sheep shelter. There's the hint of the hard ground beneath the tumble of weeds that have invaded, but I'm just grateful for the roof that only leaks in five places. There's a primary entranceway and a hole in the wall that allows another exit, should the Raiders find us in the night.

Wulfhere is unwilling to dismount, and when I finally get him to, he collapses to the ground, my tunic, used to protect his wound, sodden with blood where he's wrenched one of his stitches away.

'Is it bad?' he worries as I peer at it.

'No, but you should have said, all the same. A man grows weak if he loses too much blood.' I can't afford to have a man weak with blood loss. Wounded is one thing. Bleeding until there's no more to lose is quite another.

'If your piss is red, tell me,' I urge him, remembering comments my aunt has made in the past. He shakes his head.

'It isn't. I've been checking.' It seems I'm not the only one who listens to my aunt.

I don't allow a fire that night. The Raiders don't need any help to find us. But luckily, they don't, and the following morning the sky is brighter than it's been for days and much, much colder. The ground crunches as the horses pass over it, and I wince into the blazing light, hoping we won't come across an area that's too frozen to cross. I can't risk the horses over ice. They have too many legs to go in opposite directions. A horse with a broken leg can't go on. I won't kill an animal with my haste.

Sometime around midday, I glance back the way we've come, anticipating seeing nothing but the shape of the hill behind us, but of course, that's not what I find. Instead, I catch sight of someone watching us from the summit of the hill. Just one man, but there's something about his stance, lit against the brightness of the sun, that tells me the Raiders have found us.

Our only advantage is that they walk or run, we have our horses, and the ground is becoming flattened, if wetter, but it is so wet that no ice has managed to form even though it's bloody cold.

'We need to make better time,' I urge the men. The landscape has begun to undulate gently, and more than once, I glance back and see the Raiders seeming to advance on us. But I remind myself that they don't have horses. I've never known a man with the stamina to run for as long as a horse can. Added to which, I might have thought myself lost, but the landscape is becoming more and more familiar. We stand a chance of making it to one of the crossings over the Severn before nightfall.

In trailing us in this way, the Raiders are taking a considerable risk. If I only had my entire force, I wouldn't be at all concerned by being tracked. But at the moment, we're still exposed and will be for some time yet.

Wulfhere is better able to stay in his saddle, his face not as pale as the day before, and my warriors try and jest with one another, making this trip more enjoyable than it could be. They know we're being pursued, and it's not fear that goads us onwards but frustration. The Raiders have employed the better strategy. I'm fucking raging about that. This is my kingdom, my land. I shouldn't be making such mistakes.

'The River Severn,' Ælfgar's voice is strained as we come within sight of the river. I hurry Haden, only to rein him in tightly. Fuck. The River Severn is even fuller than the River Wye, snaking through the landscape and causing more carnage than the other river.

Somehow, in my hurry, I've forgotten the problem of crossing another river. And worse is to come. Not only have the Raiders been following us, but I can also see a ship drawn clear of the surge of the River Severn, and where there's a ship, there are always Raiders.

'What the fuck do we do now?' There's more than a slither of fear in Hemming's voice as he directs his heated gaze my way. Behind us, the Raiders are within sight, catching us at such a fast speed, I can't understand it. And from the River Severn, the other force has also seen our approach.

Not that we're out of options. Not yet. The Raiders, if this is a combined strike against me, have decided I'll aim for Gloucester and cross the River Severn there. But that's not my only option. It's probably the safest way of crossing the flooded expanse, but not when there are two troops of Raiders trying to track me down.

'Head north,' I instruct Wulfstan hastily. He nods, gnawing at his lips from Berg's back.

'We'll have to outrun them, that's all.'

'Sounds fucking easy,' Wulfred mutters darkly, but for all it sounds defeatist, he's far from giving up.

The horses turn tired heads away from where they know home lies, and the ground begins to disappear beneath their hooves as they amble to a canter they can maintain over a long distance. I keep my warriors as far from the spreading River Severn as possible. The darkness of the fields is often the only warning that they're flooded. I allow a slight smirk when I hear a cry of outrage coming from the Raiders closest to the River Severn, but outfoxing them here doesn't assure safety.

Thankful that the moon is bright, I push on with the men. No one complains, but neither is anyone laughing and joking any more. No, this is serious business. We need to be alert to everything around us.

The smell of smoke and cooking food lingers in the air, blown our way by the stiffening wind from the stray settlements we pass. None of them looks inviting. I don't see any animals grazing or people about their work on such a grim day. I envy them as my stomach gurgles with hunger. I press on. I want to feel that we've covered enough distance to risk stopping for the night. But that doesn't come until the horses are hanging their heads in exhaustion. Even I'm nodding in the saddle.

'We'll stop here,' from out of the gloom, a small copse has appeared, no doubt well-tended by its owner, but for now, deserted, even the trees little more than skeletal at this time of the year. There's no promise of cover, but the line of marching trees should offer some protection from the wind.

'We should press on,' Osmod announces, his words echoing with exhaustion. 'It's not far from here.' He's probably not the only one to decipher my intentions as to how we're going to cross the River Severn.

'I know, but we can't traverse at night. Better to get some sleep now and make the crossing in the morning.' There's something to be said for pressing on. We might wake in the morning surrounded by the Raiders. Still, if we try to get over the rickety old bridge, I'm leading my men towards, merely pieces of wood hopefully held close together, rather than a properly constructed bridge at this time of the day, I can't see it ending well. After the rain we've had, it might even be more derelict than the previous time I came this way, but it's the only option available to us.

'I'll keep first watch,' I order my milling warriors. 'Wulfstan, you'll take the middle watch, and Ælfgar the third.' It would be good to rely on more than one man for each watch, but I'll not order more of them. Hemming is exhausted, Wulfhere wounded, whereas Osmod, Cuthwalh, Eadfrith and Cealwin are beyond weary. That leaves only Eahric and Wulfred, and they can't take all three watches between them. If they even attempt it, they'll be no good to me tomorrow. No, I hope that if the remaining warriors wake in the night, they'll join those on watch duty, but I won't order them to do so. I need someone to be alert for the following day.

As my men make themselves as comfortable as it's possible to be, the horses are left saddled and ready to go. There's a large enough hollow in the ground that they can drink from it without having to go to the surging river some distance away. Better to stay together.

'How are you?' Wulfhere finds the trace of a grin on his tight face.

'Surprisingly well,' he offers. 'I mean, it hurts like a bitch, but I can cope with it. And it's stopped bleeding.' He pulls his tunic high, wincing but not sweating as he does so. I'm amazed by how quickly he's healing – it must be his youth or the fine food we've enjoyed of late. But he's probably just lucky. Some people just recover well, I know that.

'Good, you're doing well,' I reassure him. 'Others would be mewing with such a wound.'

'Well, I'd sooner be in a bed, but here I'm distracted from how uncomfortable I am.'

'Nothing like a healthy dose of fear to heal a man,' Cuthwalh comments sourly, his words hollow with exhaustion..

'Aye, nothing fucking like it,' I confirm, clapping Wulfhere on the shoulder and moving away. Haden eyes me from where he scours the ground for grass he deems worthy of his attention. His look is inscrutable. I don't doubt he's been in enough scrapes like this to know how much peril we're in, but he'll gallop and gallop if he must. I know he will. The other horses will labour to keep up with him, and if he should falter, Jethson will take his place. Haden won't need reminding of that.

I take up a position a little away from the trees, where I can get a clear view all around me, both towards the river and behind. The Raiders could come at us through a small gap in my vision, but to get to that place, they would first need to cross the open expanse, which is exposed before me and offers nowhere to hide. I don't feel safe, but I'm doing all I can.

My watch duty passes quickly, the moon bright enough to see by, the sky devoid of clouds as the temperature drops lower and lower. I shiver, thinking I might prefer the threat of rain and less visibility to watching my breath steam before me every time I breathe.

Wulfstan comes to me when I'm stifling a yawn, my legs jittery from being awake too long.

'Did you get some sleep?' I demand.

'Yes, but not enough,' his words are sleep muddled as he turns to empty his stream into the grass. The smell is pungent, and I wrinkle my nose.

'I could do with some ale to taint it,' he chuckles, yawning widely, as he surveys the area.

'The bridge you're aiming for will be a wreck after all the snow and rain,' he muses, not a criticism but a warning.

'Yes, I fear the same. But we can't take any of the fords, not with the river so bloody high.'

We're not trapped, but it could happen if we're not careful.

'I'll hope for a good outcome then,' and Wulfstan sends me on my way. But when I lie down to sleep, my mind floods with images of what might happen the following day. It doesn't make for a restful night's sleep.

Water dripping onto my nose wakes me, and I blink, sitting quickly, a loud noise disturbing the silence of the day. I'm on my feet even more rapidly, seeking out the source of the sound. My warriors are waking slowly as well, so I'm not alone in being woken by the cry.

Bending low, I make my way to Haden, thinking to mount up, so

I get a better view of everyone around me, but the horse I reach first isn't Haden. Turning in confusion, I can't even see my mount. And then I hear the words and realise what's happening. Slowly, I relax the hold on my seax and walk towards Ælfgar. He and my horse are having a fine old yap while they stand guard duty.

'What's all this?'

Ælfgar grins at me, shaking his head, so that rain tumbles onto his chest. We could have done without more rain.

'The old men slept, so Haden kept me company.'

'Really?' I demand to know. Ælfgar's nodding.

'I swear, as soon as Wulfstan started snoring, Haden appeared, and he's stayed by my side ever since. I confess he's a bloody good listener.'

I grin at the surprise in Ælfgar's voice.

'He's a funny fucker,' I confirm, running my hand along Haden's inquisitive black and white nose. It's still grey and hazy, true dawn some time away. Now that everyone is awake, we may as well press on.

The groans of my waking warriors make me shudder in sympathy. But in no time, everyone is mounted once more. We're almost home. That can drive even the most exhausted of men into his saddle.

'Now, we're going to Kempsey. The bridge isn't the best. But it's endured through bloody terrible storms before, so it should be strong enough. Once there, we'll nearly be home. If we can, one of us will race back to Kingsholm and summon the rest of the men and those from Gloucester as well. Then we can get back to Kingsholm.'

It sounds like a half-decent plan, but it isn't. I hope we can cross the flooded River Severn. I hope we'll be able to make it to Kingsholm. If Edmund were here, he'd ridicule me for such poor planning, but here, alone and cut off from the rest of my force, chased from behind, and the River Severn, there's fuck all else I can do.

The problem, of course, is that even if I make it back to Kingsholm, I still need to find the rest of my warriors. I said I'd meet them in Hereford. And I should have been there by now. If Pybba has his way, they'll come looking for us, and that could send them right into another battle.

Everything I've tried in the last week has been a fucking disaster, and it's far from over.

Wulfhere quickly assures me he can ride when we're ready to set out once more, and so I set a fast pace. The ground is frozen in some places and not in others. The sound of a vast amount of water in flow drags me towards the River Severn once more. I risk riding closer than we have since spotting the Raider ship yesterday.

Here, the River Severn is too tumultuous to risk a ship on it. If there were one, it would be smashed to pieces in no time at all. The water churns a dark muddy colour, and there are twigs and tree trunks and the occasional dead animal being tossed and turned by the water. I'm reminded of the marooned cows and spare them a thought. I hope they've escaped.

Quickly, I scan the river, seeking out the bridge, and see it just ahead. It's visible as a thin strip crossing the river, but easier to see if I sight the stone struts at its base. It looks complete enough from where I stand, but the closer I get, the more I appreciate that pieces of planking are missing on one section of it, the remaining walkway just big enough for a horse to make a crossing.

Not that they're going to like it. Haden will be a fucking arse about it. I don't blame him, not when I'm close enough to appreciate the height of the fall into the water and the derelict nature of the entire bridge.

But, now is not the time to falter. I've been aware that we're once more being chased, the Raiders finding us with the growing daylight. The Raiders are still far behind us without the horses to hurry them, but I don't want to linger.

And then I pause, a dilemma I'd not anticipated. Should I go first, showing my warriors and the horses that it's safe, or send another across? The water is loud here, not a roar, more than that, making it impossible to hear anything else. I take comfort from the fact there's no ship, but still, the bridge is bloody lethal looking as it is.

What I don't need is for a Raider to step onto the bridge in front of me, eyes crazed, a wicked-looking war axe in his hand. He's not alone, either, for three more men appear at each shoulder, and a loud crack draws my eye to where timbers are turning end over end in the churning mass of the River Severn.

Their ship. Daft fuckers should never have risked coming so far up the River Severn.

These bastards have got nothing to lose.

Chapter Eighteen

'Wulfstan, Ælfgar and Eahric, protect the rear.' I bark the order, Haden dancing beneath me, his tail swishing through the air in unease. I keep my eyes focused on the much-longed-for bridge and those who block our passage across it.

'My lord, we should carry on, find another crossing,' Osmod calls the suggestion, but I shake my head, dislodging the cold rain as I do so. It pours over my already drenched shoulders.

'This is the only place with a decent crossing. It's here, or we run until we reach Worcester.' What I don't say is that Worcester is too far away. We'll never reach it without having to fight those who chase us.

On a good day, with mild weather, a gentle sun overhead and the River Severn far from its current flooded temper, it wouldn't be a difficult task to cross to Kempsey, even if the bridge is more imagined than real. But, today, with the river extending far beyond its banks, the grey water menacing and mocking, there's no assurance that the other crossing at Worcester will be passable either. And it'll be impossible for the ships to help us, even if they're docked there. The river is wild with snowmelt and rainwater.

I'll have to fight these fuckers, and kill them all. Even if I have to do it alone. We must make it to Kempsey.

Seven men against me, on a precarious strip of an ancient wooden bridge, held upright by stone so old and wizened, in places it's as though a man stands guard, forged from the power of the water, that's formed shoulders, waist and even legs, not stone at all. A quick death is promised far below, beneath the churning water, with a misstep. What's there to fucking worry about?

I slide clear of Haden's back. I'm not going to risk him. Not here. I'll do this alone. Better that I'm wounded than he is. I make a better patient, although my aunt might disagree with that suggestion. She would, I know it.

'My lord, you can't,' but the cry is half-hearted. Old Cealwin knows there's no choice, and his tone reflects the aching knowledge that it could all end here. I have to do this, and I must bloody win. It's the only chance we have to survive. For all of us to outlive this failed expedition to the River Wye.

Gripping my shield in one hand, I step onto the wooden bridge. It creaks alarmingly, the gentle wind fiercer here, explaining why the Raiders' hair is gusting so violently from their position at the middle of the bridge, where they block our forward advance—the bastards.

My second step is poorly placed, old, brittle wood shattering with my weight. I stagger, lose my balance before reclaiming my flailing foot from beneath the surface of the bridge, placing it beside the other on the firm piece of wood that holds my weight. I try not to notice how slick the wood is thanks to the rain that's been falling.

Beneath me, I watch as the pieces of the shattered plank are caught by the churning foam of the flooded river, disappearing from view quickly, stolen by the surging force of the filthy water.

I swallow down my unease, content not to have lost hold of my shield with the shock of the wood splintering. I redouble my grip on the strap, just to be sure, pleased my hands are enclosed in gloves.

I can't hear my warriors. I can't perceive the sound of the Raiders, but I can see their mouths opening and closing before me. I know they're jeering my efforts.

I eye the planks carefully, determining a path that's stronger than the fractured piece of wood I first tried. On light steps, holding my body tight, alert to the dangers of the combined rushing wind, slippery surface and the water beneath me, I come within shouting distance of the Raiders.

The seven of them are standing firmly, legs equally paced, absorbing the force of the wind with practised ease. They have the advantage of being shorter. The wind is less fierce lower down. I don't have the same benefit, buffeted by the wind, seax in my hand. I think I'm too tall as my hair whips into my face. I'm grateful that my helm keeps it from stinging my eyes.

'Lord Coelwulf,' the first Raider taunts, the words as sharp as any blade, his eyes on what's happening behind me and not on me. I don't turn aside. My warriors are there. They'll protect me. Such an obvious tactic won't fool me. The wind tries to blow the words away, but I hear them well enough.

'And who the fuck are you?' But the man shakes his head, eyes flashing darkly, as I shout my response. If I didn't shout, I wouldn't be heard.

'My men and I will allow your warriors to pass, provided you give yourself up to us. We'll take you to Jarl Halfdan.'

I shake my head, bemused to realise this is another group of men who have no idea how far events have moved on since they left Repton last summer. I consider where they've been? Perhaps in Dublin? Certainly somewhere that doesn't know of Jarl Halfdan's defeats.

'Jarl Halfdan is dead.' I don't know why I tell them, but it seems wrong that they should die believing they're about to win the acclaim of their jarls and leaders. 'Repton is in the hands of my ealdorman.'

But the man laughs, his mouth wide open, his chest heaving with the action. I didn't think it was one of my finer jokes, but what the fuck do I know?

'Ah, the games you Mercians play.' His accent is sharp, the words spoken carefully, no doubt to ensure they're the correct ones.

I tilt my head to one side, considering whether I'd believe the words of my enemy. Probably not. I should just shut the fuck up.

'Jarl Halfdan is not dead. I would know, as would the men and women of Dublin.' At least that answers my query about where they've been since last summer when my men and I reclaimed Repton from the Raider jarls.

I smirk, shrugging my large shoulders, the action reassuring me that my byrnie sits correctly over the top half of my body.

'I have no problem ending your lives if you still want to fight to win something for a man who's already bones that the ravens have picked clean.'

I don't take my eyes from the spokesperson, but I detect one of the others speaking, perhaps telling the others my words in their language. I sense the shift of unease from the remaining Raiders, but they have nothing to lose. Not now.

I anticipate the spear thrown from the group's rear, flashing brightly beneath the gloomy sky, the shimmering wood, the blackened blade. I take my time moving aside. I might stand on wood that feels secure enough, but there are other pieces, close by, that look as though they might fall into the water with the lightest of pressure. This bridge is in desperate need of repair. It really is little more than some remnants of ancient stonework with some twigs perched on top.

The lethal-looking spear clatters to the ground not far from where I'm standing. There's a crack, and then both the spear and the split plank begin a lazy spiral to the water far below. I watch it, aware I'm not alone in doing so. Again, I sense apprehension coursing through the assembled men.

They're not wrong to be terrified. I don't appreciate the fucking feeling either.

'You lie,' and this time, the man explodes with rage, rushing me. I watch him, unable to take my eyes from his haphazard approach as I hold my shield, ready to defend myself, should he come close enough to attempt an attack.

I can't see it, though. In his wake, more and more of the bridge tumbles away. Fucking cock, at this rate, there'll be no bridge left for us to escape across. That boils me.

I don't intend to fight for something useless to me.

I ready myself, reasonably content that I stand on a firm piece of the bridge. He comes closer and closer, eyes blazing with fierceness. Only then he drops, his forward momentum not enough to save him as a horse's length of wood fractures and tumbles away, taking him with it.

Frightened brown eyes meet mine, a shock of long, coiled hair whipping in the wind, but he doesn't even get a hand on the intact bridge, and even if he did, I can't see that I'd save him.

The man re-emerges and then bobs along the surface of the bubbling river for a heartbeat before being subsumed once more, arms flailing, mouth opened in horror. Dragging my eyes away from the sight of him fading beneath the torrent, I glance at the remaining Raiders anticipating their next move.

There are six of them now.

I might have expected them to run away, but instead, another man stands in the place of the lost Raider. I've not noticed him before, but I suspect him to be the spear-thrower because he seems curiously bereft of weapons. He bites his lower lip, waist-long brown hair straggling across his face, a long beard similarly rippling in the wind.

Will he negotiate with me?

No, he fucking won't. That doesn't surprise me.

Instead, he flicks a finger on his right hand, and two of the Raiders begin a slow advance. They stand to the edges, where the bridge is more securely held together, a continual run of wood meaning they don't need to take much care with their steps. Instead, they menace me, the one jabbing his seax toward me, as though we fight closely together, the other thudding his war axe handle into his other hand.

Posturing, just what I need, standing on a fucking bridge above floodwaters and with the wind trying to topple me over the side.

I note that neither has a shield. Other things are missing from their war gear as well. These men have been shipwrecked. They have the clothes they wear, the weapons they saved, and little else. They're desperate but probably quite skilled. None of them is youths, that much I can tell from the height of the hairline, the pieces of grey that fleck what hair remains. These men have fought for their lives before. But they've never battled against me, of that I'm fucking sure. Well, as sure as I can be. That they still live confirms we've not previously fought one another.

I hold my ground, allowing them to come at me. All the risk should be theirs, not mine. I toy with the idea of hacking at the wood they stand on, but I don't know how much more damage the bridge can take before it shatters to nothing. I still need the river crossing. There's little point in killing the Raiders if I remain trapped here, with my warriors, on the wrong side of the bridge, away from the aid of my warriors who live at Kingsholm, with the remaining Raiders not far behind us.

The warrior who carries the war axe has impressive looking shoulders. A man used to swinging his weapon. But his byrnie is torn, a rent showing a flash of brown skin beneath his right arm. An easy place to attack him if I chose to, but of course, he'll be expecting that. I think he'll come at me first, but then the seax wielding warrior speeds his steps. He has short, cropped black hair, grey threading it, a broad forehead, thanks to his receding hair, and the promise of a mean jaw as he clenches his teeth. He's a little shorter than I am. He'd be a good match if the odds weren't so stacked against either of us surviving this attack. With firm ground beneath our feet, I might be worried.

With the wind, rain and the promise that the bridge will collapse if we misstep, I'm sure that the chances are not as even. He'll die here unless he can swim or transform himself into a seal or some other creature capable of surviving the torrent below us. Perhaps even a raven to fly above the storm-wracked landscape. The thought makes me smirk.

I raise my shield to counter the attack, half an eye on the war axe. Of course, the Raiders work together, the war axe flying free from the first warrior's hand. I know what they want me to do, but I stand my ground, crouching and veering slightly to the left to avoid the weapon as it rushes towards me. I don't move my shield aside. Why would I? After all, that's what they want me to do.

The war axe falls harmlessly over the side of the bridge. A fine weapon, that much is apparent in the glance I get of it, the runic symbols calling to me of some arcane knowledge, only to be sent to the depths of the river. One day, I imagine, someone will recover it, just as we sometimes find old weapons and abandoned parcels of iron, bronze, and even ancient coins buried in the ground. It's a waste, all the same. Although not for the person lucky enough to discover it.

The seax Raider still rushes at me even though I can rebuff his attack with my shield quickly enough. I imagine they both hoped the war axe would imbed in it and take it to the watery depths as well.

The axe-less Raider takes another weapon from his belt, this one somewhere between a sword and a seax, a curious weapon. I'm not used to seeing such blades, but I'll counter whatever they want to bloody try. So far, they've lost a spear and a war axe. They can't have an unending supply of blades. Perhaps, I should just encourage them to throw all of their arsenal at me. That would make it a fuck sight easier.

The wood at my feet gives out a strangled groan, and my body tenses, ready to jump if need be. The seax Raider now shares my wood. I'll have to move him aside as soon as possible. He leers, eyes flashing with malice. I flick my blade forward, and while he watches that with wild, staring eyes, shove my shield into his seax. The impact is immediate, his crushed hand dropping the knife to the floor, where we both watch it roll just once, awkwardly over its handle, before coming to rest, half on and half off the bridge.

I menace with my seax, standing between him and his weapon. The seax-warrior doesn't have another on his weapons belt. The man who threw the war axe responds quickly. Two lost weapons were just careless, another, and it would look to me as though they were trying to lose this fucking fight.

I slick my seax at the black-haired warrior who's lost his seax as he tries to bend, slicing long his mean jaw. First blood is held stationary in the air for just a moment before the wind whips it aside to add it to the surging river water. The Raider staggers backwards, scurrying without thought for the precariousness of the bridge. It's not a deep cut, but he wasn't expecting it.

His comrade, the man who threw the war-axe at me, charges me, pounding on the wood with no concern for the water beneath him, for the shrieking wind, falling rain or howling planks. I extend my shield, expecting the flurry of an attack, but it doesn't come. Instead, he stops, reaches down, hand outstretched to collect his ally's lost seax.

I brace and kick out, taking him just below the neck, in the gap between his byrnie and his head. He gasps, unable to inhale, for the time being, his half-seax, half-sword wavering in his hand.

Rolling my eyes at such ineffectual fighting, I kick aside both man and weapon and fuck me, he screams as he falls, the sound rising above the thundering water. That's four weapons gone and two men, and I've barely moved.

The short-haired, weaponless man shrieks as well, rushing to the side of the bridge as though expecting to see his friend there, holding on by any means. But all he witnesses is the sight of him disappearing beneath the water, arms and legs thrashing to stop the inevitable, as though they might just grow feathers and enable him to fly free.

The remaining Raider turns more quickly than I anticipate and runs at me, spittle flying from his open mouth, face puce with rage, his short hair stuck to his forehead by the rain. I thrust my shield before me, braced once more for his attack and when it comes, it forces me back one step and then two. I can feel the join in the wood beneath my back foot. I'm no longer on my sturdy ledge. Not that my enemy seems to notice. He continues to seethe at me, hands reaching for my throat, even though my shield is between us, and I'm using it to attack him.

I believe he'll continue to force me backwards, but abruptly he stops, and I'm not prepared. Both hands curling around one side of the shield, he attempts to wrench it from me, one gloved hand, and one not, gripping tightly to the metal rim. I try to get my seax to his fingers, but I'm holding my shield on the right side of my body, although my left hand holds it. There's no room to slice the fingers because they're on my left side. I'd need my arm to grow, snake around my body to cut him.

Instead, I lift my seax arm high and stab downwards, driving my shield low. The two forces are a strain on my arm, but my blade comes away bloody. It's not a deep cut on his shoulder, but it's something. I just need many, many more.

The pain rouses him from his frenzy. Again, he surprises me by dropping his hold on the shield. It was never going to work, but I stagger two steps forwards, and now we both stand on the piece of wood that I believed sturdy enough to take my weight without a problem. I can see where it bows beneath the heft of two men, the far end hanging so low beneath the next plank of wood, I catch a glimpse of the roiling river beneath my feet once more, the rushing greyness of the water giving me pause for thought.

Not that I need reminding of the precariousness of my fucking position. Not at all.

I've not noticed, but another two of the Raiders have been making their way towards me. They're close enough that I can determine eye colour. They wear mean expressions, the one riddled with puckered skin down the side of his face, perhaps from a burn or where someone tried to cut his skin aside. It looks excruciating, and that torment is mirrored in his hate-filled twisted mouth and blank, staring eyes.

This man lives for battle and giving pain. It would be better to put him out of his misery. So focused on his face, I don't notice the weapons he carries for a moment, a seax in one hand, a war axe in the other. He also has a weapons belt filled with more glinting blades. Perhaps he should have shared them, the selfish bastard. Then the first two men might have killed me without his aid, and without giving up their lives.

The remaining man's eyes show fear, and for him, I have some respect. The others are all crazed bastards, without thought for survival. This man wants to live, and that makes him the easiest to kill. Men who are scared of the heat of a blade will do all they can to avoid the feared cut.

With half an eye to the straining wood, I move forward quickly, rushing the short-haired Raider with my shield jutting before me. He hurries backwards to avoid me. I feel the wood shriek with relief, even over the sound of the water and the howling wind, as I'm the only one left standing on it.

My foe balances carefully on two wooden planks, one foot on either. His eyes are narrow, hatred leaking from him, for all he doesn't speak, or taunt, or do anything but eye me. I'm unsure what he plans to do next, but with the arrival of the two other Raiders, I appreciate that they mean to overwhelm me.

It might be fucking easy as well. I don't fear death, but I do fear the consequences of it. Mercia will flounder. That bastard King Alfred of Wessex or the fucking Raiders will take her, and that, more than anything, drives me on. I'll not take reckless risks if you exclude standing on an unstable bridge far above a flooded river while it rains or at least attempts to do so. I'll ensure I make as few movements as possible to bring about the desired death of my enemy.

The over-weaponed man comes at me first. I refuse to be distracted by the scarring on his face, or the fury in his tight stance, instead watching him, determined to decipher his preferred means of attack.

For a long moment, all four of us hang there, as though time slows, and then two of them charge me. I'm far from surprised.

Might often wins, I won't deny that, but here, in such a position, it can't help. It really bloody can't.

A blade flashes brightly in the many-weaponed man's hand, and the short-haired Raider I forced backwards, who has no weapons after his seax went over the side with his ally, comes as well. The one means to distract me, perhaps with fists or kicks, while the other will cut me. I don't much fancy either.

My shield is my protection. I drive it into the face of the man with his weapons, thinking he should have aimed low or high and not just randomly at my body. With my seax, I stab out at the weaponless man, and he howls with fury as my blade slices across his bunched knuckles. Again, the seeping blood takes its time before falling.

The over-weaponed man tries to push me backwards, all of his weight behind the seax he threatens me with, and now I prepare because I can read his intentions.

A wild blow from the short-haired bleeding man has me ducking, and it's that which saves me. My shield falls low, blocking the reach of the blade in the hand of the over-weaponed man that thinks to slice open one of my ankles. The seax blade sticks in my shield, instead of my ankle. It's not light, and I grimace as I have to adjust to the changed weight, my hand already aching inside the strap. It's bloody heavy at the best of times.

I rush the weaponless man, driving him back and then further back until one of his feet hovers over a gap and not wood. Then I turn to the many weaponed man. Not that the short-haired flailing man has fallen yet, but I can't see it'll be long. Not unless he's fucking lucky or someone leaps to his aid.

I have one man to either side of me. My shield is awkward, my shoulder starting to protest against the strain. The frightened man might be the easiest to kill, but the other warrior, with his temper and his burn and his scars, is so wild that it's easy to focus on him. I force my shield forward time and time again, ignoring the ache in my shoulder so that he's driven to risk broken planks of wood, to look behind him to make sure he won't follow the fate of the other three men because by now, the other man has lost his balance and joined his comrades in the water.

I'm aware of the fucking absurdity that has seen these men killed by the very means that has allowed them into Mercia – the water.

The terrified man plucks up some courage and comes at me with his blades. His shrieks of ire and fear fill the air before they stop, mid-breath, and a loud splash reaches my ears.

Really? The daft bastard. Has he not been watching what happened to his fellow warriors?

With the many-weaponed, scarred Raider distracted by the drop of the terrified man, I look to the two remaining warriors, the spear-thrower who's sent his men to fight, and the one I've not yet battled against.

Only then, the many-weaponed warrior glances at me. It's not so much rage that burns in his eyes but a fierce determination to kill me, once and for all. His steps are sure as he comes towards me, war axe and seax menacing me.

I fend him off with my seax and shield, but he has some skill and sooner or later, he'll get beyond my guard if I'm not careful.

I consider what I should do, but I already know the fucking answer.

I charge him, seax to hand, as I make a fist so that I punch him full in the nose, my seax trails after the blow. Blood wells from the broken nose as his right cheek bursts open from the force of the seax's edge. It hurts like fuck, and I feel the sting of pain up my arm, but the man crumples to the ground, the blood making it difficult to see what I've accomplished. It's too easy to reverse my hold on the seax and slice open the back of his neck as his head hangs down, hands trying to clear his vision.

He seems to deflate before me, a soft sigh escaping his mouth as he curls into a ball. Poor bastard. I have some sympathy for him.

That leaves only the spear-thrower and one another. The spear-thrower hops from wooden plank to wooden plank, not seeming to check them with his feet but using his eyes to ensure he doesn't choose one of the fracturing pieces.

He comes closer and closer. He's taken a blade from somewhere because he weaves it in front of me. I brace myself for his strike, thinking he'll attack me from directly in front, but nothing happens. Time passes, and eventually, I lower my shield, expecting to see him leering at me. But he's not there, or rather, he's not standing.

I look down and then down again, and staring eyes greet me, a flung spear stilling his heart forever, the spear vibrating at its sudden stop—a fitting end for the bastard.

I risk looking behind me, my wet hair stinging my eyes so that it takes a moment to see Osmod grinning from the far side of the bridge, where he's still mounted on his old horse, the gaps in his teeth visible even from here. He might move with the speed of a slug, but that man can throw.

Fuck me. Did he teach Hereman how to throw his spear? It wouldn't surprise me.

I'd thank him, but there's still one more of the enemy to kill. This Raider has done little but watch so far. Is he craven? I doubt it. A weakling would stand no chance with such fierce warriors. I arch my eyebrows at him, for all he can't see beneath my helm. But there must be something about my posture because his face twists.

He wears weapons at his belt, a fine sword over his back, and it's that for which he reaches. I don't think this is the place for a sword fight, but what do I know?

I leer at my fresh opponent. I appreciate that he's a slight man. He moves quickly, almost as though dancing, and not once does the bridge creak or moan at his passage. I can't rely on the planks to break and send him to the raging river below.

'Fucking fine,' I say to myself. I have the time to kill another if I must.

The Raider leads with his sword, and I let him come towards me. I'm happy for him to take the greater risk. I just need one strong gust of wind, and the way he's flinging the weapon about, he'll be swept over the side of the bridge. When my warriors and I come this way, we'll have to lead the horses. It won't end well if we ride.

'*Skiderik*,' the man calls to me.

'If you fucking like,' I reply, shield poised for what will come next. I can't see that Osmod will have another spear to throw. This Raider is for me to kill. And I will when I can reach him.

Now that he's made his intention known, the Raider takes his time. I could grow tired waiting for the attack to come. But if he thinks to lull me, it won't work. I've fought every kind of man and woman; the slow, the fast, the fat, the thin, the undecided and the downright terrified. I'll see what he offers me.

And then he bloody well surprises me. I think he'll slash at me with his sword, but instead, he comes within seax reach and only then moves to stab into my shield with the sword. The movement has no chance of success, and I consider whether he knows what he's doing or not. Thin wisps of blonde hair are visible beneath the helm, but there's no beard, only a smooth chin. A woman, I consider, but it's impossible to tell from beneath the dark helm that covers the head.

Not that a woman wouldn't know how to kill. The Jarl Guthrum's sister was an evil bitch. She knew how to battle.

I deflect the blow with my shield, feeling the impact through my arm, but my foe feels it more, teeth snapping together audibly, grip failing on the sword. Instinctively, a hand reaches out and snatches for it, holding it tight between both hands rather than risk losing it like so many other weapons before.

I feint with my shield, but it's my seax I want to use. My enemy interprets my next move correctly, and the sword is there to stop me from landing a blow. I grit my teeth, my healing hand aching from the crash of the two metal weapons.

I could reach for my sword, but I don't want a fucking sword fight here, no matter what my foe intends. No, I need to kill my opponent and get it done quickly. For the time being, the bridge has settled. The creaking and groaning have died away, the wind momentarily backing off as well, even the rain stopping, but it won't last.

My opponent spits at me and then spins, taking the sword with them, twirling it so that I almost lose sight of it. Only instinct protects me, as I hold my shield before my head, forgoing my lower legs for the time being because the sword is high in the air. I think they mean to stab down at me or to slash across my midriff. I hold my shield steady, my seax in the other hand, and as the Raider twirls into me, I thrust my seax to where I hope their belly might be.

I hit something, but I can't tell what, as the flying movement crashes into me, and I fall to the bridge, the creaks and groans immediately returning. My opponent hasn't landed tidily, legs splayed to either side although they still hold the sword, but I've noticed the slash of bright blood, and I know my blow was a good one; a fatal one as well.

I struggle to my feet, moving backwards as I do so, still gripping my shield and seax, although how I've no idea. I eye the dying Raider for a long moment, considering what I should say to them.

'*Skiderik.*' The shriek rips through the air, but I've got other things to worry about now.

Chapter Nineteen

The Raiders who faced me might be dead or nearly dead, and I might be forgiven for thinking, I'd almost won the bridge, but I can feel it shuddering over and above anything our collision might have caused. For a moment, I think it's about to fall in on itself. Only then I catch sight of people moving on the Kempsey side of the river.

I thought there were only a few Raiders, survivors of the shipwreck, but now another twenty or so Raiders have arrived at the far end.

Bastard. I can't face them all alone. I step backwards and then take another step with growing dread, feeling the wooden planks buckle and give beneath my weight. I take my shield with me, despite the worry of the weight with the blade impaled in it. I need to stand with my warriors. Only as I look behind them, I can see that the Raiders who've been following us from the River Wye are close, too close. Fuck. While I've been pissing about on the bridge, killing those who thought to face me, we've been surrounded.

With the far side of the River Severn so near, I can almost smell the foulness of the tannery in Gloucester thanks to the wind, but it's become out of reach. And I have only myself to fucking blame.

'Form a shield wall,' I order my warriors when I finally turn my back on those advancing over the bridge and stride towards my warriors. Osmod watches my back, poised, ready to launch another weapon, this one a heavier axe than the spear. Is there anything he can't aim well?

I'm not anticipating the Raiders risking crossing the bridge, but they undoubtedly will if they sense an easy victory.

The horses are milling around in confusion as my warriors dismount, claiming shields and weapons. There's too few of us to hold off the coming attack, I know that, but I'm not about to give in. I've beaten worse odds before. I'll fucking do it again.

'Wulfhere, stay mounted,' I urge him, knowing he's not well enough to fight in the heat and press of a shield wall. I think he might argue with me, but he doesn't. 'You and Osmod will watch the bridge. If the Raiders try and come at us, you must stop them. Use the horses to help you.'

Osmod nods sagely. He's remained mounted as well. They'll be able to see the Raiders coming before those on the ground if they're higher up. And the land is slick with water, the mud churned by the hooves of the animals. If I had to decide on a place to hold a fight, this sure as shit wouldn't be it.

The ground to either side of the river falls away severely, a fall onto the rocks and mud of the riverbank, sure to be as fatal as tumbling from the bridge itself. I need to make sure it's not my warriors who lose their balance.

I turn my shield, pulling at the impaled weapon there, frustrated when the seax refuses to move. It'll just have to stay there.

Eahric and Wulfstan take up position on the opposite end of our small shield wall. Ælfgar stands with me, Hemming, Cuthwalh, Eadfrith and Cealwin falling into place between us.

'This is going to be fucking nasty,' I call. Grim faces greet my words. 'But we'll beat them in the end,' I finish not by questioning my statement but by shouting it loud enough that they could probably hear it in Gloucester if the wind catches it just right.

I spare a thought for Edmund, my lost warriors on the far side of the River Wye, and my wounded men and horses. I could curse the weather, and my God, and everyone else for that fucking matter, but the truth is, we face an enemy that scatters and disperses like the wind. It's impossible to keep track of them all when they act in such a way. I just have to ensure we kill them.

I watch the Raiders form up in front of me on the landward side of the bridge. There aren't as many of them as there should be, and some of them have heaving chests and faces flushed with exertion. Their force has been split, and those at the front don't seem eager to wait. They should. There might be few of us, but we can still over-power them. I'm sure of that.

'Brace,' I call as the Raiders begin their forward march. I think it'll be a slow and staid advance, as the men prepare themselves to fight tooth by jowl with their enemy, but suddenly they're running at us. And I shake my head.

'For fuck's sake,' I complain, trying to find a means to buttress myself on the slick mud. Something hard hits my ankle, and I look down, grinning to see a few small stones and pebbles in the earth. I'm not sure who threw them my way, but it makes it a little easier to bolster myself, the rocks providing some much-needed traction against the polished mud. I should have thought of that myself.

The sound of rushing men fills the air. I focus only on killing once more. These bastards should really find another means of coming against me, something more devious, because meeting me in open combat will never work, no matter how small my numbers are and how large their own. Have they not learned that yet?

When their shields hit ours, I feel the Mercian shield wall giving. For a moment, I worry about the long fall at our back, but then their advance comes to an end in a hot pit of stinking breath and furious shrieks of rage. We hold them, for now. Every man uses his strength against them. I should never have doubted our success.

Blades hammer against my linden-board, another trying to sneak between my shield and that of Cuthwalh, who stands to my right. I hack at it with my seax, as Cuthwalh does the same to a blade at his right. I risk turning my head, unsurprised to find the horses in some semblance of order at the command of Osmod and Wulfhere. The twenty or so Raiders at our rear haven't yet made it all the way over the bridge. I consider whether they will do so, only to have my attention snapped back to those before me.

A war axe hammers against the top of my shield, trying to force it down. I strain to hold firm against the weapon. I assume that means that the man before me has another behind him. If their shield wall is twice as thick as ours, they can attack twice as ferociously. I glare at the offending war axe, wishing I could batter it aside, but I don't have enough hands to do so. I focus on holding my shield steady, my seax battling the enemy seax. I feel my rear foot begin to slip on the mud; the stones cannot support me when so many press against me.

I can see that the rest of my warriors are as compromised, and I hear the outraged whinny from one of the horses behind me.

Fuck. This is bad. Really fucking bad.

As my foot slips, my shield drops lower, trapping the enemy seax, his hand as well. Quickly, I run my seax over the squeezed hand, two of the fingertips neatly severed. I try to find some grip in the mud, to stand tall once more, but my shield wavers, the war axe managing to drag it downwards so that I'm greeted by the tight lips of the man I've cut, as well as the menacing glint of the mad-eyed bastard behind him. Both of them wear helms that have been knocked slightly askew.

The shield wall shifts back one step, quivering as it does so. All of my warriors are struggling. I force my shield high again, digging my back foot into the mud, questing with my toes for something to hold me upright. But my men are again compelled to withdraw.

Behind me, I can feel the empty expanse of the river bank. We can't risk retreating too far.

I can't turn to see how Wulfhere and Osmod fare. If they're

retreating, as we are, it won't be long, and we'll be fighting back to back.

And then I have a thought.

I've gone about this the wrong way round. I should have used the horses to fight the shield wall. One or two of us, mounted, would have been able to drive the bastards back. But it's too late to make the change now. I risk both sets of Raiders overwhelming us if I do so.

But something needs to change, and quickly if we're to stand a chance of winning. Or, maybe it doesn't. If we can just hold our ground, the Raiders will tire, eventually. There's nothing more tedious than trying to beat back a line of shields that has no intention of collapsing. If only the ground weren't so muddy, we might well succeed.

For now, the shield wall stands firm, although I can hear the heavy breathing of my warriors. I can even peer along the line and see almost everyone apart from Eahric and Wulfred. They're just out of sight where the shield wall curls back slightly, protecting our rear from any who might think to slip behind us, to join my mounted warriors.

Those on the bridge are calling encouragement to their allies on the opposite side of the shield wall. I don't understand all the words, most of them whipped away by the growing wind, but it's evident they jeer at our defence. Bastards.

And then, from the bridge, an ominous creak splits the air, quickly followed by shouting and cries. Have the fuckers over-whelmed the wooden planks, even though they do little but watch? Cocks. I hope they've all fallen to their deaths, but Osmod's words spoil the illusion.

'Four have fallen,' he calls almost sadly, as though knowing only a few are dead that will reinforce our determination to win. Four is at least four less, but it would have been much better if all of them had tumbled to their deaths.

The cry, perhaps understood by our enemy, gives them renewed purpose. I find myself dropping back again, three steps in rapid succession, the entire shield wall forced to do the same.

Ælfgar grumbles to my left as I encounter the back end of one of the horses, the smell of him ripe in the air. Fuck. We must be close to the actual bridge. I wrack my mind, trying to think of something we can do to stop them from overwhelming us, but there's nothing.

A flicker of worry begins to grow that on this occasion, I might just have fucking overreached myself. I can't be responsible for the deaths of all my warriors. Not here. Not so close to Kingsholm.

I shove my shield against that of my immediate enemy, the movement jarring my arm. I reach over the shield, stabbing down, hoping to get at his face, or his throat, or any part of him so that he bleeds, the pain making it difficult for him to carry on fighting. But instead, my seax is snatched from my hand. I'm forced to give it up or risk losing my fingers as I did to my foe.

Ælfgar staggers beside me, turning terrified eyes my way as I see him fall, the shield covering his head, but little else. The shield wall lurches, more of my men falling as it fractures away, to be left with nothing but the enemy shields against which we battle.

I keep hold of my shield, but few others do. Hemming stumbling forwards into the enemy shield before my eyes.

'Hold,' I snap, the command not enough to maintain the shield wall. Some of the Raiders have already realised what's happening, as they snatch away their shields and stand, man to man, facing my men. Some stand, others are on the slick ground, and we're all exposed. There's only me and my shield, between the Raiders and us, while behind, I hear the terrified whinny of more than one horse.

Fuck. This isn't going to end well.

I stand firm, shield before me. I'll take any of the bastards that want to try their luck.

The man with the missing fingers is the first to have a shield rammed into his nose. He drops back, crushed by the advance of the next man who wants to get at me.

Around me, my warriors are trying to regroup, to come together in some semblance of the shield wall, but our foe has rushed to stand on fallen shields. I can see Hemming, white-faced, hammering against one of the Raiders as though a tree trunk to be felled. Cuthwalh is stabbing upwards as he struggles to his feet. Ælfgar can't get enough room to stand, as not one but two of the enemy attack with their blades.

I abandon my foe, rushing to assist Ælfgar. I reach for an abandoned seax on the ground, aware it's not my weapon, but it'll have to do.

I slash into the one man with my borrowed weapon, opening a long, gaping wound on his forearm, as I insert myself between Ælfgar and the remaining foe-men. But, I'm only one man, and what I need is a shield for every one of my warriors.

Wulfstan has retreated as far as Cuthbert, trying to mount him so that he can scythe the Raiders as though wheat, but it's agonisingly slow. I've not even been able to check on the Raiders behind me. We might be fighting just to encounter yet more of the fuckers, even if we're lucky enough to overwhelm these lot.

With my help, Ælfgar can wobble to his feet. His breath is laboured, his face muddied and probably bloodied as well beneath the sheen of thick grime.

'Eadfrith,' he heaves, and I look to where he points. Eadfrith is trying to hold his own against three men, all of them angling him closer and closer to the sharp drop to the side of the bridge.

'I've got it,' and I leap over two men brawling in the mud, unable to determine which is my warrior and which is the enemy, to get to Eadfrith's side.

The older man fights with firm strokes, no hint of fear or fury, even as he's forced to retreat, one step at a time, back towards the sharp drop. I could do with a horse here, but they're in a chaotic group, Osmod and Wulfhere at their centre, Wulfstan at the edge. They're as beleaguered as I am, and the horses only have hooves and teeth to protect themselves. All the same, they seem to be holding the

Raiders back, the sound of heavy impacts assuring me they're using their hooves to attack.

I notice that the wind has picked up so close to the yawning chasm below, and worry speeds my steps. I take one of the Raiders through the back, my blade making short work of his ragged byrnie. I thrust him aside, aiming him so that his falling body tangles with the legs of one of his allies, so they both thud to the ground.

Not that such a movement helps Eadfrith. He glances at me, a tired smile on his lined face. I think I know what's about to happen, but then a projectile impacts his foe from nowhere. The man stills before dropping to the ground, dead or dead to the world. I turn, catch sight of a grinning Hemming through the melee but only for a moment before he's absorbed in the fighting once more.

'My thanks,' Eadfrith puffs through his cheeks, the words almost too weak to be heard. But another imminent disaster has caught my eye. The Raider numbers might be depleting, but it's impossible to tell for sure. Three horses have become removed from the rest of their number, Aart and Jethson amongst them. Even while Wulfstan and Cuthbert attempt to drive back the Raiders, racing amongst them, hooves and war axe sending blood and chunks of flesh high into the air, two Raiders try to mount the horses, no doubt to drive Wulfstan away.

'Fuck,' frantically, I glance around, but I'm still the only one with a shield, and what good can I do against so many others with shields?

I need to protect the horses, but equally, Hemming is overwhelmed, Wulfred and Cealwin fighting back to back, Osmod and Wulfhere being menaced by those who remain on the bridge even as they attempt to protect the horses. And I have one shield.

One fucking shield.

Chapter Twenty

Only then I don't. I hear the rumble of the ground, and my heart sinks. Fuck. The bastards have horses.

But, there's something about the sound that's achingly recognisable, and a spear impacts the ground, right through the open mouth of one of the Raiders trying to steal the horses, missing Jethson by no more than a handspan. I hear a familiar roar of outrage and find a grin for my cold, wind-buffeted face. Jethson lifts his head and begins to move away, forging a path through the battling men and slippery mud as though it's no more than a canter through a grassy expanse. Not as though he's almost just been stolen or killed by Hereman's spear.

The enemy warrior is skewered to the ground, alive, for now, with his hand on seax and war axe, but he can only fight if someone comes at him. He's pinned to the ground, and if he moves the smallest amount, he'll be dead. I eye him, considering who'll kill the man, only for Aart to crash into the man in his haste to escape, sending him thudding to the floor, the spear haft finishing the job the spearhead began.

One less to fucking kill. That cheers me, even as I try to make some sense of what's happened.

I was alone, with one shield and too many men to protect, but now, thundering from the west, or at least I assume from the west, I can hear my warriors. And I know who delivered that spear.

My missing warriors are here. I don't know how, but no one, not even Osmod, would have been able to make such a shot from so far away. Hereman must have seen the need.

'You fucking cock. That's my bloody horse,' Edmund bellows at his brother. The barked reply of laughter assures me that Hereman took such a shot just to rile his brother, even if it did save his horse.

I turn then, trying to place the sounds because I believe the two voices remain separated by distance. Did they come together? Is that where Edmund went? None of it makes sense, and now isn't the time to fucking think about it.

I stagger to Hemming, insert myself between him and the towering giant forcing him into the ground with every blow of his seax against the younger man's raised war axe. Chips of wood fly free, and I thrust my shield before my eyes so that I don't get blinded as I take the warrior with a slice through his byrnie. It does nothing other than ripping it open, but the warrior turns to me, green eyes flashing with fury, while Hemming surges to his feet, war axe swinging to graze the man's upper thigh.

The Raider screams, the sound high and eerie, seax stabbing at Hemming, not at me, because I have the shield and Hemming doesn't. Hemming remains the easier target.

No matter how many times I land a blow on arms or back, the Raider keeps going, pushing Hemming closer and closer to the rickety bridge and just when I fear he'll tumble to his death in place of Eadfrith, who I saved earlier, there's a flash of colour.

Everything happens too quickly for my eyes to take in. I feel the force of wind pass my face, and Hemming, eyes wild with terror, making a break for it.

I blink. Swallow heavily, and grin at the bastard that tried to kill Beornberht's son.

'Come on then, you fucker,' I leer at him. We're still in a desperate situation, and I don't know how many of my lost men have returned to me, but I believed we could win this before, and now with Hereman and Icel, Edmund as well, that belief redoubles itself.

I need to kill as many of the Raiders as possible. A Mercian will be that little bit safer for every life I take, and that's enough to drive me onwards.

My body aches, my cut hand, throbbing, but still, I glower at the man.

He returns the look, blood weeping from a wound above his right eye, and that gives me my opportunity.

I rush into him, trusting his vision is compromised. Hemming cut his upper thigh. Now I aim for the slit in his byrnie, the sight of his stained tunic calling to me. I need to land a blow there, stab through his belly, bring him to his knees.

Some sense alerts my enemy to what's happening, and he swings his war axe towards me, forcing me to use my shield to stop the advance. I slash out with my borrowed seax, but it's not enough, and the man has already moved aside.

I follow his steps, aware he turns me, leading me with his footsteps, but I don't fucking care. He's not going to be alive for much longer. If he wants to think this a victory, then he's welcome to it.

His war axe targets my body once more, and I swing the shield to hold it off. But now I'm too far away from the enticing slit in his byrnie to have any chance of attacking him. No, I need a new ploy, something he doesn't suspect.

Head down, I eye the ground but find nothing there to help me. The earth is churned a reddish-brown, the mud of snowmelt and rain water turning ever slicker.

Again, his war axe flickers in the air, and this time, I don't use my shield to counter it but rather skip within its reach. He can't wound me if his blade is behind me instead of in front of me.

His eyes widen in shock at my action, and I smell him. He's far from terrified, even as my seax moves through the small space between us, almost at the rent in his byrnie.

He thrusts me aside with his other hand as the war axe hits my back and then moves over my shoulder. I want to knock it aside, but my hands are both full. My enemy grins, thinking he's won, as he crushes me closer to his body with the action.

I grip my seax, pointing outwards, waiting for the right moment, only then he drops his war axe, spinning away from me, releasing both of us. My intentions were too easy for him to decipher.

Into his hand, he palms a seax, just like my borrowed one, and now he charges me, mouth open in a wide grin, seax held tight to his chest as he thinks to repeat the movement, only armed with something other than the heavy war axe.

I take one step back, angling myself away from where I believe the axe has fallen, only to tangle one of my legs with the wooden handle of his lost blade. Fuck.

I strain for balance, but the ground is too slick. I feel both of my legs failing me, the one slipping one way, the other seeking somewhere flat for it to rest other than on the rounded wooden handle of the war axe. My seax whips into the air, my shield clattering me in the chin, and I taste blood.

The Raider grins at me, his momentum increasing, not decreasing. Remembering Icel's words outside Gainsborough, I give up on my quest to stay upright and instead collapse to the floor.

My knees land first, far apart and a yelp of surprise escapes my tight lips. The Raider's seax grazes the air where my head just was, and on he runs, unable to stop himself, the slope beside the bridge taking him closer and closer to the sharp drop.

Seax on the ground, I lift myself, first bringing my knees together, feeling the mud seeping into my trews. A cry of alarm drifts on the air, and I turn towards my foe, thinking he's fallen over the edge, only to see him gripping onto his seax, embedded into the ground, as he attempts to haul himself upwards.

'Will you just fucking die,' I huff, pushing myself upright, and gripping my shield. I place my borrowed seax on my weapons belt as I lift the pestilent war axe with my healing hand.

The Raider screams for help, but no one other than me heeds his cries. The attack between the two shield walls has doubled in ferocity, but I don't look, my intention only to kill the man who thought to kill me.

Behind his prone body, I see his legs flailing in the air, the drop of the river behind him, the grey and brown water almost transfixing me with the menace it contains. The slope is so steep, I consider the wisdom of my movements.

Both of my enemy's hands grip the seax handle, one over the other, but the mud isn't holding, and I pause, watching as the seax begins to lift from the ground.

Frantic eyes greet mine, words I don't understand pouring from his mouth, but I don't need to understand the words to appreciate the intent. This man who tried to kill me begs me to aid him now from a terrible death in the crashing water far below.

I don't fucking think so. Instead, I lift the war axe, his war axe, taking careful aim, and as blood sheets my face, I hear a cry of pain and terror. I glimpse two hands, one wrapped around the other, but they're no longer attached to the rest of the body. The man is gone, only his war axe and seax left behind. I kick the two curled hands, sending them tumbling after my enemy.

'Damn bastard,' I huff, heaving breath into my body and finally taking the time to try and determine what's happening.

The shield wall is once more in place, reinforced by some of my warriors. The horses have been led to my right side, away from the precarious drop beside the river and away from the bridge which crumbles before my eyes.

The Raiders who've chased us here, fight on. They could run, but they don't, even as I watch Icel and Rudolf battering aside two enemy shields to place slick cuts on two exposed throats. The Raiders die, and the pair of them wade into the next row. Beside them, Gardulf and Lyfing are engaged in a bitter fight with three Raiders.

I try and take a reckoning, but it's all confusion. Certainly, there are both more Raiders now and also more of my men. How did they know to come here? I want to shout to Icel, to Rudolf, even to Hereman, who's the most unlikely to give me a straight answer, but I hold my tongue. Now isn't the time to know everything.

Hemming is with the horses, Wulfred beside him, but I've lost sight of the wounded Wulfhere, which worries me. Osmod is missing, although he was there a moment ago. I hope the two are together, but I can't take the time to find them, not yet, because although Icel and Rudolf have penetrated the shield wall of my enemy, it's starting to move forwards once more. They'll be stranded on the far side.

Whatever reinforcement the Raiders have, they're using them well. I look to Wulfred and Hemming, consider whether they can do what I think needs to be done, but before I can shout anything to them, the Raiders begin to hurry onwards. Gardulf and Lyfing disappear from sight, the crash and screams almost making me wince, even as I rush towards the advancing shield wall.

The Raiders means to force us onto the bridge to be crushed between them and the men there or into the churning river. The two different objectives might well be the same in a short amount of time.

That's not going to fucking happen.

'Siric, Wærwulf.' They're the closest to me who aren't already in the reconstructed shield wall.

'Quick, get behind the others,' I shout, bending to run my hands through the mucky gravel to spread it more evenly over the ground. It's not going to be enough, and my jubilation at the arrival of my new warriors is already starting to fade away. Have they merely delayed the inevitable?

I rush to fill the gap left by Icel and Rudolf. I don't know where they are. I don't even know why they're this side of the shield wall and not attacking the enemy's rear.

Shield in front of me, I thud into the advance, bracing my legs, and hoping to bring the quick steps to a halt.

'My Lord,' Goda hails me above the crash of wood on wood, his voice gruff with the effort of maintaining his stance. Osbert is to the far side of him, I notice as I flick my head one way and then the other.

'How did you get here?' I demand to know, but the words are lost beneath the onslaught of shouting Raiders, and although I watch Goda's mouth open and shut beneath his helm, I can't hear the words.

'How did you get here?' I call again.

'We followed you,' Goda manages to raise his voice loud enough for me to hear. I furrow my forehead. It makes no sense.

'The Raiders on the far side of the River Wye are all dead. It was an easy battle,' Goda continues. I nod. That pleases me, even as I want to ask where Owain is and what Lord Cadell was thinking to demand my warriors for such an easy attack to defeat.

But there's too much happening around me.

Siric thunders into place to my left, Wærwulf next to him. The hole has been filled, and for a moment, I think our reconstructed shield wall will now hold against the Raiders. Perhaps Rudolf and Icel will kill the men on the far side, aiming for their exposed necks, lower legs, or even beneath their armpits. I could do with at least half the number suddenly stopping, but despite the gravel beneath my feet and my warriors at my side, our shield wall isn't enough.

Slowly, almost imperceptibly at first, the Raiders begin to advance again, even as I'm considering where Pybba is. I've not seen him.

'Where's Pybba?' I demand from Siric, but Siric is fiercely engaged, seax and shield being used to beat against our foes. I turn to Goda, but likewise, he fights against our enemy.

I'm not sure what's happening on the bridge. Are the Raiders still there? Will they attack us soon? I wish I knew. And now I realise that although I've heard Edmund's outraged voice, I've not seen him. I'd expect him to be in the heat of the battle, but he isn't.

I lick my lips, taste the salt there, and swallow down the bitterness of failure. This isn't going to end well, and it's my fucking fault. I thought it was bad enough to be responsible for my small band of warriors failing, but now that failure is doubled. Mercia's greatest warriors are here, battering against a force of Raiders that might only just outnumber mine.

We need to do better.

My borrowed seax stabs downwards, piercing the slit between one shield and another. But it's not close enough to draw blood. I yank it back before my hand's crushed. Above the rumble of battle, I can hear Rudolf and Icel shouting one to another, and now I feel a stab of fear.

Their voices are indistinct, but I sense an edge of desperation within them.

'Siric, follow me and the rest,' I huff the words to the man to my side and then turn to Goda.

'Goda, follow me, bring the others. We go together.'

Both acknowledge my words, and now all I need to do is make sure I time it tight.

The Raiders are trying to send us into the river. The Raiders on the bridge are trying to kill us from behind. I've had enough of this bloody mess.

I turn, just to check my warriors are where I think they are. I don't see the horses. Neither do I see Eadfrith, or Hemming or the others that worry me. I do see something on the bridge, but that must be the Raiders. They're the only ones there.

'Now.' I bellow the order. Immediately, I snatch my shield to my chest, holding it tight there, even as I turn side-on. This has to work, or some of my warriors will be left behind.

The shield that faced me wobbles for an agonisingly slow amount of time, and then the Raider begins to fall. Side on, I stab down with my seax, up with my shield. I feel others moving around me, and then I'm amongst our enemy, as my foeman buckles at the chin from my shield and at the middle from my seax.

I can still hear the indistinct voices of Icel and Rudolf. My hands continue to move, seax a blur as my shield impacts arms, chests and chin. The Raiders behind the face of the shield wall have no shields, or if they do, they're above their heads. There's not enough time for them to have realised what's happened and brought them into play.

The ground is churned by mud, feet and splayed bodies. I can see where Icel and Rudolf have forged their path through the shield wall, but I still can't see them. I'm aware that Goda and Siric are with me. I can also detect that those at the front of the shield wall are down or overbalanced. I'm breathing heavily, eyes alert, seeking out all who come at me and all who are easy prey.

Sweat drips down my nose, and I scrunch my eyes shut to clear them of the sweat that's formed in the hair just above my eyes. I've been cold for days, and now I'm too damn hot.

Blood drips and flies through the air, the grunts of warriors guttural.

I can feel myself getting closer to Rudolf and Icel. And then a warrior steps into my path. He eyes me with dark eyes, a fierce expression on his face, jaw tightly clenched so that his teeth must be held clamped together.

If he thinks to stop me with his war axe, I'd like to see him fucking try.

Even though exhaustion dogs my steps, I rush at him. I feint, thrust my shield towards him so that he dodges aside, only to land my helmed forehead against his nose, pushing upwards with my borrowed seax into his nose. Better to get this over and done with quickly.

Blood touches my chin, and he drops. His war axe just missing my foot.

'Bastard.'

I step over him. I still have no idea of how many Raiders there are. If my warriors could get here without me being aware of them, then so could more Raiders.

My hands never still, and with a thrust of my seax beneath an unguarded man's armpit, I finally catch sight of Icel and Rudolf. I gasp in shock, surprise and growing admiration.

The two of them battle together, back to back, the taller man and the slighter youth, the Raiders taking it in turns to come against them. They think to beat them, just two Mercians against all of them, and there are a great deal of the bastards, but the pile of bodies and the shrieks of mewing men fills the air.

'Fuck me,' Goda speaks for us all, the awe in his voice impossible to disguise, even as he casually knocks aside a questing seax with his shield from one of the Raiders who hasn't turned aside from their primary purpose. He dies all the same from a slash across his neck.

'This is bloody carnage,' Goda continues. And it is, and I don't know what my place is amongst it all. I don't know if any of us have a place besides Icel and Rudolf, but we've fought our way here, and now we'll do what we always do.

A shrill neigh rings through the air, and I turn to where the horses were. I can see many heads, all of them looking the other way. Squinting, I decide they're far enough away from the bridge now. With luck, Hemming and Wulfred will lead the mounts to safety. There's no need for them to linger.

'What do we do?' It's Siric who asks, his words catching as he breathes deeply, trying to suck much-needed air into his starved lungs.

'We fucking kill 'em all,' I announce, looking one way and then the next. Behind us, those Raiders who still stand are only just realising what's happened. For now, we have the initiative.

'Siric, lead your men against the remains of the shield wall. Goda, you and I, and the rest of us will aid Rudolf and Icel.'

Neither man indicates what he thinks of such a division, and I'm already moving forwards, clambering over the dead and dying, stabbing downwards where I believe a blade will end a man's suffering more quickly.

The smell is terrible, even with the wind rushing through the slaughter field. These men haven't bathed for days, and that's the least of their worries now.

Two figures rear up before me; both the same height, one blond, the other entirely bald. The blond woman eyes me with rage in her hate-filled eyes. I consider the relationship between the two, but it's irrelevant when they're both about to die.

She lashes out with a long sword, and I find a smile for such a move. Swords can be too cumbersome in the shield wall. But here, we're neither in the shield wall nor out of it. And I have my double-headed eagle sword over my shoulder.

I admire the flash of bright sunlight over the rippling blade. The woman carries a shield as well, this one covered with the black shape of a raven. Her sword reverses, the movement quick and assured. I thrust my shield towards it, knowing it's likely to miss it altogether, but that's not my intention. While she reclaims her sword, ensuring the hold is firm, I dash forwards, shield extended, but behind it, my seax is preparing to take yet another of the Raiders.

Goda has engaged the bald Raider, their movements far from as subtle as those I share with the woman. As she spins aside, hand gripping the sword, I jab out and open a slice on her upper shoulder. The blade digs much deeper than I expect it to, blood dripping in a steady torrent before she's even aware that I've played her for a fool.

Spittle accompanies a shriek of pain, and I twist my lips together. A good sword deserves to be in better hands than this. For a brief moment, I think she'll drop the blade, the cut making it impossible to continue. Instead, she flings the shield to the side, and her sword is quickly in that hand. Her one arm might be wounded, but that's not going to stop her.

I admire someone who can fight well with both hands. It's not an easy skill to learn.

She takes two steps back, creating the room to be able to swing her sword. I watch her, curious as to why she insists on keeping the weapon when she wears a seax around her waist. It's much the better tool for such close fighting.

Something thuds into my back, and I'm flung forward, the sweat of another sprinkling my face, and now the woman, eyes flashing beneath her helm, thinks to take an easy blow against me. And it should be easy. I'm off balance. My shield arm is thrown high so that I have to double my hold on it to keep it under my control.

But my borrowed seax, well, any seax is genuinely just an extension of my arm, if a man could live with a blade at his wrist instead of four fingers, a thumb and the palm of his hand.

Eagerly, she flicks the sword towards me, but it's not accompanied by any brightness from the sun. I keep my eyes on it, watching to determine her next attack. It comes quickly, as with lithe steps, she's trying to land her own blow onto my shoulder. I let her come, enticing her closer, offering my shield as some defence but not really defending myself from the impacts.

She's not close enough to truly hurt, not yet, as one blow bounces from my shield so that she has to turn the blade quickly, aiming for the other shoulder on the return blow.

Beneath her extended arms, I stab upwards with my seax, the blade drawing blood in the small gap between her gloves and wrist guard. My seax bites deep, even as I'm once more jostled, but this time by the blow from her sword.

She grins at me, offering a mouth full of reasonably straight teeth. She's not felt the pain yet, too caught up in the victory she perceives. I thrust forward with my head, knocking into those teeth as she shrieks with outrage. And then my borrowed seax is slicing up her arm, the wrist guards unable to stay intact against the precise work.

My seax only comes to a stop as it hits her silver arm ring, high on her shoulder. Then, I grip my weapon tightly and stab beneath her armpit. She bleeds from too many wounds now, and her mouth opens and closes as though wishing to speak. I stand back, breathing evenly, half an eye to Goda. The man he battles, the bald man, is fighting fiercely, his back to the woman. If he realises the warrior he fought with is dying, he gives no indication of it.

The woman wavers, blood pooling down her legs where her

hands hang limp, the sword loose in her hands. I wonder which will fall first, the weapon or the woman.

'Coelwulf.' The shriek startles me from my thoughts, and my seax and shield are already before me as the bald man comes crashing into me. He snarls, his lips curled back to reveal a line of cracked and black teeth. I can smell his sweat and fear and thrust my hands out to either side to protect against a heavy landing.

The air is knocked from my body, even though I hit the wet floor. I'm just grateful there are no weapons there, but in the action, my borrowed seax has spun out of control, and rather than having my shield for protection, I'm lying half on it. It's not comfortable, not at all. I feel my legs bend the wrong way around the shield as the bald Raider lands fully on top of me.

I can see little but the grey sky above my head, the sudden resumption of rain, splattering into my mouth. I try to breathe in, but it's impossible. Abruptly, my vision dims, patches of light forming at the edges. I can't even shout for help.

The Raider has somehow stunned himself with the attack. To the side of me, I hear something heavy fall, followed by a softer clang. As my vision dims even further, I appreciate that the woman Raider fell before the sword did. How odd.

And then the weight is lifted from me.

'Get the fuck up,' Goda bellows at me, casually punching the warrior who felled me in the back. The man's eyes startle open at the pummelling he's receiving. Sucking air into my body, I roll onto my side, coughing and heaving all at the same time. My handle scrabbles for my borrowed seax, but it finds my shield strap first.

'You fucker,' I roar, swinging it behind me as I rear upwards. Its rim clatters into the man's open mouth, as he bucks, from Goda's attack. Blood pours from his open mouth, and I thrust my shield higher, wishing I didn't feel so weak. This time it hurtles into his nose, so he gasps and flaps like a fish out of water.

'Finish the fucker off,' I shout at Goda, using all of my breath to do so. The Raiders' mouth opens ever wider into a bellow of rage, but there's a seax at his neck, and the bastard dies with his mouth open and his throat slit.

I bend over, hands on my knees, shield again forgotten about, as I try to recover myself.

'My thanks,' I pant, but Goda merely grunts, standing as my guard, posture tense as he waits for me.

The sound of battle fades away, and I shake my head, hoping to God I'm not about to pass out. I concentrate on breathing, on stilling my thundering heart and rapidly moving chest.

Slowly, sound returns to me, and I can hear the shouts of men fighting against one another, the less pleasant sounds of flesh being ripped apart and the shrieks and sobbing of the dying and wounded. Only the dead make no noise today.

When I finally feel able to stand, I do so without any of my weapons, entirely dependent on bearded Goda to stop any blows that might be aimed my way.

'You alright?' He demands to know, meeting my eyes with his chin raised. I try and crack a smile, but even that tiny movement hurts. I'm impressed he thinks to ask.

'You look like fucking shit,' Goda continues, and now I do smile. So much for some care.

'Aye, I'm bastard winded.'

'Not surprised. He was a heavy bastard. I think you killed his wife, or perhaps his daughter.' While the battle plays on around us, Goda is examining the dead man and woman with interest.

'You'd spend your time more wisely seeking out the next blade.'

'Aye, perhaps, but I'm more curious about those two,' and Goda toes the body of the dead man. I watch as the byrnie ripples with the movement, flesh spilling from the waist and the leg, as though he's been tied into something too tight to fit him.

I scurry to collect my shield, noticing the dent on it and my borrowed seax, which has ended up beneath the dead woman's right foot. I move it away, retrieve my seax, even while I eye the sword with which she thought to end my life. It's a good weapon. A pity she didn't possess the skill to kill me with it.

'Right,' I huff, aware that while the rest of the men to the side of Goda are fighting to aid Rudolf and Icel, I've done little of worth other than nearly dying from lack of air. A fine warrior king I fucking make.

'Come on,' I try and lumber to a run, but Goda's hand on my shoulder pulls me back.

'They're doing it,' he offers, his tone dark. 'We should move around them, to the Raiders who're too craven to fight in the shield wall. Look, there's enough of them.' I follow his finger and realise what he means.

There are those fighting on the slaughter field, and there are the many dead, but there are also at least fifteen Raiders who merely jeer at what's happening. And they're the ones preventing us from having free access to the path we took to get here. I turn to sight the bridge, trying to determine if that way is yet clear, but a loud crack fills the air.

It might be, for now, but it won't be for much longer.

Damn the Raiders. It's been a fragile thing ever since I can remember, and yet many have used it, if only because some were too scared to do so, and it gave a quick means of evading either the Gwent Welsh or whoever was chasing you. Now, alongside rebuilding the walls of London, I'll have to decide whether the bridge at Kempsey is worthwhile restoring as well.

It's all going to cost a great deal of coins, but then, I'm not alone there. The members of the witan will have to pay their fair share as well.

I follow Goda, stabbing down every so often when a stray hand reaches towards me or the foot of a splayed Raider tries to trip me. They really will try anything.

Besides Goda, Lyfing and Ordheah join us. I scan the battle site looking for those I've not yet seen, Edmund and Pybba most noticeable of all. In the distance, Siric and my warriors are ensuring the shield wall can't reform. They fight with mean determination. I wish I could stand and watch it. It could almost make me weep. Fuck, they're lethal bastards.

Despite the shouts of the wounded and dying, we must make too much noise because I suddenly feel fifteen pairs of eyes on me. I find a smile for my mud and blood-encrusted face, aware that beneath those two colours, my cheeks are red with cold, my nose if it could be seen beneath my helm, pink-tipped and starting to ache with the cold of the wind.

I watch as the Raiders decide what it is they mean to do. One, at the centre, perhaps thinks to control the others. He reaches for his seax, even as he slides his hand beneath his shield.

He makes a fine figure, tall, almost regale, his shoulder-length black hair blowing in the wind. But I'm laughing. He might think to fight, but the Raiders at his side have no intention of joining the fray. Some share looks. Others merely turn tail and begin to run back the way they've come. Where they think they're going to get to is beyond me.

Not that it matters. I have no intention of allowing any of the pestilent scum to leave here.

Goda takes the man who stands, his swivelling head showing that he's only just realised the shield wall is merely a man holding a shield.

I skirt him; my breath restored to me, although my chest aches. My cut legs from the battle beside the River Wye will be covered in bruises as well come the morning. I'll be every colour of the rainbow in no time at all; a red nose, blue and green bruises shading to purple and all the colours in between. And when some of those bruises start to heal, they'll turn yellow, as my cuts might do as well, with all this exertion when they're not yet healed.

'What's orange?' I muse to myself, hurrying my steps to the men who flee. One slips into the mud, and Lyfing is on him immediately. Even as the man tries to turn onto his back, to batter aside the flurry of seax thrusts, Lyfing stabs into his side, opening up a cut that runs from one side of his waist to the other. Red and white flash beneath the grim sky.

'Shut him fucking up,' I huff, the shrieks reminding me of a labouring woman. I have far more sympathy for her than for him.

A gurgling cough and I hurry onwards, trying to watch where I step, aware that Ordheah is ahead of me. Goda's heavier steps can be heard coming from behind as well.

I ache. And still, I can think of nothing orange. Perhaps a tunic, but no, I'm not known for bright colours. Fuck it. I'll be every shade of the rainbow apart from orange. What do I care?

I bend and scoop a rock into my hand and throw it at the Raider in front of me. It tangles his feet, and he falls to the ground in a clatter of arms and legs, weapons as well. By the time I'm standing over him, bubbles have formed in the mud. I pull him aside with one arm, seax ready to stab downwards, but the bastard is dead, drowning in the brown sludge of the flooded landscape.

I drop him, Lyfing and Goda joining me as Ordheah powers onwards. Because they've not been fighting for their lives, the Raiders have more speed than we do. I want to tackle them, but I'm finding it hard to breathe. I should have called for Haden.

Only then, Hemming and Wulfhere thunder into view, joined by some of the riderless horses as well. I eye Wulfhere with unease, his pale face gleaming with sweat but his eyes alight with joy. I grip Haden's saddle, hauling myself upright, so his legs take the weight and not mine. Goda passes me my shield, and while I wait for him and Lyfing to mount, I turn back the way I've just run.

I can see Rudolf and Icel at their grizzly task, and they've been joined by Siric and a handful of other warriors. There are few enough of the enemy still standing. And still, the sky pisses it down.

Hemming rides Perry with great speed towards the Raiders. As soon as he's close enough, he leans precariously away from his saddle and leaps onto one of the Raiders backs.

'I would have thrown a fucking seax, not myself,' Goda offers eyebrows high over the thunder of the horses.

'It is a little flamboyant,' I confirm, the sound of both bodies hitting the ground reaching my ears, even here.

'That's going to bloody hurt,' Goda continues.

'I suggest you show the youngsters how it's done,' I smirk, and he nods.

'Aye. I'll show 'em how to kill without killing yourself,' and Goda spurs Magic onwards. I'm impressed that Hemming and Wulfhere were able to bring the correct mounts for us. It seems they've given more thought to their actions than I have to mine. Goda might be showing the youngsters how it's done, but perhaps I could learn something from them.

'Come on,' I encourage Haden. Eagerly, he begins to follow the other horses, Lyfing close to me. I catch sight of Hemming standing gingerly from his attack, a rueful expression on his face after he's stabbed the fleeing Raider through the back. Not that the man could stand.

I glance to Wulfhere, hoping he won't attempt to do the same with his barely healed wound. He doesn't. Like Goda, he sights and throws with his seax, the man in front of him, crashing to the floor when the throw is a good one. The seax quivering in his back.

I direct Haden towards two men, both of them dashing from side to side. They know they're being hunted. Not that I know where they're heading. We found little or no shelter as we made our way towards the bridge. Do they know something we don't, or are they just desperate?

The sound of the surging water begins to fade, but the ground is no less wet. If anything, the ground seems wetter than when I came this way. Haden's hooves are almost entirely covered, and I have to slow him.

"Ware,' I call to my mounted warriors, not that they need the warning. It's easy enough to see. The water edges upwards, and as it does so, it becomes more and more perilous.

'Fuck this,' I huff to myself, reaching for a knife at my weapons belt. I won't lose my borrowed seax. It has a good weight to it. I slow

Haden, not that he's moving too fast anyway, and take careful aim. I'm not Hereman or Osmod. I'll probably miss it altogether.

The knife skitters through the air, aiming for the shoulder blades of the dark-haired warrior, the slower of the two. The other is way in front of him, leaping high to avoid obstacles, upturned branches, jagged stones. I eye him curiously. Will his luck fail him? I'm not sure, but I won't allow my warriors to chase him any more.

A splash sounds in the air, and I turn, a delighted smile on my face, as I look to where the man was that I aimed to kill. He's no longer there.

'And good fucking riddance,' I offer, deciding there and then that gloating of this to Hereman is not worth it. He'll merely remind me of all the other occasions when I missed my target entirely. For now, I'll keep this one to myself.

'Come on, lad,' I rub my hand down Haden's sleek neck, revelling in his warmth on my cold fingers. It's possible to feel it even through my leather gloves.

I turn him away from the flooded landscape before me, aware that it's beginning to grow darker and darker.

'We got nearly all of them,' Goda admits grudgingly. 'Just the one escaped.' And that one was mine to kill, so I accept the complaint in his voice.

'And all the others?' I've lost sight of Wulfhere and Ordheah. Perhaps I've ridden for too long, and they're far behind us. In fact, I can't see the river from where I am, and certainly not the bridge.

'Dead or dying. Ordheah's a fast bastard when he sets his mind to it.'

'Hemming,' I call for him because he's slowly picking his way through the deep waters, his mount picking his feet elegantly, as though it's possible to stay clear from the flood altogether. I didn't see Hemming mount up again.

I see Hemming raise his hand, and content that he knows where to come, I sit back in the saddle, gazing at Goda.

'Tell me, what happened when I split our forces.'

He shakes his head; his beard sodden with more than just water. I think he won't answer, but I am his lord, and we don't lie to one another. Well, not very often.

'The Raiders on the far side of the River Wye are all dead. It was an easy battle, and then we followed you here.' I already know that. I wait. If I demand answers, he'll tell me nothing. Instead, I give him time to consider what he should say.

Goda takes a deep sigh and then begins.

'Owain led us to the far side of the River Wye. We quickly lost sight of you through the deep woodlands, but it was easy enough to follow the meandering river course. Almost immediately, Icel came to me saying he didn't trust the bastard. We all agreed with him. Owain was nervous, too nervous for a man who was leading warriors to help his lord.'

'We kept a close eye on him, and Icel ordered Pybba and Rudolf to hang back, just in case.' I open my mouth to ask about Pybba, but Goda presses on, giving me no time to ask about him.

'It didn't take long to realise that Owain had no sense of direction. When Icel asked him how far it was, he said we'd arrive soon, but we never did. He grew more and more fearful, and eventually, Icel called a halt and demanded answers from him.'

'The cowardly bastard pissed himself as he explained how he'd been forced to encourage Lord Coelwulf to the far side of the River Wye. There were two ships filled with Raiders just waiting to kill him. Icel killed him there and then. He didn't even ask for more details.' I recoil at the thought of Icel's swift justice but stay silent.

'We hunted them down from there. It didn't take long. They had smoky fires and wouldn't have been able to hide even if they'd found an old barrow to shelter within. We attacked them the next morning, well, it was barely morning, but Icel warned the weather was going to turn, and he wanted it done. I think by then, he'd begun to regret not asking for more details. You know, if there were Raiders on the River Wye, where else were there Raiders.'

'So you killed them all?'

'We did, yes. All of the bastards, and then we turned and headed back the way we'd come, but it started to rain. We thought it would never stop. We had to wait for it to clear to cross the River Wye. And then we came after you, but by then, you were already being pursued.'

Goda heavily swallows as he finishes, and I turn to him, a question on my tongue, but a cry from in front has me encouraging Haden onwards.

It seems that while I'm about ready to stop fighting, the Raiders are far from fucking done.

Chapter Twenty-One

It takes me a while to determine what's happening before me.

A pile of bodies lies close to where Icel and Rudolf fought, but Icel and Rudolf are no longer there. No, they've made their way closer to the riverside. Haden picks his legs carefully through the churned mud and stink of blood. Even the fierce wind can't drive it entirely away.

Goda, Hemming, Wulfhere and the remainder of my warriors who followed me in chasing those thinking to escape are as perplexed as I am. Why have we been called away? What is happening?

Only then I can see, and my forehead furrows beneath my helm.

'What the fuck?' It's Goda who asks the question. I'm only a moment behind him. Indeed, what the actual fuck is happening here?

It takes me a while to make sense of precisely what I'm seeing.

My warriors are close to the rickety bridge. It sways in the wind. That's not good. But neither is the fact that there are Raiders on that bridge, both close to this side and close to the Kempsey side, and in the middle of them? Well, I can hardly believe it, but I can see Edmund, his long hair blowing in the wind even though his helm fits tight over his head and face. He's not alone either.

'How the fuck?' I can't help it. There's no other word to use.

There are Mercians on that bridge, beside Edmund, but what concerns me even more, is that somehow, Jethson stands beside his master as well. I thought the bloody horse was with the rest of them. Certainly, he was when I looked earlier. I have no idea how Jethson has made his way to Edmund's side. The horse is more loyal than my warrior, that's for sure.

I pull Haden to a stop before we reach the precipice. A long way before we reach it. The ground isn't churned mud any more; no, it's slick with water and other bodily juices. My warriors stand there, mostly watching, clearly feeling as helpless as I do at this fucking mess. I can't begin to imagine that we can resolve it without losing some of my Mercians, Jethson and Edmund included in that number.

Rudolf is doing an excellent job of keeping control of an enraged Icel, who gesticulates wildly. In turn, Icel attempts to contain Gardulf and Hereman in the gaps between his own pacing and shouting.

It would be foolish for them to follow Edmund. It'd be fucking deadly. I can't see that's going to stop them. I'm particularly concerned about Gardulf. He's young and athletic enough to attempt reaching his father. I look to Rudolf, wanting to thank him, but he's busy arguing with the three of them now. He stands before them, his skinny body before three raging warriors. Fuck. He's a brave bastard. Better to take on Raiders than his comrades.

'Bloody hell,' the words explode from me in a flurry of frustration. None of this is good.

'How the fuck did he get there?' I demand of no one, aware I shout for all the words are blown from my mouth. I imagine someone on the River Wye hears them, not the River Severn.

'He came from over there,' and it's Wærwulf who points towards Kempsey. It's a small settlement. Smoke billows roughly into the air from the fires inside homes. I'm pleased to see it still stands and doesn't burn. The Raiders have been more concerned with my appearance than the inhabitants of Kempsey. That said, I can see men and women watching what's happening. They carry anything they have that could be used as a weapon.

I admire them. Should the Raiders turn, they'll not be gaining entry to Kempsey without a long and bloody battle.

'What, he wasn't with you?' I ask Wærwulf of Edmund. There are too many pieces of this puzzle to make sense of what's happened in the time my two forces have been split, and Edmund has been missing.

'No. He was with you, and now he's on the fucking bridge.' Wærwulf's eyes are filled with confusion at my questions. I swallow heavily. Now really isn't the time to work out who was where and why. It seems that Edmund hasn't done what I expected him to do. Not at all.

A shriek of strained wood rings through the air as Gardulf redoubles his attempts to get to his father. Icel holds him in a bear hug, and still, Gardulf makes some progress forwards. Rudolf watches, worry on his face as Icel gets closer and closer to the gaping chasm below.

Hereman has given up his attempts to win free from Icel. Now, he bends and retrieves any item he can find lying on the surface and flings it high into the air, aiming for the backs of the seven or eight Raiders who believe their only chance of survival is to make it to the Kempsey side of the bridge.

At the same time, the Kempsey Raiders aren't about to turn down the chance of a bloody good battle.

And in the middle of it all stands Jethson, tossing his chestnut head with fear, foam at his mouth, while Edmund tries to control him by reaching for his reins, even as Jethson steps first one and then another. He shuffles forwards and then backwards. He's so close to the side of the bridge, I can barely tear my eyes away from him.

'Leave the horse,' I add my voice to the others all shouting, somehow expecting our words to be heard, even though they won't be.

I can't see well enough to know who stands beside Edmund,

doing their best to avoid the terrified horse, but the fact the men are with Edmund tells me they're Mercians.

'There'll be no one left at Kingsholm,' I complain with frustration, but that's not really what worries me. All the bloody Raiders are here, or at least they were before I started killing them. While they're here, they can't attack anyone else, but equally, they block our path just as surely as we block theirs, and none of us is about to give up, no matter the state of the crossing.

The bridge shrieks again and is followed by an alarming creaking of wood.

'The bridge is going to fucking go.' I don't need Wulfred's sour comment to know the truth of that. It was barely hale enough for me to stand on and battle when there were many fewer of us on it than there are at this moment. Now many more men and a bloody horse are standing on it. I'm amazed it hasn't already fallen into the fast-flowing murky grey water surging beneath it.

'What do we bloody do?' The fact it's Rudolf asking me, his eyes round, his mouth hanging open, from behind Icel and Gardulf, worries me more than it should. If there's anyone here who might have devised a means of escaping this fucked up mess, it should be him.

'We need rope,' I shout, hoping there is some, somewhere.

Hemming has scampered to find what he can, if anything, lying on the ground, perhaps dislodged during the battle or mislaid by a cart passing this way. I'm thankful that the futility of it all does not freeze him.

'What about the Raiders?' Sæbald asks about our enemy. His face is tight with worry, a flicker of unease there as well. He's not blind. He sees what I fucking do. This situation is entirely impossible.

'Hereman, kill all the fuckers. Osmod, help him. And the rest of you. If you think you can take one of them down, do it. But be wary. The blows need to land cleanly or miss entirely. We can't add more weight to that framework of a bridge.' I shake my head, surprised by the calm edge to my voice as I issue such a desperate command.

Hereman is already doing as I said. Osmod, more slowly, leaps to follow his lead. They could pick off the Raiders one by one with more time, but we don't have that time. The bridge is near to collapse.

'What about Jethson?' Wulfhere retorts, staying mounted and trying to remain out of the way because his breathing is laboured. He shouldn't have been battling, not with his wound far from being healed.

'He can jump if need be.' I dismiss the beast from my thoughts. He's a canny bastard. He'll find a way to survive. I have to rely on him now. I try not to consider the fact that he'll only do it if Edmund lives. And Edmund needs to live, or my aunt will roast me alive. She won't much care about Mercia's fate and whether there's a king of it or not if Edmund is dead. I'm sure of that.

Hereman picks his targets carefully. Quickly, he takes out the two to the sides of the bridge. They might be the easiest to plunge into the flooded river, but it also opens up a space into which the Raiders in the middle of the bridge can fall.

I watch them, noting how they move carefully but with purpose. The Raiders test the sturdiness of the wood they want to stand on and only then move to it. They appreciate the frailty of the wooden planks on which they stand. I consider whether we should move aside, allow them to pass, but I doubt they'd believe us if we did so. They fear death on the edge of our blades, and such fear will drive men onwards, even towards a greater threat.

Osmod's efforts with anything he can throw are joined by Icel and Goda, both passing good at long-distance throwing. But only Osmod's first throw hits true, and then it knocks a Raider aside, but not into the water. Instead, he falls heavily, rolling away and over the already straining planks of the bridge. Icel's attempt is wide of the mark. Goda's just too short.

What it does do is to alert the remaining five Raiders that they're being hunted. Goda's retrieved spear hits close to one of the Raiders feet, making him jump high into the air. He lands off balance, one leg behind him, the other just gripping the wood in front of him. The entire bridge shudders at such an action.

'Apologies,' Goda bellows to me, not to the Raider he nearly killed, even as Icel's war axe spirals, end over end, before tumbling harmlessly into the foaming river. The four of them bend to retrieve new objects to throw. Hemming has returned with three or four lengths of rope, all different sizes, and none of them long enough to reach any of the beleaguered Mercians.

'Get them tied together,' I shout to Sæbald and Lyfing. They rush to Hemming's side, eager to assist, but it's not going to be enough.

There's a crack, loud enough to make me startle, Haden as well, and with disbelieving eyes, I watch as the entire section of the bridge, about ten steps out from the side where I stand, sheers away from the river bank. For a long moment, I can't be the only one who holds my breath, but then, everything moves too fast. The wood cracks, splinters, and fractures, throwing chunks into the air and others down into the roaring river.

Hereman rushes forward as though he intends to jump the gap, only to stop, overbalancing, both arms flailing as he realises he can't make the jump. Something, and I don't know whether it's blind luck or skill, keeps him on his feet as he thrusts his head backwards.

The Raiders closest to the broken parts of the bridge shriek with fear, their sounds shrill, and Jethson, God's love the bastard, stamps his hooves. Edmund moves to calm him once more, but the horse is beyond caring. He stamps and rears, his whinny of fear not quite as shrill as that of the Raiders, and then the rest of the bridge begins to tremble as well.

'Get the bastard rope,' Gardulf roars, his fear evident in the sharpness of the words. But I can't see that the rope will be any good. Not now.

'Fuck.'

The Raiders spur onwards towards the Kempsey side of the bridge, only a handful of steps from crashing into the Mercians, Edmund and Jethson.

'Kill them,' I command, trying to keep my voice calm. Hereman is already throwing yet another projectile, which spins, end over end, a piece of the bridge or a spear without an arrow, and it neatly knocks one of the Raiders over. He struggles to retain his balance, hands flailing on the floor, but he trips over his own feet and between one glance and the next, he's entirely lost his balance. He screeches while he falls, but it might just be the best outcome for him.

Maybe he stands a chance in the swirling current. There's no chance to stay on the actual bridge, and as he's fallen before all of the wood, he might miss being hit by it or even impaled and dragged to the depths of the river.

'Go towards Kempsey,' I roar at the Mercians and Edmund, hoping they'll hear. Of them all, it's Jethson who moves the quickest. No thought for the others, he rushes onwards, dragging Edmund with him while Edmund flounders for the mislaid reins.

Jethson's movements shudder through the bridge. I wince. The whole bloody thing's about to go. I just know it is. And what can I do? I feel helpless, and I don't like it.

'Throw the rope,' I instruct Sæbald and Lyfing. Sæbald nods, only for Osmod to hear and snatch the end from him.

'I'll do it,' he states flatly, not allowing any argument, moving quickly to tie it around a spear he's found. I watch him, unsure what he's doing. I bite down on my demand that whatever he's doing, he does it fucking quickly. It's not going to bastard help.

'My Lord,' there's a warning in Gyrth's voice, and I snap my gaze to where he looks. One of the Mercians is running towards us, not away, eyes white with fear, forcing his way through the Raiders, going the other way. The man means to leap the vast gap. It's too far. I know it. But he's a Mercian. We must do all we can to save him.

'Be ready, but don't do anything fucking stupid.' I hate giving the command but know it's necessary as I shout the order, dismounting and sending Haden away from the precipice with a gentle slap of my hand to his hind leg.

The man, hair wild beneath his helm, darts his way through the ragged Raiders, desperate to go in the opposite direction. I hold out a hope that he'll make it, despite my misgivings.

In front of me, Gyrth and Sæbald are standing together, ready to support one another, and I only wish there was more rope to hand, but who rides with rope when war is on the mind? Osmod has flung his spear, cord attached, and somehow it lands, just in front of the feet of another of the Mercians.

The shriek of outrage can be heard from here, but I don't look. My eyes are on Gyrth and Sæbald, on Leonath, Ingwald and Wærwulf, who are all doing what they can to anchor themselves, digging feet into the muck and slime, stabbing down with seaxs and swords, into the slick surface. I think of going to help them, but there's no time.

The man runs, rushes, goes ever faster, and then, just before he's about to leap, the bridge gives another shriek, and the surface begins to collapse. The man, not seeing the problem, or no doubt choosing not to, kicks off with both legs, chest flung backwards, legs scything through the air, and I realise I'm not even breathing.

He hangs, suspended over the raging water, over the empty air that the bridge used to dominate, nothing holding him up. Nothing but hope and a perverse feeling that he shouldn't die, not here, not with the bastard Raiders.

Gyrth is lying on the ground now, unheeding of the mud coating him, Sæbald beside him, both of them with hands outstretched over the gap. Leonath is behind Gyrth, Wærwulf behind Sæbald and more of my warriors are ready to assist should the man make it, and one of them gets a hand to his outstretched ones.

Although I'd rather not, I watch, and by some power, I don't fucking understand, Sæbald and Gyrth both manage to grip the reaching arms of the man. Heart in my throat, I watch the two of them slide forward, the weight of another too much for them to bear when there's nothing to grip, even though they share that weight.

'Help them,' I roar, but my men have seen the danger. More and more of them grip the man in front, and slowly, so slowly it's painful to watch, Sæbald and Gyrth reappear from where they've slid over the precipice, followed by a sobbing Mercian, so much mud on his face it's as though he sobs the stuff.

But it's not over. The twang of the taut rope recalls me to Osmod's attempts, and now I understand. It's not much, but the spear embeds deeply in one of the supporting struts of the bridge, while Osmod, Icel and Hereman hold it tight from this side of the bridge.

A man can swing from the rope. If he's brave enough to risk it and the fierce winds, the possibility of death should his grip fail.

One of the Mercians has seen it, but so too has one of the Raiders. The Mercian has decided to take his chance. He's followed the rope, crawling towards the end of the splintering bridge, rope in one hand, and now he swings on it, one hand over the other, as he makes his way towards us. But the Raider isn't far from doing the same.

'Fuck. Kill the bastard,' I order, bending to seek amongst the pile of bodies for discarded weapons to throw across the divide to stop him from overwhelming the rope.

'We can't. We risk taking the rope with it,' this comes from Osmod in a huff as he strains to hold the rope tight against the Mercians' weight. I know he's right. I also know we need something other than three men to hold the cord in place. But there's nothing. The closest tree is too far distant, even if there was enough rope. I consider the horses, but there's no surety that they'll be able to take the weight and do as we ask. It would just be our luck for the one we chose to run towards the bridge, not away from it.

I turn fierce eyes, trying to determine a way out of this mess. But it's impossible. I can't build a bridge in a heartbeat. And if I could, it wouldn't last.

My eyes flash to Jethson. He and Edmund have carved a path through the Raiders, who only now seem to appreciate the danger they're in on the bridge. I shake my head at their antics.

'Mad bastards,' I comment, even as I handle the spear I've found, thinking to throw it, but knowing I'm more likely to kill my Mercians than a Raider.

Now, Edmund and Jethson are on steadier land, the bridge to the far side, still intact and sturdier, so what do they do? Run for safety? Of course not.

'Fuckers,' I breathe, but I admit, I'm impressed by his determination.

I don't know where to look; too much happening to either side. The hanging Mercian has stalled in the middle of the rope. I can see him puffing there as he hangs, feet far above the churning waters. The Raider is down on his hands and knees, feeling for the rope, panic on his face, and fierce determination. My warriors are doing all they can to urge the Mercian to cross the rope. The rest of the Mercians haven't even seen the rope. They're trying to follow Edmund and Jethson through the crush of the enemy. And the Raiders on the bridge? They fight on, of course. Daft bastards.

At their backs, Jethson and Edmund are fighting; Edmund with his seax, Jethson with his hooves. I watch as one of the Raiders buckles to the ground, one of the Mercians jumping over him, and onwards, to where there's the promise of solid land.

A slicing sound and I turn back to the men on the rope. The Mercian is moving once more, almost within reach of Gyrth and Sæbald, who still dangle over the precipice, the man they saved moved away from the edge, his chest heaving as he lies on the sodden ground, entirely spent. But behind the Mercian, the Raider is gaining, and although I'm not alone in holding something I could throw, it can't be risked.

And then it starts to rain. One moment the sky is grey and sullen, the next fat, cold raindrops are falling onto my face, and it's not what the man on the rope needs.

'Hurry the fuck up,' the words burst from my mouth, unbidden. The rope will become slick, the tired Mercian already struggling. The Raider is almost on him, the rope bowing alarmingly towards the water. And the Raider is a slight man, his arms able to support his body, whereas the Mercian seems almost double the height and certainly double the weight.

Osmod, Hereman and Icel have more of my men supporting them now, Beornstan, Goda, Ingwald and Ælfgar gripping what parts of the rope they can find. I just can't see that it's going to be enough. The Mercian might lose his grip on the rope. Equally, my warriors might not be able to hold it.

I dare not look away, knowing that if I do, the man will fall. Instead, I run to Sæbald and Gyrth, sighting the distance. The Mercian is getting closer and closer. I can see his chest rising and falling as he struggles to breathe, to hold himself steady, and the bastard Raider behind him begins to laugh, the sound coming to me more by the opening of his mouth than anything else.

His hair is drenched, his lips almost blue, and I exactly know what he's going to do next.

I turn, look around and find an abandoned piece of chain curled in the mud. I've no idea what it's for, but I don't sodding care. I dig for it, using my hands and ignoring the wince of pain from my cut, as more and more of the chain reveals itself beneath my frantic movements. I don't think what it was there for, and I ignore the red tinge of rust on some of the ancient links. This needs to work.

It's heavy and unwieldy. Siric notes my actions and quickly understands. The chain is moored tightly against one of three pieces of stone that stand to this side of the bridge. We wouldn't have had the rope to curl around it, not and still reach the Mercians, but it already circles the stone. It's all I can offer the Mercian.

I keep pulling, more and more of the long-abandoned chain revealing itself. It will have to be enough. I hope it fucking is.

'On three,' I call to Siric. He nods. The chain is too heavy for one of us to throw that distance alone.

'Mind your heads,' I caution Sæbald and Gyrth, unsure if they hear me from their place dangling over the gap between the bridge and the land.

The Raider has started to bounce the rope up and down as he

moves along it. The bastard has more energy than I do. My warriors struggle to hold it tight with the sharp movements, the ground turning ever more slick with the cold wash of rain, and the Mercian? His eyes are wild with fear. He knows he can't hold on, not while the rope bumps and thrashes. He's weighed down with his byrnie, his weapons belt as well. And his clothes are growing wetter and wetter with the falling rain.

'One, two, three.' Siric and I reach out as far as we can, throwing the chain towards the Mercian. Only then do I realise that to catch it, he'll have to release his hold on the bouncing rope, and I don't think he bloody will. The chain falls frustrating short, and still, the rope jumps and bounces.

'Bugger,' I huff, reeling it back in. It's sharp against my hands, rust mixing with the mud, so it's as though I bleed. Siric moves quickly, his thick arms pumping with the actions, reminding me that his arm was broken not long ago. He bites his lip now, pulling it white, and I appreciate that neither of us is the best people for this particular task.

A shriek and the Mercians' hand slips. He fumbles, hanging by one arm, and then somehow manages to push upwards by kicking his legs to hold the rope two-handed once more. I startle then, recognising him as one of the two men on the bridge at Gloucester, Elfwy or Cynelm. What the fuck is he doing here?

My warriors shout encouragement to one another, words tight with the strain of their task. On the bridge, Edmund and Jethson have managed to kill more of the Raiders blocking their path. Three Mercians remain trapped behind the Raiders who try to flee, but Edmund isn't giving up, even when the bridge shrieks once more, and even I see the wobble through the hail of rain.

'Shit,' another part of the wood sheers away. Osmod's spear embedded in the wood is dangerously close to the next part of the bridge to give way.

'Throw it at the bastard, not the Mercian,' I mutter to Siric through gritted teeth. The chain is bastard heavy, and my hands are aching from handling the rusty links while my arms scream from hauling the weight. Siric's eyes startle at the words, and then he nods in understanding.

'It's further away.' He cautions, his words just as tight as mine.

'Yes, but we don't need to be half as fucking careful. Bunch up as much as we can.' It's going to be an effort, but if we can get the bastard Raider off the rope, even if the line snaps on the bridge, my warriors will be able to haul one man up, just as they did with the Mercian who jumped for his life.

But the chain is so bloody heavy. We need to get as much of it thrown outwards as possible. I bunch it into my hands, threading it in circles, testing it to see if I can still move my arms even with such a weight. They shake. I've fought in a shield wall, I've ridden down my enemy, and still, the task of protecting my men and Mercia from the Raiders is far from complete.

The Mercians' cries are desperate now, Gyrth and Sæbald extending over the riverbank as far as they can to reach him, but it's still not close enough. And the rope is jumping, higher and then lower. Damn the bastard. The Raider gurgles as he moves, legs fleeing from side to side as he seems to paddle in the air, using them to push his body up and down. He has far more strength than the Mercian or than any of my warriors.

'Now,' I throw the chain as far out as I can. I'm mindful of Gyrth and Sæbald, of the rope that's all that holds the man clear of the river. Even while the bridge continues to collapse behind the Mercian, shrieking of its fury.

Two things happen at once. The bridge gives yet another outraged shriek, and the Raider is affected first. Feeling the movement, he wraps his right hand in the rope as though that'll save him. At the same time, Siric and I fling the heavy chain. It doesn't go as far as I'd like, but it doesn't need to with the belling out of the rope. More by chance than skill, the heavy chain misses the Mercian, as he holds tight to the rope, hands and now feet entwined around it, or as much as they can be so that he hangs by four limbs, not just the two.

But the Raider? Well, he looks up, face ripe with laughter,

thinking that he's won, and the ancient chain smacks into his face, breaking his nose in a splatter of bright maroon. Before he can scream in pain, the chain continues its downward fall, and he goes with it, the weight ripping his hands free so that he dangles precariously upside down, the chain only doing part of the job of evicting him from the rope.

But it's bloody useful. For a moment, there's a clear gap to sever the rope, and Gyrth takes it, flinging a seax at the fraying edges. The cord gives in both directions, my warriors surging backwards with the removal of such a weight, the Raider falling downwards to where a tree lies tangled in the vast stone struts that hold the wooden bridge in place.

I don't look away, even when the Raider lands against one of the struts before ricocheting into the water, a bloody trail in his wake. I'm just grateful he's not impaled on a stray branch.

Not that I have time to enjoy the moment. A terrified whinny, and my eyes are drawn once more to Edmund and Jethson. The Mercians are scampering to safety, but Edmund faces two determined Raiders, and Jethson is bleeding. I can see the stream of blood above his right eye, darkening the chestnut of his coat. Edmund stabs down, trying to impale one of the men, but the other is free to try and shove him clear of the saddle.

Jethson is once more terrified, Edmund helpless, and then the Raider stills in death. I screw my eyes tight against the onslaught of the rain.

'Cock,' Hereman bellows. 'Get the fuck out of there.' While the single Raider remains alive, Edmund finally appreciates the peril he's in and turns Jethson towards the Kempsey side of the bridge. I focus on Jethson's chestnut tail, willing him onwards.

The single remaining Raider leaps as though to mount the horse, but he misses and instead thuds into the wood, causing it to break, taking him with it. But the action sets off more and more. Where before I thought half the bridge was hale enough, now parts of it tumble into the surging water with no reason at all.

'Hurry the fuck up,' Hereman urges his brother. I would echo his words, but I can't speak. I can't look away, and neither can I close my eyes. He needs to make it.

It's a race to see whether the bridge will hold and Jethson will escape.

'Bloody bollocks,' Rudolf heaves beside me. My warriors stand together, all of us urging Jethson on, even Haden emitting a shrill whinny that I take to be a hurry-up. Then we all exhale. Jethson has made it to the far side, just as with a final sharp crunch, the bridge entirely tumbles into the churning floodwaters.

I puff through my cheeks, feeling relief flood through cold fingers and dripping hair, even as the rain falls even harder. Edmund turns Jethson towards us, raises his arm because we're too far away to see any movement smaller than that. A ragged cry drifts towards me, and I appreciate that the Mercians have survived whereas the Raiders haven't. And then Hereman chuckles, Osmod as well. I turn towards them, wondering what the fuck has made them smile after such a monumental fuck up.

But then I see it as well.

'Poor bastard,' Rudolf offers, but Hereman shakes his head, water dripping from his helm to sheet over his shoulders.

'Target practise,' he counters, and Osmod nods, his eyes alight with dark fire. The daft fucker. One of the Raiders has managed to find something to cling to in the middle of the bridge, one of the stone standings which once held aloft the wooden planks of the bridge that connected the two landward sides divided by the River Severn. How he thinks to escape from there, I have no idea. None at all.

'Do what you bloody want,' I state. Despite the sheeting rain and slick mud, my body feels shaky, and I need to sit down. I glance to Haden, ensuring he's well and far away from the chasm of the River Severn. Content that he and the rest of the horses are no worse for their experience, I turn my mind to something else that's been plaguing me ever since my other warriors arrived from the far side of the River Wye.

'But first, tell me, where the fuck is Pybba because he's not here?' I hold my hands to either side, indicating that everyone else is accounted for on the side of the river.

I look to Rudolf first of all my warriors, and he does me the courtesy of looking down at his mud-splattered feet, water pooling down his neck, his shoulders low, entirely deflated even after such a victory against the Raiders.

I don't want to hear this story, of that I'm sure. And still, I must know where he is and why the fuck he's not here, fighting for Mercia. If he even lives.

Historical Notes

The events that take place in this novel are entirely fictional. Coelwulf's whereabouts isn't known during the early months of 875. In the past, this period has been written about to show Mercia, and Coelwulf, as entirely subordinate to the Vikings (Raiders) who claimed Mercia in 874, according to the Anglo-Saxon Chronicle (ASC), allowing Coelwulf, 'a foolish king's thegn' to rule for them. This is no longer the case. Careful reading, and understanding of the source material, and new archaeological finds (coin), shows this interpretation to be far too simple. The ASC was a Wessex document at its inception. Mercia didn't have its own set of chronicles, although it's believed such might have once existed but were destroyed by the Raiders. Mercia has no narrator to speak of its triumphs with the sort of blind-sidedness that Wessex, and before it, Northumbria, was to enjoy. This is a pity, but a wonderful opportunity for a writer of historical fiction.

As such, I get to decide what Coelwulf was up to, and so, I've given him some old enemies, some new enemies, and some enemies who might actually be friends. The intention is to recreate the chaos of this period. Mercia was under threat, and enemies were all around, but Mercia was still standing at this time.

Unlike when I wrote about the River Trent in The Last Warrior, I have struggled to find details of ancient river crossings over the River Severn. There was a crossing at Kempsey but I doubt it was as I describe it in this novel. Apologies for my flight of fantasy on this occasion.

The names of the ealdormen, bishops, and some of the other characters, are taken from the few surviving charters that King Coelwulf II witnessed in Mercia. These can be found on the Online Sawyer, and number Sawyer 215 and 216. It is possible to work out where the bishops held their bishoprics, often because it is mentioned in the charters – in the case of Sawyer 215 and 216 both charters are concerned with Worcester and name Bishop Wærferth. It is not as easy with the ealdormen as their designated 'areas' are not given in the charters, and so I have assigned them areas based more on luck than any great skill.

For those interested in charters, the survival of any charter is purely happenstance. Kings would have issued many more charters than now survive and the survival of any of them is usually because the charter, at a later point in time, benefited someone mentioned in that charter. Royal charters to religious institutions were particularly relied upon when these sites came under attack from much later rulers – if they could 'prove' their land had been gifted to them by a previous anointed king and queen they were more likely to be able to hold on to it. This did, unfortunately, give rise to forgeries which modern historians must try and weed out from the remaining stock – although, of course, they do have relevancy for the period they were forged.

It's often said that the Welsh kingdoms weren't as badly affected by the Raider attacks as England and other kingdoms because of the difficult terrain, but there were many rivers and the Raiders were persistent. It might simply be that we don't have the records to show the scale of their attacks, just as in Mercia.

Cast of Characters

Coelwulf's Warriors

Ælfgar – one of the older members of the war band

Athelstan – killed in the first battle in The Last King

Beornberht – killed in the first battle in The Last King

Beornstan – one of Coelwulf's warriors

Cealwin – one of the older warriors from Kingsholm, first appears in The Last Shield

Coelwulf – King of Mercia, rides **Haden**

Cuthwalh – one of the older warriors from Kingsholm, rides **Aart,** first appears in The Last Shield

Edmund – rides **Jethson**, was Coelwulf's brother's man until his death. Brother is **Hereman**. Loses an eye in The Last Warrior.

Eadberht – one of Coelwulf's warriors

Eadulf – one of Coelwulf's warriors

Eadfrith – one of the older warriors from Kingsholm, first appears in The Last Shield

Eahric – one of Coelwulf's warriors

Eoppa – rides **Poppy**, dies in The Last Horse

Gardulf – first appears in The Last Horse – Edmund's son

Goda – one of Coelwulf's warriors, appears from The Last King onwards

Gyrth – one of Coelwulf's warriors, appears from The Last King onwards

Hemming – son of Beornberht, a young warrior from Kingsholm, rides **Perry**

Hereman – brother of Edmund, rides **Billy**

Hereberht – dies at Torksey, in The Last Warrior.

Hiltiberht - squire

Ingwald – one of Coelwulf's warriors

Icel – rides **Samson**

Leonath – first appears in The Last Horse

Lyfing – wounded in The Last King

Oda – one of Coelwulf's warriors

Ordheah – one of Coelwulf's warriors

Ordlaf – one of Coelwulf's warriors

Oslac – dies in The Last King, one of Coelwulf's warriors

Osmod – one of the older warriors from Kingsholm, first appears in The Last Shield

Penda – first appears in The Last Horse – Pybba's grandson

Pybba – loses his hand in battle, rides **Brimman** (Sailor in Old English)

Rudolf – youngest warrior, was a squire at the beginning of The Last King, rides **Dever**

Siric – first appears in The Last Horse

Sæbald – injured in The Last King, but returns to action in The Last Horse

Tatberht – first appears in The Last Horse, normally remains at Kingsholm. Rides **Wombel**

Wærwulf – speaks Danish, rides **Cinder**

Wulfstan – one of Coelwulf's warriors

Wulfhere – grandson of Tatberht, rides **Stilton**

Wulfred – rides **Cuthbert**

The Mercians
   Bishop Wærferth of Worcester
   Bishop Deorlaf of Hereford
   Bishop Eadberht of Lichfield
   Bishop Smithwulf of London
   Bishop Ceobred of Leicester
   Bishop Burgheard of Lindsey
   Ealdorman Beorhtnoth – of western Mercia
   Ealdorman Ælhun – of area around Warwick
   Ealdorman Aldred - of western Mercia
   Ealdorman Æthelwold – his father, Ealdorman Æthelwulf, dies at the Battle of Berkshire in AD871
   Ealdorman Wulfstan – dies in The Last King
   His son – (fictional) dies in The Last King
   Werburg – (fictional) his daughter
   Ealdorman Beornheard – of eastern Mercia
   Ealdorman Aldred – of eastern Mercia
   Lady Cyneswith – Coelwulf's (fictional)aunt

Raiders
   Ivarr – dies in AD870
   Halfdan – brother of Ivarr (above)
   Guthrum - one of the three leaders at Repton with Halfdan
   His sister, who dies outside Northampton
   Oscetel - one of the three leaders at Repton with Halfdan
   Anwend – one of the three leaders at Repton with Halfdan
   Anwend Anwendsson – his fictional son
   Jarl Thorgills – Raider on the River Wye
   Jarl Ottar – Raider on the River Wye
   Egil

The royal family of Mercia
>**King Burgred of Mercia**
>m. **Lady Æthelswith** in AD853 (the sister of King Alfred) they had no children
>**Beornwald** – a fictional nephew for King Burgred
>**King Wiglaf** – ninth century ruler of Mercia
>**King Wigstan**- ninth century ruler of Mercia
>**King Beorhtwulf** – ninth century ruler of Mercia
>**King Coelwulf** – ninth century ruler of Mercia from AD874

Misc.
>**Cadell ap Merfyn** – fictional brother of Rhodri Mawr, King of Gwynedd (one of the Welsh kingdoms)
>**Coenwulf** – Coelwulf's dead (older) brother
>**Wiglaf and Berhtwulf** – the names of Coelwulf's aunt's dogs, Lady Cyneswith
>**Wulfsige** – commander of Ealdorman Ælhun's warriors
>**Kyred** – oathsworn man of Bishop Wærferth of Worcester
>**Turhtredus** – Mercian warrior
>**Eanulf** – Mercian warrior
>**Beornfyhrt** - Mercian warrior
>**Heahstan** - Mercian warrior from Northampton
>**Denewulf and Eahlferth** – inhabitants of Newark
>**Owain,** a Welsh man
>**Cynelm,** guardsman in Gloucester
>**Elfwy**, guardsman in Gloucester
>**Irfara**, one of Bishop Wærferth's (of Worcester)lay brothers

Places Mentioned
>**London** – more strictly Lundenwic and Londinium at this time
>**Gainsborough,** in north-east Mercia.
>**Northampton**, on the River Nene in Mercia.
>**Grantabridge/Cambridge**, in eastern Mercia/East Anglia

Gloucester, on the River Severn, in western Mercia.

Worcester, on the River Severn, in western Mercia.

Hereford, close to the border with Wales, on the River Wye

Lichfield, a diocese of Mercia. Now in Staffordshire.

Tamworth, capital of Mercia. Now in Staffordshire.

Repton, important Mercian mausoleum. St Wystan's was the name of royal mausoleum.

Gwent, one of the Welsh kingdoms to share a border with Mercia.

Powys, one of the Welsh kingdoms to share a border with Mercia.

Gwynedd, one of the Welsh kingdoms to share a border with Mercia.

Warwick, in Mercia.

Torksey, in the ancient kingdom of Lindsey, part of Mercia

Passenham, in Mercia

River Severn, in the west of England

River Trent, runs through Staffordshire, Derbyshire, Nottingham and Lincolnshire and joins the Humber

River Avon, in Warwickshire

River Thames, runs through London and into Oxfordshire

River Stour, runs from Stourport to Wolverhampton

River Ouse, leads into the Cam/Granta, runs through Bedford (Bed's Ford)

River Nene, runs from Northampton to the Wash

River Welland, runs from Northamptonshire to the Wash

River Granta/Cam, runs from Cambridge to King's Lynn (East Anglia)

River Great Ouse, running from South Northamptonshire to East Anglia

Kingsholm, close to Gloucester, an ancient royal site

The Foss Way, ancient roadway from Lincoln to Exeter

Watling Street, ancient roadway from Chester to London

Icknield Way, ancient roadway from Norfolk to Wiltshire

Ermine Street, ancient roadway from London to Lincoln, and York.

Kempsey – a river crossing on the River Severn

Lincoln – in eastern Mercia

River Witham – passes close to Lincoln

Sincil Dyke – close to Lincoln

What to read next?

I hope you've enjoyed Coelwulf's newest tale. If you'd like to keep reading about Saxon England, and Mercia in particular, then please consider this series of interconnected titles, which I term 'The Tales of Mercia.'

<u>Gods and Kings (Seventh century)</u>
    Pagan Warrior
    Pagan King
    Warrior King

<u>The Eagle of Mercia Chronicles (Earlier ninth century)</u>
    Son of Mercia
    Wolf of Mercia
    Warrior of Mercia
    Eagle of Mercia
    Protector of Mercia
    Enemies of Mercia

The Lady of Mercia's Daughter (Tenth century)

A Conspiracy of Kings

<u>The Earl of Mercia Series (End of the tenth century)</u>
The Earl of Mercia's Father and subsequent titles (please note, perversely, I began this series first).

Enjoy

Meet the Author

I'm an author of historical fiction (Early English, Vikings and the British Isles as a whole before the Norman Conquest) and fantasy (Viking age/dragon-themed), born in the old Mercian kingdom at some point since AD1066. I like to write. You've been warned! My first non-fiction title is also now available.

Find me at mjporterauthor.com. mjporterauthor.blog and @coloursofunison on twitter. I have a monthly newsletter, which can be joined here. All subscribers will receive a free ebook short story collection.

https://dashboard.mailerlite.com/forms/699265/105452112446489757/share

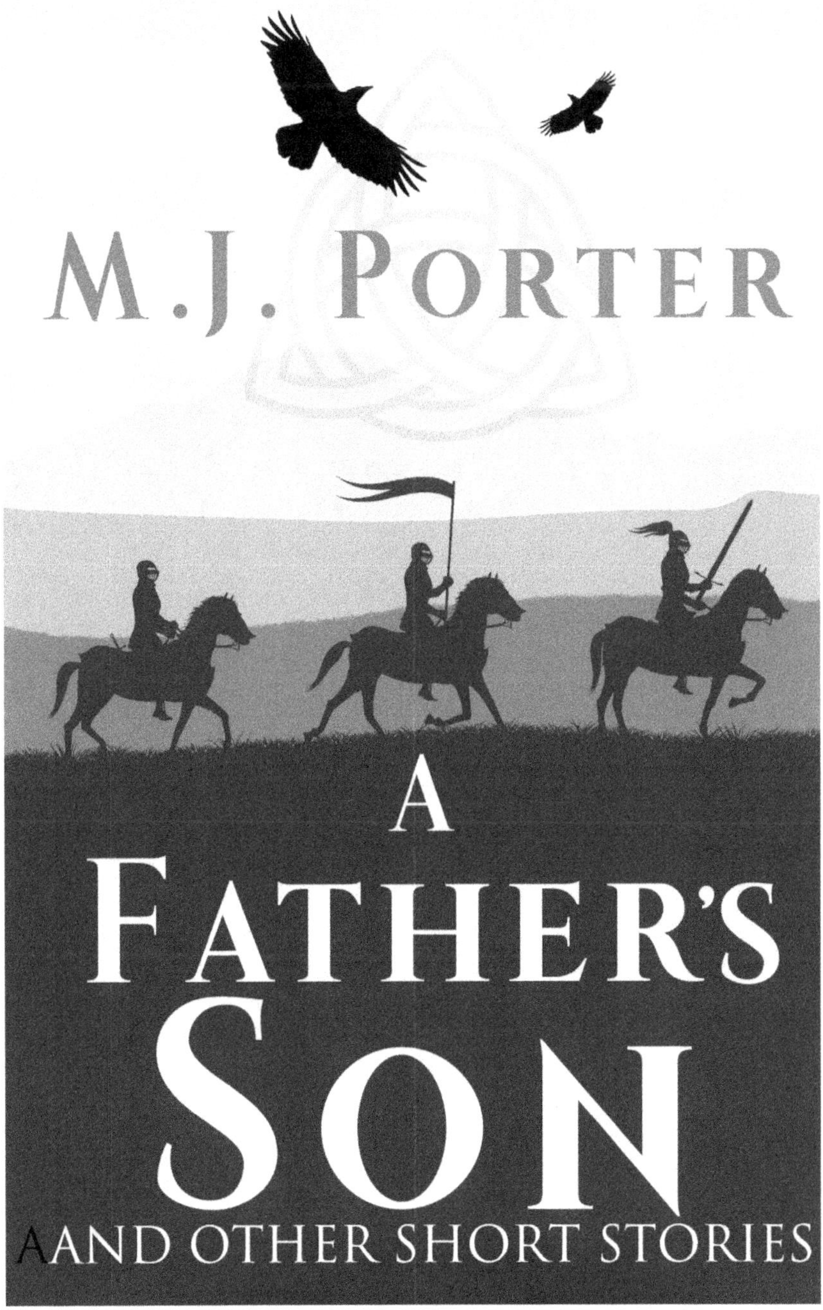

M.J. PORTER

A FATHER'S SON

AND OTHER SHORT STORIES

Books by M J Porter (in chronological order)

<u>Gods and Kings Series (seventh century Britain)</u>

Pagan Warrior

Pagan King

Warrior King

<u>The Eagle of Mercia Chronicles</u>

Son of Mercia

Wolf of Mercia

Warrior of Mercia

Eagle of Mercia

Protector of Mercia

Enemies of Mercia

Betrayal of Mercia

<u>The Ninth Century</u>

Coelwulf's Company, stories from before The Last King

The Last King

The Last Warrior

The Last Horse

The Last Enemy

The Last Sword

The Last Shield

The Last Seven

The Last Viking

The Last Alliance

<u>The Tenth Century</u>

The Lady of Mercia's Daughter

A Conspiracy of Kings (the sequel to The Lady of Mercia's Daughter)

Kingmaker

The King's Daughter

<u>Non-fiction title</u>

The Royal Women Who Made England: The Tenth Century in Saxon England

<u>The Brunanburh Series</u>

King of Kings

Kings of War

Clash of Kings

Kings of Conflict

<u>The Mercian Brexit (can be read as a prequel to The First Queen of England)</u>

<u>The First Queen of England (The story of Lady Elfrida) (tenth century England)</u>

The First Queen of England Part 2

The First Queen of England Part 3

<u>The King's Mother (The continuing story of Lady Elfrida)</u>

The Queen Dowager

Once A Queen

<u>The Earls of Mercia</u>

The Earl of Mercia's Father

The Danish King's Enemy

Swein: The Danish King (side story)

Northman Part 1

Northman Part 2

Cnut: The Conqueror (full-length side story)

Wulfstan: An Anglo-Saxon Thegn (side story)

The King's Earl

The Earl of Mercia

The English Earl

The Earl's King

Viking King

The English King

The King's Brother

Lady Estrid (a novel of eleventh-century Denmark)

Fantasy

<u>The Dragon of Unison</u>

Hidden Dragon

Dragon Gone

Dragon Alone

Dragon Ally

Dragon Lost

Dragon Bond

<u>As JE Porter</u>

The Innkeeper (standalone)

<u>20th Century Mystery</u>

The Custard Corpses – a delicious 1940s mystery (audio book now available)

The Automobile Assassination (sequel to The Custard Corpses)

Cragside – a 1930s murder mystery (standalone)